Sports Stories for Boys

ILLUSTRATED BY REG GRAY

HAMLYN
London · New York · Sydney · Toronto

The publishers wish to express their thanks to IPC Magazines Limited for permission to include *The Snatch-and Run Cyclist, Sherwood's Sharp Shooters, Masked Menace of the Boxing Ring, King of the Skating Aces, Born to Win, Mick's Greatest Innings, Push-Button Champ, Sandsprite, Trouble on the Team,* and *The Disastrous Climb.*

First published 1970
Seventh impression 1981
by The Hamlyn Publishing Group Limited
London · New York · Sydney · Toronto
Astronaut House, Feltham, Middlesex, England

ISBN 0 601 08655 4

Printed and bound in Yugoslavia

Sports Stories for Boys

Contents

List of Illustrations

The Snatch-and-Run Cyclist

The Snatch-and-Run Cyclist

by Edward Home-Gall

Motor-cycle Patrolman 'Skid' Kenley sat straddling his duty machine in a shadowy gateway alongside the main road leading into Little Horton. His eyes, behind lowered goggles, were watching the double stream of passing traffic – but his thoughts were centred upon Starbridge Speedway, five miles away, and the newly-erected 'For Sale' boards nailed to its walls.

He frowned. In his mind's eye he could see half-empty stands and bankings; in his imagination he could hear again the booing and cat-calls of disappointed fans.

'We must save Starbridge Speedway somehow,' he was thinking. 'If we could only win our league match tonight against the Benmore Tigers, then perhaps our Managing Director, Jules Barton, would change his mind about selling up!'

Skid Kenley watched a black saloon car speed by towards Little Horton. He instinctively took a mental note of its registration number, and gave a start of surprise.

'That's strange,' he mused. 'That was Jules Barton's car. But that wasn't him driving it – the driver was a young fellow.'

His thoughts switched to Starbridge Speedway, and he cheered up a little as he thought of the new rider from Australia, Ron Roberts, who had been signed on last spring and had promised to ride for the Starbridge Starlings for the first time in tonight's league match.

'Maybe this Aussie is red-hot,' he speculated. 'He'll be stale after his sea-journey, and it'll be his first ride on an English speedway, but if he can notch a few points for us that'll give the rest of the team new heart – and we might be able to beat the Tigers.'

Skid Kenley was a newcomer to the Starlings himself. He had just graduated from Police College and been posted to the Starbridge district. This was his first week of solo patrol duty.

Being speedway mad, Skid had applied for permission to ride for the Starlings, and it had been granted, provided that he did not allow his speedway riding to interfere with his police duties.

He had gone straight into the Starlings' league team. But this wasn't much to boast about, because the Starlings were at the bottom of the league table, and were losing their regular riders to other speedways faster than they could find and sign on promising youngsters.

Suddenly a motor-cyclist flashed past along the road, in front of Skid. The young speed-cop couldn't help noticing the rider. Apart from the powerful overhead-valve Mawspeed machine that he was riding, the motor-cyclist was wearing a bright blue crash helmet and overalls, and the part of his face which was not covered by his goggles was obscured by a thick black beard.

'That chap must be in a hurry,' Skid observed. 'He's jumped the traffic-lights!'

Almost in one action Skid Kenley stamped his foot down on his kick-starter and dropped his clutch-lever. His powerful motor-bike shot out from the gateway as if rocket propelled, and swerved into the road.

From the gateway he had been able to see the traffic-lights controlling the busy crossroads just outside Little Horton, which was about half a mile away.

He had seen the motor-cyclist jump those lights, deliberately opening his throttle to do so.

Apart from that, it was the worst case of careless driving that

Skid had ever seen, for the rider was swerving and skidding his powerful machine through a double line of traffic.

'He's lucky not to be killed,' mused Skid, opening his own throttle and speeding through the traffic.

This was his first chase on solo patrol duty – and he didn't mean to let the bearded rider give him the slip.

The traffic-lights changed from red to green as Skid raced towards the crossroads. His speedometer quivered up to the 70 m.p.h. mark.

Suddenly he had to cut his motor, brake hard and throw his back wheel into what was almost a speedway broadside in order to avoid a car whose driver had thought he could just get across the main road before the light changed.

The driver of the car jammed on his brakes, glaring through the windscreen, his face white and indignant. His face went a shade whiter as he saw Skid's crash-helmet inches in front of his bonnet.

Skid's front wheel grazed the car's bumper as, with his skidding bike over almost flat, he jabbed his left foot at the ground to check the swing of his madly spinning rear wheel.

The radiator of the car seemed to leap straight for his face. A crash into the speed-cop's bike seemed inevitable.

But not for a split second did Skid Kenley lose his nerve. That same quick thinking which brought precious points to the Starbridge Starlings in the last bend of a league heat served him in good stead now.

Skid straightened out his mount, swerved straight for a bollard and swung the bike round it skilfully. Shooting a disapproving glance at the white-faced offender in the car, he sent his speediron roaring into Little Horton's main street.

Anxiously he looked ahead down the deserted road. Had his mishap allowed the bearded motor-cyclist to escape him?

He breathed a sigh of relief. The big Mawspeed was not a quarter of a mile ahead of him, at the other end of the village street, and it was racing along the pavement!

A few pedestrians dived frantically into shop doorways ahead of the Mawspeed, as the bearded motor-cyclist swerved back on to the road again.

Now he was grasping in one hand a black brief-case – and Skid knew that he hadn't had it in his possession when he had jumped the traffic-lights. Sprawling on the pavement behind him was a middle-aged man. Clearly the bearded motor-cyclist had just snatched that brief-case from his hand!

'A snatch-and-run merchant!' muttered Skid, hunched over his powerful bike, its throttle wide open. 'That blighter's got real trouble on his hands now!'

There were plenty of people about to look after the robbed man – and he was picking himself up, clearly unhurt. Skid knew that his job was to get the bearded motor-cyclist, catch him and recover the stolen brief-case.

As Skid raced past the owner of the case, he flashed a glance towards him and gasped in amazement. It was the sour-tempered Managing Director of the Starbridge Speedway – Jules Barton.

★   ★   ★

The road ahead led to Starbridge, winding its way around steep hillsides bordering a deep and precipitous valley.

The bearded fugitive had disappeared around the first of these bends as Skid's machine raced out of Little Horton.

But there was something puzzling Skid. Normally, Jules Barton, on the day of a 'home' league match, would, at that time, be on his way to the speedway to prepare for the evening's meeting – due to start in two hours. His own car, driven by the young driver Skid had spotted, passed through Little Horton scarcely two minutes ahead of the bearded motor-cyclist. It was heading towards Starbridge. But why hadn't it stopped to pick up Jules Barton?

'It's got me guessing,' mused Skid. 'And it isn't like Jules Barton to lend his car to anyone; he always makes a show of driving up to the speedway in it himself. Perhaps he was waiting for it when he was robbed and it turned off somewhere in Little Horton before it reached him, maybe into a garage for petrol. No, there it is!'

Skid had suddenly spotted the black saloon, rounding a lofty hillside bend about a mile ahead of him. It was travelling fast – towards Starbridge.

'Then it must have passed Jules Barton in Little Horton!' Skid concluded. 'It isn't likely that its driver didn't spot him. Then why didn't it stop to pick him up?'

Skid decided to put the mystery out of his mind for the time being, and concentrate all his attention on catching up with the motor-cyclist.

But one thought persisted in his mind. Had the brief-case just been handed to Barton by one of the men in the car as it had passed through Little Horton? And was that the reason the motor-cyclist had followed the vehicle down the main road – and why he had jumped the traffic-lights? From those cross-roads he could have seen the car stop and the brief-case handed out to Jules Barton.

'That's not for me to puzzle out,' pondered Skid. 'My job is to catch that fellow with the beard – and get the brief-case back!'

He skidded his mount around a corner in a screaming high-speed turn – just in time to see the motor-cyclist roar round a bend two hundred yards ahead.

'Gee, this fellow knows a bit about broadsiding,' thought Skid. 'It's a pity a fellow who rides like that turns out to be a crook.'

The more Skid saw of the bearded fugitive's riding, the more he was convinced that his quarry was a born speedway rider.

Two miles from Starbridge, Skid rounded a bend in a daredevil broadside, and gave a low gasp of triumph.

He had reduced the fugitive's lead to a bare fifty yards. The motor-cyclist swung his Mawspeed round a sharp left-hand bend in a well-controlled slide.

'There's a straight stretch through the woods after that bend,' thought Skid. 'It's uphill – so that's where I'll get him. I'd say that Mawspeed hasn't been properly run in yet – otherwise I would never have caught up with him.'

Skid rounded the bend in a terrific slide, straightened out, and opened the throttle wide.

The bearded rider was just approaching the fringe of the wood. Beyond that point, to the left of the road, the trees thickened, while, to the right, there was a slope down to the edge of a precipice – a sheer drop of about three hundred feet.

The bearded speedster turned to glance back at Skid. Then, suddenly, as he turned his head again, the Mawspeed's front wheel bounded high into the air, like a bucking bronco.

The next moment the bike was hurtling sideways towards the right-hand side of the road. The black brief-case flew from the man's fingers as he was catapulted bodily from his saddle. He shot between two trees lining the road. The Mawspeed somersaulted between two more trees and began to slide rapidly down the slope.

Next moment the bearded motor-cyclist and his machine were hurtling over and over, side by side, towards the edge of the cliff.

Skid Kenley braked his roaring mount. It looked now as if he wasn't going to get his man after all – death was going to claim him first. There was nothing to save his quarry from going over the edge!

Then Skid saw a footpath leading along the brink of the cliff – and, in a flash, his mind was made up.

He twisted his throttle wide open and headed for the path. If he went flat-out, he would be able to reach the rolling man before he hurtled into space.

The rough road flashed by beneath him; to his right there was nothing but a yawning void. If he throttled down now he would crash into the fugitive. The only hope of saving the bearded rider was to sacrifice his patrol motor-bike, and risk his own neck. This was a thief on the run, but his life was at stake!

The Mawspeed ran into a tree and stopped, but there was nothing to save its rider. When Skid drew level with him, still going flat-out, the man was only a few yards from the brink.

Skid tilted his speediron over towards him, and then hurled himself from the saddle in a headlong dive. His bike skidded away beneath him and disappeared over the edge.

Skid landed, with terrific force, alongside the bearded man. He grabbed him firmly and then tried to anchor himself with his feet.

But there was no foothold to be found. The two rolled together towards the brink of the precipice.

Skid felt its sharp edge dig into his side. Then he felt himself slipping. There wasn't a thing he could do to save himself. His hips slid over the edge, his feet swung down beneath him. His chest scraped against sharp stone.

There was no sense in dragging the motor-cyclist after him to his death – and this he would certainly do if he kept hold of him. Skid Kenley deliberately released his hold upon the fugitive.

He started to drop. Then, next moment, something closed like a steel band around his wrist, and his fall was checked.

He looked up – and saw a hand, with a bruised and blackened thumbnail, gripped tightly around his wrist. A smiling, bearded face was peering down at him.

'You're in a bad jam, speed-cop!' he said. 'I suppose you realise that if I let go of you, you're a gonner?'

Skid nodded his head grimly.

'And if I pull you up,' the motor-cyclist continued, 'you'll arrest me!'

Skid gritted his teeth, but remained firm.

'I shall have to charge you on three counts,' he said, tight-lipped. 'Driving dangerously, jumping the traffic-lights, and robbery!'

'I see,' murmured the bearded motor-cyclist. 'It'd mean about ten years in prison for me – at least ten years – and that's a long time. No one would be any the wiser if I let you drop. In fact, there were no other policemen about when I took that brief-case, and I doubt if anyone but you has got the registration of my new Mawspeed. It would save me a lot of trouble if you weren't around! If I pulled you up, would you promise to forget all about me?'

Skid, not daring to look down, shook his head resolutely.

'I'm a police officer – you can't bribe me!' he said brusquely.

'Good for you!' said the bearded man with a low laugh.

Then, to Skid's amazement, the bearded speedster hauled him bodily up over the edge of the cliff. Now he was out of danger.

'Watch yourself!' cried his rescuer. 'You're on your own now!'

And so saying he bounded towards his Mawspeed and, snatching it up from the tree, began running it downhill towards the footpath. Skid struggled swiftly to his feet.

18

To Skid's amazement, the speedster hauled him up.

'Stop!' he panted. 'In the name of the law!'

'Sorry, copper – can't stop!' shouted the bearded motor-cyclist.

As Skid bounded forward, the Mawspeed's engine roared into life. Next moment the motor-cyclist had swung himself into the saddle, and was speeding away recklessly along the narrow footpath.

Skid, with his own motor-bike lying a total wreck some-where at the bottom of the precipice, could only stare helplessly after him with a feeling of mingled dismay and relief. How else could he feel, when the man he had set out to arrest had ended up by risking his liberty to save the policeman's life?

'Anyway,' he mused, 'I've recovered the brief-case – he didn't stop to go back and get it!'

Skid climbed to the road – only to hunt in vain for the black brief-case. He had seen it fall from the bearded fugitive's hand, but now it had vanished.

'What's happened to it?' he wondered. 'And, come to think of it, why did he have that pile-up? It couldn't have been a burst front tyre – because he was able to ride away on the Mawspeed. What the heck . . .'

His eyes had come to rest upon a tangled strand of wire, with one of its ends secured to a tree at the side of the road. The other end of the broken wire girdled another tree on the opposite side of the road.

'He was crashed deliberately by someone,' mused Skid, 'someone who wanted to get that brief-case from him. But he'd only just stolen it himself!'

His thoughts flashed once again to the black saloon car. The two men in it, after giving the brief-case to Jules Barton in Little Horton, could have seen the bearded motor-cyclist rob him of it from these hills. And then, as if to confirm his theory, Skid heard a car start up somewhere in the thick woods and head off towards Starbridge with a loud roar.

But the woods were too dense for him to be able to catch a glimpse of it.

After a brief wait, Skid got a lift in a passing car back to Little Horton police station. The inspector listened to his report with great interest.

'Well done, Kenley,' he said at length. 'Mr Barton reported the robbery, and now that you've given us the motor-bike's registration number we should be able to pick up this bearded character. But, of course, all that you've told me about Mr Barton's car is only supposition on your part – and may be far from the truth. Anyway, you're off duty now, so get along to the speedway – and good luck to you tonight!'

Skid hurried back to his lodging to change out of his uniform, and half an hour later he was riding his roadster into the Riders' Car Park at the Starbridge Speedway.

Turnstiles were clicking, and a stream of fans were pouring into the ground. From the pits, as Skid hurried in that direction, arose the high-pitched roar of speediron engines.

As Skid entered, and headed for the dressing-room, Chuck Keene, the Starlings' skipper, raised a hand from his machine to give the young speed-cop a welcoming wave.

'Hallo, Skid!' he cried. 'Glad your police duties have allowed you to get here! We may be able to give the Tigers a surprise tonight. Our new Aussie rider, Ron Roberts, turned up about an hour ago – in time for a spin round the track before the gates opened. He's riding my spare bike – and, by the look of him, he's hot stuff. Come and meet him!'

Seconds later, Skid was shaking hands with a tall, bronzed young man clad in crash-helmet, racing leathers and gauntlets. His handshake was like a grip of steel, and the new rider's eyes greeted Skid warmly, sparkling with friendly welcome.

'I'm glad to meet you,' he drawled. 'The boys here have given me such a glowing account of your riding that I feel that we aren't meeting for the first time! Maybe we'll be able to collect a few points together, out on that track.'

'I hope so!' grinned Skid. 'And maybe we'll be able to talk our Managing Director into taking those "For Sale" boards down if we beat the Tigers tonight!'

The league match started off none too well for the Starlings. Chuck Keene was beaten on the last bend by the Tigers' crack skipper, after his partner had piled-up in the second lap.

On the scoreboard flashed the score: STARLINGS 2. TIGERS 4.

In Heat Two, Skid Kenley faced the starting-gate grimly. When the tapes flashed up, he was first away. He led for two laps – and then his engine suddenly packed up, and he had to swerve on to the grass verge, and push his speediron back to the pits. His partner overslid his broadside in the next bend, and that left the two Tigers' riders to win five clear points for their team.

Then the new Aussie, Ron Roberts, made his first appearance on an English track – and settled down at once to show everybody that he was a red-hot cinder-shifter. Screaming around his second lap as if jet-propelled, he broadsided his roaring mount into the lead – and scored the Starlings' first winning points of the evening amid wildly enthusiastic cheers from the crowd. His partner chased him home, and on the scoreboard flashed the figures: STARLINGS 7. TIGERS 10.

The new Aussie's magnificent victory gave fresh heart to the Starlings, and for the next three heats they shared points with the Tigers.

In Heat Seven, Skid and Ron Roberts went out to the starting-gate together. Before the Tigers' two riders came out from the pits, the new rider shot a warm smile across to the speed-cop as if wishing him luck.

'Now for it, eh!' he said. 'Maximum points from us two, now, and the Starlings will start the second half of the match one point in the lead!'

From the moment that the tapes flashed up, the crowd were on their toes, thrilled and surprised. A second later they were yelling their heads off. For the first time in many a long day, they saw two riders wearing the Starlings' colours take the lead on the first bend.

For lap after lap, riding expertly together, with Skid on the white line, the two home-riders defied every effort made by the Tigers' pair to overtake them. Bedlam broke loose as, finally, they rode side by side past the chequered flag in a thrilling photo-finish.

The half-time score read: STARLINGS 18, TIGERS 17.

Skid throttled down, wildly excited. This was his dream come true. At last the Starlings had found, in Ron Roberts, a cinder-shifter who, before the season was out, could put them back where they ought to be – in first place, at the top of the league.

Back in the pits Ron Roberts and Skid took off their gauntlets and helmets.

'Well, Skid, we've done it,' cried the Aussie. 'What did I tell you? This is the turning point for the Starlings – from now on we're going to be the crack team of the league!'

But Skid couldn't open his mouth to reply. Beneath the grime of the cinder track, his face was as white as a sheet. His eyes were glued to Ron Roberts' hand. The thumbnail on that hand was blackened and bruised. He had seen that nail before, barely two hours ago, on the hand which had saved him from falling to his death.

The Starlings' new Aussie cinder-shifter, Ron Roberts, was the bearded motor-cyclist – the man it was his duty to arrest on sight!

★ ★ ★

Two minutes later, Skid Kenley was speaking tensely into a telephone close to the Starbridge Speedway pits.

It had been hard for Skid to drag himself away from the pits, where his friends were crowding round congratulating Ron Roberts on his magnificent ride. But even though Skid knew that he was about to bring the Australian's speedway career to an end, he didn't hesitate.

'He's here, Inspector – the bearded motor-cyclist!' he said in a low, hoarse voice. 'But that beard was a false one, and he's not wearing it now. He's our new rider from Australia – Ron Roberts.'

Skid's voice almost broke. He knew that, with those words, he was probably robbing the Starlings of victory over the Tigers in tonight's league match. He knew, too, that he was striking a death-blow at the Starlings – for after another defeat Jules Barton would undoubtedly close down the speedway.

'I've phoned you for orders, Inspector,' continued Skid. 'I'm off duty, and not in uniform. Ought I to arrest Roberts now, or wait?'

'No, hold everything!' interrupted the inspector. 'He doesn't suspect that you've recognised him, eh? I'll bring a squad car over at once. Don't let him out of your sight until we reach the speedway – and be careful about it; he knows you're a policeman, and he may try to give you the slip if he thinks you're watching him. Got that?'

'O.K., Inspector,' answered Skid miserably.

24

Skid turned slowly from the telephone booth. This would certainly win him a good mark in the police force, but Skid couldn't help thinking that it would make him very unpopular with the rest of the Starlings.

He returned, heavy-footed, to the pits. He looked glumly around for Ron Roberts.

But the Aussie speedster was no longer in the pits. His speed-iron was propped against a post, beside a large pool of oil – and there was a set of oily footprints leading clearly away from it, towards a little-used door at the back of the pits, giving access into a yard behind the speedway's offices. There wasn't a shadow of doubt that Ron Roberts had slipped off quietly from the pits, unknowingly leaving that trail of oily footprints in his wake.

But he had only just arrived in England from Australia. How had he known about that back entrance to the pits, by which anyone could leave the speedway practically unseen?

Outside, in the yard, Skid saw Jules Barton's black car. It was where he usually left it during a speedway meeting. Then, through the half-open door of a shed, Skid saw the back wheel of a motor-bike – and he recognised it immediately.

It was the bearded motor-cyclist's Mawspeed. Now he had conclusive proof that Ron Roberts was the wanted man – the thief who had grabbed Jules Barton's brief-case.

Suddenly Skid heard a faint scraping sound, high above his head. Looking up, he saw Ron Roberts, thirty feet from the ground, climbing a slender drainpipe up the wall of the office building.

In a flash, Skid realised the mystery speedster's objective. Just to one side of the drainpipe, at the top of the building, was the open window of Jules Barton's private office.

'Burglary, now, eh?' thought Skid, grim-jawed. Swiftly he

formed a plan. He raced back into the speedway, through the pits, and then up a wide flight of office stairs.

If he burst into Jules Barton's office he would catch Ron Roberts red-handed – perhaps forcing open Jules Barton's safe, and about to steal something.

Skid reached the office door, and threw it open. Then he stopped dead, staring wide-eyed into the room. The office was empty. The door of the safe stood wide open.

And inside it was the black brief-case.

Then his guesses had been right! It had been the two men in Barton's black car who had stretched the wire across the road to make the bearded motor-cyclist crash. They had recovered the brief-case, and returned it to Jules Barton. Ron Roberts had been climbing the drainpipe to recover it.

But where was he now? On the other side of the room was a closed door. Skid crossed to it, and tested it. It was locked.

Then he heard a faint sound in the yard below. He looked cautiously through the window, and gave a gasp of amazement.

The two men he had seen before in the car were carrying a long bundle across the yard. Without a shadow of doubt it was Ron Roberts wrapped inside a rug.

Those two men must have been waiting for him inside the office, and, as soon as he had climbed in by the window, had overpowered him and carried him away through the door, locking it behind them, and down the back stairs.

Skid thought swiftly. It wasn't up to him to solve the mystery of the black brief-case. His job was to get Ron Roberts.

The large safe stood a few inches away from the wall. Darting across to it, Skid snatched the brief-case out from it, and wedged it into the narrow gap between the back of the safe and the wall. There it was completely out of sight.

Then Skid darted back to the window, and, climbing reck-

26

lessly out over the sill, swung himself on to the slender drain-pipe. It creaked and groaned under his weight – but he slid down it at daredevil speed.

When he reached the ground the black car was being driven out of the yard, with the long bundle lying across its rear seat. He saw it turn right – away from Little Horton.

Skid dashed into the shed. In a large pannier alongside the Mawspeed's rear wheel he found, as he had half anticipated, the bearded motor-cyclist's light blue overalls and thick, bushy black beard.

Skid donned them, beard and all, in record time. Seconds later he was riding the Mawspeed out of the yard in the direction taken by the black car.

He knew that every policeman in the county was on the look-out for a bearded motor-cyclist wearing light blue overalls and riding a Mawspeed.

Almost at once a whistle shrilled at his back. Then he heard the roar of an accelerating car and, looking back, he grinned broadly as he saw a speeding police-car swooping down from out of the hilly road. His own inspector was in the seat beside the uniformed driver of that car – pointing excitedly ahead at him.

Skid opened the throttle. For two miles he sped along with the speedometer at 80 m.p.h., and by now two other police cars and four motor-cycle patrolmen had joined in the chase. Then, suddenly, just ahead of him, Skid saw the black car.

He almost overtook it, and then, throttling down, allowed the inspector's squad car to draw level with him.

The inspector opened the window at his side and began to shout to him to draw over to the side of the road. Then Skid pulled off the false beard.

'He's in the back of the car ahead!' shouted Skid.

The police car accelerated, drew level with Jules Barton's car and, edging it to the side of the road, forced its driver to pull up.

Soon the car was surrounded by policemen. Skid jumped off the Mawspeed and tore open the rear door. Beneath the rug he unearthed Ron Roberts, gagged and securely bound, hand and foot.

'You've got me!' grimaced the speed ace as soon as he was released. 'Jules Barton has been too smart for me. If I'd still got that brief-case there'd be a different story to tell. But by now all the proof I've got against him will be destroyed!'

Ron Roberts was driven back to the speedway and taken up to Jules Barton's office to be identified as the man who had robbed him in Little Horton's main street.

The door of the safe was now closed, but everything in the room bore the appearance of having been recently moved. Jules Barton had evidently made a frantic search for something – and Skid guessed what that something was.

'Oh, so you've caught the thief?' Barton said, making an effort to regain his composure. 'Smart work on your part, Inspector! And it turned out to be our new rider, Roberts, eh?'

Then Ron Roberts saw Skid take the black brief case from behind the safe, and an amazing change came over his face.

'It won't be me who's in for trouble when the police see the contents of that brief-case, Barton!' Ron Roberts said with a smile.

He turned towards the inspector.

'My father is the legal owner of this speedway,' he said. 'But, six years ago, this man Barton hid the proceeds of a £10,000 jewel robbery somewhere in the speedway, and, with faked evidence, made it look as though my father had committed the crime. We had to take assumed names and bolt to Australia to escape arrest.

'It has taken me six years to collect proof of Barton's guilt and my father's innocence. As soon as I stepped ashore in this country, I intended to take the evidence to the police, but, while I was buying my new Mawspeed, two men in a black car snatched my black brief-case from my hands and made off with it.'

Stern-faced, the inspector was examining the contents of the brief-case. He nodded towards Jules Barton, and a policeman moved to each side of the speedway manager.

'And you knew that without these papers Jules Barton could have you arrested for a six-year-old crime?' asked the inspector.

'Yes, so I dashed into a shop and bought that false beard,' continued Ron Roberts, 'and then I headed at top speed for Little Horton, knowing that Jules Barton lived there. I jumped those traffic-lights because I saw the black car pull up, and the case given to Barton. I managed to get the case from him, as you know, but the men in the car were too smart for me, and got it back. A short while ago I tried to reach this office, but his two thugs were waiting up here for me with Barton, and the three of them overpowered me!'

The inspector turned with a warm smile towards Skid.

'Well done, Kenley!' he said. 'This is quite an achievement for a young constable in his first week of solo patrol. You've not only got your man, but you've also proved his innocence, and from the look of the papers in this brief-case, you've proved his father the rightful owner of Starbridge Speedway!'

Ron Roberts gripped Skid by the hand, a thrilled grin on his face.

'Thanks a million,' he said. 'I don't know what I would've done without your help!'

Skid was about to reply when the snarl of speedirons and the roar of the crowd came from outside.

'The match – I'd forgotten all about it,' Skid gasped. 'Come

29

on, Ron. We'll have our work cut out to hold the Tigers in the second half.'

The two speedsters dashed from the room, leaving the glowering Jules Barton in the safe hands of the inspector and his men.

Skid and Ron reached the pits as the first heat of the second half finished. The Tigers were fighting back. After a tight struggle with the two Starlings riders, they crossed the line in first and second place, to put them back in the lead.

The Starlings' luck seemed right out again, for in the next heat Chuck Keene had the misfortune to fall on the last bend and his partner could only manage third place. The Starbridge team was trailing badly.

Skid was down to ride in the third heat.

'Get in there and show 'em what you can do!' Ron Roberts said with an encouraging slap on the back, as the speed-cop rode out to the starting-gate.

Skid waited tensely for the start, his jaw set grimly. He had to win this heat; otherwise the Starlings would lose their confidence and the Tigers would build up an unbeatable lead.

The tapes flashed up. Skid hurled his bike in and out of the first bend with a dazzling burst of speed, already yards in the lead. And he didn't lose that lead! To the cheers of the crowd, he romped home first, with his partner following him over the line.

From then on the match became one of the most thrilling the Starbridge fans had ever seen. First one team took the lead, then the other. The result was in doubt right up until the final heat. Then Skid Kenley screamed past the chequered flag, hotly pursued by Ron Roberts, to win the league match for the Starlings by 43 points to 40!

Thanks to speed ace Skid Kenley, P.C., the future of Starbridge Speedway was assured.

Luala Lagoon

Luala Lagoon
by Darry McCarthy

Simon waved his parents good-bye, and went on waving as long as he could see the launch at the far end of the lagoon. His father, the Resident at Luala Island, had decided to go for a short holiday to Apia. Simon's mother had at first been a little dubious about leaving a fifteen-year-old boy on his own, but Simon assured them he would be all right.

Now, as he stood waving from the end of the pier, he was not quite so sure. It was the first time he had been left alone and he hoped that nothing would go wrong.

The launch passed through the gap in the coral at the far end of the lagoon, and then around the cape, out of sight.

He was alone now. Simon turned and scuffed back along the pier, poking at the nails with the toes of his sandals. It wasn't fair. Why couldn't they take him? But he knew the answer, even as he asked himself. It was very unlikely that there would be an emergency during their absence, but someone had to stay and look after Luala.

Simon returned to the Residency, where their Polynesian maid prepared a meal for him.

'Simon, lad, don't worry,' Huia told him, smiling. 'Your parents will be all right.'

'I'm not worrying,' said Simon. But he left half his fish, although it had only been caught that morning and was delicious. Then he ate only one slice of fresh pineapple, and just nibbled at the fresh coconut.

Huia looked at him anxiously and said, 'It isn't good for a boy your age to be alone. Why don't you go out and play football?'

'Too hot,' said Simon briefly. Indeed, it had become very hot, and the air was damp and sticky. Even the coconut trees seemed to be wilting, their fronds hanging down in the oppressive air.

'Tell you what,' suggested Huia, 'you go and see Rangi. He will think of something.'

'Good idea,' Simon agreed. Rangi, who was Huia's son, was Simon's best friend. The island was too small to have a proper school, but Simon's mother ran a classroom, and there was a time when Rangi and Simon had shared a desk. Then, when he was twelve, Simon went away to boarding school. Since then, Rangi had left school, and Simon felt young by comparison. He felt as if Rangi, although the same age, was already a man. In Simon's holidays they always resumed their friendship, though Rangi was the boss now.

Simon went out into the garden, noticing the flowers hanging heavily on their stalks. He crossed to Huia's house, a round, Polynesian house, made of hand-made bricks with a thatch of coconut fronds. Inside, it was cool and dark.

'You there, Rangi?'

'I'm here, having a rest,' called Rangi. 'But I'll get up now. What shall we do?'

Rangi stood, rubbing the sleep from his eyes. He wore a khaki shirt and long khaki trousers. He was already six feet tall, and broad-shouldered.

'I'm bored,' admitted Simon. 'I was hoping you would think of something.'

'Let's walk to the cape,' suggested Rangi.

The friends set out along a white path beneath the coconut palms. As they went, Rangi talked in a deep, manly voice about prospects for this year's copra crop. Simon hardly listened. His shirt was sticking to his back with sweat. He thought he had

34

never felt so hot as he did then on their walk to the cape.

They sat on a boulder at the cape, looking out over the still, blue Pacific. The sky was clear blue with a fringe of white, woolly cloud on the far horizon. A slight breeze was coming from the sea.

'I'm hot,' said Rangi suddenly. 'How about a swim, friend?'

His brown eyes were twinkling, and Simon nodded readily. His parents had often told him it was dangerous to swim near the cape, that he ought to swim near the pier. But they were miles away by now, and what did it matter? They need never know.

They took off their shirts and sandals. Then Rangi grabbed a coconut frond, and, with wild whoops of joy, swung backwards and forwards, working up speed. At the critical moment, when the frond was above the water, he let go. He went feet first, still whooping, into the placid water of the lagoon, not far from the entrance to the open sea.

Simon looked dubiously at the palm. He would have liked to copy his hero, Rangi, but he was a little afraid of letting go at the wrong moment, and landing with a crash on the rocks.

He decided to be cautious. He ran along the cape and dived into the sea.

That was wonderful! It was super to be cool at last, to feel the sweat being washed away, to duck his head over and over again into the soothing salt water.

Rangi was shouting with pleasure. He swam with the agility of a porpoise. The two boys started playfully to splash each other, and soon the calm water was covered with foam as they laughed and yelled. Then Simon turned on his back and began to float idly, gazing at the clear sky.

Soon Simon was in a bay where the water was very deep, and there were sheer rock cliffs above him. He was beginning to tire, and he looked for a foothold, but found none. He turned and

Simon saw a pointed fin coming his way.

began to swim to another part of the lagoon. Then he saw, amidst the foam, a pointed fin, coming his way.

'Shark!' Simon shouted. 'Shark!' Rangi looked, saw the fin, and with a great turn of speed made for the shore. He shook the water from his brown skin and stood there, calling, 'Hurry, Simon, hurry!'

But Simon was trapped. The shark was between him and the only way out. Rangi ran to the top of the rocky cliff and stretched down his hand, but he could not reach far enough. Treading water and stretching his hand up, Simon was still at least six feet away. Rangi then clutched desperately at a coconut palm, trying to break off a branch, but the sap was green and the palm would not break.

Simon turned to face the shark's fin. He had some obscure idea that if he had to die, then he would not die with his back to the enemy. He remembered that it was because sharks some-times came through the entrance to the lagoon that this part was considered unsafe for swimmers. But it was too late now.

'Simon,' called Rangi, 'show no fear! He will only attack if you show fear!'

Behind the fin, the waves were beginning to swell. Simon looked around at the island hoping that someone had seen them. But the boys were too far away. They were completely depen-dent on their own initiative.

From the cliff, Rangi began throwing coconuts at the shark to distract it. Most missed it. One, however, hit it on the back. Instead of being distracted, the shark was angered. The fin disappeared. This was the dangerous moment, Simon knew. The shark was preparing to attack.

And then, so suddenly that Simon hardly saw it happen, Rangi dived. He dived right in the path of the shark, creating such a foam and shouting so loudly that the beast was diverted for a moment. Taunting the shark, Rangi turned his back and swam towards the lagoon entrance.

Undecided, the shark hesitated. Then the fin appeared again. Simon was safe for the moment. The shark began to follow Rangi, and Simon edged around the rock, fumbling for a hand-hold.

But the shark had decided that its first victim was easier prey. It turned again, and once more followed Simon. Rangi was splashing as much as he could, but making no impression, while Simon had his hands around the long roots of a coconut palm, trying to haul himself up.

Then Simon saw that the frothy water was stained with something red. Blood! He knew he hadn't seen or felt the shark bite him. The blood was coming from somewhere else – from the coral. Rangi had deliberately cut himself on the sharp coral reef, and turned himself into human bait. The shark, following the smell of blood, left Simon and turned to the Polynesian boy.

Kicking hard with his bleeding leg, Rangi swam round and round, spreading the blood, and diverting the shark. Breathless, Simon hauled himself on to the bank and watched.

Soon the salt in the lagoon had closed the wound on Rangi's leg, and the blood stopped flowing. But the shark had gained on him.

Simon was now in Rangi's position. He threw coconuts and shouted, but he could not create a diversion.

However, Rangi knew what he was doing. He scrambled up on the sharp coral, leaving a trail of blood from fresh cuts, and stood there as the shark made a greedy gulp for him.

The shark leaped, open-mouthed, towards its victim, and landed upside-down on the sharp coral. It lay there bleeding and gasping for breath.

Rangi laughed. He called out, 'What your father would call a good show, eh? But a good thing he wasn't watching.'

Simon merely nodded. He felt ill at the sight of his friend, bleeding from many wounds, and he felt sorry for the shark, gasping out its last breath on the coral, as it thrashed about in a vain attempt to find the water again.

Rangi ran his hand over his eyes, and tried to get back into the water again. But the sting of the salt water on his many deep cuts was too much for him.

Simon watched anxiously. He had always thought of Rangi as almost supernaturally strong, but the Polynesian boy was finding difficulty even standing. He had exhausted himself and the sight of so much blood in the water and on the coral upset him.

'Hang on,' called Simon. 'I'm coming!'

He jumped in and helped Rangi to solid land. Then he laid him under a coconut tree to rest.

'Sorry, old friend,' said Rangi. 'Very undignified, having to be helped to shore.'

'You've been growing too fast,' Simon said. 'That's why you hadn't the strength to swim ashore. Thanks for saving my life.'

'It was nothing,' said Rangi sleepily. Then he fainted.

Simon covered him with both their shirts. It had turned chilly; the fronds were waving in a fresh breeze, and the sea was choppy. Rangi started to shiver, lying on the dark undergrowth beneath the coconuts.

He did not wake, and Simon thought he had best run for help, as it was impossible to carry someone so big, unaided. He ran back to Luala.

There was a stretcher amongst the first-aid equipment in the Residency. He fetched it, and a blanket, then found two other boys and a girl, who ran back with him along the path to fetch

Rangi. By this time it had been pouring with rain for several minutes.

By the time they reached him, Rangi was awake, but his body was hot and he was perspiring. He was drenched with rain. As they carried him along the path to his home, he became delirious.

They laid him on his own bed, and fetched Huia, who made him comfortable and looked after him. His fever continued, and he was in considerable pain. His cuts were beginning to fester, and he had lost much blood. And the chill he had from the rain didn't help.

Simon wished desperately that his father were there; his father would have known what to do. But there was no one to whom he could turn and the villagers could not give Rangi the urgent medical attention he needed. Unless Simon could think of something to do, there was no telling what might happen to Rangi. A poor return for saving Simon's life!

Simon left the hut, telling Huia he would be back soon, and went back to the Residency. In his father's office there was a small two-way radio set, with which his father made daily reports to Apia.

As the rain drummed on the tin roof, Simon called over and over: 'Hello Apia, hello Apia, can you please contact my father, Mr Davis? This is Simon Davis. There's an emergency here at Luala. I need advice.'

Perhaps the operator at Apia thought the boy was joking, for there was no reply for an hour. Eventually, however, a voice crackled through, on a slightly different wave length.

'It's the Royal New Zealand Air Force. Can we help?'

Simon explained the situation and said he wanted his father's advice. The airman said somewhat impatiently, 'You don't need your father. You need a doctor.'

'Then get me a doctor,' implored Simon. 'He saved my life, and I've got to save him.'

'You need a doctor with penicillin,' the Air Force spokesman said casually. 'I'll see what I can do. Stand by.'

Impatiently, Simon waited, while the sound of native voices drifted up to the Residency from Huia's hut. All the relations and friends had gathered from surrounding huts to be near Huia and her sick son.

Eventually the Air Force replied. 'Sorry, young fellow. There's a storm on, in case you hadn't noticed, and orders have gone out that all planes are grounded.'

'You can't give up,' implored Simon.

'What can we do? We've looked up Luala on a map, and you've no landing strip.'

'But couldn't you drop supplies by parachute, with instructions?'

'Sorry. No. We can't risk a whole crew in this storm.'

'Can't you defy orders?' asked Simon desperately.

'Sorry,' said the airman, 'we don't want to be dismissed from the service.'

But then a new voice took over. 'Hello, hello. It's Dr Mark O'Reilly here, the Air Force doctor. Describe the patient's symptoms to me, please. I might be able to give you some advice.'

Simon explained Rangi's condition as well as he could.

'It's very bad,' commented Dr O'Reilly. 'I don't think anything I could tell you to do would help. Your friend needs antibiotics, and he needs them soon. If the infection from his wounds is in his blood stream, he may die.'

'Can't the Air Force fly you over?' begged Simon.

The doctor hesitated before he replied. 'I took my medical oath before I took my Service oath. I know which comes first.

But the flying men are grounded and I can't expect anyone to fly me there. Besides, where would we land when we got there?'

'On the water,' suggested Simon. 'On the lagoon.'

'That's a marvellous idea!' the doctor exclaimed. 'Is there enough room for a flying boat?'

'Yes,' said Simon eagerly. 'There's loads of room in the lagoon. But you'd have to be careful of the reef.'

'How's the storm?' asked the doctor.

'It's abating,' said Simon. 'But I think I should tell you it's getting late. It'll be dark in half an hour.'

'And no moon,' said the doctor. 'Oh, well, not to worry. We've an old duck flying boat here, left over from the war. One man can fly it. Me. Then no one else in the Air Force need be involved. Now, Simon Davis, listen carefully. I don't want to break my neck. You'll have to show me where the lagoon is. Too much to expect you've any landing lights?'

Simon laughed, in spite of the gravity of the situation. He was beginning to get a picture of this Dr O'Reilly as a defiant Irishman who liked nothing better than winning against impossible odds. 'No,' said Simon. 'But I'll make you some. We'll light fires all round the lagoon and two lines of parallel fires where the pier ends. If you point your plane towards the parallel lines, you can then taxi to the pier.'

'If I live,' said the doctor brightly. 'Well, no time to waste chatting. Get on with that fire lighting!'

Simon rushed down to Luala village, and burst into Rangi's house, where his relations were standing very quietly around his bed. The boy's face was covered with perspiration and the cuts were festering ominously.

'Listen, everybody!' he called. His voice had deepened. He had adopted his father's pose of authority, in order to end the panic which had gripped the village. 'A plane is coming, a sea plane, with a doctor. He has to land on the lagoon. That means he wants fires. You've all got to help. Get the dried-up fronds from the copra sheds. Make fires all around the lagoon, as near the shore as possible. Hurry!'

He picked some of his classmates as leaders, with five people to every fire. The youngest were responsible for lighting the fires on the two capes. They had to run in the dark along tracks under the coconut trees. The oldest people had the more exacting work of laying fires for the parallel flames near the pier.

There was not enough dried frond for the fires to burn long, so damp branches were added, and villagers had to run back and forth carrying petrol, taken from the boat-store, and pour it on to each pile.

The mood of the village had changed. Despair had gone, and the atmosphere was hopeful.

As soon as the drone of the old aircraft's engine was heard above, Simon gave the order for the fires to be lighted.

One by one they sprang up around Luala lagoon, and the brown skins of the people were outlined by the flickering light, as they gazed hopefully up into the sky.

The 'duck' turned, and came in to make a somewhat bumpy landing. Then it taxied towards the pier.

Simon waited at the end, as he had seen his father wait, with his hands behind his back and a solemn expression on his face. Then he walked forward and helped the tall, moustached officer to climb from the aircraft to the pier.

'Welcome to Luala, sir,' he said, in a voice like his father's.

'So you're Simon Davis,' said Dr O'Reilly. 'Chip off the old block! I knew your father during the war. Now, where's the patient?'

'This way, sir.'

Simon led the way to Rangi's bedside. As soon as she heard a doctor was coming, Huia had put the kettle on and tidied the room. Rangi was still delirious, but within a few minutes the doctor had pumped the precious life-saving antibiotic into Rangi's veins.

The three of them kept a vigil throughout the night, while outside the whole village sang and danced. The village, unlike the doctor, had thought his very appearance on the scene was enough to save Rangi.

In the morning, cool but sunny and still after the storm, the weary doctor, and mother, and friend, knew that they had won the battle, and that Rangi, smiling weakly at them, would be all right. His wounds were healing and his fever had subsided.

Slowly, scuffing his heels, Simon walked back to the Residency. He was deathly tired, but somehow he felt exalted.

The red light on the radio set was gleaming. He tuned it in, to hear from his father, who had landed safely in Apia after a stormy night at sea.

'Anything to report?' asked Mr Davis.

Simon hesitated. He wanted to boast of his task in persuading the Air Force doctor to come and save Rangi's life; he wanted to tell of the fires, and his own new-found authority. But, he thought, boys boasted and men did not. He felt every bit a man, like Rangi. Almost, he felt that he, too, would soon be six feet tall.

'No,' said Simon casually, deepening his voice like his father's. 'I could cope with everything that happened. Don't worry, Dad. Leave everything to me.'

Then he switched off, and, with long strides, his hands behind his back, went whistling into his bedroom, to catch up on his neglected sleep.

Sherwood's Sharp Shooters

Sherwood's Sharp Shooters

by Ray Marr

Arrows bit deep into the archery target. Terry Hawkins was shooting with deadly accuracy across a small field surrounded by the tall oaks of Sherwood Forest.

It was not the spreading forest of Robin Hood's day – but of the present time. And though the boys wore Lincoln green, their clothes were of a modern cut. They wore the blazers and caps of Forest Glade School, situated a little way outside Nottingham, for they were Fifth Formers.

'Good shooting, Terry,' cried Alan Charters. 'You've got four golds there.'

Terry Hawkins looked in bewilderment at the target. He could see four of his arrows in the gold central ring. But he had shot six. Where were the other two?

'I'm sure they all landed in the gold,' he said.

'Come off it,' chuckled Leslie Morton. 'You must have missed the target with the other two!'

Neither of the other two had shot so well as Terry, but all their arrows were in the target, scattered mostly round the edge.

'Four golds and two greens is what you've got,' Les laughed, meaning that Terry had hit the ground with his two missing shots.

Quickly they ran to the target and began to search for the missing arrows. They found one well behind the target, almost in the hedge that bordered the little field where they had been practising. Terry eyed the shaft of gleaming aluminium tubing – for modern archers use tubular arrows which are more accurate than wooden ones. He thought he knew what had happened.

'From the way it's lying, that shaft must have come straight through the gold,' he said. 'I should say the target's leaking!' Terry knew that after heavy use a target could become soft in the middle and would sometimes let an arrow pass right through it. This was known as 'leaking'.

'The other one must have leaked through, too,' he went on. 'Maybe it's in the hedge.'

It was only then that they noticed that a motor-cycle, which had been passing at the time, had pulled up farther down the path. It swung round and came back. Its rider dismounted and stormed towards them angrily.

'Hawkins! Morton! Charter! Which of you is responsible for this outrage?'

The angry face of Mr Gribble, their school's new assistant sports master, appeared above the hedge. In his hand he held a crash helmet which was transfixed by a gleaming arrow.

'I passed this way a few moments ago,' thundered the master, 'and one of you shot this arrow at me. Now, who was it? Own up at once!'

'It – it's my arrow,' Terry admitted. 'But I – I wasn't shooting at you, sir. And that path isn't usually used by anyone.'

'You will report to my study in the morning,' rasped the master. 'In the meanwhile you will put those weapons away. There will be no more shooting with such dangerous implements.'

Gloomily the three pals watched him go.

'That really has done it,' Alan groaned. 'Now what do we do for practice? What hope have we of shooting for the Sheriff's Cup now?'

The Sheriff's Cup was the school's oldest sporting trophy. It had been given to the school by its founder, Marney Grosset, whose ancestor had once been the Sheriff of Nottingham. In his day every boy could handle a bow and he had left the cup as a trophy to be held by the school's best archer each year.

For hundreds of years it had been competed for, but gradually interest in archery had died. For almost fifty years now there had been no shoot for the Sheriff's Cup. Now, archery was regaining popularity. It was the aim of the three pals of the Fifth to revive the contest under the terms of the school charter:

'Anye ladde that shalle have skille enoughe to hit ye marke at four score paces and ten shalle have ye right to shoot for ye cup.'

Terry looked thoughtfully at the target and then at the little field where they stood.

'I don't know,' he said. 'This could be the best thing that's happened to us. This field's too small, anyway. We're shooting at only forty yards range instead of the ninety yards laid down in the conditions of the competition for the Sheriff's Cup.'

'But there isn't another field anywhere near,' Alan protested.

'There is,' Terry corrected him, 'the school playing field – and I'm going to tell Grib we want to use it.'

'What, ask him if we can use the school playing field?' Leslie gasped in stupefaction. 'After pranging his hat with an arrow? You'd never dare!'

'I don't see why not,' Terry answered with a determined air. 'I'm going to tell him we want to form a school archery club. To shoot for the Sheriff's Cup is part of the tradition of the school. Grib can't go against that. And the very fact of that accident should show him our need for a ground.'

But despite his confident words Terry hadn't much hope as he mounted the steps towards Mr Gribble's study the following morning.

His pals waited in the school's dark-raftered old main hall. High on a wall above them hung a glass case. Within it gleamed the silver Sheriff's Cup.

Terry's feet sounded heavily on the stairs as he came down towards them. And without a word being said they could tell what happened.

'He said no,' declared Alan. 'I knew it.'

'You're right. He refused point blank,' Terry confirmed.

The three of them gazed thoughtfully up at the Sheriff's Cup.

'I wonder what Marney Grosset would say,' Leslie mused, 'if he knew we were stopped from shooting for the cup.'

Terry's jaw hardened.

'We haven't been stopped yet,' he snapped. 'And I jolly well told the Grib that, too. It's stated in the school charter that any boy who can shoot well enough can take part in the competition shoot for the cup.'

'But that's just it,' Alan insisted. 'We don't know whether we can shoot well enough yet. Why, we haven't shot at over forty yards range yet – and we'll have to shoot at ninety for the cup. Where else are we going to find a bit of open land with a range of ninety yards? It's all too thickly wooded.'

Terry looked at his pals, a strange glint in his eyes.

'There's one place,' he said. 'The old priory ruins. There's plenty of room there. It's enclosed by high walls, so we won't be seen and interrupted.'

'Gosh,' gasped Alan. 'The priory. But it's supposed to be haunted! Have you forgotten – the Priory Ghost . . . ?'

They all fell silent at his words.

The Priory Ghost! All of them had heard of the strange monk-like figure that was reputed to walk the walls of the ruined priory not far from the school in a glade of Sherwood Forest.

Terry broke the silence.

'Ghosts? Nonsense!' he snorted. 'I'll start worrying about

ghosts when I see 'em. And the priory is an ideal spot for archery. What do you say, chaps? Are you game to give it a try?'

'Count us in!' came the swift reply from Alan and Leslie.

Terry made some enquiries and found out who owned the priory ruins. Excitedly he took the news to his pals.

'A real stroke of luck!' he cried. 'The priory belongs to Colonel Humphreys, an old boy of the school. And he was delighted when I asked if we could use it, for he used to be an archer himself. In fact, he was the last holder of the Sheriff's Cup, fifty years ago!'

Terry beamed at his pals.

'He's all in favour of a school archery club starting again and he's going to persuade Mr Gribble to take an interest in it himself. Meanwhile, we can use the priory all we want to!'

On their next free evening the boys took their target and archery gear to the ruined priory for their first practice. All about were the gnarled old trees, and a light mist breathed eerily around the place. The long shadows of evening were already falling across the ground.

'We'll have to look sharp,' grinned Terry. 'We don't want to be shooting in the dark.'

They set the target up and began to aim.

But after only a few arrows had been shot there came a startling interruption. From the darkness of the trees about the priory there came a loud, shuddering groan. It was repeated twice, seeming to echo and re-echo about the ancient, ruined walls.

'Gooo-o aw-a-ay,' it said. 'Go-o-o a-wa-a-ay.'

Leslie and Alan stiffened, startled. Terry let out a snort.

'Is this someone's idea of a joke?' he snapped.

But a moment later a startled gasp burst from all three.

For a strange, dark, wavering figure had appeared on the

'It's the Priory Ghost!'

ruined wall before them. Taking on the shadowy shape of a cowled monk, it began to drift slowly along the top of the wall in a weird and sinister way.

'A g-ghost!' gasped Leslie. 'It's the Priory Ghost!'

The ghostly figure moved right along the wall to the point where it merged with the forest.

Chilled by the shock of the apparition, the boys could only stare dumbly as the figure vanished among the trees. Terry was the first to find his tongue.

'It – it's a joke,' he muttered. 'It – it must be.'

'It's coming back!' cried Alan suddenly.

The apparition moved out from the trees and swayed through the air towards the ruins once again.

'Let's get out of here!' gasped Alan.

But Terry was determined not to be scared off. His bow was still in his hand, and an arrow ready on the string. He was sure the 'ghost' wasn't a man dressed up, so he took rapid aim, and –

Twang!

Straight and true the arrow flew, right towards the black, swaying figure.

And through it!

And the apparition was quite undisturbed. At the same steady pace it moved on until it vanished among the ruins.

That was too much. The boys turned on their heels and bolted from the priory.

It was only when he was alone that a sudden thought came to Terry.

'My arrow! The arrow I shot at the ghost! I mustn't lose it!' he gasped.

The arrow was one of a matched set. He would never be able to get an exact replacement – and he certainly would not be able to afford a new set with such expensive arrows.

Grimly, Terry turned.

'Ghost or no ghost, I'm going back,' he resolved. 'I've got to find that arrow.'

He hurried back towards the priory at a swift pace, determined not to be put off by the sight of this phantom figure.

'There's still time to find it before the light goes completely,' he told himself. 'But if it's left all night, the damp will ruin its flight.'

He concentrated all his thoughts on the arrow, not allowing himself even to think of the ghost as he entered the priory again and began to search the ruins.

Bow slung across his shoulder, he mounted the wall – the same wall the ghost had walked along – and tried to pick out the spot where that shot would have landed. Anxiously his eyes peered for the silvery glint of the arrow.

Suddenly the bow across his shoulder gave a jerk. He spun around. What had touched it?

But there was nothing there! It was just as if a ghostly hand had reached out to pluck it from him.

Terry felt a shiver run down his spine, yet determinedly he moved on. He had to find this arrow.

And as he moved along the bow was plucked yet again. Fiercely Terry swung round, and saw something which made him stare in surprise.

Stretching just above his head was a long length of fishing line, so thin as to be almost invisible. It was this which had caught the upper end of Terry's bow. It went from the ruin towards the trees, above the wall.

He followed the line to its end. It was fastened to a nail hidden among the ivy. As he gazed at it thoughtfully, Terry knew he was close to a solution of the mystery of the ghost.

'What's at the other end?' he wondered.

He scrambled to the ground and made for the tree to which the thin line led. Laying down his bow he began to clamber into the branches.

He was half-way up the tree when he spotted what he had guessed he would find. Hanging from a branch was a dark mass of cloth. It was a big cloak, roughly made. There was a coat hanger in it – and to the coat hanger was tied the end of another length of fishing line.

'I thought so,' he breathed.

This cloak that he held was indeed the 'ghost'. It was worked quite simply. The coat hanger would be hooked on to the stretched fishing line with the other length in the hand of the person who wanted the ghost to walk.

Then the operator in the tree pulled in on the line and the 'ghost' would move along the fixed line.

It was a simple, yet effective, trick.

'But it won't be played again,' Terry thought as he rolled up the line and put it in his pocket. 'Just wait till the chaps hear how they were tricked.'

He picked up his bow and made for the ruins again, to look for his arrow. There was a frown on his face as he began his search. He was wondering who had rigged the ghost.

'It seems so pointless,' he thought. 'Hardly anyone ever comes to the priory. In fact, I'll bet the chaps and I were the first to come near for weeks. Who was the ghost intended to frighten? Us? Was the ghost for our special benefit?'

Why should anyone go to such elaborate lengths to stop the three pals of the Fifth from using the ground for their archery practice?

Terry stopped suddenly as he saw a silvery glint amidst the ivy. The arrow!

A moment later he was staring in astonishment at what he

had picked up from the ivy and now held in his hand.

It was not an arrow at all – it was a silver cup. A trophy!

'The Sheriff's Cup!' Terry gasped. 'Now, how on earth did it get here?'

With a new interest in his eyes, Terry began to fumble amongst the ivy. Perhaps he would find something more there. He tugged at a tough strand.

An instant later a great section of the ivy pulled to one side like a screen.

And behind it there was a low, squared doorway!

Terry stared at it in wonder. Where did it lead to? How had it remained concealed so long?

'Only one way of finding out,' he told himself.

Carefully he stepped forward into the darkness. There were steps downward. Terry groped his way down them, on tenterhooks with excitement.

He had taken about a dozen steps and the entrance was a faint blue of light behind him, when he heard a sound from ahead, a steady thudding sound.

More cautiously than ever, Terry moved on. The steps ended and he found himself in a long passage. At the end a light glimmered faintly. The thudding grew louder. Moments later Terry was peering into a small room with a heavy, iron-studded door that now stood open.

A hurricane lamp stood on the floor, its light flickering. Beyond it a man was at work with a pick – digging up a section of the floor.

Even as Terry saw him, he laid down his pick and with a grunt of triumph stooped to reach into the hole. He drew out a small but heavy casket.

'At last,' he breathed.

As he stood up Terry saw his face for the first time.

It was Mr Gribble!

Terry could not restrain a gasp of amazement at the sight of the assistant sports master in this strange place.

It was only a faint sound Terry made, but it was enough. The master looked up – and spotted him.

With one great leap he was on the boy. The master's powerful arms closed about him.

'Got you,' he snarled, dragging the lad to the light.

The cup that he had picked up fell from Terry's grasp. Mr Gribble snatched it up and looked at it, a curious glint in his eyes.

'So you wanted to win the Sheriff's Cup?' he said. 'Well, you can have it now – and much good may it be to you. It has served its purpose.'

From his pocket he drew a spool of the same fishing line that had operated the 'ghost'. Deftly he began to tie Terry's wrists and ankles with the tough material.

'There,' he grunted at last. 'You can't loosen that in a hurry.'

'But, sir!' Terry protested, hardly able to believe that it was really happening to him. 'What are you going to do?'

'Make sure you keep out of the way long enough for me to vanish without trace,' snapped Gribble.

'And with me will go this box of stuff worth fifty thousand pounds if it's worth a penny!'

He patted the casket gleefully.

'All the loot I'm after is contained in this,' he breathed. 'The family treasure of the late Marney Grosset.'

Gloatingly he told Terry how, in an ancient manuscript, he had come across a clue to the existence of the hoard. Details of the hiding place were engraved in the silver of the Sheriff's Cup. He had posed as a sports master in order to get his hands on the cup.

'So that's why you were so against our archery club starting!'

Terry exclaimed. 'It's all so clear to me now.

'Exactly,' said Gribble. 'I couldn't risk any chance of the cup being examined. And then you decided to use the priory ground itself. And that cut across my plans, too. You might have heard me at work.'

'And so you rigged the ghost to frighten us away,' Terry mused.

'Just so,' agreed the bogus master. He lifted the casket and made for the door. 'I'll bid you good day,' he smiled mockingly as the door began to creak shut.

'Hey!' Terry protested. 'You – you can't leave me here! Suppose no one finds me?'

'That will be just too bad for you!' came the callous reply, and the door clanged shut.

Terry wrestled furiously with his bonds. He was in a grim position. Apart from his desire to get free, he had to warn someone that the bogus master was a crook – and stop him getting away with his haul.

But his struggles only made the line bite into his wrists.

Deliberately he forced himself to lie still for long moments while he looked around his prison. Perhaps there would be a sharp edge of stone that he could rub his bonds on till they parted. But everything in the little room was old and smooth with age.

For a long time Terry lay motionless, racking his brains. Surely there must be some way of freeing himself.

Then his gaze rested on the lantern which Gribble, in his haste, had left behind.

'Of course!' he exclaimed as he wriggled his way towards it and held his wrists over the funnel. 'This line's made of plastic — and it won't stand heat.'

As the line warmed it began to soften. Terry had to grit his

58

teeth against the pain as his wrists were burned. But the line gave before Terry suffered any serious harm. He quickly proceeded to untie his ankles.

Free at last, he stood up in relief and rubbed life back into his wrists and ankles. Then quickly he made for the door.

But as he pushed at it, his heart sank. The door was firmly fastened on the outside. He was still a prisoner. For a moment despair was near. Then the thought came to him that the air in the room was fresh. At least he would not suffocate.

But why should it be fresh? There was no entrance save the tightly closed door.

With fresh hope he seized the lantern and began to walk round the prison with the lamp in his hand. All the time he watched the flame. At one spot it flickered wildly.

Yet there was no sign of any opening in the wall.

Terry held the lamp higher. There must be an opening. The lamp flickered more than ever.

And only then did Terry think of looking upward.

In the low ceiling above him there was a square hole which might at one time have been a chimney.

But though the hole was there, it was beyond Terry's reach – and even if he could have reached it, it was too narrow for him to climb up through.

Longingly, he stared at it. He could see the sky far above, already almost dark.

'Trapped!' Terry groaned. 'Trapped within sight of freedom!'

How long would it be, he wondered, before anyone noticed he was missing? Perhaps people might search the priory but would they ever find that cunningly concealed entrance?

If only there was some way of getting a message out of the cell. Gloomily he paced round and round the little cell, trying desperately to think of a way to escape. He tripped over his bow as he went and automatically stooped to pick it up.

And as he did so, the idea came to him – the one way of getting himself out of his prison.

From his pocket he snatched his archery score pad and began to scribble a message on it. Then, with trembling fingers, he tied it to the shaft of an arrow with a piece of the fishing line!

'If only my aim is true!' he muttered.

His heart beating with anxiety and hope, he notched the arrow on the bowstring and moved to the floor beneath the chimney.

He could still see the sky above, outlined in the chimney shaft. The shaft looked very narrow now, so narrow that he could hardly hope his plan would work.

He swung the bow up and aimed long and carefully. The bow sang, and the arrow shot upwards. Breathlessly Terry waited for the grating sound that would tell him it had struck the side of the chimney, that his shot had failed.

But the shot had been perfect. Straight and true up the centre of the chimney soared the arrow to vanish into the gathering night.

Then there was nothing more that Terry could do. He could only hope that the arrow would land somewhere where it would be spotted quickly.

Terry settled down to wait. But not for long.

Ten minutes might have passed from the shooting of his arrow when he heard a sound at the door. It swung open and Alan and Leslie came bursting in.

'Terry! You're all right!' they cried, relief on their faces.

'I'm O.K.,' he said. 'But – quickly – let's get out of here. We've got to make sure that Mr Gribble doesn't escape!'

Rapidly Terry explained what had happened, and the pals sped back to school. The headmaster at once phoned the police,

The bow sang and the arrow shot upwards.

and the bogus master was apprehended before he could get away from the district.

'Thanks to your splendid shot with that arrow,' the Head told Terry when he had heard of Mr Gribble's arrest, 'the thief didn't get away. I don't think I can give you a better reward than to tell you that I shall give my personal backing to the formation of a school archery club.

'As soon as a number of you have mastered the art of shooting at ninety yards' range, we will re-institute a competition for the Sheriff's Cup as in olden times.'

'Gosh, that's a super reward, sir!' cried Terry. 'I couldn't ask for anything better.'

Masked Menace of the Boxing Ring

Masked Menace of the Boxing Ring

by John Marshall

Biff Bailey and his manager Barney Sullivan were watching a contest from the gallery of a boxing hall. They could have had ringside seats, among other famous sporting characters who were at the fight, but Biff was a modest lad and he preferred to enjoy being a spectator without being noticed by his fans.

In the ring the Masked Marvel, the latest heavyweight sensation, was hammering the stuffing out of his reeling opponent, Clem Gallie.

'The Masked Marvel has won all his fights by knockouts so far. None of his opponents has been able to stay the distance with him, let alone defeat him,' said Biff. 'I'd like to have a crack at him. I think I could beat him.'

Biff was intently watching every move made by the men in the ring. The Masked Marvel was right on top. He was landing punches almost as he liked.

Biff, like everyone else in the boxing game, was intensely interested in the Masked Marvel, whose eyes were completely hidden by a close-fitting rubber mask, too tight to be dislodged by punches.

No one except the Masked Marvel's manager, Arty Peters, knew his identity. His career had been deliberately wrapped in mystery. He always wore the mask in public. He was smuggled in and out of boxing halls and the Peters' gymnasium with great secrecy. No one knew where he lived. Newspaper reporters were never allowed to interview him, but that didn't keep his name out of the papers. On the contrary, it prompted the sports reporters to write many columns of speculation about him.

Biff had to admit that Peters and his unknown fighter had hit on a clever publicity idea. Because of all the mystery that surrounded him, the Masked Marvel was getting far more attention from the newspapers and the public, and making more money out of his bouts, than many better fighters who deserved more notice.

The clever trick would continue to pay off for as long as the Masked Marvel continued to win fights the way he was doing tonight, but one day somebody was bound to call his bluff and flatten him for the count. Biff was eager to get the chance to do that, but as he made his request his manager shook his head.

'I've tried it, but Arty won't play,' Barney said. 'Every heavyweight in town is trying to get a crack at the Masked Marvel. Arty can pick the opponents he wants, and he isn't likely to give a bout to anyone like you, who might spoil the Masked Marvel's record. Once he gets beaten, the public will lose interest in this stunt, and Arty knows it. He isn't taking any chances.'

Biff scowled. 'Perhaps we can find a way to make him change his mind,' he said.

At that moment the Masked Marvel let fly a terrific right hook to the chin of his reeling opponent. Gallie hit the canvas like a ton of bricks, and stayed there for the count.

There were several other bouts on the card, but Biff had seen all he wanted.

'Let's get out of here,' he suggested, rising to his feet.

He had almost reached the exit door when he overheard a chance remark from a man sitting in the back row.

'I've heard an interesting rumour, Jack. Plenty of people are saying that the Masked Marvel is that fighter of Barney Sullivan's – Biff Bailey.'

Biff halted at the top of the stairs, and turned to his manager. 'Did you hear that?' he demanded.

Barney nodded.

'The newspaper boys haven't got hold of it yet, but there's a strong rumour going round the gyms that you're the Masked Marvel,' he admitted. 'After all, he's a lot like you in build and style.'

'People really believe that?' Biff asked.

'If it happened to be true it would get you a lot of publicity and earn you a lot of money,' Barney noted.

'But it happens not to be true, and we've got to stop it,' scowled Biff. 'This masked man idea is a cheap stunt that turns a boxing match into a circus act. I don't want my fans to think I've got anything to do with it. Who started this silly rumour anyway?'

'Wouldn't mind betting that it was Arty Peters himself, as soon as he spotted the resemblance between you and his man,' growled Barney.

'Then all the more reason why I should meet the Masked Marvel in the ring, and prove to everyone that we're two different people,' declared Biff. 'Come on. We're going to settle this right now.'

Biff led the way downstairs to the dressing rooms. Two burly men were posted outside the door of the Masked Marvel's room. As Biff and his manager neared the door, one of them made a menacing move towards Barney.

'Nobody is allowed in here. Beat it,' he growled.

Biff thrust himself forward.

'We want to talk to Arty Peters. Open that door,' he rapped.

The tough bunched his fist as if preparing to punch Biff, then recognised him, and hurriedly thought better of it.

'But – Mister Bailey – please – I got my orders from Arty.'

'I'll take responsibility for that,' Biff said, sticking out his jaw aggressively. 'Open the door for me immediately.'

The tough gulped uncomfortably, and looked appealingly at his pal, but he got no help there.

'Yes – Mister Bailey – sir –' gulped the first man.

Biff and Barney strode into the dressing room.

The mystery boxer, still masked, was on the rubbing table being attended by his seconds. Arty Peters swung around with an angry cry.

'Sullivan! Bailey! Who let you in here? Nobody is allowed to meet the Masked Marvel!'

'We're on special business,' Biff said sharply. 'I want a match with your mystery man. I've brought Barney along to fix the contract with you.'

Arty Peters grinned mockingly.

'Sorry. I've already got more offers than I can accept. The Marvel fights Tiger Wilson on Saturday – and after that, why I could keep him going for a year on the offers I've had already.'

'You've got to let him fight me,' Biff insisted. 'People are saying that I'm the Masked Marvel.'

'All the more reason why you two should never meet in the ring. It would ruin a good stunt,' chuckled Arty.

Biff began to grow red and angry.

'I've had to fight hard to gain a reputation for myself, and I'm not letting you play around with it,' he snapped. 'If you won't give me a bout I'll simply tell the newspapers and everyone the truth – that I'm not the Masked Marvel.'

'That wouldn't do any good,' chuckled Arty. 'If you kick up a lot of fuss denying it, people will only think it must be true.'

Biff clenched his fists in rage. Barney was afraid that he was going to throw himself at the rival manager and grabbed hold of him, pulling him towards the door.

'Come on, Biff, there's no sense in starting a fight,' he pleaded. Biff allowed himself to be dragged outside, but once they were clear of the dressing room he faced his manager grimly.

'I'm not giving in,' he promised.

'What are you planning to do?' questioned Barney anxiously.

'We can't talk here. Some of Arty's pals might overhear us,' he cautioned. 'Let's get back to your gym, and I'll tell you my plan.'

Half an hour later they were back at Barney Sullivan's gym. The place was cluttered with ladders, planks, trestles and cans of paint. Part of the gymnasium was being redecorated. Barney picked his way through the obstacles to his private office.

'We can talk here,' he said. 'What's this wonderful idea, Biff?'

'It's simple, really,' said Biff. 'All we have to do is find out who the Masked Marvel really is, then threaten to tell the truth if Arty refuses to let me fight him.'

'Simple!' choked Barney. 'Everybody in the boxing game has been trying for months to find out. No one is ever allowed to see the Marvel without his mask. Nobody knows where he disappears to after every fight. He's got a hideout somewhere, but Arty Peters is the only person who knows where it is. The Masked Marvel never does any training at Peters' gym. He does it at his hideout, using sparring partners who are taken there blindfolded in Arty's car.'

'Suppose we followed the car,' suggested Biff.

Barney scoffed at the suggestion.

'Arty is no fool. Plenty of newspaper reporters have tried to do that, but he takes good care that he is never followed,' he said. 'He has thugs stationed wherever he is to make sure no one is following him, and he always manages to lose anyone who tries to tail him.'

Biff was silently thoughtful for several minutes. He gazed distractedly at the cluttered gym with its ladders and cans of paint. Then suddenly his eyes lit up. 'Arty is probably on his guard tonight, after our squabble in the dressing-room. So we'll lay low for a few days to give him time to forget about it; but I mean to get to the bottom of this affair before the Masked Marvel has his next fight, and I think I know how to do it.'

★ ★ ★

It was three evenings later that Biff drove his car into a narrow turning about a hundred yards from Peter's gym. He backed his car into the opening; then switched off his lights, so that he could watch without being seen.

There were lights on in the gym, but there was no one outside. Arty's car was parked in a side entry.

Biff took a can of white paint from the seat beside him. After making sure that the street was deserted, he darted across to the entry, and dropped flat beneath the rival manager's car. He hooked the paint can beneath the car. With the blade of a pocket-knife he jabbed a small hole in the bottom. Immediately little blobs of paint began to drip from the can.

Biff wriggled clear, and ran to a telephone kiosk.

He dialled the number of the manager's office and heard Arty answer.

'I think you had better get out to the Masked Marvel's place,' said Biff. 'There's trouble brewing out there. Somebody's found out your hiding place and is trying to get in.'

He heard Arty splutter and gasp.

'Who's speaking? What the – what's the game? What do you mean?'

Barney hung up without answering, and raced back to his

own car. He hadn't long to wait. Things soon began to happen across at the gym.

First came the two toughs who had guarded the Masked Marvel's door. They looked up and down the street.

A taxi was approaching.

'Hold it, boss,' one of them warned.

The taxi went by. For a moment the street was clear. Then two people turned the corner, walking slowly. The tough eyed them suspiciously. They waited until the two strangers were out of sight and the street was empty again.

'All right now, boss,' one of the toughs said.

Arty came storming out of the doorway.

'I wish I knew who made that telephone call,' he snarled. 'If this is someone's idea of a joke –'

He climbed into his car and drove away. Biff was given no chance of following him immediately, for the two men stood in the street, watching. They waited until the car's tail-light, small in the distance, turned a corner and disappeared.

They stepped back inside the building. Biff's hand reached for the self-starter, then halted.

He spotted that the two men were in the entrance-hall of the building. They were hidden in the shadows, still watching the street to make sure no one trailed Arty.

A full five minutes passed, then the two shadowy figures, satisfied that all was well, disappeared into the building.

Arty by now must have been a couple of miles away, and normally it would have been impossible to pick up his trail, but Biff was putting his trust in the hidden can of paint.

He started the car up quietly, and eased slowly out of the alley, turning in the direction Arty had taken. Ahead of him was a widely spaced trail of shining white paint spots that had dripped from the car.

Biff had to drive slowly to make sure that he didn't miss the tell-tale trail. Arty had doubled and twisted through a maze of quiet suburban streets. Evidently it was all part of his plan to try to make sure that no one followed him.

Biff judged he had driven at least ten miles to and fro before he spotted Arty's car parked outside a detached house in a quiet street not two miles from the gymnasium.

Biff left his car and approached the house cautiously. If he could only catch a glimpse of the mystery man without his mask, and recognise him, his quest would be over.

He prowled round the house. Lights showed behind a curtained window on the ground floor, but all windows and doors were firmly locked.

Determined not to be beaten, Biff crept back to the front of the house. Suddenly his eyes fell upon a coal chute in the path up to the front of the house. Biff silently lifted the iron cover, and let himself drop through the hole. He landed on a pile of coal, eased his way down it without making any noise, and cautiously groped his way across the cellar to a flight of wooden steps. Quietly he climbed up.

The door at the top of the steps wasn't fastened. He stepped out into a passage, and heard a murmur of voices coming from behind a door. Grinning to himself he tiptoed towards the door, and put his ear to it as he recognised Arty's snarling voice.

Biff felt that, with luck, he might hear Arty call the mystery boxer by name, and that would be all Biff wanted to know.

'I don't like it,' he heard Arty say. 'If there's nothing wrong here, why did somebody telephone me? You're not trying to double-cross me, are you? You're sure some reporter didn't sneak in here and bribe you to keep quiet about it?'

'Don't be a fool,' came the impatient answer. 'Why should I? I've got everything to lose if I let my identity be known.'

'So long as you understand that,' growled Arty, 'and do as you're told against Tiger Wilson, we'll both clean up a packet.'

The mystery man chuckled.

'I've got to hand it to you, Arty. It was a clever idea. We've built up the Masked Marvel as a man who can't lose. He's beaten everybody he's met so far, including Curly Howard and Clem Gallie. Now he meets Tiger. Curly stopped Tiger Wilson in three rounds, Clem put Tiger out for the count in just under two minutes. So all the mugs who like to have a little bet will think it's a certainty for me – the Masked Marvel – to make mincemeat of Tiger.'

'But you won't,' warned Arty.

There was another chuckle from the mystery man.

'Not likely. This time the Masked Marvel loses, the mugs will lose their money, you and I will share the winnings, and the Masked Marvel will never be heard of again!'

'Nothing must go wrong,' Arty said. 'We've worked hard to pull off this stunt. Now that we're so close to the end of it, I'm getting jumpy. That telephone call tonight –'

'Forget it. Just somebody's idea of a joke. Or perhaps some smart reporter thought it up and meant to follow you, but changed his mind when he saw your men on the watch.'

'I hope you're right,' muttered Arty anxiously. 'But I think I'd better be getting back to the gym before –'

Biff backed swiftly and silently from the door. He hadn't learned the identity of the mystery man, but he had learned enough.

The Masked Marvel stunt wasn't just a novelty to attract the fans to fights. It was a clever swindle!'

Biff left the house silently, the same way as he had entered it, and within an hour he was in Barney's office, angrily repeating what he had heard.

'I'm not altogether surprised. Arty always was a bit shady,' Barney declared.

'If the Masked Marvel is beaten, the gamblers are going to suspect that they've been cheated, even though they can't prove it,' Biff pointed out. 'And don't forget that because of this rumour that Arty started, a lot of people think that I'm the Masked Marvel. For the rest of my career there will be a lot of fans who'll suspect that I was once mixed up in a swindle!'

Barney groaned.

'But what are we going to do?' he demanded. 'Suppose you go to the boxing authorities and tell them what you've overheard? You've no proof. Arty will simply deny it.'

'I've got a much better idea,' Biff answered grimly. 'Once I asked you to get me a fight against the Masked Marvel. But I've changed my mind. On Saturday night I'm going to *be* the Masked Marvel, and smash Arty's crooked scheme by giving Tiger the hiding of his life.'

Barney looked thunderstruck.

'How can you be the Masked Marvel?' he asked, bewildered.

'Just for one night. I've got it all worked out,' chuckled Biff. 'Listen.'

Biff wagged his finger at Barney.

'To help build up the mystery of his identity, the Masked Marvel always insists on having a dressing-room to himself,' Biff went on. 'He also likes to be left alone until it is time to go into the ring. Give me just a few minutes with him on his own in that room, and I'll make sure that I'm the one who fights Tiger.'

'You'll never pull it off,' protested Barney. 'Arty has the Masked Marvel more closely guarded than the crown jewels, from the moment he goes into the dressing-room.'

'But I'm not going to try to pass Arty's musclemen after the Masked Marvel has gone in,' explained Biff with a grin.

'I'm going to be in there waiting for him!'

'But – how?'

Biff led Barney from the office and out into the gym, which was still in the midst of being redecorated.

'A pot of paint helped me make a fool of Arty once,' he said. 'I think it might come in useful again!'

★ ★ ★

That Saturday evening, an hour before the fight programme was due to start, the fans were already queuing outside the stadium, waiting for the doors to be opened. Once again they had been drawn by the magic name of the Masked Marvel.

A cheer went up as a uniformed attendant appeared inside the foyer to unlock the doors.

At that moment a figure appeared on the pavement and began to push through the crowd. It was Biff. He wore a painter's long white coat and a cap was pulled well down over his eyes. He carried a can of paint and a brush in one hand and had a short ladder balanced on his shoulder.

'Gangway, please. Mind your backs,' shouted Biff briskly.

He mounted the steps just as the doors were opened. Then he halted. Arty had become more and more agitated as the day of the big match approached. Biff turned quickly sideways so that his face was hidden by the ladder.

Biff waited until Arty was out of sight and then lumbered through the doors. The attendant shot him a swift, puzzled glance.

'Which is the dressing-room that needs painting, chum?' asked Biff.

'I don't know anything about it. You'd better see the manager,' answered the attendant impatiently. 'Through the double door, turn right at the bottom, third on the left past the dressing-rooms.'

Biff nodded, grinned to himself, and disappeared through the doors. He was in!

Some time later a car brought the Masked Marvel and his two bodyguards to the stadium. The mystery man was already wearing the rubber mask which covered his eyes. The bodyguards cleared a way for him through the excited crowds. He hurried to his dressing-room, and went in alone, the bodyguards remaining at their posts outside. Then one of them locked the door.

The Masked Marvel chuckled to himself. He refused to share Arty's uneasy fears. Tonight was the pay-off.

Then he froze. He realised he wasn't alone. Biff, in boxing kit, stood waiting by the window.

The mystery man gulped wordlessly.

'Let's have that mask off,' said Biff quietly.

In blind panic the mystery man leapt at Biff, swinging his fists. It was a sad mistake. The Masked Marvel, despite the big build-up he had been given in a series of arranged victories, was only a third-rate boxer.

His wild blows swiped the air as Biff ducked under them. He tried to yell for help, but to no avail.

Biff closed the mystery man's mouth with a powerful uppercut, slammed him again, then caught him before he could make a noise hitting the floor.

Biff hauled the limp mystery man to a cupboard, sat him down inside, and peeled off the rubber mask. One look at the man's face was enough.

'Well, well. Wild-Bull Terry. That explains a lot,' murmured Biff.

Wild-Bull was an unsuccessful fighter who, about six months

earlier, had had his licence taken away for trying to bribe a referee.

Someone rapped on the door, and a hoarse voice called:

'Marvel. You're on.'

'Coming,' growled Biff.

He slipped the tight rubber mask over his face, threw the Masked Marvel's dressing-gown across his big shoulders, closed the cupboard door on his victim, and was ready as the key turned in the lock.

Biff stepped out into the corridor. Arty was waiting, and took his arm.

'Tiger understands exactly what to do,' he whispered. 'Make it look good for a couple of rounds. Then in the third he'll swing an uppercut to the jaw. That'll be your cue to dive for the floor and stay there.'

Biff nodded grimly, and behind the mask his eyes glittered.

The crowd gave him a tremendous reception as he climbed into the ring. The moment the bell rang for the opening of the first round the fans began to howl for action. They had paid to see an exhibition of fireworks from the Masked Marvel, and Biff was determined that they shouldn't be disappointed.

Tiger, confident that this was a fight he couldn't lose, came bounding across the ring, both fists working, tip-tapping at Biff's head.

Biff stopped him with a solid right to the jaw, and followed up with a smack on the nose that made Tiger's head ring.

Anger flared in Tiger's eyes. He cuffed at Biff, who promptly slammed the blow aside and countered with a hard right to the jaw.

Tiger, indignant, tied Biff up in a clinch.

'Take it easy,' he hissed. 'What do you think you're doing? Those last two hurt!'

'You're going to get hurt a lot more before we're finished,' Biff promised him. 'If you want to win you've got to fight for it!'

Tiger backed away, looking puzzled, as the referee made them break the clinch.

Biff went after his opponent, and Tiger retreated hastily.

The fans began to hoot and bellow. In the Masked Marvel's corner Arty was beginning to become alarmed, sensing that something was wrong.

Biff let his guard drop.

Tiger fell for the tempting move. He stopped his retreat and leapt at Biff with gloves swinging.

Biff ducked the flying leather, and caught Tiger as he came in, landing solid punches that rocked him down to his heels.

Tiger lost his temper, and flung himself wildly at Biff, throwing punches with both hands.

Biff met the attack coolly. He weaved and swayed, making Tiger miss again and again. Then, picking the right moment, he countered with swift hooks that had Tiger reeling.

The fans yelled in delight. Their favourite, the Masked Marvel was bang on form. He had never looked so good!

The round ended, and Biff trotted to his stool. Arty was waiting for him in a furious temper.

'What are you trying to do, you big clown?' hissed Arty. 'Stop showing off, or you'll ruin everything. You've got Tiger in trouble!'

'I know what I'm doing,' growled Biff.

Tiger was a badly worried man when the second round started. He had expected an easy fight. Instead he found himself up against a man who was a raging fury, and whose every punch was loaded with dynamite. He spent the whole round trying to dodge trouble.

Arty was livid when Biff returned to his corner at the end of round two.

'All right. You've had your fun,' he snarled. 'You've made Tiger look a fool. But this is where you have to let him turn the tables. The third round is coming up. You hit the floor and stay there!'

When the bell rang for the third round, Tiger flung himself at Biff, pushed him back against the ropes, and draped both arms around him.

'Now it's my turn,' hissed Tiger. 'This is the round when –' he broke off.

He suddenly noticed something. Bewilderment showed in his face.

'Hey! You ain't the guy who was in Arty's office when I signed the contract. His eyes were brown. Yours are grey. Who are you?'

'The name,' said Biff, 'is Biff Bailey!'

Tiger smothered a gasp of dismay.

At that moment there was a commotion in Biff's corner. The bodyguards had arrived with Wild-Bull Terry, who had managed to kick his way out of the cupboard.

Arty, his face as white as chalk, was staring first at Terry, then at the man in the ring.

Biff decided it was time to bring things to a climax.

Coolly and deliberately, Biff began to hammer the worried Tiger Wilson with every punch he knew.

Tiger tried desperately to back away from the onslaught of leather, but Biff was on him like a shot, flinging telling blows with such precision that his opponent didn't have time to think.

At last Tiger began to backtrack round the ring so fast that he almost fell over his own feet. Biff cornered him and swung a sledge-hammer punch at Tiger's jaw.

Arty aimed a murderous blow at Biff's head.

Dazed, Tiger closed with Biff, trying to gain time in a clinch. But Biff was determined to end the fight right then and there.

He pushed Tiger off and slammed a barrage of punches at him. Tiger did his best to stand up and make a fight of it, but he had no chance against Biff's thundering fists. He was bounced and hammered all round the ring until a crashing hook to the chin toppled him to the canvas, out for the count.

The fans stood on their seats and cheered like mad. But more excitement was in store for them.

Biff snatched off the mask. Instantly a great yell went up.

'Biff Bailey! So it was Biff all the time! We knew it –' Biff made a grab for the M.C.'s microphone.

'Your attention, please!' he bellowed. 'I want to tell you the real truth about the Masked Marvel.'

There was a shriek from Arty, who saw that he was a ruined man. He had gambled every penny he could raise on Tiger. Thanks to Biff, he had lost the lot.

Beside himself with rage, he grabbed up a water bottle and sprang into the ring. 'Don't listen to him –' he yelled.

He aimed a murderous blow at Biff's head. The fans howled. Biff whirled. He ducked the swinging blow. Then – wham! His fist caught the screaming manager on the jaw.

The bottle dropped from Arty's fingers. He wobbled round the ring and fell over Biff's fallen opponent.

The sensational ending to the fight filled the stadium with confusion, and by the time order had been restored it was discovered that Arty and his fellow plotters had slipped away from the building. Biff gave a full account of his actions to the stadium officials, and Arty made no attempt to come forward and challenge them. His gymnasium was sold up, and he was never seen around the boxing arenas again. Neither was Wild-Bull Terry.

The Dangerous Road

The Dangerous Road

by David C. Newton

The sun was a blazing red glow, sinking like a mighty fire over the edges of the western hills. Small ridges of cloud, like cotton wool, hung in the sky.

Upon a solitary hill there was a cottage, and outside this little building stood a curious-looking man, watching the sunset and twirling his long white moustache as he said to himself, 'Remarkable! Remarkable, I must say! I wonder how it's done?'

He stood pondering the marvel of the sunset for just a little longer, then turned his back on it and faced a car. It was of very ancient make, but so clean and bright, with its brass-work gleaming like copper in the sunset, that it might have been built only yesterday. The gentleman had bought this car in 1912 and had faithfully and carefully preserved it ever since.

He now advanced upon the machine and bent over the driver's door – it was a two-seater, although it was as long as a locomotive – and began to adjust the various brass levers and knobs which would make it possible, he hoped, to start the mighty engine.

He retarded the ignition, opened the throttle a little, shifted a great brass lever on the steering-wheel with a rasping noise from the ratchet on which it was mounted, then, throwing up the bonnet side, he opened the petrol cocks, one of which was on the top of each cylinder. Having done this he took up from the grass upon which the car stood a large oil-can which was full of petrol. With this he proceeded to squirt petrol into each cylinder cock. That done, he carefully closed the cocks, checked over his preparations, and went round to the front, where he halted facing the great brass radiator. He put on a pair of gloves, and in a tone of hope mixed with pleading he said, 'Now then, old horse! Let's see if we can do it first time.'

After that he gave a hearty bellow of laughter, bent and grasped the great starting-handle with both hands and, making a fearful grimace to the sky, he pulled the handle sharply upwards. One cylinder fired. It was a very large cylinder, for the whole engine was some forty horse-power, and it fired, unfortunately, the wrong way; that is to say, it fired backwards. Simultaneously another cylinder decided to fire forwards owing to the fact that at that moment there was a fault in the ignition system. So from the bonnet there burst out through the carburettor a mass of black smoke and, with a crack like a field gun going off, a similar cloud shot out of the exhaust pipe at the back.

Audacious Cotterell — for such was the gentleman's name — fell back on the grass and gave a thunderous roar, which compared very well in volume to the explosion from the old engine.

'Great thundering backfires!' he said. 'That was worse than the last time I tried to start it! I must take it down to the boys and have it looked at.'

He picked himself up, still undaunted, grasped the handle and had another go. One cylinder fired, the right way this time. Another one gave a loud pop, and then, like some monstrous animal waking from years of sleep, the engine began to turn over with such fury that the whole car shimmered, shivered, shuddered, juddered and shook, so that the glimmering machine began to look rather like a mirage.

'Well done, old girl!' panted Audacious.

He rushed round the car as fast as he could, hurled himself into the driving seat and opened the hand throttle just in time; for the monstrous engine was then on the point of stopping again.

Audacious now had control of the engine, and as he opened the throttle the exhaust roared – after a preliminary bang which made the cottage windows rattle – and the grass which was standing immediately behind the exhaust pipe was blown flat by the furious smoke, like the exhaust from a jet engine.

Once sure that the engine would not stop, Audacious got nimbly out and closed the shivering bonnet. That done, he ran to the five-barred gate which led from his field to the road, opened it, ran back, threw himself almost head-first into the driver's seat, and proceeded to engage the mighty gears with a crash that made the whole machine jolt suddenly. The car roared out through the gate, swerved round in the roadway, and proceeded to go downhill at a very fast pace indeed.

Audacious Cotterell had loved this car for so many years that he was rather astonished that it had lately become difficult to start. But he still had unbounded faith in the rest of it, including the two brakes on the back wheels, which had not really the power to arrest the weight of the machine once it was going at any sort of speed. So he steered gallantly down the hill to the village at the bottom, where the road he was on joined the main road at right angles.

Approaching the junction, the old gentleman honked and tooted with his great rubber horn, as a warning to everyone that he was shortly to charge on to the main road. It was getting rapidly darker and the road was greasy.

Audacious applied his brakes to slow down, the great car skidded, turned itself completely round in one lightning sweep, and thus entered the main road backwards, with Audacious struggling at the steering-wheel in a mighty endeavour to correct this sudden loss of control. He regained it suddenly, and the rear, having swung one way, now swung back the other, so that the nose of the car pointed in the direction that Audacious had originally planned to take. He was safely out of the skid.

He was still going at a good speed, in spite of these various changes in direction, and now he steered towards a big, iron-built garage on the right-hand side of the road. He thought he had full control, for the car steered across the road and towards the shut sliding doors of the garage. The old gentleman, with a sigh of relief, applied the brakes with the intention of stopping before he hit the doors themselves.

But fate was against him that evening. The brakes worked, but they did not work well enough. Audacious pulled on the hand-brake, but still it was not sufficient. He was swooping headlong towards the closed doors, knowing that he would require just a little more room than they allowed in which to stop. The doors rushed up at him like a mighty wall, and the nose of the Mercurial seemed about to crash.

Then, like a miracle – or as if someone had said 'Open Sesame!' – the doors parted in the middle and were flung back to each side, so that the car went through the opening and managed to come to a standstill in the middle of the concrete floor of the brightly lit garage.

'Gad,' panted Audacious. 'What remarkable service!'

Then, unaccountably, the mighty engine stopped, and there was a silence as two figures, standing in the open doorway, remained absolutely motionless. For the sudden arrival of the Mercurial was just as much a source of astonishment to these two as it had been to the grateful Audacious.

Audacious stepped majestically out of his old car, raised his deerstalker hat and with a low bow said, 'Gentlemen, I thank you.'

The smaller of these two surprised and dumb-stricken figures was quite a young fellow of about twelve with blue goggle eyes, standing out like marbles, and a round and jolly face.

'Gentlemen, I thank you.'

'Throw me into the bun shop!' said the small figure, finding his voice at last. 'I never seen such a bustin' and arrestin' in me life!'

'You sound, sir,' said Audacious, 'as if I had committed a burglary!'

'No, no, Mr Cotterell,' protested the small fellow. 'When I say arrest, I mean stop, halt, refuse to go, cease to move, a sort of absolute immobilisation all of a sudden – bang!'

The tall, red-headed youth beside him put his hands into his pockets and grinned.

'You must have been waiting outside for us, Mr Cotterell.'

'I was not, Gremlin,' replied Audacious. 'I assure you that if you hadn't opened the doors at that very moment, I should have crashed to a fearful death!'

'Seein' as we were right behind the doors,' put in the small fellow, 'we should've been in a simular prediculament!'

Audacious looked at the boy and twirled one end of his moustache.

'Bunst, me boy,' he said, 'I don't know where you get these words from.'

'Mr Cotterell, sir,' answered the boy, pushing his cap back on his untidy hair, 'some I knows, some I half remembers, and some just flash into my head like fireworks. But the rest,' he added proudly, 'I fabrickiates myself.'

'Which is why,' put in the red-headed Gremlin, with a broad grin, 'hardly anyone ever understands him until it's too late!'

Audacious guffawed. And while he stood chuckling and twirling his moustache, the young proprietor of the garage, John Wragg, came into the building from the gathering darkness of the road outside.

He was pale, and halted in surprise as he saw the ancient car standing undamaged in the middle of the garage floor. He breathed hard, as if he had been running and looked worried.

'By gosh!' he said. 'I thought you'd had it that time, sir! I saw you from up the road. Thought you'd hit the doors. Run straight into them!'

'No, no,' said Audacious, languidly brushing up his moustache. 'Thanks to splendid teamwork, the doors opened in the nick of time, and, under full control, I drove into the garage.'

'Phew!' whistled Wragg, mopping his brow, for he was warm both from running and from alarm. 'It looked to me as if you had no control at all, if you don't mind me saying so.'

'Well,' said Audacious, considering the remark and staring at the steel skeleton of the roof, 'there was a moment, when I came backwards into the village street. I confess I was having some difficulty with the steering then, Raggy, me boy.'

'Yes,' said Raggy, breaking into a grin. 'It looked to me rather like that. But still, no harm's done. And what can we do for you?'

'Oh, yes,' said Audacious. 'I want you to look at my –'

He broke off, and frowned with steely blue eyes at the oncoming night through the open doors.

It was clear to his audience, who knew him well, that Audacious had completely forgotten what he had come for.

'Ah!' said Audacious, and snapped his fingers in annoyance. 'Why, gad, sir! It's clean gone out of my mind!'

Bunst cocked his head on one side, eating a bun with a sort of meditative rhythm of his jaws. He was, in fact, very fond of reading the adventures of famous detectives of fiction, and from these stories he had got an ambition that he would like to be a detective himself. So now he kept his eye closed and pointed with a grimy finger at the absent-minded Audacious.

'I bet I can think what you came for,' he said, in tones of a detective accusing the murderer. 'You came to have your brakes took up! That was the reason, wasn't it?'

'Hang it, sir!' said Audacious. 'I came for nothing of the sort.'

'Oh,' said Bunst, disappointed. 'But it seems to me you do want them took up just the same.'

'Dash me!' said Audacious, leaning on the door of his car and pulling his ear. 'Dash me! What did I come for?'

Raggy grinned. The Gremlin winked. Bunst, quite unabashed and still certain that he had guessed right, pulled another bun from a pocket, and proceeded to munch.

'Something to do with the engine?' suggested the Gremlin.

'The engine!' said Audacious, smacking himself on the top of the head, as if to shake his brains into activity. 'Could it have been the engine? Let me think. Why, I do believe it was. Yes, indeed it was! I remember now.'

He frowned in a terrible way at Raggy, and added, 'It goes bang!'

He said the last word with such fury that they all jumped.

'Just like that,' said Audacious. 'Bang!'

'But where?' asked Raggy.

'Out through the carburettor when I start up. And, come to think of it, out of the back as well.'

'It bangs at both ends, does it?' asked the Gremlin.

'Absolutely, sir. At both ends.'

'Ignition,' said Raggy. 'It sounds as if your timing is wrong.'

'My timing, sir?' said Audacious sharply. 'I'll have you know I was always the most punctual man in the regiment!'

'I'm talking about the engine,' said Raggy, and opened the bonnet.

He looked inside at the great engine, with its highly polished copper pipes, brass tubes, and the forest of wires, all of which were spotlessly clean.

Raggy inspected the magneto, and the Gremlin went round to

the starting-handle, ready to turn the engine. Between them they found the fault within a minute.

'The magneto coupling has slipped round,' said Raggy, 'and it's worn. But it won't take very long to turn you up a new one.'

'Gad, sir! That's good news,' said Audacious. 'Very quick work. Very quick work indeed.'

There was a workshop at the back of the garage, partitioned off from the main part of the building by match-boarding. Behind this were work benches and machine tools, at which the trio had been working for so long in manufacturing a car of Raggy's own design. That car, white, like a shining ghost, now stood complete in a darkened corner of the large garage.

The job on the Mercurial was done in three-quarters of an hour. Meanwhile Audacious studied the fine lines of this modern white car as it stood in the corner. He went across to it. He sat in it. He had, in fact, ridden in it before, and had secretly formed the opinion that it was the best car he had ever come across. He wished that he could afford to order one from these enterprising young engineers. But the price was beyond his modest purse; also he was so fond of his old Mercurial, which he had owned for so many years that, even had he had the money, he would never have had the heart to 'hurt the old girl's feelings'.

When the job on the Mercurial was finished, he was still leaning on the side of the white Pegasus.

'You seem to have improved her since I saw her last!' he said. 'More gadgets, eh?'

'Not gadgets,' said the Gremlin, 'just things we think ought to be on every touring car.'

'By gad!' said Audacious. 'She looks fine. Like a new pin. I hear you have an order for two of them.'

'Yes,' Raggy answered. There was a worried look on his face.

'We've got the orders all right, but I'm afraid that we shall have to turn them down.'

At this Audacious stood up stiffly, and cried out, 'Turn 'em down, man? Do you mean retreat?'

Raggy grinned, but only fleetingly. Then he shrugged.

'I'm afraid so, sir. You see, it's going to cost us more than we can get to build two more of these. All our money has gone into this one.'

'Although we were hoping – –' started the Gremlin; and then broke off as Raggy gave him a sudden look.

Audacious noticed this glance between the two.

'Hoping what?' he demanded. 'Let me know, gentlemen, what the trouble is. Who knows, I may be able to lend a hand. Or at least,' he added, 'I may be able to help you find a way of getting over your difficulties.'

'Our difficulties,' said Bunst, 'are composootly financial.'

Audacious looked from Bunst to the Gremlin, and then to Raggy.

'Mmm,' he said. 'I can't help you get money to build two more of these cars. Although if you could build and sell two you would very soon get orders for a lot more!'

'We're pretty sure of that, sir,' said Raggy. 'The point is how are we going to build two? We spent everything in building this one, which is our prototype. We can't let it go. We couldn't sell this one because we'd have to use it to advertise the others we were hoping to build.'

'You see,' said the Gremlin, who was more forthright than any of the others, 'we were hoping to win the Grayfield prize.'

'Grayfield prize?' echoed Audacious. 'What's that?'

'Sir George Grayfield, sir,' the Gremlin explained, 'has offered a prize of ten thousand pounds for the best touring car of new design and ideas. Now Peggy is quite as good as anything we've heard of. I think she would stand a jolly good chance.'

'Well then, sir,' said Audacious, boldly. 'Your troubles are over!'

'You don't seem to grasp the point,' said Bunst solemnly. 'We're flat broke. We can't afford the money to let the garage be shut for a week and take part in the trial.'

'Trial?' said Audacious, 'is there a trial to it, too?'

'Yes, sir,' said Raggy, for now that the other two had let it out he didn't see any sense in keeping quiet any longer. 'You see, sir, the cars which enter for this aren't going to be judged on gadgets and new ideas alone. They've first of all got to drive from the highlands of Scotland to Cornwall over specially selected test roads, and then, finally, to take part in a speed and acceleration test in Sir George Grayfield's grounds – on the disused aerodrome – which is actually inside his estate.'

'Now it would cost us about a hundred pounds to get everything ready and for the expenses of the trip. And the fact of the matter is that we haven't got a hundred pounds to spare.'

'No, sir,' said Audacious, 'that I can well believe, as you haven't had the business very long. But still, you must do your best to try to raise it, because, if you win that competition, then,' he said, pointing at the roof, 'your fortunes are made, and you'll have nothing else to worry about! I shall look forward to hearing that you are taking part in the competition!'

'There's less than a week to go,' said the Gremlin, gloomily, 'and our chances of raising the money in that time – without selling the very car which we hope to use in the competition – are so small you need hardly think about it.'

'Never mind,' said Audacious, 'you never know which way luck may jump. Because luck, you know, gentlemen, is like a cat on hot bricks. You can't tell where it will go next.'

He got back into his ancient car and said, 'Gentlemen, I wish you good night. By gad, no!' he corrected himself. 'I haven't paid you for your work, eh? Must settle that, what? One thing about Audacious Cotterell; he's never owed any man a penny!'

His voice boomed through the place.

'How much do I owe you?' he said, taking off his gloves again and beginning to hunt through the pockets of his old-fashioned Norfolk suit.

'Oh, fifteen shillings, sir,' said Raggy.

'Very reasonable,' said Audacious, still hunting feverishly in his pockets. Then suddenly he stopped hunting and became rigid in the seat. 'Well, dash it, sir!' he cried, in a burst of rage. 'I've come out without any money! Not a single, solitary, jingling ha'penny have I got!'

'Well, leave it, sir. We don't mind,' said Raggy, grinning. 'We know you well enough.'

'Certainly not, sir!' said Audacious. 'Haven't I just told you I never owe any man a penny? You must take a cheque. I insist.'

He pulled out a cheque book and an old fountain pen of huge dimensions which shone with bands of gold.

'One of the first fountain pens ever made, sir,' he said to Raggy. 'It was given to me by my grandma,' he explained, scratching away in his cheque book while the pen made an alarming number of blots and splutters, which shot out in all directions. 'A fine old lady she was, sir. But dead these forty years, rest her!'

He ripped the cheque out of the book, and stuffed the book back into his pocket. The pen gave one last long squirt as he pushed the cap on, and covered his fingers with splotches of black ink.

He handed the cheque to Raggy, who turned to the Gremlin, and said, 'Give her a swing, Gremmy.'

The Gremlin grasped the starting-handle, while Audacious

manoeuvred the great brass controls and switches and levers. The Gremlin swung the handle up once, and the motor started with a roar and emitted a cloud of blue smoke.

'Good night, gentlemen!' bellowed Audacious from above the noise of his engine. 'I shall be seeing you very shortly, I'm sure!'

And so saying, he rammed the shift into reverse, and the old machine shot back through the open doors. It pulled up just in time to stop hitting the hedge opposite, then, turning on the headlights, Audacious engaged first gear and thundered away towards his home.

'The old chap is barmier than ever,' said Gremmy, with a grin.

'Oh, I don't think he's barmy,' said Raggy, laughing. 'He's just fond of old things and rather eccentric, that's all. Gosh! What a fountain pen that was! Blots all over the place.'

He lifted the cheque up.

'Look at this,' he said, 'you can hardly read –'

He broke off. He looked at the cheque. Then he looked at Gremmy.

'Well, can't you read it?' asked the Gremlin, coming closer.

'Yes,' said Raggy, very quietly, 'I can read it. Can you?'

The Gremlin looked and gasped in amazement.

The cheque was made our for the sum of one hundred pounds and fifteen shillings.

The Start of an Adventure

The three stood in a little group under the overhead lights of the garage, looking first at the cheque, and then at each other.

Finally Raggy looked up and said solemnly, 'Of course, we must return it.'

'I suppose so,' said the Gremlin, rather sadly.

'Return it?' said Bunst, offended. 'What for? It's a gift, that is. It was done a' purpose.'

'I know,' said Raggy, 'but we can't take it like that. It doesn't seem right somehow.'

'Listen,' said the argumentative Bunst, 'if somebody gives you something free will and willy-nilly, you aren't supposed to return it. It's like a Christmas present, that's what it is. Only it doesn't happen to be Christmas.'

'Yes, I know that,' said Raggy. 'But it isn't right for us to take it. We'll have to go up and give it back.'

'Well, of all the daft – –' began Bunst.

'Quiet, you shrimp!' said the Gremlin, although he looked almost as sorry as Bunst that they would have to give the cheque back. 'Well, we want to give Peggy a run anyway,' he added, as a sort of consolation. 'We'll pop up there now. Yes, I think that's the best idea.'

He turned towards the white car and started the engine. Raggy and Bunst got in beside the driver, and quietly and smoothly the Pegasus swept away from the garage, gleaming with the reflection of the starlight. They turned off the main road and climbed the hill to the solitary thatched cottage at the top.

'I think I'd better go alone,' said Raggy to the Gremlin.

'Okay,' said the Gremlin.

Raggy pushed open the garden gate, and seeing that the upstairs light was the only one that shone in the house, hesitated, wondering if Audacious was preparing for bed.

But at that moment the lighted window above was thrown open and, framed by the darkness, Audacious Cotterell appeared in his pyjamas and wearing a sleeping-cap. There then began a series of elephantine snorts, and Audacious's face became rather redder than usual. The snorting of his breathing was so loud that the panes of the little casement rattled in sympathy, and the ivy on the walls rustled uneasily. Audacious Cotterell was doing his deep-breathing exercises.

'Mr Cotterell!' Raggy called out.

The breathing stopped. Audacious stood with his chest so full of wind that he looked like a pouter-pigeon. He cocked his head on one side and then, letting this tremendous breath out to give force to his voice, he roared, 'Who is it?'

'It's me. Wragg, sir.'

The old gentleman came and leaned out over the sill. His nightcap, which had a bobble on the end, flopped over, so that the bobble tickled his nose.

'Hang these mosquitoes!' snapped Audacious, and at the same time hit himself on the nose. 'No, by gad! It wasn't one at all,' he said, his eyes watering from the effects of the blow.

Then, with a gesture of irritation, he pushed the top of the nightcap and the bobble behind his right ear so that it would not fall over his face again.

'Well, me boy? What's the matter now?'

'It's about this cheque, sir,' said Raggy. 'I hardly know how to put it. It was so – generous of you, and – well – I hardly know what to say.'

'Well, hang it! You've said it twice already!' said Audacious. 'Make up your mind.'

'Well, sir,' said Raggy, plucking up courage. 'I mean – it's awfully generous of you – but we can hardly take this money.'

'Take it?' said Audacious.

He stopped and thought for a moment. Then, with a cunning glint in his eye, he went on. 'Gad, sir, you aren't taking anything. I'm making an investment, that's all. I'm putting that hundred pounds into your firm. And if you're a businessman, me boy, you can't refuse it.'

Raggy was nonplussed. He did not know what to say to this.

'Well, you understand, don't you?' said Audacious, after a pause. 'It's ordinary straightforward business.'

'Oh, I – er – I see,' said Raggy, and scratched his head.

'That's good, then,' said Audacious. 'Well, good night, me boy. I must get into bed, absolutely at once. For to tell you the truth I've just struck a brilliant idea. I've decided to go to sleep.'

Audacious withdrew from the window. The interview was over, but Raggy could still hear him chuckling when he got back into the car. The two who were sitting waiting for him had heard everything, and were now grinning happily.

★   ★   ★

It was three days after the incident of the one hundred pounds that Audacious drove up once more to Raggy's garage. The sunshine was brilliant, frost sparkled on the hedges and the air was very fresh and cold.

Audacious was dressed in a huge greatcoat, with the collar turned up so that this gigantic garment reached from underneath his nose down to the ground, and only the toes of his boots could be seen sticking out of the bottom. His nose shone like a beacon from the cold, and his white moustache looked almost as frosty as the hedges.

'Ho, there!' he cried, and his breath steamed on the air like the exhaust from a locomotive.

Bunst came running out, hastily stuffing a half-eaten bun into the pocket of his overalls.

'Ah, good morning, me boy, good morning,' said Audacious, beaming with cheeks as shiny and red as his nose. 'I come

100

with great news to tell you three young fellows!'

He strode into the garage and Bunst turned to follow him.

Raggy and the Gremlin were at work getting the Pegasus into perfect tune, as they had been doing for the last two days. But as the old gentleman came in, they stopped.

Raggy withdrew his head from the open bonnet and the Gremlin stuck a head out from under the running-board.

'Good morning, sir,' said Raggy. 'What's the good news?'

'Why,' said Audacious, halting. 'I've decided to come with you on the trial!'

'Oh, good,' said the Gremlin, scrambling out from under the car, 'that will just make the four.'

'Oh, no, no. You misunderstand me,' said Audacious. 'I mean that I'm going to drive the old Mercurial along the trial course.'

'Good heavens!' said Raggy, startled. 'Are you?'

'Certainly,' guffawed Audacious. 'I'll show you youngsters there's life in the old dog yet! I propose to start off this afternoon and thus give myself a couple of days to get up there.'

'Do you think the old car will do the distance, sir?' asked Raggy, doubtfully.

'My dear feller, she's already done enough mileage to carry her six times round the world, and has enough left in her to do another six! She'll do it all right, me boy, never fear.'

'I hope everything goes all right,' said Raggy, and silently exchanged doubting glances with his two companions.

'Oh, I'm not anticipating any trouble,' said Audacious cheerfully. 'In fact I shall enjoy the trip, believe me. I haven't been to Scotland since I was the first man to fly under the Forth Bridge in 1912. That is, I would have been the first hadn't a couple of other fellers done it just before I did.'

He laughed. Standing there he looked just like one enormous

overcoat with a hat on top, and whiskers and a nose sticking out from between the two.

'And this coat, gentlemen,' he continued, 'I bought in Scotland the same year. It was in that year, gentlemen, that I drove the Mercurial from London to Edinburgh, and she was then the newest thing on the road. And now she's the oldest I propose to do it again.'

'Well, I wish you luck, sir,' said the Gremlin, grinning.

'Yes,' said Audacious, closing one eye. 'All I need is luck and about a hundred gallons of petrol. Given these I shall give you all a surprise. Expect to see me in the Highlands on Thursday night when you arrive. I shall have a good hot supper waiting for you' – he hesitated, then added – 'even if I have to get there by train!'

So saying he raised a hand in a kind of salute, then turned and went out to his ancient car, which he had left ticking over, because it had no self-starter. He clambered into the car, sat at the wheel and pointed a heavily gloved hand ahead of him.

'To Scotland and victory!'

Then with a fearful crash of gears, the old car lurched forward and roared out of sight, and all that was left of Audacious was a fading cloud of blue smoke.

Bunst pushed his cap back from his forehead, and whistled. 'I hope he makes it. A bit of a feat if he does.'

'I don't see why he shouldn't,' said Raggy quietly. 'After all, that old bus is in very good condition . . . Well, we'd better get on with our work and hope we see him when we arrive up there.'

Their work on the Pegasus took them until late the following day. They wanted to be sure that everything about the car, including their own inventions and gadgets, was in first-class condition. According to the rules of the competition, minor failure, even of accessories, would count so many points against them. Sir George Grayfield, the organiser, was determined to make the trial a stiff one, so that every part of a car entered for the competition would have to show its real worth.

By Wednesday night the white car shone like a machine ready to be pushed into an exhibition, and all that Raggy had left to do was to paint a small sign to be fixed to the garage doors saying. 'This garage will be closed until next Monday.'

While he was doing this, Bunst went home to his mother's cottage in the village and came back with a huge parcel of sandwiches, cakes, mince-pies, in fact such a variety of food that it seemed enough to carry him through a week. But by three o'clock the next morning, when they were all ready to start their journey north, Bunst had eaten nearly half the food.

'Blow me down!' said the Gremlin, seeing the shrunken parcel in the hands of the mini-mechanic. 'What have you done with the rest of it?'

'Ate it,' said Bunst tersely. 'I was so excited last night that I couldn't sleep, and I had to do something.'

'Well, it ought to keep you going for a while,' grinned Raggy. 'There was enough there for all of us in case we were stranded in the snowy mountains of Scotland for a week!'

Raggy had made sandwiches for himself and the Gremlin, and he had also brought along three thermos flasks of cocoa.

Outside the moon shone serenely down upon a world made sparkling white with frost. The Gremlin went to the window and looked out upon this peaceful scene, just to make sure that the weather had not changed since he had looked out about five minutes before.

Raggy was busy making the last check of all the things that they wanted to take with them, such as maps and heavy rugs, which they were certainly going to need before the trial was over. It was going to be a long, cold trip.

'Everything all right?' asked the Gremlin.

'Everything's aboard,' Raggy answered. 'I can't think of anything we've left behind. I've checked everything against my list,' he added, waving a small notebook in the air, 'and I think we can safely get ourselves wrapped up and started off towards the snowy North.'

'Snowy?' said Bunst, struggling into a thick coat which was rather too big for him, and the sleeves of which covered his hands. 'Who said it was snowy?'

'Midnight news on the wireless,' said Raggy, 'said snow was expected in Scotland.'

'Good,' said Bunst with eyes brightening. 'Snowball fights!'

'If we get any time,' laughed the Gremlin. 'Personally I think we'll be busy enough without it.'

'Right-ho, then,' said Raggy, 'all aboard!'

He opened the double doors of the garage, while the Gremlin and Bunst got into the car and drove out silently on to the road.

Raggy had a last look round the garage, switched off the lights, and made sure that everything was locked. Finally, he tested the padlock on the doors, saw that it was properly fastened, and then got into the car.

'This is just the right time of day to start a journey,' said the Gremlin, sniffing the cold fresh air. 'There'll be no traffic for the next four or five hours. We should get a long way on our journey by then. I reckon we shall be able to keep to our average of forty, which means we shall be up at Dorrach in ten hours.'

Raggy laughed.

'We needn't make such a rush of it as all that, old boy,' he said. 'We shall want to stop now and again to stretch our legs. After all, the real time-table we want to keep to is the one which will start tomorrow.'

'Ah,' agreed Bunst nodding wisely, 'that'll be the time. I wish we were starting now. If I stay as excited as this for a whole day more I shall be exhausted by the time we start.'

The car moved away quietly, like a white shadow, into the moonlight. It accelerated with terrific power, yet the only sound to be heard was the whistling of the wind past the bodywork. The Gremlin was driving, and for the first hour nothing much was said between the three of them.

Bunst, who was sitting in between the two, having been over-excited, found himself made sleepy by the cold, fresh air, and dropped into a doze. The Gremlin drove easily and accurately along the moonlit roads, so that it seemed the motion of the car was absolutely effortless.

At the end of the first hour they had covered a distance of sixty-two miles. The journey had been so completely smooth and quiet that even Raggy, the designer of the Pegasus, was astonished at the distance that had been covered.

'I'll be surprised,' said the Gremlin, 'if there's another car which can touch this taking part in the trial.'

'Don't be too sure,' said Raggy. He crossed his fingers in his coat pocket, and quickly changing the subject, he said, 'I wonder how Audacious is getting on?'

'I wonder,' said the Gremlin, with a grin. 'I don't know if I shall be surprised or not to find him there when we arrive.'

'Oh, he'll be there,' said Raggy. 'He always is. When he says he's going to do something, nothing ever stops him. I'll bet you he'll be there when we arrive.'

'Gosh' said Bunst, waking up. 'Is it breakfast time yet?'

The Rival

Dorrach was a small Scottish village with one fairly large and old-fashioned hotel, built of grey stone and black aged wood.

The road to it came down through the mountains, and upon this road about a dozen cars had been descending to the large square field beside the hotel. And there they now stood, mostly covered with large canvas sheets, upon which the heavily falling snow was gathering fast.

The fields around were deep with snow, and the scattered cottages which formed the village could scarcely be seen through the dazzling screen of big snowflakes. The gabled roofs of the hotel were thick with white, like icing on a cake. Above it, the sky was grey, and the flakes seemed to come down from nothing, and swell in size as they came.

The windows of the hotel shone warmly with lights. At one window on the ground floor a tall, grey-haired man was standing looking out at the snowstorm. There was a fire in the room behind him, and standing with his back to the fire was a young man of about thirty, round-faced, with narrow black eyes and a slightly twisted mouth, which made him look very bad-tempered.

'If this keeps on, sir,' he said, in an over-loud voice, 'some of the cars I've seen arrive won't be able to get away tomorrow.'

He laughed openly at that thought.

'Frankly, Grant,' said Sir George Grayfield, turning away from the window, 'I'm disappointed with the entries so far. These cars that I've seen don't seem to be particularly new in design – –'

'With the exception of mine,' interrupted Grant.

'Yes,' said the grey-haired Sir George, turning back to the window. His tone was cold. 'Yes, with the exception of yours. I must admit you've new developments on your three machines, and at present I think you should stand a good chance of winning – –'

'A good chance!' laughed Grant, interrupting again. 'By Jove!

There's no one to touch my cars. I'm determined to win this event, and I can assure you, sir, that I'm going to – –'

He broke off, for he suddenly realised that Sir George was no longer listening.

That gentleman had started, and was staring through the window with wide eyes, as if he had seen something outside which he could not believe.

'Good heavens!' cried Sir George. 'It can't be!'

'Can't be what?' said Grant, and came from the fire to the window.

Both men stood staring at the spectacle which had just arrived outside the hotel. For there, in the whirling snowflakes, the monstrous apparition of the ancient Mercurial was approaching, its wooden wheel-spokes stuffed with snow, steam rising in a cloud from its shuddering radiator, and the bright red uproarious face of Audacious Cotterell triumphantly yelling a cry of victory, as he pulled on the massive hand-brake and slid the old car to a standstill.

'What on earth – –?' began Grant, his first look of surprise fading into one of contempt.

Sir George did not hear him, for a smile broke over his face as he cried, 'Audacious Cotterell, by all that's wonderful! After all these years!'

He turned, left the room, and went out to welcome his old friend on the snowy steps of the hotel.

Audacious came up the steps, stamping his feet, and swinging his arms to and fro across his chest to get his blood circulating.

'Gad, what a day, what a day!' he said. And then he saw Sir George standing in front of him. 'Ah, there you are!' he went on. 'I thought I'd give you a bit of a surprise, George, me boy.'

'And you certainly succeeded,' laughed Sir George, seizing Audacious's large gloved hand and beginning to pump it up and down. 'You don't mean to say you've come up in that old thing?'

'Not only that, George, me boy, but broken all the records in doing it. I beat my time of 1912 by one hour fifteen minutes, mainly due to the fact that every time I tried to slow down to come down the hills, I just slid to the bottom at anything between seventy and eighty miles an hour.'

And so saying, he burst into a hearty laugh.

'Come on in. Get that coat off,' said Sir George. 'I never thought I'd meet an old friend like you up here. We'll have a lot to talk about after all these years.'

'I've a lot to talk about at any time,' warned Audacious, going into the hotel. 'After two days of driving by myself I'm pleased to have somebody to talk to, and once I start I shall probably go on for hours.'

He left his coat, cap and gloves in the broad stone hall of the hotel, and went into the room which Sir George had just left.

Both men were laughing as they came in. Then Sir George suddenly saw Grant, whom he had forgotten, and grew serious.

'Oh, by the way, this is Mr Grant,' Sir George said, 'one of the competitors.'

'Ah, yes; pleased to meet you,' said Audacious.

The young man nodded in rather a supercilious sort of way. He eyed the old-fashioned dress of Audacious curiously, but said nothing beyond a mumble which no one heard.

'Mr Grant,' said Sir George, 'has a very fine team of cars with him, which I believe stand a very good chance.'

'I'm sure,' said Audacious, jovially, 'that he stands a very good chance, but within an hour or two, I warn you, the *winners* will arrive!'

He brushed his walrus moustache with a forefinger and looked tremendously important.

108

'The winners?' repeated Sir George, startled.

'Well, not the winners yet, me boy,' laughed Audacious. 'But they will be. You mark my words, they will be.'

Grant laughed as if he believed that there was nothing likely to enter the competition which could be a serious threat to his own entries. But at the same time his eyes narrowed calculatingly, as if eager to find out more about Audacious's mysterious 'winners'.

'I'm talking of the Pegasus,' said Audacious.

'Pegasus?' said Grant, frowning. 'Never heard of such a thing!'

'You will, young man,' said Audacious. 'Oh, yes, you will.'

Grant looked more relieved than anything. Audacious's remark had made him fear at first that some big firm had suddenly decided to enter the trial with a hush–hush machine.

'Do you mean,' he asked, 'that there's only *one* car called the Pegasus?'

'Just one,' said Audacious, 'just one. Built by three young friends of mine. Very clever engineers. Very clever.'

Grant laughed with relief.

'Oh, a sort of amateur job, is it?'

'That's to be decided,' said Audacious. 'It looks pretty professional to me, and I've been driving since 1912.'

Grant looked out of the window to where the Mercurial stood in the snow, half enveloped in the steam which the snow made by sizzling on the over-heated bonnet.

'I can believe that!' he said, and lit a cigarette.

'Well, now,' said Sir George, 'let's have a chat. How are things with you, Cotterell? Tell us what you've been doing all these years.'

The two elderly men sat down in armchairs and began to talk. Grant was left out of it. He hung about for a while and then went out of the room, slamming the door behind him.

'That young man,' said Sir George in Audacious's ear, 'is one of the most self-satisfied, pompous fellows I've come across. He's been hanging on to me like a leech since he got here.'

'He didn't strike me very favourably,' agreed Audacious, cautiously. 'He seemed worried about the Pegasus.'

'Perhaps he is,' said Sir George, with a sigh. 'He's come up here to win this trial and, judging from the number of cars he has brought, he means to do it.'

'Oh, numbers don't count, me boy,' said Audacious, laughing heartily. 'You wait till you see *my* team. By this time next week, George, you'll have a Pegasus on order, and what's more, you'll have the pleasure of giving my young friends a cheque for ten thousand pounds!'

'You always were an optimist,' laughed Sir George. 'But don't forget in these trials – especially in this weather – anything can happen. And the point is there's only one Pegasus, but there are three Grant Tourers. That gives Grant a treble chance to your one.'

'Odds are nothing to me,' said Audacious. 'I'm a prophet, not a betting man.'

Then they sat back again to discuss old times.

★   ★   ★

During the afternoon, the snowflakes became smaller, thinned down, and stopped. The sky was still grey. There was a threat of more snow to come, and the mountains of the Highlands formed a range of white, ghostly peaks against the dull colour of the lowering clouds.

Grant was sitting in a chair in his bedroom at the front of the hotel, gazing into a small log fire. On the edge of his bed sat two men. One was about forty, a thin, tall man, with protruding cheek-bones. The other was younger, and had a front tooth missing. This second man was now grinning cheerfully; the gap in his teeth made him look like a schoolboy.

Grant was talking of what had happened downstairs.

'And then the old fool said that this car was going to win the trial.' Grant laughed and looked round to the man with the missing tooth. 'What do you think of that, Gappy?'

'Pretty optimistic,' grinned the man with the missing tooth.

The thin man beside him kept his jaw set, so that the muscles on either side knotted.

'Are you sure this isn't a manufacturer's trick?' he asked, in a dry, precise voice. 'They sometimes do put their cars in under other names, you know, Grant.'

'You can be sure of that,' said Grant, lying back in his chair. 'Anyone who has anything to do with that old fathead downstairs can't know anything about designing cars. After all' – he got up, took some cigarettes from the mantelpiece and turned towards the window – 'you're my designer, Marshall. You ought to know whether our tourer is the best car for the trial.'

'I believe it is,' Marshall answered, his thin face never relaxing. 'But you never can tell. I'm an old hand at this trial business. Anything can happen.'

Grant laughed again.

'My dear Marshall,' he said, and turned his eyes to Gappy, who was laughing with him, 'what do you think three young fellows could produce privately, and without assistance? Why, it will be some fantastic contraption held together with straps, years out of date, and daubed over with new paint, so that you can see the brush-marks.'

Gappy laughed, but Marshall merely shrugged.

'I don't propose to bother about it,' said Marshall, 'until I see the car itself.'

111

'You may never see it,' said Grant. 'They're coming right from the south-west of England, and the chances of them getting here are remote, to say the least! I don't think –'

He stopped by the window as something caught his eye. He stood quite still for a moment, then slowly went close to the window, opened it, and looked up towards the mountains where the road came through the pass and down the slopes towards Dorrach.

He could see a car coming down very fast, its colouring looking cream against the brilliant white of the snow on either side of the road. It came towards a bend on the steep slope, still travelling at a high speed.

'Gosh! Those chaps are asking for it!' he said. A grin spread over his face as he watched.

The two on the bed jumped up and ran to the window to look out.

'Just watch it when it comes to the bend,' Grant said. 'You might see a good pile-up!'

'Bound to,' said the taciturn Marshall.

The car reached the bend, ploughing its furrows through the snow on the road, and turned the corner as if it had been running on rails. It straightened out after the bend, and ran on down towards the village. Grant's grin faded right away. Marshall remained staring.

'Too far away to recognise it,' Marshall said drily. 'But whatever kind of car it is it holds the road better than any I've come across.'

'Luck,' Grant said very sharply. 'There's one more bend to go. We'll watch it, and if he keeps up the same speed that he's doing now, it will be the end of him, because on the other side of the bend there's a drop right down into the burn of about two hundred feet. It should make good watching!'

The white car came to the bend without slowing at all. It began to turn, then suddenly it was clear that the wheels had lost their grip. The car slid sideways towards the frail wooden fence which guarded the outside of the bend and the drop down into the burn, two hundred feet below.

'I told you – –' Grant shouted.

'Wait!' Marshall said, his voice dry.

The driver of the white car was steering into the skid, and the watchers saw the car answer. It wagged its tail briefly as if to dig itself deeper into the snow and so get a better grip. Then it came round the bend as steadily as it had done on the corner above.

It ran down to the hotel. Not one of the three men in the window said a word as it came nearer and nearer, and its smooth streamlined body became clear to them. The car rushed through the snow to the hotel door. The watchers in the window above could hear no sound from the engine. There was just the crunching of snow beneath the tyres. It stopped. There were two young men inside it together with a small boy.

'The three,' said Marshall, with a hard smile. 'That's what your "old fool" said, wasn't it? Three chaps had built this car, and you expected something tied together with rope! Somebody's made a mistake.'

Gappy said, 'Jove! That's one of the best-looking cars I've ever seen. Modern, too. Look at that line. Look at the curves from front to back. Why that's absolutely – –'

Gappy started back, his eyes watering, his words cut off. Grant had pulled the casement shut so furiously that he had hit Gappy on the nose with the handle.

Grant turned away, his face red. Marshall was standing by, showing no emotion at all.

'Still sure you're right?' said Marshall quietly.

Grant went to the fire and turned round, flushed with rage.

'If I'm not right I'll make myself right,' he said, 'so there's nothing else to bother about. We've three cars, haven't we? Three against one ought to win. True, it's too late to try to stop the overheating trouble on the tourers, but we can make pretty sure of winning.'

Gappy was startled by his tone.

'I don't like that talk, Grant,' he said. 'If there are going to be any of the old racing tricks in this trial, you can find another driver in my place.'

Grant stood quite still for a second or more, and then his muscles relaxed and he smiled one-sidedly.

'Don't be a fool, Gappy,' he said, keeping his voice under control. 'Naturally I don't mean that I should go in for any dirty work.'

'Well, in that case,' said Gappy, 'you'd better keep your temper. You've hired me as your driver, and I'll drive for you, provided that you want a straight driver. But if you try anything funny, count me out!'

Marshall stepped between the two.

'You've both lost your cool,' he said very quietly. 'After all, why should you be so worried by this car? Granted it isn't what you expected. It looks better than ours, but how do you know that the inside is any good?'

Grant turned suddenly to the fire.

'Quite,' he agreed. 'We don't know that the inside is any good. But one thing I do know – that all the run up here we suffered from that cursed overheating trouble. And if we've got a fast competitor in this trial, I shan't feel too sure that we shall get away with it.'

He turned suddenly back to Marshall and spoke through his

teeth, violently now and in deadly earnest.

'And you know too well, we've *got* to get away with this! We've got to win it. Otherwise we're broke!'

Marshall sat down on the edge of the bed again.

'We'll win it all right,' he said, and for the first time he almost smiled. 'After all, they are very young, these chaps. You saw that just now. They couldn't possibly have the experience in designing that I've had.'

Grant smiled, and then suddenly his smile grew into a laugh.

'Of course not,' he said. 'What am I worried about?'

When the Pegasus had been parked in the field with the other cars, and covered with a canvas sheet, its crew went over to the hotel, where they were boisterously greeted by Audacious.

They showed no surprise over the arrival of their old friend, because they had already seen the ancient Mercurial outside the hotel entrance, but all three were still rather dumb with wonder that the machine had actually made the journey.

'Ah, here we are, gentlemen!' said Audacious, breezily. 'Come in. Get warm. You'd probably like a wash and brush up, eh? Well, I'll find out where your room is and make sure it's comfortable for a good night's rest.'

Raggy had booked a room in the attic of the hotel, where three iron bedsteads were ready for them. This was the cheapest way he had been able to get accommodation, for he had long decided that he was not going to spend more of the famous one hundred pounds than he had to.

They washed there, that is Raggy and the Gremlin did, but Bunst abstained, saying, 'You don't want to wash the dirt off in weather like this. Dirt helps to keep you warm.'

He sat on his bed and opened the remnant of the once giant parcel his mother had given him. During the stops which they had made on the way, Bunst had used his time in buying additional buns, all of which had gone save one. In the last twelve hours he had eaten a dozen sandwiches, nine sausage rolls, six meat pies, eleven apples and twenty-seven buns. He was now munching on the twenty-eighth.

Raggy laughed, and then pulled from his pocket a sheet of paper, upon which he had carefully printed out the specification of his car.

'I must go and find Sir George Grayfield,' he said. 'The rule is that the specification has to be given in to him as soon as the competitor arrives. I'll pop down and find him.'

He left the other two by the small smokey fire in the attic, and made his way down to the hall of the hotel again.

There were several other drivers sitting and standing about, smoking and exchanging tales of their trip into the snowy Highlands, but above the buzz of their voices could be heard a sudden hearty guffaw which Raggy could not fail to recognise. He turned towards a closed door on his left, from behind which the guffawing was still going on. He knocked and went in.

It was the same room from which Sir George had seen Audacious arrive, and now the organiser of the competition was sitting at a table with some papers before him. These were specifications of other cars which had been handed in to him.

Audacious was standing with his back to the fire smoking a great, curved calabash pipe, and the smoke from this fearsome object practically obscured his face behind a blue cloud.

'Ah, there you are, me boy', he cried. 'Come on. Meet Sir George Grayfield. This is my young friend, John Wragg.'

Sir George stood up and shook hands with Raggy.

'I'm glad you're able to take part in the competition, Mr

Wragg,' he said. 'I wish you luck.'

'Thanks, sir,' Raggy said, and handed him the paper. 'This is our specification, which I believe you want straightaway.'

'Thank you, yes,' said Sir George. 'Oh, by the way, that's Mr Grant, a rival of yours.' He pointed to the window-seat where Grant was sitting, smoking a cigarette.

Until now he had made no movement, and therefore Raggy had not noticed him. Grant nodded to the young man, and Raggy smiled back.

Raggy looked younger than his twenty-one years, owing to his untidy hair and the rather studious look which he always had about him. From the moment that Grant saw him, he felt that he had been worrying too much about such a rival, for clearly Raggy was far too young to have entered any car which could compete with the experienced design of Marshall.

'Well, now,' said Sir George to Raggy, 'let's have a quick look through your list. I must say that up to now we've had very little that is new. Only Mr Grant seems to have struck a new note. However, let's see what we have here.'

He began to read it quickly, and then his frown deepened and he began to read certain parts out loud.

'Well, this is a change!' he said, looking up at Raggy. 'You seem to have got something new from stem to stern!'

He began to read from the specification.

' "The engine is fitted with twin ignition, single carburettor incorporating automatic supercharger, controlled entirely by the demands of the engine, thus ensuring an even mixture throughout, however hard it may be driven. Brake horsepower 220 . . ." '

Grant was sitting forward on the window-seat. By the fire Audacious was smiling through his smoke at the ceiling, like a proud father listening to his son winning the first prize at school.

Sir George's eyes were gleaming.

'You've certainly given a lot of thought to this, young man,' he said.

'Well, sir,' said Raggy, 'I designed the car because it was the type that I'd like to have, and I was determined to cut out all the inconveniences of the ordinary type touring model.'

Sir George grunted, and went on. ' "Fully automatic transmission," ' he read out, ' "with a lever provided on the steering column if the driver wishes to use the gears in sporting events. The hood is motor-driven, both up and down." Good gracious me! You've thought of everything. "All wheels independently sprung. Hydraulic jacks operated from the engine and fixed to the chassis, so as to minimise the unsprung weight." '

He broke off and sat back and looked at Raggy.

'It sounds the sort of car I want myself,' he said, and then laughed. 'Why, this has cheered me up no end.' He looked across at Grant. 'Did you hear that, Grant? It seems as though we've got another Royce with us.'

Grant said something that could not be heard, and then aloud, 'Gadgets don't mean much. Just a lot more to go wrong. It's the performance of the car that really counts.'

'Well,' said Sir George undaunted, 'we'll see tomorrow whether it has got the performance or not. Meanwhile, it looks as though you've got a very serious competitor, Grant.'

'It seems so,' agreed Grant.

He got up, stubbed out his cigarette in an ash tray, and left the room.

'Difficult man, that,' said Sir George, giving Raggy a sidelong look. 'I think you've been a bit of a shock to him, Mr Wragg. Anyhow, I'll go through these details of yours more closely in a moment. I think you'd better get your supper and turn in. You won't get much sleep in the next day and night.'

'I know, sir,' agreed Raggy. 'I could do with a kip, too. Well, good night, sir.'

'Good night,' said Sir George.

'And mind you do sleep well, me boy,' said Audacious, 'because if you don't win, I've promised to eat my hat, moths and all!'

He laughed again, and Raggy went out.

'There, what did I tell you, George, me boy?' said Audacious, taking his pipe out of his mouth and pointing the stem at his old friend.

'Well, it almost seems,' grinned Sir George, 'that you've been telling me the truth for once.'

The Breakdown

The next morning brought brilliant sunshine and clear skies; and though the air was frosty, it was bright and fine. Breath steamed on the air in clouds, and the faces of the enthusiasts in the car park were ruddy and cheerful. Some of the engines were going, purring smoothly in sharp contrast to the normal shattering racket of a racing event.

There was an atmosphere of fellowship everywhere. Cars were uncovered, and although Bunst was inclined to scowl when anyone came near to look at the Pegasus, Raggy and the Gremlin were in high good spirits, and only too eager to meet the friendly advances of the other drivers.

Grant was one of the first to come across to the Pegasus crew, smiling as if Raggy and the Gremlin were his oldest friends. He ignored Bunst, who had an expression on his face as if about to take a hard crack at the fat-faced Grant with his catapult. It was fortunate, perhaps, that he had not got that fearful weapon with him. Grant addressed his words to the others.

'Nice job you've got here, Wragg,' said Grant.

'We hope it's going to be the best one here,' Raggy answered, smiling. 'Anyhow, we're going to give it a short trip this morning, just to make sure everything's running all right.'

'You are?' Grant said. 'We'll probably be following you then. I'm trying one of mine. So often things go wrong at the last minute.'

He laughed. His bad temper of the day before seemed to have died right away, and both Raggy and the Gremlin, who would rather have made friends than enemies, returned this sudden friendship.

'When are you setting off?' Grant asked.

'Oh, we'll push off any minute now, I think,' replied the Gremlin, looking at his watch. 'The sooner the better, and the quicker we'll be back to lunch.'

'Lunch!' echoed Bunst, suddenly forgetting his suspicion of Grant. 'Thank goodness for that. I'm starving!'

It was difficult to see quite how Bunst was starving, since for breakfast he had had six sausages and eight slices of toast, and that had been only an hour ago.

As they spoke, a rattling roar from nearby drowned the sound of the other engines in the field. Raggy turned, and in the far corner he saw Audacious jumping back victoriously from the starting-handle of the old Mercurial, which was now shivering, exploding and throwing out clouds of black and blue smoke from the back.

'Looks as though Audacious is going somewhere,' said Raggy. 'I wonder where he's off to now?'

'You never know where he's likely to go,' grinned the Gremlin, watching Audacious clamber into the seat of his enormous car and begin to thunder across the fields towards them.

'What on earth is that crane affair over his head?' asked Grant curiously. 'It's a very odd-looking thing.'

'It's a launching ramp for his model aircraft,' said the Gremlin. 'He's an expert at radio-controlled aeroplanes.'

'My hat!' said Grant. 'I shouldn't have thought he was an expert at anything.'

'Oh, yes, he is,' said Raggy. 'And bang up to date with it, too.'

'It's about the only thing that's up to date about that contraption as far as I can see!' said Grant, and laughed.

The Mercurial came to a shuddering standstill in a flurry of snow and steam.

'Ho there, gentlemen!' cried Audacious, shouting at the top of his voice so as to make himself heard above the thunder of his engine. 'All well for the journey?'

'We think so, sir,' said the Gremlin. 'We're just going to take a short run now to check up on things.'

'Good idea, good idea,' said Audacious, nodding. 'I'm just giving mine a run up so that I shall be ready to start in about an hour's time.'

'Where are you going?' Raggy asked.

'I'm going over the trial course,' replied Audacious, brushing his frosty moustache with his forefinger, 'and I expect to be there not very long after the rest of the competitors.'

Behind Audacious, Gappy, Grant's driver, had appeared, and was looking at the Mercurial, his face quite blank with wonder. When he heard Audacious state his intention to drive four hundred miles in this antiquated thing, he looked up with considerable interest and the broadest grin he could manage.

'Well,' Gappy said to himself, 'that's courage, that is. I admire the old chap. I hope he makes it.'

Then he passed on to one of the dark-red Grant Tourers,

climbed into the driver's seat and started it up.

'Well, we'd better get going,' said Raggy, 'and then we shall be back in time to see you off.'

'Well, best of luck in case I don't see you,' said Audacious, and laughed heartily as if he knew that they did not need much luck to win the prize.

The white bonnet of the Pegasus headed swiftly towards the zig-zag road up the mountain, the engine pulling steadily and so quietly that only the crunching of the snow under the wheels could be heard. Some distance behind, the red Grant Tourer, with Gappy at the wheel and Grant beside him, was making its way along, keeping a level distance between itself and the white car ahead.

The climb was becoming steeper, although the bends which helped to form the zig-zag roadway were smooth and even.

'Going perfectly,' said the Gremlin, steering a course round a curve. 'She's got power to spare. Shall I step on it and let him see what we can do?'

Raggy and Bunst looked back.

Raggy laughed, and said, 'Yes, let her have her head for a bit. We might as well have some fun while we're here.'

The Pegasus pulled away, gathering speed up the steep wide slope. She was holding the road beautifully.

'Go right on up to the top,' directed Raggy. 'Then we'll turn and come back. As far as I can see, she's perfect!'

The red-headed boy at the wheel grinned as the car went faster. They approached the next bend, which swung to the left. The Gremlin flicked the little lever on the steering column and the car changed silently into third.

He kept close to the ditch on the bend and steered round accurately; there was no suspicion of a skid. As they went on higher and higher up the mountainside, it was clear that the road alone limited the speed of the Pegasus.

The red tourer behind hung on. Gappy was a good driver and knew his business. He kept behind easily for a time, and then he began to slacken.

'What's the matter?' Grant asked quickly.

'Look at the temperature,' said Gappy, pointing to the dial on the dashboard. 'She's starting to overheat.'

'Never mind about that,' Grant snapped. 'Keep up behind the white car!'

Gappy accelerated again, but his grin was fading. He began to look worried.

They went on up for another half mile, keeping behind the white car, then he began to slacken again.

'She's getting too hot,' he protested. 'You can hear her.'

'I told you to keep up behind!' Grant shouted. 'She'll cool down in a minute.'

'It doesn't feel to me as if she'll cool down,' Gappy answered. 'But anyhow, it's your car.'

He changed into third round a bend, but with the increased revs the engine began to lose power, and the white car drew steadily away ahead of the pursuers.

'It'll wreck the motor,' said Gappy. 'I'm not going to push it any farther. There's something wrong with this engine!'

'There's nothing wrong with it!' cried Grant. 'You're pushing her to the limit, that's all. She's bound to overheat.'

'I don't see why, unless the design's faulty,' Gappy said.

'There's nothing wrong, I tell you! Keep on with it.'

Grant was in a towering rage. He had no time to look at the tell-tale instruments on the dashboard, but kept his eyes on the white car drawing steadily ahead up the zig-zag road towards the summit.

'All right,' said Gappy, resignedly. 'If you want to wreck it, let's go. But I tell you, this engine is no match for the one they've got. We can beat most things; but we can't beat that.'

He accelerated again, but the engine began to waver. It felt for a moment as if the brakes were being slowly and steadily applied.

There came a furious knocking from under the bonnet, a noise so loud that it could not be mistaken for anything but a breakdown inside the engine. Gappy took his foot off the accelerator, pushed out the clutch, and switched off the engine. He drew into the deep snow at the roadside. From the bottom of the radiator in front a thin cloud of steam was hissing out. Grant and the driver clambered out quickly and threw the bonnet open.

'Well, what's the matter with it?' Grant asked.

'She began to seize up,' answered Gappy. 'And now it sounds as if you've got a main bearing gone. You made me push the darned thing too hard. She won't stand for it. I told you she's no match for that other job.'

Grant looked quickly up the mountainside to where the Pegasus was still climbing steadily and easily towards the top of the rise.

'Let's get back quickly,' he said. 'They mustn't see this. Nobody must know about it.'

Gappy looked round at him quizzically.

'Why?'

'Because I say so,' Grant answered. 'We can roll down the hill, and she'll be cool enough then to start again. Come on, shut that bonnet and get in!'

Gappy shrugged and did as he was told.

'Well, this puts me out of the trial anyway,' he said, as he let the car roll backwards into a turn across the road.

He judged his turn beautifully, for once on the other side

of the road he had the car at such an angle that he could now roll forward and swing on to the downhill path again. They began to gather speed down the snowy slope. As the cold air rushed in through the radiator grill, the engine temperature began to fall.

'Of course,' said Gappy, 'I didn't find anything wrong with her yesterday. But then I didn't push her like I did just now. It seems to me that Marshall made a boob of this design. Are the other two the same?'

'Marshall's is the same as this one,' Grant said, between his teeth. 'It was his confounded idea to drill out the crankshaft to the limit and get more revs. He did it to two cars, but he didn't do it to mine.'

'So that means his car isn't any good either,' said Gappy. 'The same thing will happen to that.'

'Only if he has to push it hard,' said Grant, staring ahead through the windscreen.

'Well, he *will* have to push it hard,' Gappy answered, 'if he's going to keep up with that Pegasus. So you might as well say good-bye to the prize.'

'You don't think I'll give in because of a thing like this, do you?' Grant said angrily, and turned on his driver, his face pale. 'I'll make sure that we *don't* have to push too hard! I'll make sure of it, don't you worry.'

There was silence for a moment. Gappy narrowed his eyes.

'Oh,' he said, slowly, 'so it's that kind of a game, is it? I rather wondered why you got so upset last night, and now I know.'

They were running down to the bottom of the slope and there was a small lane leading off to the left, bounded on both sides by high hedges.

'Well, remember what I told you. Any funny business and I'd

be *out*,' said Gappy.

He pulled the car to a standstill on the slope.

'I'll walk, if you don't mind, Mr Grant,' he said. 'It isn't very far. The exercise will do me good.'

He got out and stood in the snow. Grant moved over into the driver's seat.

'You can do as you like,' he snapped. 'But if you tell anybody down below what's happened – –'

'Don't worry about that,' Gappy cut in. 'I shan't tell them. I shan't need to. They'll find out soon enough.'

Grant released the brake and let the car roll on down the slope to the little turning on the left-hand side of the road. He swung round into the lane and let the car roll along until it could no longer be seen from the main road behind it. Then he stopped, the two near-side wheels in a ditch, and got out.

He stood for a moment undecided, then got back into the car and started it. The run down the mountain had cooled the engine sufficiently, but instead of the quiet tick-over which there had been before, there was now a regular knocking.

Grant listened for a moment and then switched the engine off completely.

He turned and trudged back through the snow to the main road. He arrived at the hotel only a few minutes after Gappy had got there.

The Pegasus was back in the field with its crew, who were now leaving it and heading for the hotel for their lunch, although it was still quite early.

When Grant came into the hotel hall he saw Marshall studying a map which was hanging on the wall. Grant went up to him.

'Number Three's gone up in smoke,' Grant said.

Marshall looked round quickly.

'What do you mean?'

Grant told him what had happened in the fewest possible words.

'I told you,' he added fiercely, 'drilling out that crankshaft as you did created too much whip. She's burnt the centre main bearing clean out. You can hear it a mile off! And if you ran it another five miles the big-ends would be gone as well.'

Marshall swore under his breath.

'The calculations worked out all right,' he said. 'I can't understand it. Mine was overheated yesterday, remember.'

'I know,' Grant said. 'Probably the same thing will happen to that one as well, which means that there's only my Number One to be relied on.'

'And you say this Pegasus actually got away from you?' Marshall said.

'It walked away!' said Grant, sarcastically. 'But we could have held it if Number Three hadn't begun to overheat like that. She began to seize up altogether. That's what it felt like.'

Marshall said nothing for a minute or more.

'Then all we can do is to make certain we don't have to go all out,' he murmured, his grey eyes cold as stone.

'That's the only thing,' said Grant, and turned away.

Gappy had gone upstairs to get his things from his room, but in the corridor above he came face to face with the tall figure of Audacious Cotterell. Gappy stopped, staring at that gentleman as if halted by a sudden doubt. Then he appeared to make up his mind and approached Audacious.

'Excuse me, sir,' Gappy said.

'Why certainly, absolutely, me boy,' said Audacious.

'I was going to take part in this trial,' said Gappy quickly, 'but I've had a bit of bad luck, and I shan't be able to do it.'

'Oh, bad show, bad show,' said Audacious, looking very

concerned. 'I'm sorry to hear it.'

'Oh, that's all right,' said Gappy, 'but the only point is this. I overheard you saying this morning that you were going to drive over the course in that interesting old car of yours.'

By using the word 'interesting' Gappy had gone straight to the heart of the great Audacious.

'Interesting, by gad! Yes, I'll say she is, sir! One of the finest machines ever put on the road, and incidentally, she's my oldest friend. I've had her, sir, well over fifty years and more . . .'

Audacious rambled on enthusiastically for about five minutes before Gappy could get in another word. And when the sporting driver was able to speak, he said, 'Could you take a passenger with you on your trip down?'

'Passenger?' said Audacious. 'Only too glad of the company, sir. But who do you suppose would want to come with me?'

'I would,' said Gappy.

'Good lord!' said Audacious, startled. He recovered, broke into a hearty laugh and patted Gappy on the shoulder. 'You're a man after my own heart,' he added. 'We'll start in fifteen minutes.'

The Chase

The first of the small cars left Dorrach Hotel at four o'clock, and thereafter others followed at intervals according to their handicaps.

The sky was clear, and in the West the sun was gold, dropping down towards the sparkling white of the mountain-tops like a copper ball. As other cars followed the first, and the intervals of the handicap drew longer, the sun gradually vanished behind the mountains, and against the darkening sky the white landscape began to shine with an eerie radiance.

The Pegasus and the two Grant Tourers were handicapped so that their time of departure was not until six o'clock. Grant and Marshall stayed in the hotel until the last minute, studying maps and the directions for the route. Raggy, the Gremlin and Bunst had already memorised their orders by heart, and were ready to go nearly fifteen minutes before six o'clock.

The route was so planned as to lead through Scotland and down to the south-west of England to the small seaside town of Oldquay, where Sir George Grayfield's estate lay. Part of his estate had been given up during the war for a great airfield, which had been used by Coastal Command, and it was upon the wide concrete runway of this gigantic drome that the final speed tests were to be carried out.

Along the route there were twelve stopping places, called checks where every car had to report and refuel according to its needs. If a car was behind its schedule for arrival at any check it could lose up to five points, and the points allotted for the whole trip down therefore amounted to sixty. Twenty more points were to be allotted for unique design, which must prove itself during the long run, and the final twenty points were for a high-speed test and acceleration on the aerodrome.

The Gremlin was counting the possible points they would score; in fact he and Bunst had been counting them nearly all day.

'I think,' said the Gremlin, for the twentieth time, 'we should get a good eighty-five, even if we have bad luck.'

'Tripe!' said Bunst tersely. 'A hundred.'

'I've told you before,' said Raggy 'not to count chickens too soon. The state of the roads is likely to put us back a bit.'

'I think they've got too many checks,' grumbled Bunst. 'It means stopping every forty miles.'

'I've tried to explain to you before,' said Raggy, 'there must be frequent checks in order to make sure that people don't roar through thirty-mile limits at sixty. And as it says in the rules, there will be people watching in some towns or villages to make sure that nobody *does* break the limit.'

Bunst grunted.

It was three minutes to six when Marshall and Grant came out for their cars. In their big coats and caps they looked huge as they tramped quickly across the snow to their waiting machines. There were only three men at the gate: two timekeepers, who were comparing watches, and Sir George Grayfield.

The seconds ticked on. The Gremlin's finger was ready on the starter button. Then from the gate came the shrill note of the starting whistle. The Gremlin pressed the starter and the faint mumble of the engine came in reply. From across the snow at almost the same time came the louder noise of Tourers' exhausts.

Grant started off in a flurry of snow as the Gremlin steered towards the gate. The Pegasus slowed down as Raggy called out, 'Let them get out first. He's kicking up so much snow he'll block our windscreen right at the start. We can catch them up easily enough.'

Grant swung out through the gate, making the timekeepers and Sir George duck away from the snow which was coming up from his car. Marshall raised his hand towards the Pegasus, then followed his employer out of the gate. The Pegasus came a split second afterwards. As they went by they heard Sir George call out, 'Good luck!'

They turned on to the road and accelerated away up towards the pass in the mountains, the headlamps of the three cars running like broad yellow fans of light over the snowy ground. Overhead the sky was dark, and the tops of the mountains shone queerly, like white jagged clouds with no foundation, as the slanting beams of the rising moon caught them in its silver light.

The trial was on, and upon its result depended the fate of the Pegasus and its builders. If they failed to win, this Pegasus would be the only one ever to be made, and the time and money which they had spent on it would be wasted.

On the winding gradient, Marshall was drawing away from Grant, going very fast indeed. Behind Grant the Pegasus was accelerating so rapidly that Grant could see it was useless to try to stop it from passing him. He drew into the side of the road and raised his hand. The Pegasus pulled out and slid by in hot pursuit of the red car ahead.

At the summit of the peak there was a quarter of a mile between Marshall and the Pegasus, for Marshall's car was going extremely fast – as fast as the road conditions permitted.

The road became narrower, running in between stone walls. The Pegasus began to catch up on the car ahead, but Raggy gave a caution.

'No need to try to pass him, Gremmy,' he said. 'Just hang on to his tail. We don't want to risk a skid into the walls at the side of the road. They'd be too tough for our wings!'

'Right,' the Gremlin answered, and settled down to follow Marshall.

Behind them Grant was coming along steadily, but the performance of his car was not quite good enough to keep up with the two in front. He contented himself with hanging behind the Pegasus. He knew that he had a good enough performance not to lose any points all the way along, and though his average might be slightly less than the others, he had a good chance of making a high score at the end of the long run to the South.

He could see now that when it came to the final speed trials, the Pegasus would undoubtedly win; but as he watched the two cars a mile ahead of him on the long highland road, he realised suddenly that if Marshall's car could only make the distance, its performance would otherwise match that of the Pegasus.

As he sat watching the leaders his heart began to beat faster. Grant did not like any odds against him; he did not even like a fair chance; he liked to be certain that he would win, and it was possible for him to win now – if only Marshall's car held out.

★   ★   ★

For an hour now Marshall had led the swift way over the mountains and down through the pine forests of the valleys. The moon was bright, and the carpet of snow made the road easy to see.

In the Pegasus behind Marshall, the Gremlin had followed with the coolness of an expert. But there was one advantage which Marshall had, and which his driving revealed with every passing minute; this was his vast experience of racing driving in all conditions, spreading back over a number of years.

They could see his head and shoulders over the back of the big red open car, managing his car as if he were a part of it.

The Pegasus was running with silent efficiency. Raggy was keeping a careful check of the time and the distance they were covering. At the end of sixty minutes, having averaged forty miles an hour over the winding roads covered with snow and ice, Marshall slowed down as he ran into a small village set in the middle of a forest.

Outside a small inn there, five people were waiting, flinging their arms about and stamping to keep themselves warm. It was the first check. Marshall pulled evenly to a standstill beside them, and the Pegasus came up behind him.

'I'm going to tell you now,' said the Gremlin, who had hardly spoken all the way, 'that there's practically no difference between us. I couldn't have passed him on that road if I'd wanted to.'

Raggy exchanged glances with him.

'Yes, it struck me that his performance was good,' he said. 'Still, we must keep on. I'll take over now until the next check.'

One of the muffled checkers noted down their number and time in his book, though he had to blow on his fingers before he could write anything.

'Nice freezing night for you chaps,' he said. 'But I'd sooner be you than stand round here waiting. Thank goodness there's only one more to come!'

He looked round as through the trees on the bend the lights of Grant's car appeared, and said, 'And here he is, I'm glad to say.'

Marshall started his engine again and pulled away. Raggy was in the driving seat of the white Pegasus, all ready to go.

'Okay, chaps,' said the checker. 'Carry on,' and turning, he went to meet Grant.

The other four checkers disappeared into the warmly lit inn, their vigil in the snow now finished.

The Pegasus accelerated away after Marshall, and once more the silent chase began through the deserted Scottish countryside.

The red car kept steadily ahead, travelling fast. And now one or two of the earlier starters appeared. They drew in to let the faster cars pass them, and raised their arms in cheerful signals as first the red car, and then the white, hurried past.

Raggy was following Marshall more closely than the Gremlin

had done, but now with the skilful use of gears, and the advantage of leading, Marshall began to gain.

He passed one car; Raggy could not get by, and had to wait for several seconds. By that time Marshall was farther ahead and passing another. Raggy had to drive as well as he knew how to try to diminish the advantage of Marshall's lead. He passed the last car in sight, and then slowly began to overtake Marshall, but it was very, very slow, although they were driving as fast as the road permitted.

'You're right, Gremmy,' he said. 'It looks as though if we're going to win this, we shall have to win it on design alone, because the performance seems to be pretty even.'

'It's funny,' Bunst said, looking back, where in the far distance he could see Grant, just passing one of the smaller cars. 'There seems to be a jolly big difference between the two. The two red ones, of course, not us and him,' he added, jerking his thumb through the windscreen towards Marshall. 'The one behind hasn't got the performance of his pal in front. Looks queer to me.'

Raggy laughed, amused at his constant suspicions.

'Everything looks queer to you. You're too suspicious, Bunst. It's quite likely that Grant's holding his car back. Saving it in case the first one is in trouble.'

'P'raps,' said Bunst, 'and on the other hand, conversively, p'raps not. I don't trust those two,' he added very darkly.

'I don't suppose Grant trusts you either,' said the Gremlin with a laugh, 'after the way you've been scowling at him all day!'

'All right,' said Bunst, 'you don't believe they could be up to any harm, but I just don't trust them.'

'Well, they haven't done anything we know of,' said Raggy, his eyes fixed on the rising road ahead, 'so we must give Grant the benefit of the doubt.'

All three now turned their eyes towards the front, for Marshall was slowing down once more to a spot where two cars had been pulled off the road.

It was the second check, and this time they had taken ten minutes under the hour to cover the forty miles.

Again there was a small band of checkers standing ready, and beyond the parked cars one of the competing cars had been stopped. As Raggy drew up behind Marshall, a checker came across to them, his nose shining like a red beacon under his cap. The nose, in fact, was all that they could see of the heavily muffled figure.

He jotted down the time and the number and said, 'You've been hitting it up, boys, but you want to watch the limits. This chap in front has been caught doing forty-five through a village a few miles back. That's five points off.'

'We're watching that,' said the Gremlin. 'We don't want to throw our chance away.'

The checker laughed into his muffler.

'Right-oh, then. Off you go and drive carefully.'

Marshall was away. Raggy started after him. This time they did not see Grant behind them before they left the checking point.

Once again Marshall was flashing up to his high speed, and this time it seemed that he was out to make a lead for himself and to keep it.

★ ★ ★

Meanwhile, miles ahead of the competing cars, the mighty Mercurial was thundering its way at a steady twenty-five miles an hour towards the third check. It had been delayed first of all by a puncture, and owing to the fact that the old-fashioned tyres could not be bought, Audacious and Gappy had had to repair the puncture by the snowy roadside.

Some distance farther on, the bottom of the radiator had frozen up, owing to the intense cold and the fact that Audacious had driven into a small snowdrift, which had blocked half the radiator with ice. This had resulted in the two men being partially obscured in clouds of steam, which necessitated a halt until the heat of the engine unfroze the bottom of the radiator again. These two incidents had taken some time, and so the Mercurial was still a few miles from the third checking place.

Now Audacious raised his voice above the thunder of the engine and cried, 'Gad! We shan't get there before they do. We must make up time!'

And so saying, he accelerated to thirty-five miles an hour, which took a minute or two, but as it appeared to be a level road Audacious thought he was quite safe.

Suddenly the road dropped away in front of him into a long, steepish hill, where the packed snow and ice shone dangerously in the moonlight.

'Gad!' roared Audacious. 'Caught napping!'

The great car began to descend the hill, gathering speed.

'For heaven's sake, don't put the brakes on!' bawled Gappy, clinging to the door.

'Gad, sir, no!' roared Audacious. 'That would mean a skid. We'd lose control.'

The fact of the matter was that, although Audacious did not know it, he had lost control already.

The snow which covered the hedges, the road and the fields beside the road made it difficult to see that at the bottom of the hill there was a bend round to the right.

As far as Audacious could see, all he had to do was to go

straight on. And so the Mercurial went faster than it had ever done in its life towards the hidden bend.

'She's holding well!' shouted Audacious. 'She still answers the helm!'

The racketing roar of the over-driven engine was now becoming so loud that Gappy, who had met all kinds of dangers in the motor-driving business, began to fear that the whole machine would explode into a thousand pieces and blow them both to eternity. But he had no time to worry about that, for with a look of horror upon his face, Gappy suddenly saw the bend ahead of them.

At the beginning of the bend there was a five-barred gate in the hedges, which led into the field on the nearside of the bend.

'Look out!' he shouted, his voice faint and thin amidst the roar of the death-dealing descent.

'Good heavens!' roared Audacious. 'It's a bend!'

And the intrepid gentleman, who had flown himself into more crashes than any man on earth, and escaped to tell the tale, became rigid with alarm, until his old army training came to his aid.

'Hang on!' he cried, with a sudden revival of confidence. 'We'll just about do it.'

Gappy hung on, but he knew that no car could have made the bend at the speed they were going, let alone this ancient and top-heavy automobile. So he shut his eyes.

Audacious pulled the wheel round with the intention of going round the bend, and to his amazement – though not to Gappy's – the car refused to turn, but kept straight on, heading for the five-barred gate.

The gate rushed up at a dizzy speed, while Audacious still held the wheel over at full lock in the hope that somehow, by some magic, the Mercurial could still get round the bend. Then it became obvious to him that all his four wheels were skidding, so he spun the steering-wheel in a good many directions to try to control the skid. It spun very easily, for the front wheels had long since lost interest in the whole affair and refused to grip anything.

Above the thunder of the engine and the wild shout from Audacious to 'Look out!', there was a crack, and it seemed that the whole of the gate, whose wood was rotten, burst upwards in a fountain of a thousand splinters, and rained down upon the driver and his paralysed passenger like fantastic jagged hailstones.

The Mercurial charged on across the field with Audacious steering first one way and then the other, all the while shouting, 'Just made it! Lucky the gate was there!'

Gappy opened his eyes, but still did not look any more pleased. They went on over the slippery, frozen field like some grotesque toboggan heading for disaster. And immediately ahead, like a frosty mirror, appeared the surface of a frozen pond.

The Mercurial slid on to the pond, and then, as the rear wheels bumped over the edge of the pond and on to the ice, they gripped for a second, and the whole car spun completely round in one dizzy sweep. The scenery flashed past them in a sideways rush; trees, hedges, hills, all swept past in the windscreen, like a shot from a crazy film.

Audacious had no idea by this time which way he was heading. The car bumped again, and came off the pond, sliding sideways through the snow for some yards, with Audacious putting on all the brakes he had, and trying to get the car under control. Finally the front wheels gripped, and he found himself steering directly towards a gap in another hedge, which after the

They slipped over the field like a grotesque toboggan.

gyrations of the last second or two, seemed to have appeared like magic.

There was no question of stopping the car, but by rapid juggling with the wheel, Audacious got it through the gate. And to the astonishment of himself and his passenger, he found himself once again on a road.

He skipped first to one side, then to the other, and finally, as if tired of playing games, the Mercurial came back into control again.

'Gad!' said Audacious, quite undaunted. 'That was a pretty clever way to cut off a corner!'

Gappy let go the door and partially collapsed in the seat.

'That will go down as one of my reminiscences!' said Audacious.

'It nearly went down as your obituary,' said Gappy, and scrambled in his pocket for a cigarette to soothe his nerves.

The Fake Car

Marshall was a cold machine of a man. Accurately, calculatingly, he had driven all that way like an automaton, a perfect part of the machine he had designed. But even within his chilly heart the warm thrill of near success had begun to flow.

He had been driven much faster than he had wanted to go by the pursuit of the white car, which had hung behind like a ghostly spectre. He was afraid of it. He felt that in a short and rapid test, his own car would outpace the Pegasus, but he was far from certain now that his would stand the distance.

He was beginning to get rattled, and the reason was that after he had covered four miles from the second check, with the Pegasus coming up behind him, he saw the temperature of his engine beginning to rise – only slightly at first, but it was rising.

For a while he kept on, holding the same very fast pace, for he knew that if he lagged at all the Pegasus would be up and by him. The two cars were almost evenly matched, but Marshall knew that in his last-minute alterations he had cut things too fine.

He was as firm in his seat as before, taking every bend with accurate certainty, using his gears exactly to suit his engine. But the white car behind him was beginning to press now. It was coming up faster then he had thought it could. Once more his narrow eyes flicked down to the thermometer.

The temperature was rising still, slowly but surely. He knew what had happened to Number Three. He knew now what was likely to happen to his.

The temperature was rising towards the boiling point, yet still he kept the speedometer between sixty and seventy, even more at times, in order to try to get away from the white, steady-riding car that followed him like a shadow. He could see it in his mirror every time he glanced up, steady, solid, like a thing that would never be shaken off.

He looked from the mirror down to the temperature again. Higher still. In the speedometer the miles were clocking up closer and closer to the third check. His car was going as well as before, but automatically the engineer in him was making his foot lift from the accelerator. His speed began to drop, his turns round the corners were slower, and suddenly he knew that if he wrecked this car, as Number Three had been wrecked, his chance would have gone. The Pegasus would win.

He clenched his teeth tight, so that the muscles of his jaw knotted, and in that second he made a lightning decision.

He slowed down still more, but in such a way as to give the impression that he was a man who had set the pace and was willing to let it slacken for a while. He drew in close to the verge and signalled the Pegasus by.

The white car came up and passed, smooth and sleek in the moonlight, and only the faint spray of hardened snow was left in its wake. Marshall's speed dropped down to forty, and now he began to look back at the road behind him.

By slackening off beforehand he had already slowed down the Pegasus, which had given Grant time to catch up the two miles that he had been left behind. And now, as Marshall looked back, he saw the unmistakable shape of Grant's car rapidly closing in towards him.

He turned his eyes to the front again, looked quickly from one side of the road to the other, and then four hundred yards ahead he saw a narrow turning leading off to the left.

Grant came close up behind him. Marshall looked back behind Grant, and along the white road saw no other car. He made a swift signal with his arm, then slowed right down and turned into the narrow lane.

Grant stopped opposite the lane, as if uncertain what to do.

'Here, quick!' Marshall called, then drove on round a slight bend, so that his car was obscured from the view of anyone passing on the road.

Grant followed him and stopped. Marshall got out of his car and came up to Grant's.

'What's the matter?' Grant said.

'Can't stand the pace,' Marshall said, shortly. 'She's starting to overheat. Been doing well, but she won't carry on. I've been pressed too hard. I'm certain I could beat that Pegasus in the speed trial, but I haven't the stamina to keep up for the whole of the trial at the pace those boys are making.'

'Well,' Grant snapped, 'what do you propose to do?'

'I've thought it out,' Marshall said quickly. 'Instead of them competing with one car, they'll have to compete with *both!*'

He was speaking between his teeth, and Grant was surprised at the emotion he showed.

'What do you mean? Quick!'

'I'll tell you what I mean,' Marshall snapped. 'We've got to change these number plates over. I'll say that your car, my Number Two really, has had an accident and fallen out.'

'What the deuce good is that going to do?'

'It means this,' Marshall said. 'You can make a short cut right down to the end of the trial. You can save a hundred miles, take it easy, and save my car while I go on through the whole trial in your car. I shouldn't lose many points on the checks. The Pegasus is my only rival, and I can drive pretty hard without anything going wrong. Therefore, when we reach the end there shouldn't be much between us.'

'True enough,' said Grant. 'But what's the rest of the story?'

'When I arrive,' said Marshall, his eyes glinting in the moonlight, and a faint smile appearing on his face, 'we change the number plates back again, and our fastest car will then be in a position to beat the Pegasus to bits.'

Grant was quiet for a second.

'Heavens! You've got it!' he said. 'Let's get to work at once and change the plates!'

Marshall had a spanner ready. The business of changing the number plates took some minutes. That done, Marshall got into Grant's car, drove back to the main road, where he halted to make sure there was nothing coming in either direction, then started off and accelerated away towards the third check, driving as fast as he knew how.

His jaw was stuck out. Apparently the halt had not given time for any of the smaller cars, which had already been overtaken, to come up past the turning. Therefore the road to the village, where the third check was situated, was empty of traffic.

'Lucky,' he said tersely.

Then, as the lighted windows of the cottages of the village came into sight, his eyes dropped to the clock on the dashboard. His self-satisfaction evaporated. He had thought the halt he had made had been short, but that, in conjunction with slowing down beforehand, had made him seven minutes late. That alone would lose him several points.

He was confident that Grant would get the other car to Oldquay, but he could not afford to lose any points unless the Pegasus lost some too. And as he drove into the lighted village, slowing down beside the hotel which was the checking-point, he said aloud to himself, 'I think I can arrange that.'

* * *

In the hotel courtyard, many of the trial cars were parked. A group of checkers were waiting by the road to mark off each car and the time it came in.

This halt was to be one of two hours' duration, Sir George's idea being twofold. First, it would allow the drivers to get hot food and drinks and a warm-up after driving in the bad weather. Secondly, it would also let the cars grow gradually cold standing outside in the freezing wind, and would therefore create a test for quick starting.

Marshall stopped at the entrance of the inn courtyard, and, as he was checked in, his eyes quickly found the white Pegasus amongst the other cars there.

144

'Lost a bit of time, old chap,' said the checker cheerfully.

'Yes,' Marshall said, betraying none of the anger which he felt. 'What do I lose on it?'

'Let's see,' the checker said. He looked at his wrist-watch, then at his notes. 'You're over seven minutes behind,' he said. 'That's a loss of four points for your type of car.'

'What about the white car over there?' Marshall said. 'I was following them for a long time.'

'They're doing well,' said the checker. 'Haven't lost a point so far.'

'Hm,' Marshall grunted. He drove his car into the park, switched off the engine and went towards the inn. He had another plan to put into operation. Then he spotted a group of tough teenagers standing about in the alley by the hotel. He went quickly up to one of them.

'I want you to do a job for me,' said Marshall in a low voice. 'What's your name?'

'They call me Smudger,' said the leader, sourly, 'and that'll be enough for you.'

Marshall chuckled.

'I see that you don't trust me,' he said. 'But look.'

And as he spoke he pulled from his pocket some pound notes. He counted off five and held them out in a fan like a hand of cards.

'See that? It's for you if you would like to do a simple little job for me.'

Smudger had a round pasty face with small eyes, rather like a pig's. In the starlight his eyes had been no more than slits, but as he saw the money his little eyes widened. Automatically he put out a hand to touch the notes, but Marshall laughed and held them back from him.

'Not too quickly, Smudger,' he said. 'You don't know what I

want you to do yet.'

'Is it crooked?' Smudger said.

His mates were standing close behind him, silent, but now one said. 'Must be, at that price.'

'Well, it isn't', said Marshall. 'I want to play a joke, and I should think you're just the chaps who could do it for me.'

'Joke, eh?' said Smudger, eyeing the notes again. 'Pretty good joke for that price. What have we got to do?'

'See that white car?' said Marshall. 'In about an hour and a half that white car will be starting off from here, and I want you to see that it is decoyed off the road, and the crew detained for an hour or more.'

Smudger stroked his cheek.

'Well, that isn't going to be so easy,' he said.

The fellow behind him who had spoken before said, 'Yes it is, you fool.'

'You shut up, Snapper,' said the gang leader.

'Not me,' said Snapper. He had a sharp and metallic voice and he snapped out almost every word he spoke. 'You know Barnes Lane about a mile up on the right-hand side? Hang it! All we've got to do is to get them to turn off and drive down to the old rectory. You know, the empty one. The one they say is haunted. We can keep them in there without any danger of being found out.'

Smudger grunted. He agreed with the idea, but he was annoyed that he had not thought of it himself.

'Sounds exactly what I want,' said Marshall. 'Right-oh, chaps, there's just one thing I'd like to know. How do you expect to get them to turn off the road?'

'I'll wait in the hedge on the main road,' said Snapper, quickly. 'As they come along I'll rush out and get them to stop. Tell them a friend of mine has had a bad accident. Nearly killed

146

himself. Ask them to come down and give me a hand and get him along to hospital.'

His head jerked from Smudger to Marshall and back again with the swift nervousness of a quizzical sparrow.

'Splendid,' Marshall said. 'Right-oh!' He gave the money to Smudger. 'There's the cash.'

Smudger grabbed it and stuffed it into his pocker, but the others were pressing very close behind him as if they feared he might try to get away with it.

'But I tell you,' Marshall went on, with a sudden cold fury in his voice, 'if you fail, I shall come back here, and when I've finished with you you'll be sorry you ever met me.'

★ ★ ★

Through the frosty night the thunderous, racketing, bucketing form of the Mercurial steamed on upon its fateful journey. Audacious was still at the wheel, muffled up to the nose. That appendage and the bushy moustache under it were the only visible parts of him. The brass-work of the Mercurial was glittering now, as if silver powder had been sprinkled on to it, for the dew was settling in ice.

Through the bare forests of the night, round the dangerous bends, the old chariot kept on its way. Audacious was surprised to notice that he did not recognise the road at all, although he thought he had driven up that very same way only the previous day.

Gappy was huddled in the seat, doing his best to read a map by the moonlight, for there were no dashlights inside the ancient car. He was turning the map this way, that way and upside-down, and often dropping it from his frost-bitten fingers, until he, too, had a queer sensation that all was not well with them.

'I don't think we're on the right road,' reported Gappy at last, shouting desperately to be heard above the noise of the engine.

'Gad, sir!' said Audacious, through his muffler. 'I was just getting the same idea myself. Now how could we have gone wrong?'

'There's only one thing I can think of,' said Gappy, working his fingers to and fro to make sure they would not freeze stiff, 'which is that when you made your "short cut" through the bend where the pond was, the road we came out on to on the other side wasn't the one we should have been on, but a different one altogether.'

'Gad, sir, I do believe you're right!' Audacious said. 'What on earth are we going to do now?'

'I don't know,' Gappy said. 'But this road is getting more like a lane than a road. In fact, I'm sure it isn't a main road at all.'

'Confusion, confusion!' roared Audacious. 'This is a fine kettle of fish. In fact stinking fish. We shall have to stop at a house and ask where we are.'

'Stop at a house?' said Gappy. 'Why, we haven't seen one for the last twenty miles. And from the look of it, we shan't find one for another twenty.'

'Don't be faint-hearted,' said Audacious, with a cheerful laugh. 'If we get lost, we can only freeze to death. And judging from the numbness of my feet, I can't imagine that we'd feel anything at all.'

Then he guffawed and sent the Mercurial bucketing along a bit faster, as if to get to the end before the road stopped.

The Hold-up

Raggy, the Gremlin and Bunst waited impatiently for the end of their enforced two hours' halt at the inn. Raggy had finally

148

prised Bunst away from guarding the Pegasus, and rewarded him with a good hot meal in the hotel. All three felt refreshed as they went out into the frosty moonlight towards the end of their rest.

Several of the smaller cars had started up and gone on their way towards the South. Overhead the moon was icily clear, like a great hollow snowball with a light inside it. Marshall strolled out, putting on his gloves. He gave the boys a cheerful signal as he passed them and went to his car.

The courtyard was rapidly emptying as the other cars drove away. Then the timekeepers gave the signal to the Pegasus. As it started off and swung out of the courtyard, the road ahead of it was clear.

The last car before them had vanished round the bend in the road, and the trees on either side of the white way cut off the twinkle of its rear light. The Pegasus swept away in hot pursuit of its competitors ahead.

The moonlight flickered through the naked branches of the trees, standing like nobble-jointed fingers against the silver sky, and threw weird distorted shadows across the road. The Gremlin was again at the wheel, and driving fast. They rounded the bend, then went on to where the four snow-blasted arms of a finger-post marked a crossroads. Automatically the Gremlin slowed down, for the trees, which had lined the road, had temporarily given way to high hedges, which blocked the view of any vehicle which might be coming out to cross the main road.

It was a good thing he did slow down, for as they approached the crossing, a figure ran out from the right-hand side of the road. It stopped, turned suddenly towards the car, and began to make frantic signals to the Pegasus to stop, waving its arms and calling out.

'Hullo, what's the matter?' asked Raggy.

'Looks like some chap in distress,' answered the Gremlin, slowing down to a standstill.

'Hullo, there!' he called out. 'What's the matter?'

Snapper, second-in-command of Smudger's gang, came up to the side of the car. He was panting as though he had run a long way and was pointing urgently up the little country lane behind him.

'There's been an accident,' Snapper said excitedly. 'Up the road here. A chap's seriously hurt. I can't get him to hospital by myself. Will you come along and give us a lift?'

'Of course we will,' Raggy said at once.

'Here!' Bunst broke in. 'We shall lose time if we do.'

'Can't help that,' said the Gremlin sourly. 'Come on, hop into the back, old man,' he added to Snapper, 'and show us which way it is.'

Snapper got into the back as the car started off again.

'To the right here,' said Snapper, leaning on the back of the front seat. 'Then keep straight along . . . .'

The car turned right, down the high-hedged lane where the snow was deep and soft, as if no traffic had been along it all that day.

'Keep going,' said Snapper. 'It isn't far.'

As they went along, they saw through the naked trees the shape of an old gothic-style building with sharp gables rising into the sky, like inverted icicles gleaming in the snow which outlined them.

'I left him inside this house,' Snapper said. 'Just turn into this drive.' He pointed to a gate on the left-hand side, which stood wide open.

The Gremlin swung the Pegasus through the gateway, round the short drive, and to the front of the house. He stopped by the steps and they all looked towards the house.

'Well, where is he?' asked Raggy, turning his head sharply to Snapper behind, for the panes of the windows in this house were dark and empty, sparkling with the frost which had gathered like star-cracks on the glass.

Around them were a number of great bushes, heavy with snow. There was no sign of a movement anywhere.

The Gremlin noticed that the front door of the house was slightly ajar. For a moment Snapper almost grinned. But his trap-like jaw was under full control, and he merely answered, 'I left him just in the hall. I thought it would be warmer for him. Will you come in and give me a hand to get him out?'

And so saying, Snapper jumped out of the car.

Then through the open door there sounded a faint groaning voice.

'Is that you – come back at last?'

'Yes, it's all right. It's me,' said Snapper, and ran up the front steps.

'He sounds bad,' said Raggy, getting out of the car. 'Come on, we must see what we can do.'

Bunst and the Gremlin tumbled out of the car together, and followed Raggy up the steps into the dark hall.

It was a big, broad hall with the doors on either side of it standing open. The moonlight on the snow outside painted the ceilings with a clear, white light. Yet even with that brilliance they could see no sign of Snapper, but only of a man lying covered in rags just inside one of the rooms to the right-hand side of the hall.

This fellow groaned, as if in some pain. Raggy went to him immediately and knelt down by his side. The Gremlin half followed, then stopped in the doorway as Bunst, close behind him, said, 'Here, where's the other chap?'

'Here!' said a voice behind Bunst, and a number of figures came running across the hall from the open door of a room on the other side.

At the very same moment, Smudger, who had been playing the part of the sick man, jumped to his feet with the rags falling off him, and hit out at Raggy's head with a fist like a leg of mutton.

Raggy was quick. He had heard the sudden remark from Bunst, and the sound of boots in the hall. And as Smudger swung at him he automatically backed a step, warded off the blow with his left, and at the same time swung a powerful right fist into Smudger's solar plexus.

It was Smudger's weak point, and he began to double up, so that his jaw came forward just as Raggy brought his left fist round in a cracking blow to the chin.

Smudger was half-dazed, and staggered away, but not before Raggy had hit him for the third time, and the blow landed under the bully's jaw and cracked the back of his head against the wall.

Smudger crumpled up and went to the floor on his knees, while Raggy turned to his companions, who were now in the thick of a scrum in the middle of the hall.

As Raggy ran into the hall, he could see the tall figure of the Gremlin hitting out all round him, and he could also see one lout, who had got round to the Gremlin's back, about to bring a stick down on Gremmy's red head.

Then suddenly Raggy saw Bunst. The little fellow came like a flash, head-first between the legs of the attacker with the stick. He barged into the legs and straightened up as he got his head and shoulders between them. The youth gave a loud yell and dropped face down to the floor with a crash that shook the boards, and caused a cloud of dust to rise like silver smoke in the moonlight that flooded into the hall.

Another of the gang, struck by a swinging blow from the Gremlin, tripped over his fallen comrade, and he, too went down. It left the Gremlin fighting three, but not for more than a second.

Raggy went into the fight with the same coolness with which he had dealt with the treacherous Smudger. Seeing the face of Snapper immediately in front of him, he crashed his fist into it with a crack. Snapper let out a wild yell of pain, and attempted to draw back out of the fight.

At that moment the Gremlin crashed two heavy punches into the chest of one of his two remaining adversaries. That youth, too, went back, knocked almost out of breath, his arms raised to protect himself.

Bunst came round the Gremlin and charged at the fellow as he went back, lowered his head and butted him hard in the chest. It was the final blow. The lout spun round, lost his balance, and fell against the wall.

It seemed at that moment that the trio had got the better of their attackers. But two were getting up off the floor. One of them did not trouble to get to his feet. Instead, he grabbed the Gremlin round the legs and brought the big red-head down to the ground.

At the same time, Smudger had recovered his breath and came thundering out of the doorway to try to catch Raggy unawares.

'Look out behind!' Bunst called from across the hall.

The warning was just enough to let Raggy half turn and see Smudger come rushing at him, but not enough to give him time to bring his arm back for a blow.

Smudger hit out, and his fist glanced off Raggy's shoulder. Raggy then swung round fully towards Smudger and hit him

153

hard against the chest, but Snapper now saw his chance.

He leapt across the floor like an ape, and jumped on to Raggy's back. Bunst had seen this new move, and leaving his own man, he darted across and rushed straight in between Smudger and Raggy, taking two heavy blows from the bully's fist as he did so, one of which caught the side of his head so that for a moment his brain spun.

Raggy staggered back with the weight of Snapper on him, and was fighting for breath against the steely grip of the Snapper's hands round his throat.

Bunst hit out wildly at Smudger, although his brain had not cleared enough for him to see properly. And small though he was, the very fury of his attack made the bully retreat in front of him.

Meanwhile the Gremlin, struggling with one youth on the floor, now found another one sufficiently recovered to scramble over and join with his companion in trying to get the red-head down and keep him down. The Gremlin fought as hard as he could, but the weight of the two upon him was almost too much. He knew that at any moment he would be out of this fight.

There was a crash as Snapper, with a violent twist, brought Raggy and himself to the floor. And Snapper began fighting in the only way he knew how. He kicked, punched, bit and scratched. Raggy had all that he could do to hold off the savage attack.

Smudger, driven back against the wall by the fiery Bunst, suddenly kicked out. His boot cracked agains the boy's shin and carried his leg clean away from under him. Bunst went down and rolled over on the floor, his leg numbed with pain.

It looked like the end of the fight. The superiority in numbers had told. It had been two against one the whole way through,

154

and it could have had only one ending.

The lout whom Bunst had butted against the wall had now recovered, and came to throw himself down upon the helpless boy to take his revenge on him. But as he went, he looked to the glass-panelled door at the back of the house. It was the door which led to the garden. Suddenly he stopped and his eyes widened.

'Good grief!' he shouted. 'Look!'

Smudger, frightened by this sudden cry of alarm, followed his companion's trembling finger to the glass door. For through the frost-starred pane of the door there showed a mis-shapen, unreal figure in glistening white. And as the figure moved its head slowly, the panes distorted more and seemed to make the face grow long and one-sided, like a nightmare scene in a curved mirror.

'It's – it's the *ghost*!' Smudger roared, and the panic in his voice stopped the struggle throughout the hall.

The louts attacking the Gremlin stopped and looked round.

'Here, let's get – quick!' said one.

The rear door of the house rattled. The Thing was trying to get in.

'Run!' shouted Snapper, letting go of Raggy and jumping back on to his feet. 'It's coming in!'

The handle stopped turning, and the door began to open. The weird glistening figure from another world let in a cold dank wind which blew, like a terrifying breath, down the hall.

'Drop it! Let 'em go!' Smudger screamed, and ran to the front door.

Snapper was after him like a shot. The door opened fully, and into the weird light of the hall stepped a figure which had no face, but which shone with a strange luminous light.

Through the door there showed a mis-shapen figure.

'It *is* the ghost!' repeated one of the fellows, and began to scramble away towards the front door, although the Gremlin was still trying to cling on to his trouser leg.

The apparition stopped in the doorway. And then from it came a terrible voice which rang and echoed in the empty house.

Snapper and Smudger and another tough were heading for the front door, running for all they were worth. They had heard of the rectory ghost and now, at last, they had seen it. They dared not look back at the awful sight, as they ran headlong out to the steps towards the snow of the drive.

★　★　★

The Mercurial raced on upon the thick, snowy road which led between the naked trees. There was no sign yet of a house, but the snow was growing deeper, and ahead of the radiator, which was now giving off little bursts of steam, there appeared a bend to the right.

'There's a bend ahead,' yelled Gappy, remembering the adventure over the frozen pond.

'I have everything under control, by gad!' responded Audacious, shouting through his muffler.

There was no hood up in the car, and Audacious, tall and upright at the wheel, was gradually being frosted over. His moustache glistened; his deerstalker hat was beginning to shine as the frost coated it, and, in fact, he was beginning to look like a frozen man encased in a light sheath of sparkling ice.

He brought the car round the bend with only a slight skid, and roared on through the wood, his ancient tyres flinging up sprays of snow which gathered behind the car like the wake of a speed-boat, and fell in disorder upon the newly rutted road.

The Mercurial, in order to catch up time, was now going all out, and the speed was over thirty miles an hour. Everything shook from the pounding of the powerful engine, including the windscreen, which was shimmying before the frozen gaze of Audacious, and the more apprehensive eyes of Gappy.

'Gosh!' shouted Gappy. 'I never knew a driver quite like you before.'

Audacious laughed through his muffler, though the sound of his laugh could not be heard above the thunder of the engine. Then ahead he saw a sign standing upright on the left-hand side of the road, but so plastered with snow that it was unreadable.

'I wonder,' said Audacious, 'what that meant?'

'Cross-roads or something,' said Gappy. 'But you can't stop now anyway.'

The sign was very near to the crossing and Audacious fully realised the truth of Gappy's statement.

They descended upon the cross-roads just as a big, red touring car appeared, crossing their path. The hedges on either side of the road had cut off all sight of it until suddenly it arrived. Audacious knew now that it would be useless to apply the brakes, as that would only result in a skid into the ditch on one side or the other of the road, and probably stop them for several hours.

'We'll have to bang through!' he cried, although the red car's side was now only a foot or two away from his bonnet.

'Bang's the word,' said Gappy, and closed his eyes.

Audacious steered to the right in order to try to miss the red car. At that time, the red car suddenly accelerated, and Audacious charged across the main road with an inch or two to spare. He entered the road on the opposite side of the crossing, where there were tracks of a single car.

'Anyhow, somebody's been down here,' said Audacious hopefully. 'Probably one of the competitors.'

'I don't believe that,' argued Gappy. 'This isn't a main road. I'm pretty certain we should have turned left at that crossing.'

The Mercurial was still thundering on, but now losing speed.

'Why, hang it, sir!' bellowed Audacious. 'I couldn't have turned left there. I was going much too fast,' he added rather proudly.

'Yes, I know that,' replied Gappy. 'But – –.' And as he saw a house appear between the trees he added, 'By Jove! There's a house. We ought to stop there, and ask the way.'

'Hang everything, sir! I believe you're right. There's an open gate on our left and a car's gone in there. You can see the tracks,' said Audacious, pulling back his monstrous hand-brake. 'But unfortunately I don't think I can stop in time.'

That was very true, for the Mercurial slid straight on past the gate, and by the time it pulled up it had stopped by a small gate in the hedge, which was obviously the tradesmen's entrance to the same house.

'I'll dash in and ask,' said Audacious.

'I'll just get out and stamp my feet,' Gappy replied. 'I'm frozen to the bone.'

Audacious got out, covered in frost, and appearing like some monster from another world, breathing steam from his nostrils. He pushed open the small gate and trudged through the snow towards the back of the house.

The snow deadened the sound of his footsteps, but from inside the house he could hear what sounded like a large party in progress. There were shouts and yells, bangs and thumps. Audacious paused and listened.

'Gad!' he said to himself. 'Sounds a cheerful spot.'

He went on and up the steps to the back door. For a moment he stood there at the glass pane of the door, looking on either side for a bell-push, which he could not find. He then tried the handle, which turned easily, and to his astonishment he found that he could push the door open. He walked slowly into the hall, worried because he was an intruder and did not like to walk in on somebody's party.

He was about to speak when suddenly he recognised Bunst sitting on the floor rubbing his shin. He shifted his eyes and saw Raggy lying on the floor trying to grab at a big youth's legs as that lout began to run away towards the door. Then his eyes turned in another direction and he saw the figure of the Gremlin doing almost the same thing as Raggy, but lying in a queer position so that at the same time as he was trying to grab another fellow's leg he was also swinging his leg round as if to trip his victim as well. He also saw three or four figures running towards the open front door. Outside, Audacious, from his great height, could see the well-known shape of the white Pegasus. And it was at this moment that Audacious stopped trying to find a word to say, and instead let all his boiling feelings rise into one fearful shout, which echoed in the empty rooms of the house, and ran away into the wings, echoing like a thousand tiny shouts. 'Thieves and vagabonds! I knew there would be dirty work on this trip!'

And so saying he ran forward, just as the Gremlin and Raggy were scrambling to their feet to pursue the bullies who had already run out of the front door. Poor Bunst was still so hurt in the shin that he could not get up.

'You all right, me boy?' cried Audacious, as he charged through the big hall.

'Yes, sir,' answered Bunst quick as lightning. 'Just paramalized in the leg, that's all. You go after them, sir; I'll be all right.'

Audacious thundered past in pursuit.

Meanwhile Gappy, finding that stamping on the ground did his feet no good, had decided to run gently up and down the road outside. At the end of his first trot, he turned to go back opposite the open gate through which the Pegasus had gone. As he turned he saw the shape of the white car in the drive, and he stopped suddenly.

'Well, well!' he said. 'It's the Peggy.'

He went into the drive, and as he came to the car he heard several sudden shouts from inside, which to his confused hearing sounded like: 'It's the ghost! Let 'em go! Let's get out of here!'

Although these were not quite the words which were used, that was the sense which Gappy got from them. And being a curious young man, he went up the steps towards the front door at a very fast pace indeed, for it suddenly occurred to him that the Pegasus should not be there, and that it might be some trick which had brought it there.

When the first youth – who happened to be Smudger – came running out of the door, he got a glimpse of the moonlit hall which told him in a moment that some sort of a fight had been going on. And so, as Smudger ran out, white and scared. Gappy decided that this was one of the people in the hall who should not have been there.

Gappy had been a professional boxer, a middle-weight, and had all the art of the ring in his fists. Gappy was a quick thinker and a very much quicker hitter. Smudger did not even see Gappy before something hit him on the side of the jaw. He went headlong down the steps and smack into the snow, knocked out.

Gappy, with a professional pride in the blow which he had just dealt, turned just in time to see Snapper coming out of the front door. Snapper was quick, and would have halted, but the snow was slippery, and so he slid on, like a man on skates, straight into the fist of Gappy, who had it ready for him. Snapper went over the side of the steps and into a bush, which shook and heaved and let loose an avalanche of snow from its heavily laden leaves. A third member of the gang soon lay by his side.

At this time Gappy heard the voice of the great Audacious from within, and with a short laugh he went in through the door in time to collide with another of the gang, who was trying to run out of it. The ex-boxer was never slow, and as soon as the bully staggered back from the collision, Gappy brought his right fist smack into the fellow's ribs. He followed this with another, using his left this time. And then he said, 'Sorry, old chap, but you'd be better out.'

And he gave one final right to the jaw, which sent the fellow sideways across the hall through an open door, where he clung to the handle for a moment, and then collapsed in a mass of useless limbs.

'Right-oh, you chaps!' Gappy shouted. 'All stop where you are!'

But he was a little too late, for Audacious, seeing one of the remaining two in front of him, swung his mighty gloved fist, and to his great astonishment hit the fellow on the side of the head. The result was that the youth, big and burly as an ox, seemed to do what was an eccentric dance, with all his limbs flopping and his head wobbling turning round in a kind of pirouette, from which he finally lost his balance, and, staggering, fell face upwards on the stairs.

'Gad!' said Audacious. 'I didn't know I had it in me.'

By this time, Gremmy and Raggy had got Bunst to his feet, and all three were standing there grinning. The one remaining member of the gang was leaning against the wall shivering. His eyes moved from Gappy to the Gremlin; from the Gremlin to Raggy; and finally to Audacious and back again to Gappy. It was a lost battle and he had given in, although he had been the youth who had tried to knock out the Gremlin with a stick.

'Well, now,' Audacious said. 'This is a fine kettle of fish. What's happened? You should be on the road, me boys.'

'We're going to be in just about two seconds,' said Raggy, through his teeth. 'Thanks to you, sir, we weren't held up for good.'

'By gad, yes!' said Audacious. 'You've got to get away at once. The only thing is,' he said putting a gloved hand to his frozen moustache, which looked like glass in the moonlight, 'I'm hanged if I can understand why they thought I was a ghost. Why, I don't look like a ghost, do I?'

The Gremlin grinned.

'If I didn't know you,' he said. 'I should have run away myself!'

'And now we've got to make up time,' said Bunst. 'Come on! Let's get going.'

'Yes, you must be off,' said Audacious. 'But just before you go,' he added quickly, 'keep your radio tuned in to my wavelength, just in case we find out what's at the bottom of all this.'

'Right-oh, sir, we will,' said Raggy. 'Now, come on, chaps, we must, move.'

Gremmy and Raggy helped Bunst out of the front door, past the prostrate forms of their attackers, and scrambled into the car. Raggy started up. The car swung round in a wide sweep and disappeared out of the gate.

Audacious turned to the one shivering member of the gang left, as he crouched against the wall.

'Now then, me man,' he said. 'Who put you up to this?'

'Yes, who did?' asked Gappy, his eyes narrowed.

'I don't know,' the shivering fellow answered. 'It was some-body we met at the inn. Smudger took the money from him, but we only saw him really in the dark, and I can't tell you who he was.'

'Did he come in a car?' asked Gappy.

'I th – think he must have done.'

'What car was it?' said Gappy.

'I didn't see, sir,' said the fellow, shivering. 'I didn't see at all. There were lots of cars there.'

Audacious was about to say something, but he realised that Gappy was the better questioner, and he also realised that Gappy had a strong suspicion in his mind, which he meant to confirm.

'Carry on,' said Audacious.

'Right, sir,' said Gappy. 'There's only one more question. What was this man like?'

'I didn't see, I tell you!' said the fellow, so frightened now that it was obvious that if he had seen, he would have told.

'Right-oh,' said Gappy. 'We've finished with you. Now you and your friends had better get out of this place before I call the police. If there are some of them who can't walk, you'll have to carry them. But as far as I'm concerned you've had your punishment.'

'Thank you, sir, thank you,' the fellow said, hardly able to believe his good luck.

'Don't bother about thanking me,' said Gappy. 'Which is the main road?'

'Why, sir, just up to the top, and then turn left.'

'Good,' said Gappy, and turning to Audacious he added, 'it

was the road we slid across. Come on, I think we should get going.'

'Very lucky,' said Audacious. 'Lucky that we did take the wrong road. I think our young friends were having a rough time of it.'

A Clue to the Trick

The Pegasus was travelling very fast now in an effort to try to make up as much of the lost time as possible. The crew were all suffering from bruises of one sort or another, and Raggy's knuckles were bound round with a handkerchief where he had hit someone too hard.

Raggy was driving coolly, but he knew that it was impossible they would get through without loss of marks after that delay.

'I would like to know,' said Bunst, 'what that was all about. I have come to the conclusion that it must have been organised.'

'How could it have been?' said the Gremlin sharply. 'It looked to me like an ordinary hold-up. They thought probably we had some money with us.'

'It's about the only sensible solution,' said Raggy, without turning his head.

'Well, I don't agree with it,' said Bunst obstinately. 'I bet that fellow Grant organised it.'

'Grant?' echoed the Gremlin, 'He couldn't have had anything to do with it. He never even reached that check. He's out of the running; didn't you hear that? Broke down some way back.'

'Hmm,' said Bunst. 'Well, it all seems very superstitious to me.'

The little fellow looked dissatisfied, and frowned ahead at the racing road as if trying to think of a way in which Grant could have reached the last check. But he could not, and had to give it up. As if by way of a consolation he pulled two thick sandwiches out of his pocket and began to eat.

The Gremlin was watching the clock on the dashboard.

'We're making up a bit of time,' he said. 'But not enough. I think we're going to be down on this lot all right.'

'Well, we ought to tell them at the next check what happened,' said Bunst. 'Then perhaps they wouldn't take any marks off.'

Raggy grinned faintly.

'No, that wouldn't make any difference, Bunst,' he said. 'Any hazard counts in this game. Whether it's a burst tyre, or smash, or even a hold-up! It's all part of the luck.'

They began to pass one or two smaller cars and, as more miles sped by beneath the wheels, it seemed for a time as if they might make up enough time to lose them not more than two points at the most. And then on the road ahead there came a sight which dashed their hopes.

There was a sports car lurching in the ditch where it had skidded a minute or two before, and the driver and his companion were signalling to the Pegasus to stop.

Raggy groaned.

'This is just the one time I really don't want to play the good Samaritan,' he said. 'But still, we'll have to see if we can help somehow.'

Bunst was so annoyed with this that he threw his half-eaten sandwich overboard, and muttered things under his breath as the Pegasus drew to a standstill by the ditched car.

The driver came up to Raggy.

'Sorry, old chap,' he said. 'I know you can't afford the time, but could you give us a hoist out of this ditch? We've got a tow

166

rope fixed to our front. Do you mind if we sling the other end over your bumper?'

'Certainly not,' Raggy said. 'Carry on. We'll see if we can get you out, although the road is a bit slippery here.'

'You're telling me,' said the other driver ruefully. 'We spun round twice before we got in the ditch.'

Raggy moved the Pegasus into position. The driver put the looped end of his rope over the rear bumper of the white car.

The other machine was well in the ditch in three feet of snow. It was five minutes before the Pegasus slowly dragged the car out and up on to the road again. The driver took the rope off the Pegasus and shouted out, 'Sorry, old man, didn't think it would take that long.'

'Okay,' yelled Raggy, and accelerated away, all hope of making up time now lost.

They ran on very fast to the next check, where the checker made a note of their time.

'Better look out, chaps,' he said. 'Your average is falling. You've lost a whole five points on this run. Still, carry on, you may catch up yet.'

The Pegasus started off after a halt of only thirty seconds. The crew said nothing. The Gremlin wrote down the times in the log which they had been keeping from the beginning of the trial.

'Five down,' said the Gremlin at last. 'That puts us one behind Marshall, and I wonder how far he is ahead.'

'I don't know,' said Raggy grimly, 'but we'll catch him up sooner or later, don't you worry.'

★   ★   ★

Audacious and Gappy came out of the haunted rectory and went down the steps to where Smudger was sitting up in the snow and rubbing his jaw.

'No harm in trying to find out who did this,' Gappy said, halting. 'It won't take a minute.'

He stood over the sullen Smudger.

'Who's the leader of this little lot?' he demanded.

Smudger grunted.

'There's no leader,' he said.

'Do you know you can go to prison for this?' said Gappy.

Smudger started. He had not realised that what he had done was criminal.

'Prison?' he shouted. 'But it was – just a joke. A fellow put us up to it. Practical joke he said it was, on some pals of his.'

'Practical joke?' said Gappy. 'Did he pay you anything for it?

Smudger hesitated.

'Yes. He gave us some money.'

The gang leader was now thoroughly cowed, and he shivered, but not because of the cold of the snow in which he was sitting.

'I didn't think it was serious,' he said. 'I thought it was just a lark.'

'What was the man like?' said Gappy, ignoring Smudger's protests.

'Well,' Smudger said rather breathlessly, 'he was tall and thin. Sort of didn't smile much. Hard chap altogether.'

'Good,' said Gappy. 'And now you and your gang had better get off or else I'll have the police straight down on you.'

Smudger needed no second invitation. He scrambled up in the snow and stood for a moment as if not sure whether to trust Gappy or not. Then he turned like lightning, ran towards the gate, and out of it.

'Hmm,' said Audacious, brushing his frozen moustache. 'That description doesn't fit our friend Grant, does it?'

'It doesn't,' Gappy agreed. 'But it fits his second driver Marshall.'

'Gad!' said Audacious, 'so it *is* dirty work! In fact dirty work at the cross-roads.' He laughed, as he always did at his own jokes. 'I tell you what we must do, me lad. We've got to warn those boys, and we must do it at once!'

'Warn them?' said Gappy, 'How on earth are you going to do that?'

'I'll send my plane after them,' said Audacious. 'Come along we'll get it rigged up now.'

With this mysterious remark Audacious began to walk away through the snow towards the lane.

'What plane?' said Gappy, following him.

'I've a model radio-controlled aircraft in the back of my car,' said Audacious briskly. 'It has a speed of a hundred and twenty miles an hour, and should catch them up within a very short time.'

'But how? How is it going to find where they are?'

'My dear fellow,' said Audacious, arriving at the car and opening the huge dicky, 'remember I told them to keep their radio tuned in? My aircraft is radio controlled and is tuned to a certain wavelength. My radio set in the dicky of the Mercurial can control it to climb, fly and land. But once I cut my radio, the plane flies to the nearest radio which is tuned to the same wavelength. So it will fly straight to the Pegasus and circle round that aerial until I decide to switch on my radio and bring it back to us.'

Audacious was now tenderly lifting out the wings and fuselage of his big model. It was designed to break into pieces so that it could be reassembled within a matter of seconds. Audacious worked with his gloves off, and before the astonished eyes of Gappy, the plane was built in no time.

'It's launched, as you see, from the ramp over the top of the car,' said Audacious, fixing the wings in position on the fuselage.

'So that's what it is,' said Gappy. 'I've been wondering what that was supposed to be for ever since I first saw it.'

'Just hang on to her by the middle of the fuselage,' said Audacious, 'while I start her up.'

Gappy took hold of the plane firmly while Audacious began to flick over the propeller several times. The engine spluttered, then started with a high-pitched whine, which suddenly ended with a pop, and the propeller stopped.

'Confound the thing!' said Audacious. 'I suppose it's too cold.'

Once more he began flicking the propeller, but the engine would not start. It was some time before it went properly, and then it went well.

'Okay,' bawled Audacious in relief. 'Give me a hand to hoist her up on the ramp.'

Both men lifted the model up to the crane-like ramp on top of the car, and Audacious fixed it in position.

'Better stand back,' Audacious said. 'She's rocket launched, and there's a bit of a blast from the rocket on the travelling cradle as it shoots forward and launches the plane.'

'You think of everything,' said Gappy in admiration. 'Your machinery is ancient *and* modern.'

He grinned.

Audacious stood back for a moment and reached for the radio control inside the dicky.

'Off she goes,' he said, and pressed the button which electrically fired the rocket on the launching cradle.

A jet of fire shot out from behind the cradle, and for a moment the shriek of the engine was lost in the hissing roar of the exploding rocket. The plane was shot forward to the end of the ramp, and then flew off under its own power, and began to climb away into the night sky, like a streamlined hawk.

It climbed to about three hundred feet under Audacious's radio control, which he was operating with nimble fingers. Gappy watched the machine until its nose pointed towards the south.

'Now then,' said Audacious. 'I throw this switch over so that instead of my controlling it, the aerial on the Pegasus will take charge, and the machine will fly straight there.'

He threw over the switch. The little aircraft turned a few degrees towards the south-west, and then droned away out of sight.

'Yes, that's all jolly fine,' said Gappy, 'but you haven't put a message in it. How are they going to know what it means?'

'Aha!' said Audacious, and tapped the side of his nose. 'There's a little signalling light under the belly, which I operate by this morse tapper here.' He pointed to a morse key which was fitted alongside his control knobs. 'And as I send the message in morse, so the lamp under the plane will flash it down to them.'

Gappy looked at the old gentleman in amazement.

'You know, there's more to you than appears on the surface,' he said with a grin. 'There's just one thing more I want to know,' he added, 'and that is this. How will you know when the plane is above the car?'

Audacious switched on a light fitted inside the dicky, which showed a map. And across this map a tiny light shining from underneath it was moving slowly south by south-west.

'Radar, my friend,' said Audacious. 'That light shows the position of our plane, and the minute it stops going forward and begins to circle, we shall know that she has arrived.'

'Well, if I'd known that this old junk-box –' Gappy broke off as he saw Audacious give a sudden frightful glare – 'this fine old car had got all this stowed away in the back, I should have been playing with it all the way down, even if I'd had to sit on the rear number plate to do it!'

An Intentional Accident

In the Pegasus, the drivers had changed over. Raggy had done his spell coolly and efficiently, and now the Gremlin had taken charge.

But the Gremlin was red-headed and fast-tempered. He was ready to be angered even if something incalculable, like the weather, got in his way. He was driving very fast indeed in order to make up the time which had been lost. He drove so fast that Raggy from time to time looked across at him, but the Gremlin's face was set as hard as rock. His eyes were straight ahead, his hands firm on the steering-wheel as he watched the white, icy glass of the road ahead.

Once or twice the back of the Pegasus began a slight slide, but each time the Gremlin was quick to rectify these incipient skids.

Bunst, sitting in between the two, seemed to have lost all interest in his packet of sandwiches, and was staring from the road to the speedometer and then to the clock. Several times he looked at Raggy's log-book and asked, 'How are we doing?'

Each time Raggy replied, 'We're making up. Don't worry.' And each time Bunst grunted, looked miserable, and stared ahead at the shining white road again.

The road was by no means straight. On the bends the Gremlin

shifted down and kept his wheels close to the frozen inside of the curves. Thus he made his best possible speed wherever the road turned. Hills made no difference to the extraordinary power of the smooth engine. The Gremlin had only to curb it when the car rose over the crest of the hill and began to go down the icy slope on the other side.

The freezing wind made a faint whine as it passed over the windscreen and round the sides of the car. And now and again, as the tyres rode over a frozen ridge of ice on the road, there was a brisk crushing sound.

For forty miles the white car passed through woods, broke out into the open again where only hedges bounded the sides of the road, then plunged once again into pine forests, where the great firs stood like Christmas trees on either side of the road. Finally it slowed down to enter the village where the timekeepers were frozenly waiting in the midnight frost.

The Pegasus drew up, and a muffled timekeeper came up to make his check. Raggy compared his log-book with the checker's pad.

'Jove!' said the checker. 'You've been moving, haven't you?'

'We had to,' said Raggy grimly.

'Well, you've averaged sixty-seven miles an hour from the last check,' the muffled figure said. 'Are you chasing somebody?'

'We're after the Grant Tourer,' the Gremlin said.

'Oh, him!' the checker said with a laugh. 'Well, you're getting pretty close up behind him now. He's only a few minutes ahead of you.'

'Good,' said the Gremlin, as he engaged the gear and set the Pegasus off.

The acceleration of the white car was so great that it seemed to create a wake of frozen air behind it, which made the checker stand back as the leaves of his notebook fluttered in the sudden disturbance of the air.

Bunst looked back, and then turned round to the front again.

'Near blew the pad out of his hand,' he said. 'It's the best take-off we've had so far.'

Raggy was busy jotting his calculations down in the log book he was keeping and did not hear what Bunst was saying.

'The trouble is,' Raggy said, 'we can lose marks on this trip, but we can't make any. Once we've lost them, they're gone. The only thing we can do is to try to make up our time so that we get in at least level with the Grant Tourer.'

'He's only a few minutes ahead,' Bunst reminded him. 'It won't take long to catch up.'

'You're a wishful thinker,' said the Gremlin, slackening his attention from the road for a half-second. 'It takes a long time to catch up minutes with a car which is probably doing seventy or eighty the whole time.'

'But it's only, say, ten minutes off,' Bunst protested.

'Yes,' said Raggy. 'But we're only overtaking him at a rate of about ten miles an hour. If he's doing seventy and we're doing eighty you can see where the difference comes in.'

'Thundering crankshafts!' said Bunst. 'I didn't realise that. I was thinking of it as if it might be a tree standing still while we was approaching at a rate of knots.'

'Well, you see,' Raggy said, 'it isn't a tree, it's a car. And it's moving away from us at a rate of knots, so that we're only overtaking it – I expect – at ten miles an hour.'

'If only those fellows in that house hadn't got up to their tricks – –' said Bunst, and broke off.

Then in a moment he went on, '– still, it's no use wishing it hadn't happened, because it did; and there you are. Just bad luck, eh? Just a gang of hooligans up to a bit of dirty work. But it's unlucky they should have caught us, eh?'

'Jolly unlucky,' said the Gremlin, and shut his jaws together.

Raggy looked across at him.

'You made that sound as if those fellows tried to stop us getting on,' he said quietly.

'I'm so jolly annoyed I don't know whether to think that or not,' said the Gremlin.

'But it must have been a pure accident that they picked on us,' said Raggy. 'Surely gangs of chaps like that don't wait around to interfere with people competing in the trial?'

'No, I suppose not,' said the Gremlin with a short laugh. 'It's just that I'm bad tempered about the whole thing.'

Then suddenly a broad grin spread over his face.

'But I must say I enjoyed the fight,' he said.

Raggy laughed. Bunst frowned.

'You dropped off five miles an hour while you were talking,' Bunst said. 'So you'd better stop nattering until we've caught up with Mr Marshall.'

'All right,' said the Gremlin.

Ahead of him the ice and snow were still packed tight on the road.

'If only we could get away from this wretched snow,' he said, 'we could average more than we're doing now.'

Raggy agreed, but he said, 'You're doing well enough, Gremmy, and there probably won't be any snow as we get farther south.'

They began to pass several of the smaller cars; the Gremlin went by them as if they were not there. He was travelling very fast indeed now. In the next few minutes more and more of the smaller cars appeared and seemed to swell as the Pegasus overtook them, and then vanished into the moonlit whiteness behind. Then suddenly Bunst, whose little eyes had never missed a detail of the cars they had passed, said, 'Look! Straight ahead! It's Marshall!'

His two companions said nothing for a moment. The smaller cars had dropped so far behind they were now out of sight, and ahead was just the one large Tourer, its twin rear lights showing up like beacons against the shining snow of the road.

'It is,' said the Gremlin. 'It must have been going slower than we thought.'

'No,' Raggy said pointedly, 'I think it's more a case that we've been going faster than we ought.'

'Well, we've got to catch up,' said the Gremlin, his eyes fixed on the big red car ahead.

Steadily the Pegasus overtook the Tourer. The road ahead of them ran straight in a gradually rising slope, like a road leading direct to the moon. Hedges and fields on either side flashed by in a white blur as the Pegasus swept on nearer and nearer to the rear of the car ahead.

In the moonlight the three pursuers could see Marshall's head turn and look back. It took him only a split second to recognise the car behind him, and his head jerked back towards the road again. He began to draw in towards the side of the road as if to give the Pegasus room to pass.

'Sporting, anyway,' said Raggy.

The white car came up until its front was level with the back of the Tourer.

Then suddenly it seemed that the red car skidded out towards them. As if in a nightmare the Gremlin saw the narrow space through which he was passing grow narrower still, as the red car swung out towards him.

It was no moment to cram on the brakes, for the road at that point was like glass. He merely eased his foot off the accelerator, and the Pegasus began to fall back. But the rear of the red car struck the Pegasus' bumper a glancing blow, and at the same time Marshall steered into the skid. This brought the Tourer hard across the road, swinging wildly and losing speed, so that the Gremlin, still on the offside of the road and with his wheels on the very brink of the ditch, was trapped.

'Hang on!' the Gremlin shouted, and very lightly applied the brakes.

But it was too late. He was driven so far over by the skidding red car that his offside wheels were smashing through the frozen snow at the roadside, and the jagged white fringe had the hardness of rocks. The front tyre suddenly exploded.

The white car's springing was so well designed that for a moment the car retained perfect balance; but then the hard snow seemed to catch hold of the deflated wheel and turned it into the ditch.

Their speed had now dropped right down, but the Pegasus plunged into the snow-filled ditch with a crash that threw the three forward in their seats. It ploughed through the snow for some yards before it stopped.

Just ahead, the red Tourer had come to a skidding standstill broadside on across the road. Marshall backed towards the white car as the three scrambled out of it into the deep snow.

'Heavens!' Marshall cried, jumping out of his car. 'I'm sorry about that, chaps, but my car skidded right out of my hands, and I hadn't room to control it with you just in the act of passing me. Any damage?'

The Pegasus crew hardly took any notice of him, but Raggy answered, 'I know a tyre's gone, but I hope the rest is all right.'

'Tyre gone, eh?' said Marshall, his hard eyes narrowing.

'Burst, by the sound of it,' said Raggy shortly.

The Gremlin and Bunst were pushing snow aside from the front of the car with their hands, in order to see what other damage had been done.

'We've got a spade in the back,' said Bunst. 'I'll fetch it.'

'It doesn't look as if there's much wrong,' Marshall said. 'But you can't tell when it's lurching in all that snow like that. Is there anything I can do?'

The Gremlin straightened up, knee-deep in the snow of the ditch.

'You can give us a tow out, if you like,' he said.

'Tow?' said Marshall. 'I can't do that.' The man seemed surprised. 'You know very well that it's against the rules to tow another car.'

'Against the rules?' said Raggy, surprised.

The Gremlin stared at Marshall. And Bunst, who had just come up with the shovel, stopped still on the icy road. He was carrying the spade over his shoulder, like a rifle, but in his surprise he let it slip, and the blade of the spade hit the rear wing of the Grant Tourer. The sudden clang made him jump.

'Sorry,' he said hastily, and bent down to rub the mark off the wing with his sleeve, but unfortunately he had scratched the paint away.

'Don't worry about that,' said Marshall. 'Probably get worse scars before we're through. Is there anything else I can do for you, apart from towing?'

'Nothing at all, thanks,' said Raggy. 'We'll just have to put up with it. Bad luck, that's all. There's no need for you to hang about and lose time.'

'Right-ho!' Marshall said. 'Though I say again, I'm sorry, but it just couldn't be helped.'

He got into his car, raised a hand, and drove off with a hard smile on his face.

'Quite a neat little trick,' he said to himself. 'But a pity it was necessary. The fellow Smudger couldn't have been very good at his kidnapping. In fact it was a waste of money!'

His car raced on along the moonlit road.

★　★　★

Meanwhile, on a road many miles to the west, Grant, in the duplicate car, was driving easily and steadily down towards Oldquay. He was nursing the engine carefully to make sure that in the morning it would be in perfect condition to win the final part of the trial.

The Warning in the Air

The Gremlin had dug the snow away from under the front of the Pegasus, and now Raggy was in the driving seat. He pressed the button which operated the offside automatic jacks, so that one side of the car was slowly lifted out of the snow until it was almost on an even keel. Bunst had the spare wheel ready to clamp on, and the Gremlin had the faulty wheel off in fifteen seconds.

'Good job I practised this,' the Gremlin said, as he carried the wheel and put it into the back of the car.

Bunst, staggering under the weight of the spare, clamped it into position just in time for the Gremlin to return and put back the hub cap. The wheel was fixed.

The Gremlin now began shovelling the snow away from in front of the car to give it sufficient clearance to be driven out of the ditch. Raggy let the jacks down again and started the engine. When a path was roughly clear he drove slowly out.

Now and again the wheels lost their grip on the frozen snow, but the Gremlin and Bunst were pushing with all the strength they had, and at last the car climbed up on to the road again. As it

From the plane's belly, a signal light flashed.

went, both the Gremlin and Bunst, who had been pushing a little too hard, went face down into the snow. They were up again in a moment, and this time they did not get into the front with the driver but into the back.

As Raggy accelerated away the two behind him began to mend the wheel. The team work had been splendid, and no professionals could have got out of such trouble in less time.

Then, as the car drew away, there was a sudden high-pitched scream which grew louder behind them.

It was Audacious' aeroplane shrieking down upon them from a height of about two hundred feet.

Raggy slowed, and the plane flashed by overhead. It went on for about fifty yards and then banked into a turn and began to circle over the top of the car as the Pegasus travelled on along the road. Then, from the belly of the machine, the little signalling light began to flash.

'It's Audacious trying to send a message,' Raggy said, without taking his eyes of the road. 'Better get your pencil ready.'

The Gremlin reached over into the front seat and picked up the log-book and the pencil which was tied to it by a piece of string. His eyes watched the flashing light as the aircraft went round and round in the night sky above, and slowly spelt out the words of the warning.

'Look out for Marshall stop.' The light spelt the words out swiftly. 'Foul play stop. Kidnapping faked by him stop. Look out for trouble and keep away from him stop.'

The Gremlin shouted out the message to the driver.

'So that's it!' said Raggy between his teeth. 'If only the plane had caught us up a little while ago we should have known what to expect.'

'You mean he faked the skid?' asked Bunst.

'Must have done,' Raggy answered. 'Well, we know what to

expect, but it's going to be a long time before we catch him up now.'

He began to accelerate, and at the same time switched off the small radio set in the dashboard. Immediately the plane ceased to fly round the car, turned and screamed away back to the North, disappearing against the silver sky as if it had been swallowed up. But the message which it had brought had come too late.

'We shall lose another three marks,' said the Gremlin sourly.

'We might lose even more than that,' said Raggy. 'I didn't know it was against the rules to tow somebody else.'

'I didn't either,' said the Gremlin. 'But now I come to think of it, there was a paragraph in the rules which said, "No assistance must be given by the crew of one car to the crew of another." Of course I didn't think it meant just a tow out of a ditch,' he added bitterly.

'Neither did I,' said Raggy.

'It just shows you,' said Bunst, 'that it's no good being kind-hearted. We might even get disqualified for it.'

'Don't you start being cheerful,' said the Gremlin sharply. 'Give me a hand with this tyre.'

And for a long time no one in the Pegasus said anything. It seemed that their chances of winning were slipping away, and through no fault of theirs or of the car's.

★ ★ ★

Mr Cotterell's moustache still glistened with frost in the moonlight as he bent over the radar screen in the back of his car. He was watching the small yellow blip returning across the screen, which signalled that the little aircraft had delivered its message.

Gappy was already watching the moonlit sky as if expecting to see it shoot into view over the distant hills.

'She won't be back for a few minutes yet,' Audacious said. Gappy grinned.

'No I suppose she won't.'

And he turned his eyes from the sky to the old gentleman's stern but cheerful face.

'By the way,' he said. 'How did you ever come to get such a name as Audacious?'

'It's a nickname, sir,' said Audacious, pulling himself up to his full height. 'I was the first man to fly a sea-plane from the battleship *Audacious* over thirty years ago.' He paused and cleared his throat, then added cautiously. 'That is, I would have been the first, but there were three others who did it before me.' He guffawed.

'Oh, you've been a pilot as well, have you?' said Gappy.

'*Been* a pilot, sir?' Audacious exploded. 'I still am! I held one of the first licences which were issued in the country, and I've always kept in practice.'

Gappy did not answer at once, but he was thinking.

'Now, listen, Mr Cotterell. I have an idea,' he said at last. 'Grant and Marshall have made trouble for your chaps already, as you know, and I don't trust those two. I think the Pegasus will probably win through on the long-distance trial and, if it does, you can look out for some dirty work at the speed trial when they get to Oldquay. It seems to me that one of us must be at Oldquay before the speed trial begins.'

'Hang it!' said Audacious. 'Don't you think that the warning by plane was sufficient?'

'Sufficient as a warning, yes,' said Gappy. 'But at the trial they will be too busy with the car to have time to keep an eye open for dirty work. Somebody should go, and there isn't time enough to get there in this old – in this car.'

Audacious looked at his watch.

'She could do it, you know, driven all out,' he said. 'But of course there's the risk that she won't. And as you say, I think somebody ought to be there to help our young friends. Now, how can we do it?'

'Fly,' said Gappy.

'Eh?' Audacious looked surprised.

'Fly,' said Gappy again. 'If you can fly an aeroplane, the best thing to do is to hire one. There's an aerodrome about fifteen miles from here. I know the chap who runs it.' Gappy was speaking very quickly now, and he went on, 'He will let you have a plane if you've got a current licence. I can't fly, and also I want to get this car back. I know a short cut; that is to say,' he corrected himself with a grin, 'something near a hundred miles shorter than the trial route. I could get the old Mercurial down there, at any rate, some time tomorrow. I'm thinking, of course, of all this valuable radar stuff you've got on board.'

'Too true, too true,' Audacious said, frowning. 'Yes.' He pulled his moustache, then again he said, 'Yes.'

'You think the idea is all right, then?' said Gappy.

'I think it's excellent,' said Audacious in his loud booming voice. 'Let me see, what time does it get light?'

'It's light enough to fly at about half-past six,' said Gappy. 'And you should be able to do the journey in three hours or under.'

'Mmm, yes,' said Audacious. 'Yes, you're right. We must do that.'

He turned suddenly as the faint screaming whine of the returning model sounded in the silent night.

'Ah, here she is! Now we can get going.'

The model came overhead, circled, and then its engine cut out as Audacious operated his radio controls. He brought the machine down close by the car and stalled it just above the snow.

The machine landed in a flurry of white snowflakes, and then came to a standstill.

In half a minute Audacious had dismantled it, and he and Gappy began to pack it away into the car. Audacious closed the lid of the dicky and locked it.

'Now then,' said Audacious, 'off we go. A race against time!'

He leapt into the driving seat, then let go a bellow of laughter.

'By gad! You know, I'm enjoying myself!' he shouted.

★　★　★

Audacious drove fast and furiously as he followed Gappy's directions which would lead them to the airfield. They reached it in twenty-five minutes, and drove through the open gates into the broad field that spread out as level as a giant tablecloth. Near the gates there was a small hangar, and beside this a Nissen hut, above the main door of which was a painted sign saying, 'Offices'. Silhouetted against the sky behind these two buildings was a windsock, which now hung limply in the still air of the early morning.

The Mercurial slid sideways to a standstill outside the offices, and Gappy jumped out and began knocking on the door of the Nissen hut. As Audacious clambered out of the car a light was switched on inside the hut, and as the mighty muffled figure strode to the door it opened. A tousled young man, with a moustache so wide that it almost rivalled the handle-bars of a bicycle, blinked out.

The young man was wearing a flying jacket over his pyjamas, and it was pretty obvious that he was not quite awake.

'Hullo, George,' said Gappy, gripping him by the arm. 'Remember me, you old bulldozer?'

'Why, of course,' George answered sleepily. 'Who are you?'

'It's Gappy, you fathead. Wake up!'

'Well, prang me!' said George, opening his eyes more alertly. 'So it is! And what's the idea of waking me up this time of night? What do you think I am, a barn owl?'

'This is my friend, Mr Cotterell,' said Gappy, ignoring George's query. 'He wants an aeroplane.'

'What – now?' said George.

'Well, as soon as you can manage it,' Gappy replied.

George hesitated in the doorway for a moment, then stepped to one side.

'Look here, old boy,' he said. 'You'd better come in. I'm still under the influence of sleep. I didn't quite get you.'

Gappy and Audacious went into the hut, and the door swung to behind them.

They found themselves in a compartment furnished as an office, with a desk, a telephone, and the walls covered with bunches of weather reports and danger notices which had been pinned on top of one another. At the end of the office was a door which stood open and showed a tumbled bed in the next compartment of the hut.

George dropped into the seat by the desk, yawned, then brushed his moustache vigorously, and seemed to become wide awake.

'Now then, chaps,' he said. 'What is it exactly you want?'

'An aeroplane,' said Gappy.

'Yes, so I gather,' said George. 'But it's dark, at least it's night time,' he corrected himself, looking up at the moon shining through the window. 'I haven't an aeroplane fitted for night flying; consequently I'm not allowed to let people fly at night.' He shrugged. 'Clear enough?'

'Yes, that's clear enough,' said Audacious. 'Well, how soon

can I get going?'

George started up out of his seat.

'*You?*' he asked, his eyes goggling.

For to George, Audacious looked like a gentleman who had just walked out of a museum.

'Yes, me,' said Audacious. 'I want the aircraft. I must get going as soon as it's light. I reckon that should be about seven o'clock in the morning, so that we have some time to spare.'

'Prang me!' said George, startled almost to the point of being frightened, so that he completely forgot his manners. 'You must be as old as Methuselah!'

'That, sir, has nothing to do with the case,' said Audacious. 'It's true that I have the oldest flying licence in Great Britain, but that makes no difference. The hair, sir, may go grey, but the skill is evergreen.'

And to mark his pleasure at this wit, Audacious burst into a guffaw of laughter.

'Anyhow,' Gappy broke in, 'you two fix it up together. I shall have to get going if I'm going to reach Oldquay.'

'Yes, sir, you're right,' said Audacious. 'And take great care with the old lady.'

'The old lady?' said Gappy. 'What old lady?'

He looked surprised, as if expecting to see Audacious' grand-mother hidden somewhere in the room.

'I refer to the Mercurial, sir,' said Audacious.

'Aah,' sighed Gappy with relief, 'for one moment I thought – –' He broke off and grinned. 'Never mind. Well, I'll be getting on, sir. See you tomorrow, and good luck!'

'It's you who'll need the good luck, sir,' said Audacious, with monstrous vanity, for anyone would think Audacious was safer in an aeroplane than Gappy would be in a car. Gappy went, leaving George and Audacious together.

'Now look here, sir − −' said George, and broke off. 'Why, prang me! I hardly know what to say!'

'There's nothing to say, sir,' said Audacious, and opening his huge coat he began searching in various pockets until he found an enormous wallet stuffed with papers of all kinds.

He opened the wallet, and after some minutes' searching among the papers and licences which he had there, pulled out one in triumph, which he showed to George.

'There, sir, is my original pilot's licence dated, as you will see, 1913.'

'Good lord!' said George, who had never seen one so ancient before. 'But this isn't the first one in Great Britain, it's Number 13.'

'I should have mentioned, sir,' said Audacious haughtily, 'that there was a queue at the time and, unfortunately, as I arrived a little late, twelve others got served with their licences before me. Otherwise, as I say, it would be the first one in Great Britain.' Then he laughed again.

George grinned rather uncertainly, and then said, 'But you know, I can't let you fly on this licence.'

'Of course not,' said Audacious. 'But I have a licence for every year since, except for when there was a war on.'

And so saying, he brought quite a bundle of other licences from the wallet, and put them on George's desk. The bundle represented all the licences he had ever had, including the latest, which was current. George was still clearly uneasy, did not know what to do.

'Of course,' he said at last, 'you know I'll have to give you a trial run first, just to see if you're still all right, sir?'

'Naturally, naturally,' said Audacious.

'Oh, well,' said George, and shrugged his shoulders, as if giving up the problem. 'We've got about three hours to wait.

188

What would you say to a cup of tea?'

'I would say hullo in a very hearty manner,' said Audacious, and guffawed.

George got up from his desk.

'Well, just wait while I open up the throttle on the gas stove,' he said.

Audacious nodded, brought a huge old pipe from his pocket, and began to stuff it with tobacco.

The Aeronaut

Towards dawn the cars in the trial were running into the south of England, with the worst part of the gruelling journey behind them. The snow, too, had been left far behind, and the roads were clear and dry as the stream of vehicles headed on towards Oldquay.

The two big cars remaining – they were Marshall's and the Pegasus – had been halted twice on the way in order to keep their handicap in a proper relation to the smaller cars. Since the incident of the skid the Pegasus had kept going steadily. It was impossible for the crew to make up the marks which they had lost; all that the drivers could do was to make sure that they lost no more. They were arriving at the various checks right on time, not losing any marks.

Marshall was also keeping up a steady pace, and although his car was slower than the Pegasus, by clever driving he had lost only three more marks for being late at two checks. The position at dawn was that the Pegasus had lost eight points, and Marshall, thanks to the tricks he had played, had lost only seven.

As the Pegasus sped silently on, the three in the front seat looked tired and strained.

'The whole thing depends on winning the final sprint,' said

the Gremlin, for the tenth time. 'We can't possibly make up any more points.'

'I think you've said that before,' said Raggy ironically. 'Of course it depends on the sprint, but I think we shall win that without any trouble. That is,' he added cautiously, 'provided Marshall hasn't been nursing that Tourer. He's cunning enough for anything.'

'Cunning's the word,' grunted Bunst. 'Why don't you report him? He ought to be disqualified, the dirty cheat.'

'Unfortunately we've got no proof that he's done anything to try to interfere with us,' said the Gremlin. 'You know that jolly well. You can't prove that he deliberately skidded his car into us, can you?'

'No, but what about that hold-up?' said Bunst. 'That was a deliberate attempt at kidnap. He must have fixed that up; you know that.'

'Oh, it's no good going on talking about it,' said Raggy, rather crossly. 'If we did try to report him you know they would only think that we were doing it because we were bad sports. So forget it! We'll have to try to beat him, car, cunning and all.'

Bunst gave an indignant grunt, pulled a thick sandwich out of his pocket and began to munch it.

With Marshall a mile behind, the Pegasus fled on, while the sky slowly lightened in the east.

★ ★ ★

At seven o'clock the sky in the North was turning a brilliant golden yellow, and the rising sun's rays sparkled and glinted upon the frosty surface of the snow-covered airfield and upon the frost-bitten nose of Audacious Cotterell.

He presented, then, a most curious figure, muffled up to the nose with scarves, his enormous greatcoat, borrowed flying boots, and fur gloves up to his elbows. He also wore a borrowed flying helmet which almost covered his eyes, and thereby left only the tip of his nose to be shone upon by the sun. He was standing by the side of a Tiger Moth, and George, still rather doubtful, was about to help Audacious cram his padded bulk into the rear seat of the little biplane.

Audacious, however, was very agile that morning, and clambered into the machine without any assistance at all. George's mechanics had not yet arrived on the scene, as it was too early for them, and therefore George had to start the engine by swinging the propeller. He seemed rather nervous about having to do this, for Audacious would be at the controls.

'You know the drill for starting up?' he asked, cautiously.

'Mmbullomopomba,' was all that George could hear of Audacious' voice through the wrappings of his scarf; but as the distinguished gentleman nodded his head at the same time, George knew roughly what he meant.

George went to the nose, flooded the carburettor, then went round and grasped one blade of the airscrew.

'Suck in,' he shouted.

'Fphoomah!' boomed the unintelligible answer.

George swung the propeller, then brushing his moustache up nervously, he shouted, 'Contact!'

'Ahoom!' thundered Audacious.

George swung the propeller, the engine fired, Audacious caught it with the throttle, and George beat a hurried retreat across the snow. But he was relieved because, after all, Audacious obviously did know how to start it.

The intrepid old airman kept the engine going until it was warm enough, then he ran it up, tested the magnetos, nodded his head vigorously, and raised a thumb.

George pulled the chocks away, ran round the wing, and got into the front seat. He adjusted his helmet, and plugged his earphones into the tube at his side, though it is difficult to know what he expected to hear through the several layers of Audacious's scarf.

'Okay?' George shouted into his mouthpiece.

'Humbemumba,' Audacious answered.

'Right-oh!' George cried. 'You've got her.'

'Abblaboob!'

Audacious taxied the machine into wind, and without any further ado opened the throttle wide. The airscrew became a thin, transparent circle tinged with gold in the sun, and the little machine began to race across the airfield bumping slightly over the snow.

It gathered speed. Audacious pushed the stick forward with rather more heartiness than judgement, and the tail lifted with such suddenness that the airscrew nearly went into the snow. But he corrected it almost at once, and the machine raced on, rapidly accelerating to flying speed.

'Boomandgumson!' Audacious shouted through the tube.

By now George could almost understand him.

'Oh, too many gloves on!' he translated.

And as he spoke, Audacious yanked the aircraft off the ground, and sent it up so steeply that it might have been a rocket taking off. He eased the nose down, and then, settling himself more comfortably, climbed away easily into the morning sky.

'He knows how to fly all right,' George muttered to himself. 'Just a bit too enthusiastic, that's all.'

Audacious made a circuit of the field, then came in and made a good landing in the snow.

'That's all right,' George said, as the plane ran to a standstill. 'Now you've got your maps and the route drawn on them?'

'Immebocket,' said Audacious.

'Right-oh, then,' George said. 'And you'll bring her back before dark?'

Audacious nodded in reply, then with a wave of the hand he opened the throttle and swung round into the wind, thus blowing up a hurricane of snow, which smothered George from head to foot in its frozen blast, and so the aircraft bounded away across the field, leaving what looked like a one-sided snowman staring in utter astonishment after it.

Towards the End

The white bonnet of the Pegasus crested the hill and as it began to run down the other side the crew could see the broad shape of the airfield away to the west. It lay close to the cliff edge, and beyond the red rock of the cliff the sea shimmered in the morning sun like ruffled silk. The last check was on the airfield.

Farther to the west of the airfield lay the scattered cottages which were the outskirts of Oldquay itself. They were queer, bent little cottages, like shrunken, fat, little old men squatting there waiting for the cars to come and entertain them.

'Gosh! It's good to smell the sea,' said Gremmy, sniffing hard. 'And what a morning!'

'It might almost be summer,' said Raggy cheerfully, for the sight of the end of their long run had brightened him up a lot.

'Except,' said Bunst firmly, 'that my nose is like an ice block, and me fingers fell off long ago!'

The white car slid on down the broad, gently curving road towards the airfield. It was splashed with mud and snow and yet in the bright golden sun it seemed to shine as if it had been newly washed.

The Pegasus had lost no more marks during the remainder of

the long run, but had kept steadily on, clocking in at its handicap speed with mechanical accuracy. Behind it, Marshall had had to push the Grant Tourer and to use all his wide experience in order not to have lost another mark. He had succeeded.

The winner now depended on the marks gained in the speed trial.

The Pegasus' competitor was already at Grant's garage not far from the airfield, being carefully tuned so that its engine would be able to give terrific power for long enough to defeat the Pegasus.

Marshall smiled at the shimmering sea as his car breasted the hill. He could afford to. He was a point ahead of his rivals, and his trump card was waiting ready in Grant's garage!

The hard-faced driver began to whistle. He was happy. His plan had worked after all, and the victory – with all the orders and money it would mean – was very close now.

A mile or more ahead the Pegasus slowed down and stopped at the last check. It was a hut standing at the edge of the perimeter track of the airfield, and by it were half a dozen grinning men in coats and mufflers, ready to welcome those cars which had stayed the course and come through.

Sir George Grayfield, the organiser, was foremost in the group, and as the Pegasus stopped by him he ran forward laughing, and clapped Raggy across the shoulders.

'Well done, boys!' he bellowed. 'By old Harry! I'd an idea you'd pull it off!'

'We haven't quite finished yet, sir,' Raggy reminded him with a smile. 'There's the speed trial.'

'Yes, yes, of course!' agreed Sir George, his cheeks shining like apples. 'But you've got a couple of hours' rest before that! Time to have a bite of breakfast and go over the car if you like! By old Harry,' he said again, 'I *am* glad you made it!'

As he spoke he recognised the red shape of the Grant Tourer approaching from about half a mile away, and the smile half-faded from his face as he saw it.

All this time Bunst had been staring fixedly at Sir George, and there was in his eye a look of intense suspicion.

'What's the matter, youngster?' asked Sir George, catching sight of this glare. 'You look as if I'd committed murder!'

'I was thinking,' said Bunst, closing one eye and pointing with a finger, 'that you must have cheated to get here first!'

Sir George guffawed.

'You're right!' he admitted. 'I knew I couldn't keep pace with you, so I got the night plane from Aberdeen!'

'Ah!' Bunst exploded, and the look of mystification fled from his face. 'Good! I knew you couldn't have done it fairly!'

'Right. So now you're satisfied, eh?' said Sir George, and pointed across the tarmac to where a large marquee had been erected on the grass beside it. 'That's the refreshment place.'

'Thanks, sir,' said the Gremlin, his eyes brightening. 'We'll pay it a visit!'

The Pegasus drew away very quietly, and as it went the Grant Tourer came into the check and stopped. It's engine did not make a sound, for Marshall, his face set, had coasted the last quarter-mile.

There was a bead of sweat on his forehead as he stopped. He had a good reason for feeling uneasy.

On the way down the hill one of his engine's main bearings had begun to knock. He knew very well what it meant. Even the toughest of the three cars he had designed had not been able to stand up to the grind of the trial.

'You know the rules, Marshall,' Sir George said. 'A couple of hours for rest and food.'

'I know, sir,' Marshall said. 'I wondered – –' He broke off.

'What?'

'I live only two miles away,' Marshall went on. 'Is it permissable to call in home for some food?'

His eyes were bright, his face tense. Everything depended on permission being granted, but although he had been sure it would be, Sir George's slight hesitation seemed to him like an hour's pause.

'Yes, that's all right, Marshall. And you are allowed to make slight running adjustments to the car if you wish – but you mustn't have outside help.'

'I know that, sir,' said Marshall. 'As a matter of fact, my timing chain has been kicking up a bit of a clatter,' he lied. 'I'd like to have a go at it before the speed trial.'

'Right.'

Marshall started his engine again and drove off very slowly, so that the broken-down main bearing should not be heard by the checkers at the hut.

'It'll last long enough to get me home,' he muttered as he went. 'And I only hope Grant's got the other one ready.'

He drove half-way round the perimeter track and then turned off through an open gate on to the road leading into Oldquay. The engine was knocking badly.

He coasted down the hill towards the town, then swung off into a modern garage on the left-hand side. The big sliding doors of that garage were open, although standing against one of the three petrol pumps outside was a notice saying: 'Closed.'

As Marshall swung in, Grant appeared, his round face pale with worry. His pudgy features broke into a nervous grin as he recognised his team-mate.

'So you made it!' he cried.

'Only just,' snarled Marshall, and accelerated the engine. 'Listen to that motor!'

The knocking was too loud and distinct for Grant not to know what it was.

'Heavens! Has that one gone, too?'

'You've got ears, haven't you?' snapped Marshall. 'Shut those doors and let's get these number plates changed.'

He switched off and clambered out as Grant slid the doors to behind him. Marshall lit a cigarette.

'Is the other one all right?' he asked.

'She's perfect,' Grant said, rubbing his hands together in a nervous way. 'I treated her very gently.'

'She'll last out the sprint, then,' sneered Marshall. 'And she ought to get away with it, although I warn you that Pegasus might be faster, and she's still fresh as a daisy after the trip. I heard her drive off – quiet as a ghost!'

'Never mind the Pegasus!' said Grant, with a look of sudden irritation. 'It's your job to beat it. All you've got to do is a sprint. Two miles at most. If she can't stand up to that she's no good at all.'

'They're none of them any good,' said Marshall, his eyes narrowing. 'There's a fault in the design of the centre main bearing, and if we win and get orders we'll have to re-design it and cut the performance right down.'

'It doesn't matter what we have to do,' Grant shouted in a sudden fury. 'I want that money. I don't care if the car's any good or not. It's the money that counts. Once we've won we can sell the design to some mug and let him carry the baby.'

Marshall smoked for a minute in silence.

'Well, don't you agree that's the best thing we can do?' Grant demanded.

'Of course I do,' said Marshall, with a faint grin. 'But we've got to win the sprint first. Come on, now. Give me a hand changing these plates. We haven't too much time.'

The two men set to work, and when the job was done, Marshall stood back and lit another cigarette. He was tired after the long night of driving, but his moodiness of a short time before seemed to have vanished.

'She'll do it all right,' he said with a sudden twisted grin.

'Glad you've become a bit more cheerful,' said Grant drily.

'Yes. I was tired, I reckon. But I feel much better now. I'll make a cup of coffee before I go. Nothing like coffee to keep you going.'

★ ★ ★

At the airfield the smaller cars had been arriving in handfuls and several had put up very good performances. Fourteen had failed to arrive, and were scattered somewhere along the roads from Oldquay to Scotland.

Also somewhere on the short road from the North the old Mercurial was roaring along at thirty miles an hour. Truck drivers and other motorists waved to the old warhorse as it thundered on, its brass-work gleaming in the morning sun, and a cloud of steam and black smoke streaming out behind it something like a destroyer laying a smoke-screen.

Three times Gappy had stopped to borrow buckets of water from cottages on the road to fill up the old radiator, but apart from those halts the Mercurial had kept going strongly.

It looked very much as if Gappy would keep his appointment at Oldquay almost on time.

Meanwhile, in the cold morning air above the roads, Audacious, almost frozen to the controls of his aeroplane, was speeding steadily south.

More than once he had wandered off his course owing to mistakes in his map reading, but he had come back in the right direction each time.

He did not steer a course by his compass, for he considered this to be 'new-fangled nonsense.' Instead he was following the roads, just as he had done over forty years ago when he had first learnt to fly.

For most of the journey he had been talking to himself to keep himself company, and his talk had been mainly like this:

'I wonder what that rascal's up to? I'll wager it's no good!' Gad! What can he have in mind? How can he cheat, eh? Answer me that?'

As there was no one but himself to answer he very naturally got no reply.

'What can they do? Shove a rocket behind their car, or what? Goodness knows what they've got up their sleeves, but, by Jove! I know I don't trust them! They've got something . . . yes, they've got something!

'I didn't like that Grant feller from the moment I saw him. Nasty type. Not to be trusted. Gappy's right. He's a rogue, that Grant. Gappy knows him, and Gappy ought to know – –.

'That's a funny sentence, that is! Too many knowses, some-how . . .'

Now and again he made himself guffaw by making funny remarks, but mostly he was too worried for the welfare of Raggy and his friends to laugh.

The Mark of the Cheat

A crowd had gathered on the airfield to watch the final sprints between the cars. Some of the smaller machines had already run, but the crowd was waiting for the final duel between the only two big cars in the event.

A group of interested spectators were gathered round the

199

Pegasus where the crew were just finishing cleaning the overnight mud from the body. The whole car now shone in the sun as if it had just been driven out of a showroom.

'Well, that's that,' said Bunst, mopping his face with a polishing rag and pushing his cap back on his head. 'She looks as clean as a new pin.'

Raggy was answering questions which were being put to him by the lookers-on. The Gremlin stood beside Bunst, his head turned to where the Grant Tourer was parked some distance away across the grass by the side of the track.

The red car, too, was clean and shining and a little group was standing round it asking questions of Marshall.

Bunst followed the direction of the Gremlin's eyes, and then he frowned.

'I wonder where he went off to?' Bunst said suspiciously.

'Grant's garage is near here,' said the Gremlin, 'on the road into Oldquay. I expect he went back there to wash the car.'

'Hmmm,' Bunst grunted, as if this explanation did not satisfy him.

The Gremlin laughed.

'You wouldn't trust your own grandmother, would you?'

'Yes, I would,' said Bunst. 'But I don't trust him. Remember the warning we had? That made it pretty oblivious that he's up to something.'

'Well, he can't be up to any tricks here in broad daylight, and in front of a thousand people,' said the Gremlin. 'So you needn't worry about him any more.'

'I'll keep on worrying until we've won,' retorted Bunst darkly.

They stopped talking and turned as six small cars started off along the runway, accelerating as fast as they could go, each one straining to get in front. The crowd began to shout and cheer as

200

the cars drew into the distance.

The course ran to the end of the main runway, a distance of one mile, turned sharply to the left, and came round the perimeter track, a huge semicircle that joined the runway again a quarter of a mile below the point where the cars had started. This made a total distance of three miles.

The small cars were going well, and all the people around Bunst had their heads turned away watching the race. Bunst, however, kept his suspicious eyes on Marshall, as if he thought that the racing driver might try some stealthy trick at the very last moment. Bunst was disappointed. Marshall himself was watching the race, and showed no interest whatever in either Bunst or the Pegasus.

At last, when the cars swung round into the straight and headed towards the finish, Bunst could not keep his eyes off the competitors any longer. And as the leading car came up to the finishing line, with another racing along neck and neck, Bunst forgot his suspicions in the excitement. He waved his cap in the air, and joined in with the shouts of the crowd. The cars flashed over the finishing line only seconds apart.

It had been a very close race. The cars pulled up on to the grass beside the track, and the officials went across to congratulate the winner and inform the other drivers of their times and average speeds.

Now the interest of the crowd drifted away from the small machines and became centred entirely on the two big cars. They were due to provide the greatest excitement of the day, and it was their turn next, although some little while would elapse before the judges were ready to start them off.

The Gremlin was feeling rather hot in spite of the coldness of the day, for he was going to drive the Pegasus on this sprint, upon which the whole success, or failure, of their work depended. Once or twice he looked across at Marshall lounging by the red car, and Raggy saw the slight flush of nervousness on his friend's face.

'Don't worry about Marshall, Gremmy,' Raggy said quietly. 'Just keep calm and let the old bus do her best. You know from the performance on the road last night that you've got the best of him.'

'Yes, we're faster than he is,' said the Gremlin. 'But he has the experience, don't forget, and he's up to almost any trick.'

'You won't give him a chance to pull off any tricks,' said Raggy. 'You want to get ahead at the start, and keep ahead, and he won't be able to catch you up.'

Neither of them had any idea that the car Marshall had with him now was a much faster car than the one he had driven through the night.

'Yes,' the Gremlin said, still a little nervous. 'I ought to be able to get away from him without any trouble. All I've got to do is to make sure I get the best acceleration at the start. After that I should stand a good chance of keeping right ahead of him all the way, although it's on the two bends that I may find experience counts. Experienced drivers know just how close they can cut without getting into trouble.'

'Well, after this race,' said Raggy, 'you'll be pretty experienced yourself, so I shouldn't worry.'

'I think you ought to drive her,' said the Gremlin.

'Then you don't want to think such things,' said Raggy with a laugh. 'You're much the better driver for this sort of thing, and besides which the designer is never the best driver of his own product.'

The Gremlin looked relieved.

'Thanks,' he said. 'I didn't actually want you to accept my resignation.'

They both laughed.

Bunst was lightly dusting one of the already highly polished wings, but his eyes were still on Marshall.

'He looks pretty sure of himself,' Bunst muttered. 'And yet he's smoked about six cigarettes since he's been there. I wonder if he's nervous? I don't like the look of the beggar. I bet he's still got some trick up his sleeve.'

The judges had finished with the small cars, and now walked back towards the starting line. One of the judges came across to Raggy.

'All set?' he asked.

'Absolutely,' Raggy answered.

'Good man! Now get her down to the starting line. Are you driving?'

'No, my friend here,' Raggy said, indicating the Gremlin.

'Right,' said the judge, with a quick glance at the red-head. 'I wish you luck. You know all that you have to do?'

'Yes, sir,' said the Gremlin with a quick grin. 'It's pretty straightforward, I think.'

'Quite,' the judge replied. 'Only just remember, young fellow, that the two bends you have to take are not banked, so you'll have to be pretty slick slowing down for them, otherwise with this car you might run off the concrete altogether!'

'I'll watch them, sir,' said the Gremlin.

And they all laughed.

One of the other judges had been talking to Marshall, and now the thin man got into his car and started up. He glanced quickly across at the Pegasus, and there was a queer glitter in his eye. Bunst was watching. He saw that gleam and it seemed to confirm his suspicions, but he had no idea what those suspicions meant; therefore there was nothing to say.

The Gremlin got in, started the engine, and gave Raggy and

Bunst a lift down to the starting point.

The two cars turned round and were lined up with their front wheels on the painted line. Their engines were switched off.

The Gremlin sat there alone. He felt nervous and fidgety. He glanced across at Marshall, who seemed to be sitting in his machine like something carved out of wood.

The eyes of the entire crowd were fixed upon the two drivers, and in the sudden silence which had descended over the audience, the sound of an aeroplane engine could be heard flying somewhere in the brilliant golden clarity of the morning sky. But no one took any notice of this approaching noise. Just before the starter raised his pistol the aeroplane engine was shut off. Had anyone taken notice of that warning procedure, they would have known that the aeroplane, somewhere quite near in the sky, had gone into a glide.

It seemed as if Audacious had arrived in time.

The crack of the starter's pistol was clear and sudden in the quietness. Almost as if trained together, the forefingers of the drivers pressed the starter buttons. The engines started like lightning. The gears went in, and together the two big cars started off along the runway, accelerating at a rate which made the onlookers gasp with astonishment. There was nothing in it between the two machines. They were going together, the needles of the speedometers rising at a fantastic rate as the cars raced along the runway.

And then from the whole crowd there came a sudden roar, made up of shouts of alarm and screams.

For out of the sky there dropped a Tiger Moth, gliding down to land head-on into the two racing cars!

It appeared that neither of the drivers saw this menace coming down upon them, until the very last moment, when it seemed that nothing could avoid a tragedy. Everyone could see that the aeroplane could not rise above the two cars because its propeller had stopped altogether.

Audacious had run out of petrol.

Both the Gremlin and Marshall saw the danger at the same time. The tyres screamed on the concrete as the brakes were applied. And then the Gremlin swung to the right, and Marshall to the left, off the track and on to the grass.

As the Gremlin turned off the track, the lower wing of the aeroplane swept close over his head, and he saw the under-carriage whizz past him, with its wheels on a level with his ear. He skidded across the grass, and came to a standstill looking back, while the Tiger Moth made a perfect and silent landing on the concrete of the runway.

The crowd was quiet, and then gave a great sigh of relief as they saw that disaster had been avoided at the very last moment.

★ ★ ★

The two cars, their sprint ruined, returned to the starting point, while a large number of the crowd ran towards the aeroplane, from which the muffled, stiff figure of Audacious was now descending. Several willing hands pulled the little aircraft off the runway and on to the grass, while Audacious unwound the muffler from his face. He had just uncovered his impressive features in time to see Sir George Grayfield shaking a fist right under his nose. But at that moment Sir George recognised his old friend, and let his fist drop.

'Ah!' he said. 'I might have guessed it was you!'

'I must confess, sir,' said Audacious, 'that it very nearly added one more to my list of narrow escapes. The fact of the matter is I clean forgot to look at the petrol gauge, and just as I was gliding in to land, well, hang it, I used up the very last drop. So there was only one thing to do, and I did it!'

'You did it?' said Sir George puzzled. 'What did *you* do to try to avoid an accident?'

'Why, sir,' said Audacious firmly. 'I shouted to those cars to get out of the way!'

The cars and the aircraft had been approaching each other at a tremendous speed, but even so it did not occur to Audacious that his voice would have been swept right back and over his shoulder, and could have stood no chance of reaching the cars at all. But perhaps Audacious did not *choose* to realise this.

'And I'm glad to say,' Audacious ended, 'that they obeyed my instructions instantly.'

'You old line-shooter!' said Sir George with a laugh. 'The drivers obeyed their own common-sense. Anyhow, don't let's argue about it. You've already put off the big event. Let's get back to the starting point and see them set off again.'

'I'm very anxious to do that, sir,' said Audacious.

'Well, your friends have done very well,' said Sir George. 'And as a matter of fact I think they're going to pull it off. They are, at the moment, only one point behind Grant's machine, and I haven't any doubt that they will win this sprint pretty easily.'

They had come up to the starting point now, and both cars were stopped on the startling line. Raggy was standing by the side of the Pegasus, patting the Gremlin on the shoulder.

'If you can get another start like that, old boy,' said Raggy, 'it's in the bag!'

'I'm not so sure,' said the Gremlin sharply. 'That car is faster than we thought. It was dead level with me when we had to pull off the runway. It didn't lose an inch.'

'Perhaps Marshall had been nursing it a bit,' said Raggy. 'But it looked to me as if you were going to run away from him just when the aeroplane came down.'

206

Inwardly Raggy was cursing, because the Gremlin had been keyed up for the first start, and now that had been cut short, the Gremlin would naturally be getting more nervous. He was not used to racing in public, as Marshall was, and there was the danger, as there always is with new drivers, of Gremmy becoming over-excited. That was the reason why Raggy was talking to him.

Audacious parted from Sir George and headed towards the crowd at the side of the starting line, where he saw Bunst standing absolutely still as if he had been petrified where he stood, his eyes bulging at the cars as they stood on the starting line, with the officials grouped around them.

From a loud-speaker van a voice announced that there would be a short delay as the electrical timing apparatus along the track had developed a fault, which the engineer was now putting right. The fault had been caused by Marshall's car. In turning off the runway, it had torn one of the cables which lay on the grass beside the track.

Audacious came up to Bunst and stood towering beside the small figure of the boy.

'Well, my son,' he said cheerfully, 'you look as if you've seen a ghost, by gad!'

Bunst started violently, and turned his head to Audacious.

'Oh, it's you, sir, is it?' There was a look of relief in the boy's eyes.

'Yes, it's me,' said Audacious. 'All the way from Scotland *par avion*, as the French say.'

Bunst did not seem to listen, but caught hold of Audacious's arm and looked over his shoulder at the people grouped round them.

'I want to talk to you, sir, quick!'

He began to pull the great man away.

'Gad! What's up?' said Audacious, and followed the young boy to a spot some yards off on the grass, where they would not be overheard by the crowd.

'Is there anything fishy going on?' said Audacious.

'Fishy!' said Bunst. 'That car – –' he raised his hand and pointed to the Grant Tourer.

'What about it?' said Audacious.

'It's not the one that Marshall drove last night!'

'What?' said Audacious. 'But are you sure? It sounds fantastic. Why, it's almost impossible to change over cars like that. Is the number the same?'

'Yes, sir, the number is the same,' said Bunst. 'I remember the number all right. But it isn't the same car. I know, and I think I'm the only one that does know.'

'This is a very serious thing,' said Audacious. 'You must be sure before you make any accusation in front of the judges!'

'Yes, sir. That's why I wanted to speak to you first, and find out what's to be done.'

'Right,' said Audacious. 'You tell me all about it.'

'Last night,' said Bunst, 'that fellow skidded us into a ditch, and I got a shovel to dig our car out with and I dropped it on the back wing of the car he was driving. It knocked the paint off. I saw it myself. But if you look at that car's back wing there, there's no mark on it at all.'

'Gad!' said Audacious, screwing his eyes up as he stared towards the Tourer. 'Stay here, me boy. I'll go and have a look.'

He marched across the concrete just as Raggy left the Gremlin's side and came to meet Audacious. As they met, Audacious was quite near enough to the red car to see that the paint on the back wing was unmarked.

'Thieves and vagabonds!' said Audacious.

'What's the matter, sir?' Raggy asked.

'Dirty work!' replied Audacious. 'Come back to Bunst over here. We've got time to think this thing out while they're mending the electric thing!'

'Time to think what out?' said Raggy, as they began to walk back towards Bunst.

Audacious ignored the question.

'Do you remember Bunst hitting that red car with a shovel last night? Accidentally, of course.'

Raggy frowned for a moment.

'Why, yes,' he said, 'I do.'

'Well, on that car standing there now,' said Audacious, keeping his voice low, 'there's no mark on the back wing.'

'No mark ––?' Raggy halted, his brain working fast. 'Do you mean it isn't the same car?'

'That's what I do mean' said Audacious. 'Bunst has just noticed it.'

They went on and reached the young mechanic standing alone on the grass.

'Now what's to be done?' Audacious said. 'We must have proof before we can do anything. But the question is how can we get it? You see, at present it's merely your word against Marshall's that the car was damaged last night.'

'Well, there's only one way to get proof,' said Raggy, 'and that must be to find the other car.'

'And how in blazes can we do that?' said Audacious.

'I don't know,' said Raggy, thinking fast. 'There's only one thing. I'm not going to tell Gremmy. He's getting a bit of stage fright from all these people looking on. I don't want to worry him any more.'

'Well, then,' said Bunst, 'there's one thing we can do.' His little face lit up suddenly. 'I bet I know when the car was changed. Don't you remember? Marshall went back to a garage somewhere for his breakfast!'

'By Jove! So he did!' Raggy exclaimed. 'We must be quick. We've got to go and get the evidence before we can stop this sprint.'

'Then the best thing to do,' said Audacious, 'is for Bunst and me to borrow a car and go to this garage, while you stay here and keep an eye on things. And if you can, delay them starting. Even,' he added, between his teeth, 'if you have to cut the timing cables with a pair of scissors, or something.'

'Right,' Raggy agreed at once. He knew that there was no time at all to spare.

There was a car about fifty yards away, and by it was standing Sir George Grayfield's chauffeur.

'That's the car we'll borrow,' said Audacious. 'Come on!'

They hurried across the grass to the chauffeur, who recognised Audacious and saluted.

'Sir George has lent me his car for a few minutes,' said Audacious, not very truthfully.

'He has, sir?' said the chauffeur, surprised.

'Yes,' said Audacious, and opening the driver's door he got in before the startled driver could argue.

Bunst was in the other side as quickly as he could move, and almost before the chauffeur could say another word the engine was going, and so was the car.

Audacious had taken command of the operations and, like an old soldier well used to quick decisions, he was carrying the plan into operation in as short a time as it was humanly possible to do so.

The Duel

Audacious drove out of the airfield and on to the main road

leading into Oldquay.

'Keep your eyes open for any garage,' said Audacious, tersely.

'I will,' said Bunst, grimly.

They began to pass cottages on each side of the road, which was widening. Some distance ahead they saw the concrete shape of a garage, with its petrol pumps standing outside, like red painted soldiers on guard.

'There's a garage!' said Bunst. 'And,' he hesitated as they drew nearer, 'yes, by golly, it's Grant's! His name's over the door, look!'

'Fine,' said Audacious.

He slowed down, and swung into the driveway by the petrol pumps, where he stopped with a jerk that almost shot Bunst through the windscreen. They got out of the car and saw the big notice saying 'Closed.' They also saw that the sliding doors of the main garage were shut.

'Ha!' said Audacious. 'Looks as if we shall have to do some house-breaking.'

With Bunst by his side, he marched up to the big double doors just as a small wicket-gate in them opened, and the round white face of Grant looked out.

'By hocus-pocus!' said Audacious. 'It's the man himself!'

Grant made an effort to slam the wicket, but Audacious was a second too fast, and as the door came to, Audacious raised one huge foot, placed it against the door, and pushed. Grant was taken by surprise and fell back inside the garage. The wicket swung open, and Audacious forced his great frame through the little opening.

'What the devil's this?' said Grant standing doggedly in the path of Audacious. 'What do you think you're doing, busting into my place like this? Do you want me to call the police?'

'Certainly not,' said Audacious. 'I have merely come to ask

you how you got here, when you're supposed to have broken down on the road last night.'

'I got here by train,' Grant lied. 'What other way do you think I could make it, without a car? Why are you asking?'

Bunst had slipped in through the door behind Audacious, and his quick eyes were looking about the garage.

There were about a dozen cars in the garage, three of which were entirely covered with dust sheets. Bunst did not see a Grant Tourer there.

'I wanted to have a talk with you,' said Audacious.

'I gathered you must have wanted *something* with me,' sneered Grant, 'by breaking in like that. I propose to summon you for assault, and if you won't get out I'll fetch the police to get you out. This is private property. This garage is shut. Now, get out!'

Quite suddenly Audacious realised that Grant had a perfect right to order him out of the place. Even if there *had* been a substitution of cars in the contest, it was not a criminal offence, and Audacious knew that he could do nothing about it. It was deadlock. And yet they must find out within the next minute or two whether a second Grant Tourer was in that garage, hidden under a dust sheet. It was up to him to think of a way to trick Grant into letting him find out for certain.

'I apologise for the intrusion,' said Audacious, thinking fast. 'But to tell you the truth, I came because an ex-driver of yours gave me some information about you which may affect your chances in the trial.'

'Gappy, do you mean?' said Grant, at once.

'Yes,' said Audacious.

'What information did he give?' Grant sneered. 'What information could he give? He could know nothing of me that could be of any use to you!'

'Ah!' said Audacious, quickly, 'then there's *something* that he could have known if he had stayed with you?'

Grant was silent. He had fallen into this trap too easily.

'In other words,' said Audacious, 'something has happened since Gappy left you yesterday.'

'Lots of things have happened,' said Grant, 'but nothing that would be of any interest to you. Now, will you kindly get out? I've some business to do.'

'What?' said Audacious, producing his trump card. 'You mean that you're going to stay locked up in this garage while your fortune's being won or lost a couple of miles away? My dear sir, you must be mad, or – –'

'Or what?' said Grant, the corner of his mouth beginning to twitch.

'Or frightened,' said Audacious.

Grant could see Bunst's eyes trying to pierce the covers of the sheeted cars in the garage. He knew then what they had come for, and suddenly he lost his head.

'Get out of my garage!' he said, and pushed Audacious in the chest.

'By gad, sir!' said Audacious, hardly able to restrain a laugh of triumph. 'You've struck me, and that entitles me to take my revenge!'

And so saying, Audacious bunched up a fist and hit Grant on the side of his head. Grant staggered back a pace.

'Go on, Bunst!' Audacious shouted. 'Have those sheets off!'

Bunst began to run, but as he went, Grant threw himself sideways, and charged the little fellow so that he spun round and fell heavily to the concrete floor. And at the same time Grant turned, picked up a long iron starting-handle, which had been lying on a bench close to his hand, and raised it above his head.

'Now then!' he shouted. 'Get out of here or I'll give you a taste of this!'

Audacious, for once, was prudent. He knew that the man was too far gone with anger to know quite what he was doing, and that it was likely he would hit out with this dangerous weapon if Audacious moved again.

'Keep still, Bunst!' said Audacious.

Bunst got to his feet, but remained standing where he was. His eyes shifted quickly from the calm, almost amused face of Audacious to the white, enraged features of Grant. He could see the young man's eyes blazing, and it was quite clear now that Grant would go to any lengths to keep his secret, in spite of the fact that his behaviour showed him to be guilty.

The two men were standing close to the bench by the doors, from which Grant had snatched up the starting-handle. Audacious could see from the corner of his eye that on the bench there was another long steel rod, which he knew to be a jack handle.

'Well, are you getting out?' said Grant.

'Why, no, not for a minute,' said Audacious pleasantly.

He raised a hand to twirl the end of his moustache, and Grant started, as if suspecting a trick, and almost hit out; but he stopped himself in time.

Audacious shrugged, as if in silent comment on Grant's jumpiness. He let his hand fall again, and as he did so, his fingers closed over the end of the jack handle, and like lightning he raised it above his head. Grant saw the move and struck out with the starting-handle.

Audacious stepped back a pace and parried the blow with his own steel bar. There was a terrific clang as the bars met. And then Grant drew back his arm for another blow.

'Never learnt fencing, I suppose?' roared Audacious. 'I did when I was young. A grand game!'

Clang! He parried another blow, and before Grant could do

214

'Take care or I'll have you disarmed.'

anything Audacious whipped his handle round, and poked Grant in the midriff.

'Aha!' laughed Audacious. 'Off your guard, my friend. Take care or I'll have you disarmed!'

Grant was beside himself with fury, not only at being baulked in trying to keep his secret, but also by the fact that he was being made fun of. He began to hit out like a madman.

Audacious parried blow after blow with his steel rod as the two men began to move across the garage floor.

'Go to it, Bunst!' Audacious shouted, parrying more blows.

'You bet!' said Bunst, who had been watching this fantastic fencing match.

He ran across the floor to the first covered car, and lifted the corner of the sheet. He dropped it again and ran on to the next.

The clanging of the duel was echoing in the garage. Audacious was attacking now with the intention of getting Grant's weapon from his hand. Three more times he prodded the young man in the chest and drove him back against the front of a car. Grant felt the bumper against the back of his legs and knew he could not retreat any farther.

Bunst lifted the cover of the second car. The red rear wing of a Grant Tourer met his gaze and, on the highly polished surface, there were the scratches made by the shovel on the previous night.

'Got it!' he yelled, with a shrill voice.

Clang!

With one final terrific hit Audacious knocked the starting-handle from Grant's hand. The iron crank clattered to the floor. Grant became still, breathing hard, his face white as a ghost. Audacious threw his jack handle across the garage.

'Now then, my friend, you and I will wait here and have a chat. Bunst,' he called over his shoulder, 'get back to the airfield quick as you can! Stop that sprint and get the judges here!'

'Right,' cried Bunst.

He ran across the floor, dived through the wicket-gate and went out to the waiting car. Once in the driving seat he found himself hardly tall enough to see over the bonnet. But this did not worry him. The matter was too urgent.

He swung round in the road and raced off up the hill back towards the aerodrome.

Bunst carried on until the gates of the airfield appeared on his left. He turned through the gateway, drove over the perimeter track and straight across the grass towards the crowd at the starting point.

And then, as he came close, he heard the crack of a pistol. He stopped the car. He was too late by seconds. The Pegasus and the red Tourer were already accelerating fast away from the starting line.

★ ★ ★

Grant was trembling. His shifty eyes watched Audacious with a light of cunning in them. He had seen Bunst go, and he knew now that the game was up, whatever happened at the sprint.

'Mr Cotterell,' he said hoarsely.

'By gad, we are getting polite!' Audacious exclaimed.

'Let me get away from here,' Grant demanded. 'I shan't be able to face anyone in this town after what's happened. Give me a chance, will you?'

'What's the game?' said Audacious quietly. 'You've played your little tricks, and you'll have to wait now and face the music. You've got a confession to make to the judges.'

'That doesn't matter any more,' said Grant. 'The Pegasus is bound to win. There's nothing against it. Come on now, let me go!'

'No,' said Audacious firmly. 'By gad, no! I suppose your idea is to run away and let Marshall take the full blame?'

'My idea is – –' said Grant.

He broke off, and with a sudden movement stepped forward and drove his fist with all his weight behind it at Audacious's solar plexus.

Audacious doubled up, all the breath knocked out of him. He fell back and hung on to a near-by car for support. Grant went up to him and gave him a savage blow to the jaw. Audacious went down, knocked half silly by this sudden attack.

Grant ran to the doors and pushed them open. Then he darted across to the sheet-covered Tourer, tore the sheet off and jumped into the car.

Audacious was trying to get to his feet. He heard the engine start, dimly saw the car back out into the main part of the garage, its engine knocking ominously. The gears grated, and the car started forward towards the doors.

'There'll be no evidence for you by the time I've finished with this!' Grant shouted. 'She'll be over the cliff in two minutes from now, and there'll be more than one scratch by the time that's done!'

The Finish

The roars and shouts of the crowd as the two cars raced away along the track rang in the ears of poor Bunst like a mockery. He pushed his way through the people at the starting line, and now only a few yards away from him he could see the beaming, excited face of Sir George Grayfield, who was watching the cars and showing the excitement of a schoolboy.

Bunst had meant to catch hold of Sir George at once and tell him of the trick which Grant and Marshall were trying to play, but he realised that it would do no good now; he would have to wait until the race was over.

It was a sudden shout from Sir George which made Bunst almost forget what he had come for, and to look towards the cars which were now approaching the first bend at the end of the runway.

'The white one's in front!' Sir George shouted. 'By gad! Look, he's going across to the inside of the bend in front of Marshall! Well done, boy!'

Bunst's heart seemed almost to jump out of his chest in the sudden wild excitement of realising that after all the upsets and tricks that had followed them through the trial, the Pegasus was now out in front of its rival.

In the distance, the white car slowed noticeably, and then drove round the bend on to the perimeter track, running as steadily as if it had been on rails. It rounded the bend, flashing in the sun as it turned, and began to accelerate away as the red car came round close on its heels.

Marshall cut the corner so fine that he came off the track and on to the grass, thus cutting off some two hundred yards at the speed he was going. When he came on to the perimeter track again, he was close behind the Pegasus, and it seemed that he was overtaking it.

'What's the man doing?' Sir George said, his voice suddenly angry. 'He cut that corner right off!'

'He ought to be penalised for that,' one of the other judges said. 'It's a funny thing to do in front of a crowd like this.'

'Give him the benefit of the doubt,' said Sir George. 'He may have misjudged the turn altogether. It could happen.'

The two cars were now going extremely fast round the racing track, and, owing to his smart tactics on the bend, Marshall was now level with the Pegasus. And then, to the astonishment of the onlookers, it seemed as if the Pegasus deliberately slowed down, for the red car began to draw ahead.

In the Pegasus, the Gremlin was driving as well as he knew how, and the car was answering beautifully to his touch. He was surprised when he saw the red car draw alongside, for he had not been able to see Marshall cutting the corner, and it seemed to him that the Grant Tourer had suddenly picked up a tremendous reserve of power and was going ahead. The Gremlin accelerated slightly, but Marshall was holding him.

Suddenly the Gremlin noticed that the distance between the two cars was narrowing very, very slowly. The Gremlin steered closer to the edge of the track, and still the red car seemed to draw in nearer to him. For the Gremlin to turn any more to the left would have meant going off the track, and he held his wheels on the very edge of the concrete, while the red car drew in still closer.

The Gremlin realised with a sudden shock that Marshall was trying to drive him off the track, and the ground beside that part of the concrete was rough and soft. If the Pegasus went into that, the race would be lost. He set his jaw and kept his course.

The wings of the two cars became so close as almost to be touching. Marshall could not draw ahead. The Gremlin could not accelerate any more with this threat on his right-hand side. He felt like a man trying to run along a tight-rope.

The gradual forcing of the white car towards the soft ground could not be seen by the crowds some half a mile distant. For a moment the Gremlin felt that the only thing he could do would be to give way to this pressure on his right-hand side, and risk going on to the soft ground, but that moment of terror which had made him consider this course passed as quickly as it had come.

For he realised that although Marshall was keeping level, he could not go any faster, whereas the Pegasus could. The Gremlin made up his mind in a moment. And then he lifted his foot off the accelerator.

The Pegasus slowed, and the Grant Tourer shot ahead. But Marshall, surprised by the sudden disappearance of the Pegasus from his side, lost his iron grip on the wheel, and for a moment he swerved towards the edge of the track, and had to brake in order to regain control before he ran over the edge.

Meanwhile, the Pegasus had fallen just to the rear of the red car. As it did so, the Gremlin swung to the right and accelerated. And like some great white bird the Pegasus ripped past the Tourer. Marshall regained control and tried to set off in pursuit. But the issue was no longer in any doubt. Three-quarters of the race was over, and the Pegasus was ahead. Marshall's trickery had failed to break the nerve of his competitor, but it had momentarily broken his own, and the trick had lost him the race.

He drove his car as hard as he could go, but the Pegasus was now a hundred yards ahead. Marshall glanced down. His engine temperature was rising; he was driving the car all out. Ahead of him the white car did not gain, but he could not overtake it. The performance of the two cars was well matched, but the Pegasus had stamina, and the red Tourer had none.

The Pegasus slowed down for the bend which would lead them back on to the finishing straight. The Gremlin's face was fixed in a grin which he could not alter. His heart was beating very fast. He was about to swing round into the finishing straight, and his rival was behind him.

Then suddenly, the unexpected happened. The Gremlin saw danger ahead, and his foot left the accelerator and settled hard on the brake.

Ahead of him a vehicle burst through the open gate at the end of the main runway, and with a rattle and roar and a cloud of smoke and steam, flashed across the bows of the Pegasus and thundered up the runway at nearly sixty miles an hour.

The Gremlin avoided this monstrous machine, but he had to slow right down to do it, and swiftly changing the gear, he accelerated away in pursuit. That sudden hesitation on the part of the Pegasus had let Marshall come up close behind. And now, as the two cars came on to the straight together, they accelerated almost neck and neck.

★　★　★

Audacious scrambled to his feet as Grant's car vanished through the open doors. He ran, his greatcoat flying out behind him, and arrived in the roadway just as the red car began to accelerate up the hill, its engine knocking badly.

Approaching Audacious was a car, a black, very highly polished car, and upon the roof of this there was a blue and white sign reading 'Police'.

'Stop! Stop!' roared Audacious, rushing out in front of it.

The policeman at the wheel had no choice but to stop, with the wild figure of Audacious standing dead in front of him. The policeman was alone in the machine, and Audacious ran round, flung the door open, and scrambled in beside the astonished constable.

'Follow that car!' said Audacious.

Policemen are trained to act quickly and to ask questions later so that not a second may be lost. The driver moved swiftly away in pursuit of Grant, and then said, 'What's the trouble?'

'He's going to drive it over the cliff!' said Audacious.

'Lor'!' said the constable. 'Is he? Then we must catch him!'

The policeman naturally thought, from Audacious's misleading description, that Grant was on his way to commit suicide, and he began to drive very fast indeed.

Grant, who saw the pursuers in his driving mirror, drove faster. He swung off to the left on to a road which he knew led close to the cliff top. His engine was knocking badly. Grant could not see that the car behind him was a police car. His intention was to get well ahead and jump out of his car near the cliff edge, so as to leave the machine to go on alone to its own destruction.

The road was winding, and the hedges on either side cut off the sight of the red car from the pursuers. With his engine hammering, Grant came on to the last bend. The hedges stopped, and fifty yards away from the bend the edge of the cliff rose up. Grant drove off the road and opened the door ready for his jump as the car charged across the grass.

Then, suddenly, as he was on the point of leaping to safety, the damaged engine seized up completely. The car jerked, as if terrific brakes had been applied, and skidded round on the grass, throwing Grant out like a sack through the open door. The car stopped, and at the same moment the police car came round the bend and drew to a standstill nearby.

Audacious clambered out, and so did the policeman. They ran to Grant, who was sitting up, looking dazed.

'Are you hurt?' cried the policeman.

Grant looked up at the man in uniform.

'No,' he said. 'But one of these days I'm going to hurt that old geyser,' he added, and jabbed his finger towards Audacious.

The policeman looked quizzically from Grant to Audacious, and slowly unbuttoned his tunic pocket and brought out a notebook.

'I think,' he said, 'that I ought to make a few jottings about this.'

'Hang it, sir!' said Audacious. 'We haven't time! Take us both up to the airfield and we will explain to you there.'

★ ★ ★

Ahead, hardly anything could be seen of the monstrous intruder owing to the smoke trail which it was laying down behind it as it roared on to the finishing line, to the accompaniment of shouts of astonishment from the spectators. Behind it, the Pegasus and the Tourer accelerated hard.

The Pegasus held the red car for two or three seconds, and then steadily drew ahead, the superior acceleration at last showing itself in a straight fight towards the finish. No trickery now would help Marshall to make up for the ground he was losing as the Gremlin went on, a certain victor, towards the end.

Before the Gremlin could overtake the clattering vision of the old Mercurial, that famous car bounded over the finishing line a yard or two ahead of its modern counterpart. There were roars of laughter and cheers as it went, though it was obvious to the onlookers that Gappy, the intrepid driver, had left the wheel alone, and was pulling with both hands on the handbrake in an effort to stop the car. He roared on down the runway, still making furious efforts to operate the brakes, and gradually began to slow down.

The Pegasus flashed over the finishing line, slowed down, and stopped effortlessly. Behind it, beaten by a hundred yards or more, Marshall finished the course and pulled up close to the Pegasus.

Excited by the glorious finish and the sudden comic arrival of the unstoppable Mercurial, the crowds were shouting themselves hoarse. Raggy was at the side of the Pegasus and slamming the Gremlin across the shoulders hard enough to have knocked him out of the seat.

'Good man! Well done!' he shouted. 'By gosh, I can hardly believe it!'

'Neither can I,' said the Gremlin, laughing. 'But there's just one thing I would like to do before I leave this place, and that is to have a few words with Mr Marshall.'

In the crowd at the finishing line Bunst was beside himself with excitement. He was jumping up and down, shouting, throwing his cap into the air, and laughing at the same time. It was in the midst of these wild demonstrations that the police car came up the runway and stopped beside the judges, who were now gathered round the Pegasus.

★ ★ ★

It was evening, and in the biggest hotel in Oldquay a banquet had just finished. Most of the drivers who had taken part in the trial, and who had finished the course, were present. Grant and Marshall, of course, were not there.

Sir George Grayfield had on his right-hand side his old friend Audacious Cotterell, who was laughing heartily at one of his own jokes, and almost choking himself by smoking a huge cigar at the same time.

Sir George got up and banged on the table for silence. The laughter and the chatter died down as the guests sitting at the long table turned their heads towards the organiser.

'Well, gentlemen,' said Sir George, 'the fun is over. It's now my pleasure to give the prizes to the various classes of cars which took part in this gruelling trial.'

'There are, as you know, prizes for the various horse-power classes, but the most important prize of all is for the car which showed the greatest advancement in design, performance and stamina, no matter what class it was in. You all know which car that was.'

There was an outburst of clapping as everyone looked towards Raggy, the Gremlin and Bunst. Bunst was still eating, although everyone else had finished, but he grinned with his mouth shut and his face full.

'What you may not know,' said Sir George, 'is that this car won in spite of repeated efforts on the part of its rival drivers to defeat it. Those drivers, I may add, are finished as a result not only of their bad design, but also of their cunning and trickery. We need think no more of them. They will pay very dearly for their dishonesty by the business which they'll lose as a result.'

The grimness of his tone changed, and a smile came back to his face, as he added:

'And now, here is the cheque which was promised to the winning design, and I will ask the designer, the driver, and Mr Bunst, chief mechanic and food-supplier, to come up and receive it.'

The three went up amidst cheers and clapping, their faces hot and uncomfortable. It was the worst part of the whole trial as far as they were concerned. The only one who seemed to enjoy it was Audacious, who sat back in his chair beaming, with his cigar stuck upwards like some fearsome cannon, clapping until his hands hurt.

The three went back to their seats and Sir George called for silence again.

'I have also a special unexpected prize, which I think is well earned,' he said, 'for the first car to pass the finishing mark was the property of Mr Audacious Cotterell: a Mercurial, well over fifty years old.'

'I understand that the intrepid driver, whom we all know as Gappy, entered the course and passed the finishing line because he was unable to make the brakes work. Therefore, I have pleasure in giving to Mr Cotterell a postal order for ten shillings, which I hope he will put towards the cost of having his brakes relined!'

Audacious laughed with the cigar in his mouth, and choked himself.

'Gad!' he spluttered. 'I jolly well – –' His face changed, his eyes popped, and he jumped to his feet.

'Hang it!' he bellowed. 'I must fly!'

He had remembered that he had forgotten to return the aeroplane.

King of the Skating Aces

King of the Skating Aces

by John Marshall

'Right, fellers. See if you can stop this one.' Zip King, player-coach to the Royal Park Aces ice hockey team, streaked across the rink to take a neat pass from his winger, Big Ed Dekker.

Zip hooked the puck close to the goal-mouth. A hefty back tried to block him, but Zip cleverly passed to Big Ed, beat the back for speed, and took a return pass from the winger. He shot, but the goalminder kicked the puck out with his skate. Zip caught the puck on his stick and shot again. The net quivered at the force of the impact.

'O.K., boys. That was pretty good – but you weren't fast enough. Take five minutes.'

Zip skated to the side of the rink and joined Rusty Sargent, the Royal Park Aces' manager, who had been watching the practice game.

The season was half over, and things were not going well for the Aces. The previous season had been a triumph for Zip. He had built a great team, and had taken the Aces to the top of the league. But during this season some of his best Canadian players, including his star defence men, had left the United States and returned home.

The Aces had disappointed their fans by their showing in the Autumn League. Now the National Cup Competition, which took place in the second half of the season, was about to start.

'What do you think, Zip?' asked Rusty Sargent as Zip sat on the bench next to him.

'You saw for yourself, Rusty,' Zip replied. 'We won't make

the grade until we get a stronger defence. Those backs just don't react fast enough.'

'Got any suggestions?' Rusty inquired.

'I thought you and I might take a little trip,' said Zip. 'Have you heard the news? Ledford's Leopards won't be in the National Cup. The club's being disbanded.'

Rusty snorted.

'Leopards dropping out, eh? Well, I guess they'll be no great loss. They were bottom of the Autumn League. Though, mind you, it might have been a different story if their attack had been half as good as their defence.'

Rusty broke off, the light of understanding in his eyes.

'Defence! Chuck Kowalski! Wow! If we could get him under contract to play for us it'd make all the difference to our team. I see what you're getting at, Zip. We've got to get Chuck for the Aces!'

'There's a winding-up meeting today,' nodded Zip. 'We ought to get up to Ledford and see what we can do. My car's outside. I'll have a word with the boys. Then we'll be on our way.'

Zip went to the rinkside and beckoned to Big Ed Dekker and Beaver Warner, Aces' two star wingers, who skated over.

'You two boys take charge,' Zip instructed. 'Rusty and I have business to attend to in Ledford.'

'Zip thinks we can get Chuck Kowalski to sign on for us,' grinned Rusty.

Big Ed let out a whoop.

'Say, that would be great. Chuck would just about solve our troubles,' he cried. 'Best of luck, Zip. Bring us back Chuck Kowalski and we'll win the National Cup for you.'

The pair drove away, Zip at the wheel of his car. By mid-day they were half way to Ledford, and Zip stopped at a roadside hotel for lunch.

While they were eating, Zip saw another car swing on to the hotel drive, and glide past the window of the dining room. It was a large, flashy, pale blue vehicle. Zip caught his breath.

'Bernie Clackmann's car has just pulled in,' he said tensely. 'Looks as if he's on his way to Ledford, too!'

Clackmann was manager of a team known as the Brinstead Buccaneers. He and Zip had never been friends. Zip didn't like his unscrupulous methods. Rusty Sargent chuckled.

'Clackmann, eh? He'll get a surprise when he walks in and finds us here!'

He looked towards the door, but minutes passed, and no one appeared.

'You must have made a mistake,' Rusty remarked at last. 'That couldn't have been Clackmann's car.'

They finished their lunch and returned to Zip's car. Zip let out a moan.

'One of the back tyres is flat,' he cried. 'Now we'll have to waste time changing the wheel.'

As he bent down to examine the wheel, his eyes narrowed.

'A valve cap has been taken off, Rusty,' he declared. 'I'll bet someone deliberately let the air out of this tyre.'

They stared questioningly at each other.

'Are you thinking what I'm thinking?' Rusty asked.

'I guess so,' growled Zip. 'It was Clackmann that I saw. He was coming in here for lunch but he recognised our car. He guessed that we were on our way to Ledford, so he let the tyre down to delay us. It's just the sort of trick he would play.'

Zip, seething with anger, made a quick job of getting the spare wheel on, and then sped the rest of the way to Ledford.

When they reached the headquarters of the disbanding Leopards they found it crowded with players and club managers who had joined in the hunt for spare talent to strengthen their teams.

The first man Zip set eyes on was Bernie Clackmann, fat-faced and smugly smiling.

'Well, hallo, Zip!' he grinned. 'I'm afraid that if you've come here looking for someone to improve that defence of yours, you left it too late. I've signed Chuck Kowalski for the Buccaneers!'

Rusty Sargent let out an angry roar.

'Of all the nerve!' he cried. 'We'd have been here first if you hadn't let our tyre down.'

Chuck Kowalski, tall and broad-shouldered, looked bewildered.

'But I don't understand, Zip,' he interposed. 'Bernie told me you wouldn't be coming up today. He said you'd told him that you weren't interested in getting any new players. I'd much rather play for the Aces.'

'It's too late for that now. You've signed on for the Buccaneers, and you can't back out,' Clackmann said sharply.

Zip gritted his teeth. He was furious, but he wasn't the type to take defeat so easily.

His gaze swept the room to see who else was there. Thanks to the way his rival had delayed him, most of the worthwhile ex-Leopards had been snapped up by other managers.

Suddenly his expression grew thoughtful as his eyes rested on a chunky dark-haired man standing alone in a corner. Nobody appeared to be interested in him. As Zip watched, this man walked slowly towards Chuck and held out his hand.

'Looks like this is good-bye, pal,' he said, with an undertone of sadness in his voice. 'I sure hope you have lots of luck.'

Chuck gripped his hand.

'This is tough,' he said. 'What'll you do now?'

'Go back home to Montreal, I guess,' was the answer.

'It burns me up,' growled Chuck. 'None of these darned managers has the sense to offer you a job.'

Zip whispered in Rusty's ear, indicating the dark-haired man. 'That's Joe Brown.'

'Never heard of him,' answered Rusty. 'Who is he?'

'You've seen him play every time we've met the Leopards. He and Chuck came here from Canada together, several seasons ago. They've always been partners. This is the first time they've had to break up,' explained Zip.

'I see what you mean,' Rusty nodded. 'Brown has always got by because he has been teamed up with a star player. Now that he's going to be left on his own, he's not much good to anyone.'

'I don't mean that at all,' Zip answered. 'We're signing Brown on.'

'You're crazy!' cried Rusty. 'He'll be no use. The Aces need Chuck Kowalski.'

'That's where you're wrong,' Zip answered. 'Bernie thinks he's been clever. Before I've finished with him he's going to realise that he got the worst of the bargain.'

He strolled over to Joe Brown, and put a hand on his shoulder.

'How do you feel about joining Royal Park Aces, Joe?' he asked.

Joe's craggy face lit up with pleasure. Then he shook his head.

'Thanks, Zip, but I don't want to stay in this country. I'm pretty fed up.'

But it didn't take much to convince Joe that he was really needed. Anyway, the Aces were reputed to be a great bunch of boys, and Joe was flattered that they wanted him to join.

Zip was chuckling as he rejoined Rusty Sargent.

'It's all fixed up!' he told his manager.

But Rusty only shook his head, frowning. He obviously

thought Zip had made the biggest mistake of his life. Was he right?

★   ★   ★

Zip's first action on leaving the board room was to send a telegram to the Aces.

'Success. Have signed the man we need. Am bringing him to the rink to meet you all tomorrow morning. Zip.'

The news delighted the Aces, and they were all on the ice the next morning waiting to greet Zip when he brought the new player on to the rink to meet them. Joe Brown had changed into ice hockey gear and was wearing the Aces' colours. Big Ed Dekker, Beaver Warner and the others swooped across the ice to meet him.

'Welcome to the Aces. Sure glad to have you with us,' shouted Big Ed.

'Yeah. With good old Chuck Kowalski in our line-up nothing can stop us from winning the National Cup,' agreed Beaver.

Then, as Big Ed skated closer, his jaw dropped. He stared.

'B–but, you're not Chuck Kowalski!' he exclaimed.

Zip chuckled.

'Boys, meet Joe Brown,' he announced.

There was dead silence. The Aces stared at each other. Who was this unknown whom Zip had signed on?

Joe himself was embarrassed by the dismayed silence.

'Guess I'm a bit of a disappointment,' he apologised. 'Bernie Clackmann stole a march on Zip, and signed Chuck for the Buccaneers first. I'm afraid I'm just second best.'

'Nothing of the sort,' Zip insisted. 'Bernie may think he's smart, but he's going to find out before long that he's got the worst of the bargain.'

236

'You're not Chuck Kowalski!'

There was another awkward silence, broken by Big Ed, who held out his hand to the newcomer.

'Whatever Zip does is O.K. with us,' he declared. 'Welcome to the gang, Joe.'

The others took their cue from him, and surged round the new player to slap his shoulder and make him feel that he was among friends. They were all dismayed and disappointed, but they were too sporting to let Joe feel that he wasn't wanted.

Just the same, they secretly felt that Zip must have taken leave of his senses. Big Ed tackled him the moment he got him alone.

'This is the biggest let-down you ever handed us,' he protested. 'When we read your telegram we all figured that our troubles were over. We took it for granted that you'd signed on Chuck Kowalski. What can this guy Brown do to help us out of our jam?'

'Plenty,' Zip answered. 'Just leave this to me. I know what I'm doing.'

During the days that followed, Joe Brown trained hard with the rest of the team. He showed himself to be a clever skater and a fast, workman-like player, but there was nothing about him to suggest that he would ever set the ice on fire.

'He's all right, but he's no Chuck Kowalski,' was Big Ed's comment.

The puzzled Aces talked it over among themselves. They decided that Joe Brown might show up better in match-play than he did in training, and decided to wait to see how he would perform.

The following week the Aces took part in the opening game of the National Cup series, and the players came in for an even more puzzling surprise.

Joe Brown appeared on the team bench, kitted up, but Zip

didn't use him. He sat out the whole game. The same thing happened in succeeding games.

The bewildered Aces bombarded Rusty Sargent with questions.

'What's Zip doing? Why did he give Joe a contract if he isn't going to put him on the ice?'

'It's no use asking me,' protested the manager. 'I don't understand it any more than you do.'

'I think,' said Beaver Warner, 'that Zip made a blunder and doesn't like to admit it.'

The only man who voiced no complaints was Joe himself. A good team man, he accepted Zip's decision, content to wait patiently until he was called upon.

His behaviour earned the respect and sympathy of the rest of the team. The more they knew of him the more they liked him, and the more indignant they became over the way Zip was treating him.

Zip knew that he was becoming unpopular, but he had his own reasons for what he was doing. All in good time the team would find out. In the meantime, he kept quiet.

During the early games the Aces showed no signs of being able to cure their defence-line weaknesses. The attack, especially the first string composed of Zip, Big Ed and Warner, was good enough to get plenty of goals, but it was being let down by the defence all along the line.

Then came the Aces' first home game against the Buccaneers.

In the meantime, Zip had been keeping an eye on the reports of the Buccaneers' games. Chuck Kowalski was proving something of a disappointment to his new fans. He wasn't showing the brilliant form that had made him a star with the Leopards. He didn't seem to be able to settle down.

On the evening of the match Chuck came to the Aces'

dressing-room, looking for his pal. They greeted each other excitedly.

'How are things going now, Chuck?' asked Joe. 'Bet you're setting 'em alight, eh?'

'Well, no,' admitted Chuck. 'Just can't seem to hit it right, somehow. It isn't like the old days. What about you? How are you making out?'

'I like it here,' said Joe. 'Aces are a great bunch of boys.'

'How are you playing?' asked Chuck.

'Well, I haven't actually played yet,' confessed Joe. 'Guess Zip thinks I'm not quite ready yet.'

'Not ready!' exploded Chuck Kowalski, and turned to Zip. 'You need your head examined. Here you've got the greatest defenceman who ever held a stick, and you keep him on the bench!'

'His turn will come,' Zip said quietly.

As Chuck returned to his own team, Big Ed and Warner came up to Zip.

'Any special instructions?' asked Big Ed. 'Figure we'll need to show some real powerhouse stuff tonight, with Kowalski defending against us.'

'That remains to be seen,' Zip answered with a mysterious grin.

The teams skated on to the ice. A great roar went up from the home fans when Zip won possession of the puck at the opening face-off. Everyone was eagerly anticipating a tremendous and thrilling duel between the home attack and the famous Kowalski.

Zip weaved through, and skimmed the puck to Big Ed. Kowalski came across like a bullet. Big Ed slipped the puck back to Zip. Kowalski shuttled across the ice, but he couldn't break up the attack. Zip sent Warner away. The puck went from

Beaver to Big Ed and back to Zip, who let drive with a cracking shot. Buccaneers' goalie did the splits, but in vain.

The puck was in the cage, and Aces were one up.

The Aces' fans were thunderstruck. It seemed too good to be true. But as the game wore on they realised that the first goal had been no fluke. Buccaneers' defence, even with Kowalski, was all at sea. The most unhappy man in the stadium was Joe, who watched his pal's poor performance with dismay.

Zip and Co. were so completely on top that they rammed the puck into the net nine times. It would have been a runaway victory for Aces but for the fact that their own defence was unsteady, and let the Buccaneers through to score four.

As soon as the match was over, Zip made his way to the visitors' dressing room. Bernie Clackmann greeted him with a scowl.

'I suppose you've come to scoff,' snarled Bernie.

'Not so pleased with your bargain now, eh?' asked Zip. 'It seems it was rather a waste of effort, going to the trouble of letting my tyre down.'

'All right,' sneered the rival manager. 'I made a monkey out of myself, saddling the team with Kowalski. Maybe he was good with the Leopards, but he's finished now. A washout.'

'Well, I'm not so sure,' said Zip. 'Chuck's no use to you. If he agrees, I'll take his contract off your hands.'

The rival manager's face lit up. He could hardly believe his ears. He accepted the offer eagerly, before Zip could change his mind.

'It's a deal. Take him and welcome!'

'Right,' nodded Zip. 'But I want no squawks from you if you decide you've made a bad bargain when we meet in our next match.'

'No squawks,' grinned Bernie.

Chuck Kowalski was astounded when he heard of Zip's offer, but he was eager to accept it.

'Fine,' chuckled Zip. 'Now let's go tell the team the good news.'

Meanwhile, in the home dressing room, the players were discussing the match.

'Guess Zip wasn't such a fool after all,' Big Ed was saying. 'He must have known what he was doing when he let Bernie Clackmann have Kowalski. Thank goodness he didn't bring him here. He's a wash-out.'

He stopped, his mouth open. He suddenly realised that the door was open. Zip was standing there, and Chuck Kowalski was with him.

'Boys, I want you to meet our new recruit,' grinned Zip. 'I just made a deal with Bernie Clackmann. Chuck Kowalski has joined the Aces.'

No one knew what to say. Zip was making up for his first error by committing a worse one.

The only man in the room who was pleased was Joe Brown, who grinned with pleasure.

'This is great news, Chuck! We're together again!'

'Zip must be crazy,' muttered Big Ed under his breath.

'Our next match is a return fixture against the Buccaneers,' Zip announced. 'You two boys will be first string defence. Don't let me down.'

Rusty Sargent grabbed Zip, and swung him round.

'What are you trying to do – ruin this team?' he hissed. 'A wash-out partnered by a man who hasn't yet been on the ice? Buccaneers will murder us.'

'I don't think so,' Zip said quietly.

'I think you've gone mad. I can't stand any more of this. Either you resign, or I do,' growled Rusty.

'Wait and see how it turns out,' begged Zip.

'All right,' growled Rusty, 'but if Bernie's outfit wipes the floor with us I wash my hands of this team.'

'You won't need to. If that happens I'll resign myself. But I'm sure I won't have to,' Zip answered confidently.

Aces waited with mixed feelings for the return match. Kowalski came in for some booing from the Buccaneer fans when he skated on to the ice in Aces' colours. But the booing didn't last long after the face-off. The opening minutes were sensational. Buccaneers broke away, and their attack swept down the rink looking full of confidence. Kowalski whipped across to tackle the winger in possession. Swinging behind him, Joe Brown rapped on the ice with his stick, then drove across, to meet the winger as Chuck compelled him to swerve.

Chuck left Joe to tackle the winger, and circled round the pair, almost lazily.

Joe went in and hustled the winger into making a hurried centre pass. It never reached its mark. Chuck suddenly came in, picked up the puck, burst his way through the Buccaneers' attack, and sent Zip away with a pass down the middle.

Zip was dumped on the ice before he could shoot. There was a face-off that led to a milling struggle round the Buccaneers' cage. They scrambled the puck away, but once again their attack broke up against Joe and Chuck.

If one of the pair was beaten, the other was always there to back him up. The attackers might get the puck past one of them, but never past both.

Joe and Chuck seemed to be able to read each others' minds. They played like two men controlled by one brain.

Bernie Clackmann sat and ground his teeth.

His team was getting nowhere. At the other end Zip broke through and split the defence with a pass to the wing for Big Ed to open the scoring.

After that it was a landslide. Aces were leading 6–0 at the end of the first period.

Before the end of the game Buccaneers managed to score twice, but by that time Aces had scored 12.

When the match was over Bernie Clackmann burst his way into Aces' dressing room, flaming mad.

'You dirty, double-crossing swindler!' he raved at Zip.

'That'll do, Bernie,' advised Zip. 'We made a bargain. You promised no squawking if you decided after seeing Chuck play for us that you'd made a mistake. Remember?'

'But this is different,' stormed Clackmann. 'Kowalski must have been bribed to play badly for us so that I'd be glad to get rid of him. I'm going to report this to the Control Board. Let Kowalski explain his behaviour to them – if he can.'

'I wouldn't do that, unless you want to look a bigger fool than you do already,' warned Zip.

'What do you mean by that?' asked Clackmann.

'I had the sense to see that Kowalski wouldn't be any good without Joe Brown, that's all.' Zip answered. 'These two have always played together – they've always been pals. Together, they're unbeatable. But they're nothing when they're not playing together.'

'You haven't been swindled, Bernie,' Zip concluded. 'You just outsmarted yourself.'

Born to Win

Born to Win

by Mark Aldridge

'You're not proposing to run that . . . that shaggy elephant in our point-to-point?'

Jerry Kane flushed at the mocking note in the voice of the older lad who taunted him. But he did not answer. Instead he turned back to the great golden-coloured horse he had been grooming.

Butternut was a massive horse, powerful-shouldered, strong in the quarters. But with his heavy, unclipped coat he seemed ill-chosen company for the glossy chestnut hunter that Derek Huntly-Jones was riding, as he flung his taunt at Jerry.

The two lads had never got on well, not even years ago at the village school, before Derek's father – then plain Mr Jones – had come into a fortune and added the 'Huntly' to his name. Derek had been a bully then, though Jerry had often curbed him. Now he was an unbearable snob. And his father was Master of the Pyecroft Foxhounds, whose point-to-point race meeting would shortly be held.

'Look here,' continued Derek in conceited tones, 'you can't put that creature into the race. We've got a lot of important people coming to the meeting and that beast would just make a laughing stock of us. Keep it in the shafts of the milk cart where it belongs!'

Jerry's grip tightened on the curry comb he was wielding, and for an instant he was tempted to hurl it into the other's sneering face. But with an effort he kept his temper. Drawing the comb down through Butternut's thick coat he said half to himself:

'Butternut's racing all right – and what's more he's going to win.'

'Against this sort of class?' snorted Derek as he slapped his own thoroughbred on the neck. 'Don't be a bigger fool than you look, Kane. That cart-horse hasn't a hope of even finishing the course.'

He wheeled his mount and cantered away down the lane that led to Jerry's home. Jerry turned and watched him go before he continued with his grooming. He was beginning to regret the impulse that had made him say he was entering Butternut for the point-to-point.

'All the same, Butternut,' he grinned as he wielded the curry comb, 'you're racing. Cart-horse you may be. But that's not your fault.'

Jerry's father ran a little dairy and Butternut pulled the milk cart on its daily round. It had been Jerry's idea to buy the beast as a colt when it was offered up for sale. There was something about the ungainly-looking young animal that appealed to him. They had got him cheaply for he was unusual-looking and there were no other offers. But as he grew and filled out, Jerry's faith in him had been justified. As a van-horse, he was first class, pulling the milk cart with its heavy load as quickly as a motor van would have done on the winding country roads.

Butternut was a four-year-old before Jerry thought of riding him. But when he did, he found the golden horse was a natural jumper, and fast, too.

'Dad,' he had told his father, 'it's a shame to keep him between the shafts. The race course is the place for Butternut!'

'Maybe you're right, son,' Mr Kane had agreed after seeing the golden horse's paces. 'But how can we ever afford to race him? And who would draw the cart? I'm afraid that until we have a bit of money Butternut will have to stay right where he is.'

That was the snag – money. If they had had the money they could buy another van-horse and so free Butternut to race. But a dairy is not a very profitable business and a new horse would cost at least a hundred pounds.

Then Jerry saw a notice about the hunt's forthcoming point-to-point meeting with its cup and hundred-pound prize.

It was his great chance. If Butternut could win that race, all would be well.

Helped by old Silas Martleby, a retired jockey, Jerry began Butternut's training in real earnest. In the morning the horse pulled the milk cart. In the evening it jumped an improvised course on the deserted heath.

'We've got a winner here, boy,' old Silas used to assure him. 'And I don't mean just winner of the point-to-point. That horse is going to go places – maybe even the National.'

'The Grand National!' Jerry had gasped. 'You're not serious.'

'Why not?' Silas demanded, cracking his bony knuckles. 'Other horses have come from pulling carts to the National. And I never saw as likely a champion jumper as Butternut.'

Jerry had been confident enough himself, until Huntly-Jones had belittled the animal. Now, though he continued his grooming, he was beginning to wonder. Maybe Butternut was stepping out of his class. Could a horse which had cost a few pounds hope to match something like Derek's chestnut – valued at over a thousand pounds?

'Still, if we don't try, we'll never know,' mused Jerry.

It was time then for the evening training run and he saddled Butternut and mounted lightly. Old Silas was already waiting on the heath.

'Tonight I want you to give him a real work-out,' said the old jockey. 'I want to see just what he does when he's pressed. I wish we had something to pace him.'

His wish was granted a few moments later. Cantering over a rise came Derek Huntly-Jones. He saw Butternut and his eyebrows rose.

'Why don't you take that horse to the kennels?' he sneered cruelly. 'You'd get at least ten pounds for him as dog food.'

'Dog food!' spluttered Silas. 'Mind your words, young Jones . . .'

'Say "sir" when you speak to me,' blustered the other.

'Sir indeed!' snorted Silas. 'Don't come your airs and graces over me, my lad. I remember you when you were just a nipper with dirty knees. So don't you forget it Mr bloomin' double-barrelled Jones. Go on, Jerry – let Butternut show him what's dog-food and what isn't.'

'A race?' Derek's eyebrows lifted contemptuously. 'All right. It should be good for a laugh anyway. To that coppice over there and back.'

The coppice was a full mile away and several loose stone walls and hedges lay between. It would be a good, stiff test.

'Are you ready?' Derek cried quickly. 'Then – go!'

Away he went at a full gallop, ignoring the fact that Jerry had been facing the opposite way. His trick gained him a full ten yards.

But as he felt the surge of Butternut's powerful stride beneath him, Jerry knew that he would catch the conceited lad up and pass him.

Over the first hundred yards of the race, Derek's lead increased, his chestnut striding full out, taking its jumps smoothly. Then, as they neared the coppice, Jerry began to gain. Derek's lead was decreasing, foot by foot.

As they rounded the coppice and headed back towards the excited Silas, Butternut was only a length behind the other horse.

Jerry set himself to get the last ounce of speed out of him. The big horse's hooves pounded away at the turf. Derek swinging round to see how great his lead was, got the shock of his life when he saw Butternut so close behind him.

Then his crop began to flail his horse's flanks, driving it on for one brief spurt. But Butternut answered the spurt. With less than a quarter of a mile to go, the horses were level. Butternut was drawing just slightly ahead.

It was then that Derek reined in abruptly, bringing his mount to a halt. He flung himself to the ground and ran a hand down his horse's leg.

'Going lame,' he shouted briefly as he mounted again and rode off. 'I'll have to get him to a vet at once.'

Butternut cantered up to where Silas was standing.

'Going lame!' scoffed the old jockey. 'He didn't like being beaten, that was his trouble – and he was well beaten, Jerry. You'd have led him by a dozen lengths at the finish!'

'Gee, d'you think so?' Jerry breathed excitedly. 'Then I really have a chance in the race.'

He might not have felt so sure if he could have seen the hatred in Derek Huntly-Jones' eyes at that moment.

'That hairy monster is fast,' Derek told himself grimly. 'It can win the point-to-point, and if it does, then it's good-bye to the sports car Dad promised me. I'll have to make darn sure that neither Jerry Kane nor his yellow carthorse takes part in the point-to-point!'

★ ★ ★

It was the following day, and Jerry was making a late delivery of milk at the home of the hunt secretary, Mr Barnet. He decided that, while he was there, he would put in his point-to-point entry. The secretary took down the details, then looked up questioningly at Jerry.

'You have a certificate that the animal is a *bona fide* hunter, of course?' he asked.

Jerry looked blank.

'This point-to-point is a race for hunters,' said Mr Barnet. 'To make sure that people don't enter race-horses just to get the prize, we insist that every horse have a certificate that it is in fact a hunter, and had been ridden with the hunt during the season. No one is going to risk riding a valuable race-horse in a hunt, so that ensures that the race is kept to the proper type of horse.'

'But . . . but how do I get a certificate?' Jerry demanded.

'Your horse will have to take part in a hunt,' was the answer. 'Afterwards ask the Master for a certificate.'

Jerry had not been gone long when Derek Huntly-Jones' telephone rang.

'Kane turned up all right,' said the secretary. 'But my word, he was shaken when I told him he'd have to hunt the horse. I think we've seen the last of him!'

'And a good thing too,' drawled Derek. 'We don't want that class of person at our meeting. Thanks for letting me know. I'm sure Dad will be relieved.'

Derek had allowed the secretary to think that his plan for stopping Jerry's entry really came from his father, the Master of the Hunt. Smiling smugly, Derek Huntly-Jones replaced the receiver.

'So much for Kane's yellow elephant now,' he thought.

He might not have felt so smug if he had been able to overhear Jerry's conversation with Silas Martleby that evening.

'So they want a certificate,' grunted the old jockey. 'All right then – get one. The hunt meets tomorrow at Greenstone Manor. What's to stop you hunting with them? You'll get your certificate all right.'

'What . . . me go hunting with all the nobs?' Jerry exclaimed. 'A fine fool I'd look.'

'They're not all rich men that hunt,' the jockey answered. 'No, not by a long shot. There's farmers, shopkeepers from the town, garage hands even. You'll be all right.'

It took a lot of arranging. Jerry had to start his milk round two hours earlier in order to get to the meet on time.

Hounds had arrived already and were milling round eager to be off. Mr Huntly-Jones, impressive in his coat of hunting pink, was mounted and giving orders to the hunt servants.

Jerry tried to ride Butternut into the background where he would not be noticed too much, for he was all too conscious of the big horse's shaggy appearance and his own makeshift riding clothes.

Derek saw him almost at once and a frown settled on his face.

'The nerve of the blighter!' he muttered. 'I suppose he thinks he's going to get his certificate from Dad. . . . Well, I'll jolly soon put a stop to that.'

He stared at Jerry thoughtfully. He knew it would be of no use to go to his father and ask him to ban Jerry from the field, even though the Master of the Hunt did have this power. Mr Huntly-Jones was a fair man, though inclined to be pompous. There would have to be some reason for Jerry to be banned from the hunt.

As the hunt began to move off to the first draw, Derek edged his own horse closer and closer to Jerry. He carried a long-lashed crop and he let this dangle loosely. Then, with a quick glance to see that he was unobserved, he flicked the crop swiftly. The lash flashed out to sting Butternut painfully, low on the flank. The big horse reared, whinnying.

'If you can't control that beast, you shouldn't be here,' rapped Derek. 'The brute's dangerous.'

Jerry flushed as he heaved on the reins, bringing Butternut to a quivering halt. He had no idea of the trick that had been played on him.

'Sorry,' he muttered. 'I don't know what got into him.'

Then the whips put the hounds in to search the first covert, a dense thicket of bramble and gorse where a fox was often to be found. Sure enough, the musical sound of their baying soon rose. They had found a scent.

Away streamed the pack with the Master and the whips close behind, followed by the rest of the hunt strung out across the heath.

Butternut seemed infected with the spirit of the chase and Jerry had to use all his strength to hold the great horse in. Little though the lad knew of hunting, he knew it was considered very bad form to get too close to the hounds. And he did not want to tire the big horse too much.

They jumped three hedges, Butternut soaring easily over them, before the hounds stopped, losing the scent. The horses gathered at the side of a meadow. In the lee of a hedge stood Derek, his eyes glinting cunningly. He rode his own horse to the other side of the hedge and edged along until he was level with Jerry, who was just behind the local butcher.

Huntly-Jones waited his moment. He broke off a tall weed and snapped off a section of hollow stem. From the hedge he plucked a long thorn attached to a little bit of twig. He put it inside the tubular weed stem like a peashooter.

Then, when Jerry's back was to him and Butternut close up against the horse in front, Derek's cheeks puffed out.

'Ouch!'

Jerry could not help the start he gave as something stung his ear. His whole body jerked, including his legs. His heels drummed Butternut's flank. It was the signal to go – and

Butternut went!

The butcher was almost bowled over as the big horse surged forward with Jerry tugging at the reins.

Behind the hedge Derek grinned as he heard the butcher ranting and threatening to demand Jerry's removal from the field. It began to look as if Butternut would not be getting his certificate after all. One more such incident and the Master would surely expel him.

The clamour of the hounds rose again and the field moved off once more. The butcher had no time to carry out his threat.

Thankfully Jerry settled in his saddle.

'I'll have to watch it,' he told himself. 'That felt like a wasp sting. Maybe it was a wasp that worried Butternut before.'

It was a long run that followed and steadily the field grew more and more strung out. Despite his intention to keep in the background, Jerry found himself getting closer and closer to the front. Butternut was so strong that the lad could scarcely hold him back.

The big horse was going like the wind. Ahead were only a few riders and the huntsmen, who rode close behind the pack.

'We've lost him now,' Jerry heard a man ahead call. 'He's making for the quarry.'

In the rocky quarry side there were many small caves and holes, where the fox would easily find a safe refuge.

The hounds were going well, close-packed like a brown and white carpet gliding across the heath. It was a thrilling sight, brightened by the scarlet of the hunting coats.

Jerry realised suddenly that another horse was coming up close beside him. He glanced aside for an instant – into the mocking eyes of Derek Huntly-Jones.

What followed came so quickly that even Jerry was not quite sure how it happened. One of his reins parted suddenly, and

Butternut headed straight for the massive hedge.

Jerry almost fell backwards. He fought for his balance, regained it – and then discovered to his horror that he had lost control of Butternut.

With only one rein, he could not hold the big horse. The beat of Butternut's hooves rose with every moment. His speed increased breathtakingly. Completely out of control, he was charging forward. 'Oh, heck!' groaned Jerry. 'I've had it now. They'll chuck me right out.'

For at the speed Butternut was going it would be minutes only before he raced past the Master, perhaps even past the hounds. He would be committing the worst crime possible on the hunting field

White-faced, Jerry could only cling to his saddle and try to turn Butternut with the one remaining rein. But the big golden horse was not going to turn. Its powerful neck strained against the rein. Jerry was so intent on his own troubles that he did not notice that the Master and one of the huntsmen had swung aside and were now racing flat out straight at a huge thorn hedge which must have been close to nine feet high.

The huntsman's horse baulked at the jump and the Master swung his own aside at the last moment, just when it seemed it must crash right into the thorns. Both circled back to try again. They were still turning when Butternut flashed between them, heading straight for the massive hedge.

Instinctively Jerry crouched, trying to time the jump that must come. Without reins he could not control Butternut properly. But he still had his legs. Now those legs that gripped the horse had to do all the controlling.

The huge hedge seemed to loom high overhead as Butternut thundered down on it. Jerry's mind was cold and clear, judging the distance.

'Now!'

Butternut's massive legs gathered under him and up he soared, up and up for breathless split-seconds that seemed unending.

Then he was dropping again – over and clear.

Not even Butternut could jump nine feet. But his massive body smashed through the upper part of the hedge, leaving a great gap behind. Thanks to his great thick coat, he wasn't even scratched. Through the gap, leaping a good five feet, came the Master and the huntsman. They raced after Jerry, who was crouching forward, trying to grab the dangling end of the rein. Once and twice it flicked out of his reach. The third time he had it.

But as he started to heave Butternut to a halt, he heard the baying of the pack.

'Oh, I've done it now,' he groaned.

He was right ahead of the hounds, turning towards them, riding into the pack, committing the worst offence possible on the hunting field!

While he still struggled with the reins, the Master and the huntsman swept past, their long whips cracking in the air. He hardly saw them go.

At last Butternut was under control. Lightly Jerry slipped to the ground and knotted the broken rein. As he did so, he saw it had been cut.

'So that's it!' he breathed. 'Derek did this deliberately to get me thrown out of the hunt!'

Indignation flared up in his heart. But even as it did, he knew there was nothing he could do about it. Who would believe his story?

Then, with a sinking heart, he saw the Master ride towards him.

'Here it comes,' he thought. 'He'll be furious with me. I'll never ride in the point-to-point now.'

But to his amazement, there was a smile on Mr Huntly-Jones' face.

'A fine piece of work, young fellow,' said the Master approvingly. 'We'd never have got over that hedge if you hadn't given us the lead.'

Jerry gulped silently. This was no time to say that the jump had not been planned!

'And if we hadn't got over,' the Master went on, 'I don't like to think what would have happened to the pack. Hot on the scent as they were they'd have gone straight over the edge of the quarry. . . .'

Only now did Jerry realise that he had halted close to the edge of the great cliff that was the quarry's face.

'We've hunted that fox before,' the Master went on. 'He has his den below the edge of the cliff. A fast-running pack would never pull up in time. You did us a great service.'

Jerry had his vital certificate in his pocket as he jogged homeward that afternoon. Butternut might be mud-stained and weary – but now he was qualified to run in the point-to-point.

'All we've got to do now,' he told Silas that evening, 'is to win the point-to-point. And after the way Butternut went today I don't think there's a horse around here to beat him.'

But even now Derek Huntly-Jones had not given up hope of stopping Butternut from racing.

★   ★   ★

It was the morning of the point-to-point. Jerry had completed his milk round and seen Butternut safely stabled, rubbed down and given a hearty feed of corn. Even with the race due that afternoon the horse had to go to work. But Jerry was sure he would not be over-tired.

Then, as he went for his own breakfast, a small boy came hurrying to him.

'Message from Mr Huntly-Jones,' panted the boy. 'You're to take two gallons of milk and a quart of cream up there right away.'

Jerry heard the words with dismay. Another trip for the horse – and it was getting near race time! Could he make the delivery and get back to be ready for the race?

He was strongly tempted to ignore the order completely. But then that might mean losing one of his father's best customers. That was something they could not afford – not even for the race.

With a sigh he loaded the milk and cream on to the van and headed for the Huntly-Jones' home.

It was Derek who greeted him.

'You took your time I must say,' Derek sneered. 'Well, don't just stand there. Bring the churn round to the back.'

At the back of the house he pointed to an outhouse.

'Put it in there,' he said.

Jerry carried his burden into the cool shadows of the outhouse and set it down. As he did so, the door closed behind him. He heard a bolt slide home. He was locked in!

'You'll find plenty of cockroaches in there,' came Derek's taunting voice. 'Maybe you can teach them to race, because that's all the racing you'll see today.'

The sound of his footsteps faded as he walked away across the yard. Jerry slumped against an old packing case. He had been tricked. A prisoner in the outhouse, he would never get out in time for the race!

Jerry did not bother to shout for help. He knew that Derek would never have trapped him in that outhouse if there had been anyone within earshot. Family and servants must have already left for the meeting.

The door was solid oak and there were no windows in the outhouse. Escape seemed out of the question.

'But I've got to get out,' Jerry told himself. 'Somehow I must get to the race.'

He threw his weight once against the door, but it did not even shake. A few empty crates were all the furniture in the hut. They were far too light to make a battering ram. The roof was stoutly made, and even if he could have reached it, there would have been difficulty in smashing through it.

Outside Butternut pawed the cobbles and whinnied impatiently.

Back and forward in his prison Jerry paced, his boots clicking on the cobbled floor. He had been pacing for some minutes when an idea came to him.

'Of course,' he breathed. 'Tunnel under the door.'

It was an old building and like the yard outside was floored with cobbles rammed into the earth.

'If I can pick the cobbles away at the foot of the door, I could burrow my way out,' breathed Jerry.

It was no easy task he had set himself, as he soon discovered when he set to work with his penknife. The rammed earth was almost as hard as the stones themselves.

But he moistened the earth with milk from the churn he had brought with him. Soon he had the first cobblestone out. From then on it was easier. Softening the earth with the milk, he pulled stone after stone from the floor, until there was a hollow beneath the door itself. Soon it was big enough for him to squirm his way through.

Butternut whinnied a welcome to his master.

'Come on, boy!' Jerry grunted as he reached for the reins. 'Let's go home.'

Then he halted. Had he time to go home? It would take half an hour or maybe more, pulling the heavy van. Then another half-hour to the track. How long had he been imprisoned? Was he already too late for the race?

There was only one way to find out. Fingers working deftly on the harness, Jerry freed the big horse from the shafts and then shortened the reins.

Lightly he sprang on to the horse's bare back and cantered from the yard.

★ ★ ★

On the race course the horses were gathered in the paddock for the start of the point-to-point.

Derek Huntly-Jones, his riding boots gleaming and bright jockey silks and cap immaculate, was posing beside his handsome chestnut. From the bookmaker's boards he had seen that he was favourite.

'Looks as if you'll be buying me that sports car, Dad,' he grinned at his father.

'If you win this race you'll deserve it,' answered Mr Huntly-Jones. 'Are all the runners ready?'

'One still to come,' reported an official. 'Young Kane's Butternut.'

'Oh, Kane's scratched,' said Derek airily. 'He felt he was out of his class in a race like this.'

He mounted his own horse lightly and headed through the admiring crowd towards the starter on the course.

As he did, he heard a surge of laughter from the crowd behind.

A weird figure was in the paddock, arguing with the officials, a figure smeared with mud and white milk stains.

'I tell you I didn't scratch,' Jerry insisted. 'I'm going to race.'

Butternut took his place at the starting line.

'But the race is due to start,' protested the secretary. 'You haven't time to change and saddle your horse beforehand.'

'Then I'll do without a saddle – I'll ride Butternut as he is,' Jerry retorted shortly.

'Oh dear, this is all very irregular,' the secretary muttered. 'Really I don't know. . . .'

It was then that Mr Huntly-Jones came over. He recognised Jerry and his mount at once. He asked for no explanations.

'Let the boy race,' he rapped.

The Master's word was law, and the amusement of the crowd increased as Butternut took his place on the starting line, making a startling contrast to the other immaculate horses and their elegant riders.

They were off to a perfect start.

Butternut was badly placed, on the outside, and at the first bend, the big golden horse was lying an easy last.

Far ahead, Jerry could see Derek Huntly-Jones, gliding smoothly over jump after jump on his chestnut mount. He had taken the lead from the start and was riding showily, determined to cut a dash in front of the big crowd.

The jumps did not trouble Butternut in the least. Fence after fence he cleared with ease, just as if he were on a training gallop. The big horse's pace did not slacken. Half-way round the gruelling course, he was going as fast as when he had started.

But already many of the others were dropping back. Jerry passed one, then another. Gradually he crept up the field. Soon he was lying fourth.

Now Huntly-Jones' chestnut was feeling the effect of its first burst of speed. It was beginning to tire and falter slightly at the jumps.

With less than a mile to go, Jerry was lying third. The second horse was about a length ahead and two lengths beyond was

Huntly-Jones.

Derek had not yet looked back. Confidently he rode on, sure that no one could catch him.

The second rider made a tremendous effort to gain the lead. Spurring his mount on, he caught up with Huntly-Jones. Neck and neck they went into a jump together.

As they jumped, Jerry saw Huntly-Jones' foot nudge the other's stirrup. Unbalanced, the rider swayed in his saddle for a moment and then crashed to the ground. Jerry, following up, had to put Butternut into a second jump to make him clear the fallen figure on the ground.

'That was deliberate,' Jerry blazed. 'He unseated that rider.' Butternut was just behind Huntly-Jones as they rounded the last bend.

Though Huntly-Jones did not look round, Jerry could see that he sensed that he was followed closely. He swung wide at the bend for a moment right in front of Jerry. Clouds of mud and turf showered into Jerry's face and into Butternut's eyes. Both were half blinded.

But the move was to cost the trickster dearly. For in swinging wide he had left an opening between himself and the rail.

Even though he was dazed by the spray of mud, Jerry saw the opening.

'Go, boy, go.' He urged Butternut on, his heels drumming in the horse's flanks.

Like a golden arrow, Butternut flashed forward. For a moment the two horses were neck and neck. Then Butternut was in the lead. The next fence loomed up. As he thundered towards it, Jerry suddenly realised that Butternut was not slowing, not poising himself for the jump. He was going to crash straight into it.

It was a solid brushwood jump. To crash into it would

certainly mean disaster. Yet could a blinded horse jump?

Instinctively Jerry prepared for the jump, his legs gripping the barrel of Butternut's chest.

'Now, boy,' he breathed.

Only great trust between horse and rider could have taken them over the jump. The next moment Butternut jumped, although he could not see what he was jumping. He landed safely on the other side of the brushwood and sped on towards the finish.

As they went, Jerry leaned forward to clean the horse's eyes.

Behind, Jerry heard the tattoo of Huntly-Jones' mount's hooves and the crack of his crop as he tried to force it to go faster. But it was wasted effort. The horse's strength was spent. With every pace Butternut was drawing ahead, so that Jerry was able to slow him to a canter as he neared the finishing line, a certain winner.

In the unsaddling enclosure, Derek Huntly-Jones was protesting wildly.

'Kane bumped me deliberately,' he declared, pointing at Jerry. 'It was a foul. He should be disqualified.'

Jerry's eyes blazed as he stared towards the other. But he had no chance to answer the lie. For Mr Huntly-Jones himself was looking at his son with contempt.

'Only one rider is disqualified from that race,' he said bitterly. 'That one is you, Derek. I saw through my glasses what you did as you crossed the half-way jump. Now get home. I'll deal with you later.'

Jerry hardly saw him go. For now, as the thrill of the race died down, he realised that the had achieved his ambition. He had won the point-to-point.

'You'll pull no more milk carts, Butternut,' he told the big horse. 'From now on you're a race-horse!'

Mick's Greatest Innings

Mick's Greatest Innings
by Reg Clark

Mick Smart watched the ball as it left the bowler's hand. It was an off-break, he decided, and, with calm confidence, he moved out to the pitch of the ball. His bat swung easily forward – and the ball was sent whizzing across the turf, just wide of cover.

'Yes, Ted! Come on – two!' Mick yelled to his partner at the other wicket, and both began to run.

But there was no need. The ball had gone straight to the boundary.

'Well done, Mick! Keep it up!' chuckled Ted Brown, Mick's pal, who was batting with him. 'You're doing fine.'

Before the end of the over from the slow bowler, Mick Smart cracked two more fours, putting his score up to forty-two. During their third-wicket partnership, Mick and Ted had put on more than sixty with some hard hitting.

Although he was only eighteen, Mick was fast becoming the Beston Cricket Club's best batsman, and it was well known that the county coach had been watching him in some of his recent matches. Mick, a junior mechanic at a local garage, was crazy about cricket, and would have given almost anything for a chance to join the county staff. His great ambition was to make cricket his career.

'It won't be long before you get that chance, if you put up a good performance against Malford this afternoon, Mick,' said his pal, Ted Brown, when they had discussed Mick's future before the match. 'Who knows – maybe you'll be asked to play in the Colts *v*. Second Eleven game on the county ground next Wednesday.'

Mick was playing as well as he'd ever played, and his hopes rose even higher when he and Ted hit another eleven runs off the next over, leaving Mick to face the Malford off-spinner again. But then something happened that changed everything for the young batsman.

Mick saw the Malford skipper sling the ball to a tall, dark-haired chap who had been fielding in the deep. Instantly, Ted walked down the pitch and spoke quietly to his pal.

'Watch this chap. His name's Bert Mason,' he said. 'He's played several times for the County Colts – and he's fast – blinkin' fast!'

Thanking his pal for the advice, Mick crouched confidently over his bat. He watched the fast bowler mark out his long run, turn, and then gallop up to the wicket. Down came the ball – and before Mick could play any stroke, it hurtled past his face!

Undeterred, Mick took guard again. Down came the next ball – a yorker this time. Mick just managed to stab it out of his wicket.

There was an arrogant air about Bert Mason as he walked back again to his bowling mark. And if his first two deliveries were fast, the next was a real scorcher. Whizzing like a rocket, it was a venomous, short-pitched ball which rose straight towards Mick's body. He tried to step aside – but it caught him a sickening thud on the thigh.

Mason screamed, flinging his arms high in triumph. But the umpire quickly turned his head away. Mason frowned angrily.

How Mick managed to play the next three balls from Mason he never rightly knew. Grim-lipped, he played the first to silly mid-off. The next flew wide of the off-stump, and Mick instinctively drew away from it. Determined to score off the last ball of the over, he hooked the ball courageously as it hurtled towards his face. It flashed over the head of the short leg fielder, and went for two rather lucky runs.

Mick was glad to see the end of that over. Not that he was scared of fast bowling – he never had been. He always enjoyed matching his batting skill against the bowler's speed, but Bert Mason was different from any other pace bowler he had ever faced. He was certainly fast – but he obviously relied on frightening the batsmen out, rather than bowling them. He was wild, venomous and intimidating!

But Mick had a chance to relax during the next over, for Ted kept the bowling, scoring another ten runs off the slower man. Now it was Mick's turn again – and Bert Mason was the bowler.

'I've got to hit him – and hit him hard,' Mick vowed to himself as he shaped up for the first ball. 'I'll never get a chance with the County Colts unless I can prove myself against any type of bowling.'

With a new determination, Mick watched Mason charging up to the far wicket. Down flashed the ball. It was almost too fast to see, but Mick stepped into the line of flight to drive it through the covers. But at the last moment it shot up – and rapped him on the right hand.

It was a painful blow, but the young Beston batsman gave no sign that he had been hurt. As though to prove it, he played the next ball for two.

But they were the only runs Mick managed to score off that over. In fact, it was only through his neat footwork that he avoided being badly hurt. One ball cracked him on the elbow. Another flew off the shoulder of his bat as he shielded his face, and he was nearly caught.

As the over finished, Bert Mason strutted down the pitch with an insolent sneer on his face.

'I'll get that kid in a minute,' he said to the wicket-keeper with a smirk as they changed over. 'He's scared stiff of me!'

Mason *did* get Mick's wicket in his next over, but not in the way he hoped.

The third ball of the over was one of the fastest and most erratic Mason had ever bowled, but Mick timed it beautifully, driving it high towards the sight-screen. It looked a 'six' all the way, but, unfortunately, at the last moment it dipped, and fell short.

A fielder raced towards it. He got one hand to it. The ball popped out. But then, as he fell sprawling on his back, he managed to make a second grab at it. This time the ball stuck!

Mick Smart was out.

'Bad luck, Mick!' said Ted as his pal passed him on the way back to the pavilion. 'You played a grand knock!'

Mick forced a smile of thanks – but he didn't feel like smiling. Everything had been going well until Bert Mason started to bowl – but that had ruined any chance he might have of being chosen for a trial with the County Colts.

It was about ten minutes later that Ted Brown was out – caught behind the wicket when stepping away from a Mason 'flyer'. He hurried into the pavilion to find Mick sitting there, alone and disconsolate. Ted tried to cheer him up, but without much success.

'I've spoiled everything, Ted,' said Mick dismally. 'I allowed that fellow Mason to knock me off my normal game – but why hold an inquest on it? The county won't even look at me again after this!'

'Don't talk daft, Mick!' Ted exclaimed. 'Anyone'd think you failed – but you stood up to Mason jolly well. In any case, you scored more than fifty runs – scored 'em well, too!'

'The county aren't likely to think twice about a chap who

can't play fast bowling!' said Mick. 'No – I've had it, thanks to Mason!'

At that moment there came a shout from outside the pavilion – and another Beston batsman was out. The two pals soon heard footsteps outside. They thought it was the batsman returning. Instead, a stocky, grey-haired man stepped into the pavilion.

At the sight of him, Ted Brown jumped to his feet, smiling from ear to ear.

'Why, Mr Greener,' he cried, in surprise. He turned quickly to Mick, to introduce the newcomer. 'Mick – this is Bill Greener, a senior county coach!'

Mick jumped up, too astounded to speak.

'How d'you do, Smart?' the famous cricketer began. 'Nice innings you played this afternoon. You were unlucky to be out, just when you were getting on top of Mason's bowling. I like your batting, in fact it's the best I've seen in a long time – and I want to know if you'd like a chance to play for the Colts?'

'You – you mean it?' Mick stammered, hardly able to believe his own ears.

Bill Greener smiled. 'We're playing a trial game next Wednesday between the Seconds and a team of Colts. There's a vacancy on the ground-staff, and any of the Colts who impress us in that game will be given the chance to fill it. What do you say, Smart?'

What *could* Mick say? As a matter of fact, he was too excited to say anything much – except to thank the county coach for the invitation. It was Ted Brown who finished off the short conversation.

'That's great, Mr Greener! Of course Mick'll accept! I'm playing, so I'll bring him along. He won't let you down, you can be sure of that!'

★ ★ ★

From that moment Mick Smart could think of nothing else but the chance that had been offered him to achieve the first of his ambitions – the chance to become a County Colt. It was a chance that might lead to a career in first-class cricket. No wonder he was excited.

On the Monday morning, when he turned up at the garage where he worked, he went straight to the office to see the manager. Later in the morning, he was whistling so cheerily that even the foreman was curious to know the reason. He soon found out.

'Smart's been given the day off on Wednesday to play in a Colts match for the county – lucky chap!' one of the other mechanics explained.

'H'm! Nobody tells me nothing!' growled the foreman. 'Play for the County Colts, eh? Well, I hope he'll make a better job of that than he does of his work here. All he thinks about is cricket!'

The foreman called Mick from a car at the back of the garage.

'Oh, Smart,' he began, 'seeing that you've been given the day off on Wednesday to play cricket, perhaps you'll attend to your work for a change. Get out on the pumps for the day – and don't make any mistakes!'

The foreman hurried away, leaving Mick staring after him. He knew that he had upset the foreman, but he didn't mind now. And he was still whistling softly when he went to attend to a motorist who had pulled into the garage for petrol. He wouldn't be working as a garage mechanic much longer. He was to get his chance to become a county cricketer – and he didn't intend to fail!

Later on, a big blue sports car swung into the garage. Mick hurried forward – and then the smile died on his face.

274

The driver of the car was Bert Mason, the fast bowler who had given him such an unhappy time on the Saturday!

Their eyes met, and Mason instantly recognised Mick.

'Oh, so this is where you work,' he exclaimed haughtily. 'Well, I'll have four gallons – and don't run your greasy hands on my car!'

Mick bit back the hasty retort that flashed to his lips, and started to fill the tank of the gleaming sports car.

'I hear you've been chosen to play for the Colts on Wednesday, Smart – although I can't think why!' Mason sneered. 'A chap who's scared of fast bowling will never make a cricketer – –'

'Are you suggesting that I was scared of you on Saturday?' Mick broke in, unable to remain silent in the face of such a taunt.

'It certainly looked like it to me,' Mason replied. 'I don't blame you, of course. After all, you've never had to face top-class bowling before, and I've scared far better batsmen than you!'

'I've never been scared to face any sort of bowling,' Mick exclaimed, a flush of anger on his face. 'And if you call your bowling top-class – then I don't!'

'That's an opinion that I shall ignore, Smart!' Bert Mason flashed, cutting Mick short. 'How long does it take you to fill my tank? Hurry up – and put it on my account.'

Mick said no more. Then, as the arrogant fast bowler was about to drive away, he leaned over the side of the car.

'Oh, Smart,' he sneered. 'I don't know whether you've heard, but I shall be playing in the match on the county ground on Wednesday. I shall be in the Second Eleven! You see, I'm expecting to be selected for the first team shortly, and I'm only playing in this er – trial game as a favour to the county coach. He wants the Colts to be given a thorough test: I just thought you'd be interested to know that I shall be bowling against you – that's if you don't cry off before Wednesday! And that wouldn't surprise me!'

Mason's sports car roared away from the garage, leaving Mick staring after it as though in a daze. The news that he would have to face Bert Mason in the most important match of his life left him speechless.

For the rest of the day Mick was unusually quiet and thoughtful. It puzzled the other mechanics. It wasn't like Mick to be so glum. They could only assume that he was upset because the foreman seemed to be particularly severe on him. They were wrong, as they would have found out could they have seen Mick after he left the garage that evening.

As soon as he had washed and changed, Mick hurried round to the home of his pal, Ted Brown, and told him of his meeting with Mason.

'He accused me of being scared of him, Ted,' Mick exclaimed hotly, 'and I'm going to make him eat those words! I'm determined to knock his bowling all over the field in Wednesday's match!'

'Forget Mason, Mick!' Ted put in. 'He was only trying to upset you. As for him being chosen for the county team, that's sheer baloney – wishful thinking. In any case, we all know that you weren't scared of him on Saturday. No one could have played strokes against his rotten bowling. You'll be O.K. on Wednesday!'

'I've got to be!' Mick exclaimed. 'I don't intend to let Bert Mason spoil my chance of a place on the county groundstaff. Listen, Ted, I've got an idea, but I shall need your American friend Bob's help.'

Ted Brown was amazed at Mick's suggestion, but his eyes glinted with eager anitcipation as he listened. Before Mick had finished, Ted's friend Bob arrived.

'Hallo, Bob!' Ted greeted him. 'Mick needs your help. It means everything to him. He'll tell you about it.'

Mick quickly repeated the idea that had taken shape in his mind since his meeting that morning with Bert Mason. Bob heard him in silence, and then, without hesitation, agreed to help.

'O.K., Mick,' he chuckled. 'Cricket's not my game, but this little stunt of yours will give me an appetite for my tea. Let's go!'

A few minutes later the three pals hurried along to the Beston cricket ground. The place was deserted, for there was no practice on Monday evenings.

Ted unlocked the pavilion, and Mick quickly buckled on some pads. While he did so, Bob took off his jacket and found half a dozen cricket balls. Then they went out to one of the nets. Mick took guard in front of one stump, and Bob prepared to bowl at him.

But Bob was no orthodox cricket bowler. Having been raised in America, his favourite sport was baseball. He had been the star pitcher of his school baseball team, and it was reputed that he could hurl a ball at the batter faster than any pace bowler. Knowing this, Mick had hit on his idea of getting some extraordinary practice before the Colts game.

If he could stand up to Bob's fast pace pitching he was quite certain that Bert Mason's bowling would hold no terrors for him.

'O.K., Bob, I'm ready! Let's have it!' Mick called.

Bob then wound himself up and slung a fizzing thunderbolt at the eager-eyed young batsman. The ball was almost too fast to see. Mick's stroke was too late – and the ball whistled past his shoulder!

The second dropped sharply – but again Mick missed it. He

just failed to connect with the third, too. His timing was all wrong.

'Wait for it, Mick!' Ted yelled to his pal. 'Don't be impatient!'

The next ball, even faster than the others, seemed to swerve in the air, and flashed towards the single stump, at about waist height. Mick watched it, and then – crack! Bat met ball – and the side netting bulged as the ball tried to burst through it!

'Well hit, Mick!' called Ted. 'That would have been a four!'

From then on, for nearly half an hour, Bob slung cricket balls at Mick as he would have pitched in a baseball match. It was almost terrifying for the young batsman in the net, but gradually Mick's confidence increased and his timing improved so much that he connected with nearly every ball. He brought out all his strokes, and time after time Ted had to chase the ball right across the field.

At last, puffing and perspiring, Bob called a halt.

'Phew! I've had enough!' he panted. 'How'd you feel now, Mick?'

'Marvellous!' Mick replied, with a huge wink. 'Thanks, Bob! I'll teach Mason to accuse me of being scared of his bowling!'

'Gee, I can't wait for Wednesday!' laughed Ted.

★ ★ ★

There were few spectators around the spacious county cricket ground, and there were no famous test stars out on the pitch – not even any of the regular county men. But to Mick Smart it was the most important match that had ever been played on the ground.

Padded up, he sat in front of the big pavilion, impatiently awaiting his turn to bat and wondering, would this be the last time he would play on the historic county pitch?

The Second Eleven, among whom were several promising young professionals, had taken first innings and were all out for a hundred and eighty-six. Now the Colts, mostly ground-staff boys, and three local lads who had attracted the interest of the county coach, were batting.

The opening pair, one of whom was Mick's pal, Ted Brown, were finding runs hard to get, for the bowling was good. At last, with only eleven runs on the board, the first wicket fell. Mick was next man in.

With a quietly confident smile on his face, Mick snatched up his bat and walked out on to the sunlit pitch, pulling on his batting gloves, to join Ted. He took guard and glanced around to see the placing of the field. His eyes caught those of Bert Mason, fielding at first slip, and the sneering, contemptuous look on Mason's face only gave Mick added confidence.

Down came the first ball from the Second Eleven's regular fast bowler. It was a beauty, dead on the wicket, but Mick played it easily. The next was slightly faster – but Mick drove it past cover for three runs.

This was the last ball of the over, and Mick prepared to face the off-spinner who had been bowling from the other end. But suddenly Mick saw the skipper hand the ball to – Bert Mason!

Ted Brown glanced down the pitch, trying to catch his pal's eye. Despite what had happened on the Monday evening, Ted wondered what Mick's reaction would be, now that Bert Mason was to bowl. He need not have worried. There was something really cheeky about the big wink that Mick flashed at his pal, as though to say: 'Don't worry, Ted!'

Having set his field, Bert Mason swaggered back to his mark. He turned, galloped up to the wicket and hurled down a screaming bumper.

279

Mick hit the ball high towards the boundary.

He expected Mick to duck away from it, but the young batsman did nothing of the sort. He timed the hurtling ball perfectly – and flashed it straight to the boundary! A 'four' all the way!

Bert Mason flashed a venomous glance at Mick and then bowled him a vicious full toss that should have shattered his wicket. Instead, with almost contemptuous ease, Mick killed it with a dead-bat stroke.

The next ball, travelling like a thunderbolt, swung waist-high at Mick. Swiftly moving into the ball, he played a beautiful late cut. The ball sped like a rocket through the slips to the boundary board!

This was too much for Mason. With an angry glare on his flushed face, he shifted another fielder into the slips from the extra-cover position. And then, with cool deliberation, Mick drove the next ball from Mason straight to where the extra-cover fielder should have been. It was another boundary! Twelve runs from four balls!

Mason was furious, but he took good care that Mick scored no more from the last two balls of that over. Both flew high over Mick's head, and he could make no stroke at either of them.

As Bert Mason moved to his position at slip for the next over, he passed close to Mick. Through half-closed lips he hissed at him:

'You'll pay for those runs, Smart! You'll wish you weren't here!'

At last, after Ted Brown had scored six more runs off the other fast bowler, Mick prepared to face Mason again.

'Perhaps he still thinks I'm scared of him,' he thought to himself.

Then, as though determined to prove that he wasn't, Mick cracked the first ball of the over straight past Mason to the sight-screen.

From then on Mick played like a master. He revealed style and strokes that would not have disgraced the finest county batsmen, and slowly the runs mounted – most of them scored off Bert Mason. It didn't matter what type of ball was slung at him, Mick played them all with a confident ease that brought admiration from all the fielding side – except Bert Mason.

By the time he started his fifth over against Mick, Mason had completely lost all control of his temper. Mick was making him look a fool, and he was determined to get his own back.

The first ball of that fifth over would have knocked Mick unconscious – if it had hit him! But the young batsman ducked easily away from it, refusing to make a stroke, and smiled confidently.

The next ball, head-high on the leg-side, was clouted to the mid-boundary. Even the fielders applauded that glorious stroke. But Mick wasn't finished yet.

Bert Mason hurled himself at the bowling crease in his uncontrolled fury, but Mick seemed completely unperturbed. If the ball was playable, he treated it as it should be treated. If not, then he was content to leave it alone.

Then came the last ball of the over. It was the most flagrant bumper Mason had bowled – with all the vicious fast bowler's hatred behind it. Mick watched it closely, ducked low, and then, on one knee, flashed his bat round like a scythe. Next moment, the ball soared high over the heads of the fielders – and crashed on to the roof of the grandstand! It was a glorious 'six'!

Ted Brown could not restrain his delight. He waved his bat high.

'What a shot, Mick!' he yelled. 'Do it again!'

And Mick did do it again.

Mason started his sixth over to Mick with a vicious ball that pitched outside the leg stump and came in chest high. Mick coolly took one step forward and cracked the ball firmly over the enraged Mason's head for four. That shot took all the wind out of the pompous bowler's sails. His next five balls were all well wide of the wicket and Mick flayed them to all parts of the ground. That was the end of Bert Mason. His bowling had become so wild and erratic that his skipper took him off.

Mick was almost sorry to see his enemy sent into the deep field, but by now he felt like batting all day. Not that that was necessary. Although Ted Brown was bowled, to be followed by two or three other Colts, Mick Smart remained in control. Soon he reached his century, and shortly afterwards he scored the winning hit – with another glorious six right out of the county ground!

As he walked back to the pavilion, flushed but wonderfully happy, he was quickly surrounded by team-mates and rivals. Only one of the players was missing – and that was Bert Mason! He hurried straight across to his car and left the ground.

Then, pushing through the crowd of players, came Bill Greener. He strode up to Mick and slapped him on the back.

'One of the finest innings I've ever seen, Mick,' he said. 'I admit Mason's bowling was absolutely hellish in every way, but you proved that you've got what it takes. That vacancy on the ground-staff I mentioned to you – it's yours if you want it. Think it over!'

'I don't need to, Mr Greener!' Mick exclaimed. 'This is the day I've dreamed about all of my life. Of course I'll accept – and thanks a lot. I won't let you down.'

Mick Smart flung his arm round Ted Brown's shoulder as they hurried into the pavilion to change.

'I made it, Ted!' he cried. 'And I owe it to a baseball star – your friend Bob! Come on. This calls for a celebration – and Bob must be in it. I owe him so much!'

Push-Button Champ

Push-Button Champ
by Tom Stirling

I have an invisibiliser. And what, you may ask, is that?

The invisibiliser is a comparatively simple, but wonderful scientific gadget invented by my Uncle Septimus. He's a professor, and just about the most learned man you can meet.

Actually I'm not supposed to have the thing, but Uncle is a bit absent-minded, and I think he's forgotten he lent it to me to try out.

What does it do? Well, it makes things invisible. Press the button, and out zip some special rays that cause things to vibrate faster than usual and make them invisible.

Just to give you an idea of the thing in action, suppose I'm late for school, and biking is out of the question. I stroll along to where Hoggins, one of our prefects, lives.

Now he has a motor-scooter, and can get to school in no time on that. So just when he's about to start off, I sit on the pillion seat.

Of course, he notices the weight and looks behind, wondering if the brakes are binding, but he can't see me. Why not? Because I have taken from my pocket the aforementioned gadget, which is roughly the size of a clip-on pocket torch, shone its rays on to myself, and become invisible.

Well, now that's all clear, picture me one fine morning cycling to school, for once in good time.

I was cycling along minding my own business when suddenly I heard a sharp, anguished yelp.

'Yowowo –'

Coming from a shop holding a chocolate bar was my own pal, Bob Day. He was holding the chocolate bar with one hand, and his ear with the other, while out of the shop after him came a tough, flat-eared, crooked-nosed lout.

'You young ruffian,' he growled nastily at Bob, 'you trod on my foot!'

'It was an accident. I'm sorry,' Bob apologised.

'Not as sorry as you will be,' retorted the tough. With a ham-like hand he knocked Bob's chocolate bar out of his grasp into the gutter, and then brought his fist back-handed to Bob's ear.

'Ow!' yelped Bob in surprise.

Of course, I wasn't standing for that. I don't like to see any chap bullied by some hooligan twice his size, and most certainly not when it's my own pal.

'That's enough,' I said commandingly, as I got off my bike.

The tough turned to glare at me with small glinting eyes. His general appearance suggested that someone had trodden on his face when it was still warm and plastic.

'Are you talking to me?' he said, pointing a stubby finger first at me and then at himself, as though he couldn't believe his ears.

'That's right,' I said, backing away as he lumbered forward. 'It wouldn't pay you to hit him again.'

I know it was big talk, but the tough didn't get annoyed. For a minute he looked puzzled, then he grinned, and suddenly let out a hoot of laughter.

'Hey, Jem! Look who's threatening me,' he called.

A cocky-looking type came out of the shop, weaving a bit so that he could get his shoulders through the doorway.

''Smatter?' he asked

'I'm just warning him,' I said, 'not to try to hit my pal again, or he'll have to deal with me.'

'Deal with you?' echoed the man with an amazed expression. 'Scram, sonny, before I shuffle my feet and frighten you!'

'Haw, haw!' guffawed the tough. 'And just to teach this other one a lesson, I'll squash this chocolate bar all over his face.'

Bob had just picked up the chocolate bar, which, being wrapped in paper, hadn't been hurt by the fall.

With a savage twist of the wrist the tough got it away from him.

'Now's your chance, Jingo,' said Bob with a wry grimace at me. 'Beat him up.'

Now, don't get the idea I'm a prize-fighting sort of chap. I'm not. I'm just an ordinary Fourth Former, of average weight. But I had the invisibiliser as Bob, and only Bob, knew.

'Listen, son,' said Jem, looking at me over his cigar, 'do you know who this gentleman is?'

He jerked his thumb at the tough.

I looked at the thug intently, and made a shrewd guess. 'Brother of Tarzan?' I suggested.

I backed off as I spoke, for I saw the plug-ugly's eyebrows twitch. It was towards a lamp-post that I backed, and, without anyone noticing, I took out the invisibiliser.

You may not see why straightaway, but I focused the rays on to the lamp-post, pressed the button, and made it invisible. Naturally, knowing it was still there, I took care to get on the far side of it.

It shows a chap can't be too wary, for even as I backed away the tough came towards me with his fists raised in the usual fighting manner.

'Hitting me will be just like hitting a lamp-post, you know,' I warned.

He came forward, looking really nasty, and ready to swing.

'Steady, Alf,' said Jem. 'And listen, you chicken-brained

Alf drove his fist at my face.

half-wit,' he added to me, 'this gentleman you have insulted is one of the professional boxers from the Fair Ground: Alf Slaughter, the Merciless Mauler!'

That shook me. I knew by the look of him he was some kind of boxer, but I hadn't guessed it was the Merciless Mauler.

'One slam from him would stun you!' gasped Bob in alarm.

'Take it easy, Alf,' warned Jem. 'He's only a kid. Just clip his ear.'

'Go on, clip it,' I invited, pushing my head forward so that it was against the lamp-post.

Alf brought his right round in an ear-cuffing slap, which I dare say he thought was gentle.

Boinggg! went the lamp-post as the tough's fist hit it.

'Owwl!' yelled Alf, flapping his hand wildly.

'Sure made my head ring,' I grinned, 'but it didn't hurt.'

Alf glowered at me, amazed. Then he lost his temper and drove his left at my face.

I can't tell you how glad I was that the invisible lamp-post was in between. It took that punch for me again.

'Oooowww!' yelled Alf, tucking both fists under his armpits.

I pranced about with my fists in a sparring attitude, keeping the lamp-post between Alf and myself, and pretending to be fighting.

Alf charged like a bull straight at me, and I may as well be honest and admit that for a moment I forgot the invisible lamp-post was between us. I felt icy prickles running up and down my spine.

Then Alf cannoned into the lamp-post and, quick as a flash, I darted my left in his direction to make it look as though I'd hit him.

Alf tottered back and put a hand to his forehead.

'What did he hit me with, a hammer?' he stuttered dazedly.

At that moment there was a sudden shriek of brakes, and a car pulled up near us.

'Look out, Jingo!' gasped Bob. 'It's the Head.'

The old car's door was flung open, and out sprang my Head-master.

'What is the meaning of this utterly scandalous scene?' he demanded. 'Jones, I saw you strike this unfortunate man a blow on the forehead that caused him to sag at the knees.'

'He started it, sir,' I said, quickly. 'I was trying to prove to him that bullying doesn't pay. He knocked a chocolate bar out of Bob Day's hand.'

The Head looked at battling Alf, who was just coming round from the stunning effect of colliding with the invisible lamp-post.

'Anyone speak to you?' he asked the Head, nastily.

'Besides Jones? No, I do not think so,' said the Head with a puzzled frown. 'Did you hear anyone speak to me, Jones?'

'No, sir,' I said. 'I think he's trying to pick a quarrel with you.'

'Pick a quarrel with me?' exclaimed the Head incredulously. 'Surely he cannot be so stupid as to attempt to match himself against me, when you, a mere schoolboy, and a rather weedy specimen at that, can deal him stunning blows?'

The Head threw out his chest, which has slipped a bit in the course of years, and braced his shoulders. His handlebar moustache bristled.

'Talking to me?' said Alf, nearly choking with anger.

'I am including you in my general remarks,' nodded the Head.

I saw Alf move menacingly towards the Head and summon up all his strength for a terrific right to the Head's jaw.

But there was no invisible lamp-post between the Head and Alf!

'Sir, look out!' I gasped. 'He's going to hit you!'

'Hit me?' snorted the Head in scorn. 'Let him hit me. He will regret it. Hit me if you think you can and dare,' he said scoffingly to Alf.

Now, that was a silly thing to say. With a grunting noise, Alf's right swung up and caught the Head on the point of the jaw, and stretched him out full length as stiff as the lamp-post.

When I saw the Head go flat, I gave an inward groan. I couldn't help feeling sorry for him, you see.

Jem rushed forward, dropped to his knees and started rubbing the Head behind the ears, but Alf stood back, scowling.

The Head had asked for it, but he had not seriously meant Alf to fell him like an ox.

'You'll get into trouble for this,' I told Alf.

'That gentleman is my Headmaster. As likely as not you'll get your boxing licence suspended.'

'And if you go on like this,' added Bob Day, piling on the agony for Alf, 'you'll be suspended yourself – by a rope!'

'You ought never to have done it,' said Jem worriedly to his pal.

'He only did it because he couldn't hit me,' I scoffed, dodging behind the invisible lamp-post – just in case.

Alf charged me intending, I guessed, to grab me rather than hit me.

But before he could do anything, the lamp-post felled him for the second time.

Thud! Alf fell full length by the side of the Head.

As he landed, another car drove up, a magnificent, expensive limousine with a five thousand pound glitter of chromium and gloss, and driven by a uniformed chauffeur.

At first glance, I thought it was the local constable in the police wagon, but a second glance told me differently.

Out from the car jumped a man wearing a fur-lined overcoat.

Between his teeth he clenched a long cigar and he stared at Alf and the Head for a moment and then came over to me.

'My boy!' he cried. 'I will make you a world champion!'

'A w-world champion?' I gasped.

'That's what I said,' he nodded. 'I'm Ike Jacobson, the biggest and best fight promoter. Every boxer who works for Ike Jacobson will tell you he wouldn't work for another. I treat my boys right. You're at school, eh?'

All this took me by surprise, but I soon realised that the poor chap thought that I had knocked out Alf, and was a world-beater in the making.

'Where's your Headmaster?' he asked.

I pointed to the Head, who was stirring slightly on the ground.

'There he is,' I said. 'Alf knocked him out.'

'Hey, mister,' cried Jacobson, stirring the Head with a shoe. 'I'm coming right along to your school to talk turkey.'

The Head was just sitting up, and he gave Jacobson a glassy-eyed stare.

'Huh?' he said, blankly.

'Turkey,' repeated Jacobson rolling his cigar across his mouth.

'No' f' me,' said the Head with a shudder. 'I'll just have soup and Christmas pudding.'

'Carry him to my car,' Jacobson snorted to Jem. 'I'll drive him to the school. You boys get into the back. You,' he turned again to Jem, 'warn that pudding-brained dumb-wit fighter of yours to stay away from this new find of mine. Or else –'

I glanced at Bob Day with a grim smile. Things seemed to be moving a lot faster then we could keep pace with.

Luckily the Head came round, and we helped him to his feet. He stroked his chin and looked down at Alf, who was just

294

starting to stir.

'So I knocked him out, too?' said the Head. 'Perhaps the force of my own blow sent me reeling back and I stunned myself.'

'You got knocked cold by that fair-ground dope,' Jacobson rasped. 'Then this boy of yours – this world-beater – knocked him cold with a punch between the eyes. Step in my car, Headmaster, and we'll go to the school and talk this over.'

'I have my own car,' frowned the Head.

'Then follow me! I'll take the boys, and their bikes.'

But the Head still didn't understand, and he frowned at the fight promoter.

'Are you telling me that Jones, here,' he said, pointing to me in what I thought was an off-hand and contemptuous way, 'knocked out that tough hooligan who–er–felled me?'

'That,' explained Mr Jacobson patiently, 'is what I'm trying to tell you, sir, and you'll appreciate it fully when you're more fully recovered. I'm going to take that boy Jones and make him into a world beater. He's going to be a credit to your school and you. He's going to make headlines.'

'Hm,' said the Head frowning.

After packing our bikes on behind, Bob and I scrambled into the luxury limousine, but Mr Jacobson suddenly decided that he would ride with the Head.

As our car swept off, Bob gave me a baffled look.

'Gosh, you're in for it now, Jingo,' he said in awe. 'You certainly diddled Alf, and taught him a lesson. Thanks a lot for coming to the rescue, but it looks to me as though there'll be some fireworks pretty shortly, thanks to all your help.'

'You're right,' I mused, 'I've got myself in deeper than I meant, and it's not easy to see how even the invisibiliser can get me out of this.'

But just how bad it was I didn't realise until we got to school.

It was some time later that the Head sent for me. He was alone in his study when I looked in. He was still stroking his jaw, but he looked none the worse for having been knocked out.

'You wanted to see me, sir?' I enquired politely.

The Head stroked out his moustache left and right, and stared at me.

'My boy!' he said, 'I did not realise you had such a terrific punch.'

I coughed modestly.

'I am astounded,' mused the Head, looking at me over his glasses. 'Of course, when I was young I was something of a fighter. I had a punch my companions dreaded. I sometimes lay awake at nights fearing the possible consequences of failing to realise my own strength. I might stun some poor fellow into unconsciousness. You, too, Jones must be guarded.'

'Yes, sir,' I said, hiding a grin, 'I will.'

'Let me feel your muscles,' suggested the Head suddenly.

He made me hold out my arm and then bend it at the elbow, tightening what he called the biceps. He pressed my arm and gave a start of surprise.

'Where are your biceps, Jones?' he asked sharply, as though I had hidden them somewhere.

'Well, there, sir,' I said, pointing to my arm.

'But you appear to have no muscles,' he said in a surprised voice. 'How could you deliver such a punch with no muscles?'

Of course, the very last thing I wanted was for suspicion to be aroused in such a way that the invisibiliser became suspected. I had played too many tricks on the Head for that. Once he found out the truth about one, he'd guess the truth about the others, and life wouldn't be worth living.

I had to think quickly.

'Er – I haven't always got muscles, sir,' I admitted. 'It's

possibly something more mysterious than you know.'

I took off my jacket with a flourish.

'Now, sir, there's nothing up my sleeve, is there?'

'So what, my boy?' frowned the Head.

Now on his desk was a cricket ball.

Unseen by the Head, I switched the invisibiliser on to it, and the ball vanished – at least it was still there, as solid as ever, but invisible.

I picked it up, but the Head saw nothing in my hand.

'Now, sir, observe closely,' I said, pushing the invisible cricket ball up my shirt sleeve. 'I give a touch to a muscle and, lo –'

This time when I flexed my arm, the cricket ball showed up.

'It's amazing – absolutely fantastic,' cried the Head, as he felt my arm and the cricket ball. 'That muscle is as hard as iron.'

'Now – the relaxed position,' I said.

Keeping the ball on my arm by pressing the forearm against it, I drew back my sleeve, so showing nothing but my rather skinny upper arm. Then I drew the sleeve down again, and the bulge showed and could be felt once more.

The Head looked utterly baffled. All things considered, it was a pretty nifty trick, impossible without the invisibiliser.

'Amazing,' he said. 'That probably accounts for your punch, Jones.'

'Yes, sir. It's a matter of knack rather than strength,' I explained, getting worked up a bit, and perhaps showing off slightly. 'For instance that book on your desk, it's pretty heavy, isn't it?'

'You are referring to *Economic Evolution of Medieval Europe?*' asked the Head. 'It is rather heavy in the main, but there are some good laughs here and there.'

'I refer to its weight, sir,' I said patiently. 'Do you think you could lift that book with finger and thumb from a kneeling position?'

The Head peered at me.

'Lift that book? From a kneeling position?' he said. 'Why not?'

The book lay on the edge of his desk and I knelt down and extended my arm. I picked up the book in my finger and thumb.

'Of course, it's a knack,' I smiled faintly.

The Head looked from the book to me.

'Do you seriously think I couldn't pick that book up as you did, Jones? Really, boy!' he snorted. 'I've half a mind to cane you for insolence.' He stormed over to the window and turned his back on me in fury.

Finally his curiosity got the best of him.

He knelt down, pulling up his trouser-legs so as not to crease them. What he didn't know was that while his back was turned I had used the invisibiliser again. This time I made six volumes of his encyclopedia invisible and plonked them on top of the other, larger book, but, of course, the Head didn't see them.

'Don't strain yourself, sir,' I warned.

The Head gripped the book in his finger and thumb, luckily not touching the smaller encyclopedias. He couldn't lift it. Considering there were six heavy volumes on top of it that wasn't surprising, of course, but he wasn't to know that they were there – invisible.

'That's funny,' he said, going red in the face, and getting a little peeved.

Finally he used the finger and thumb of both hands, and puffed and gasped. But still he couldn't do it.

The Head stood biting the end of his moustache. He was in such a temper I wonder he didn't tear the book up.

Luckily the telephone rang before he could do anything.

'What? Mr Jacobson. Oh yes, you have Butch Campbell

there? Well, who is he? Oh yes, the next flyweight champion of the world, eh? A killer – and you want Jones matched against him?'

The Head looked at me, and perhaps he saw me give a violent start.

'I should be very pleased to see someone take the rise out of Jones – I mean,' he corrected himself, 'it would be dangerous if Jones became over-confident. Of course, you appreciate, Mr Jacobson, that Jones' uncle would have to be consulted. The decision to launch him on to a career as world-beating pugilist is not mine to make. However, a tryout with this Butch will decide whether Jones' future really lies in that direction.'

He hung up the receiver, smirked and rubbed his hands.

'Jones, you defeated me in that little contest –'

'Only by a trick, sir,' I said hurriedly. I was so scared of fighting Butch Campbell that I was on the verge of telling all.

'Well, you will have need of all the tricks you can muster. Mr Jacobson intends to match you against a lad named Butch Campbell. If you succeed in knocking him out or making any impression on him at all, your future as a fighter is assured. Butch Campbell has knocked out his last six opponents in the first round, and three are not fully recovered yet.'

I did not make a rush to the door to get started. In fact, to be honest, I quaked.

'You-you think I ought to go on with this, sir?' I said anxiously.

'My boy! If you knocked out that tough hooligan, Alf, you must have a terrific punch. I cannot compel you to go, and would not even try to influence your decision. If you do not wish to go, say so.'

'Ahem, perhaps it would be better if I did a little sparring in the school gym first, sir,' I said uneasily.

'Very well,' agreed the Head, stroking his moustache. 'I will get Sergeant Bellow to try on the gloves with you. He was a boxing instructor in the army, and should be able to assess your worth. If you can knock him out,' he added with a glint in his eye, 'that will be proof indeed that your future lies in boxing.'

'You'd like me to knock him out, sir?' I asked.

'Certainly. May the better man win,' said the Head with a smirk. 'Take care not to injure Sergeant Bellow, but by all means knock him out, my boy.'

The Head went off, purring, to make arrangements, for I was well aware that he would have liked the chance of knocking out the sergeant himself. The sergeant had been wished on to the Head by one of the school governors who had an idea that the Head didn't know how to discipline boys, and kept offering the Head advice which he never took.

I had piled up trouble for myself in plenty. Thanks to the cricket ball and the invisible volumes, I had convinced the Head that I was strong, but that hadn't got me out of the jam.

How was I going to convince the Head that I wasn't a good boxer, and yet let him believe I had knocked out Alf? And how was I going to stand up in the ring against Sergeant Bellow?

If the sergeant made me look silly, and I ran out of breath after two minutes, the Head would refuse to let me fight Butch. That would be dandy – except that I wasn't looking forward to being biffed around the ring by a heavy-handed sergeant who hadn't a clue to his own strength. He once put a prefect out for ten minutes in a boxing lesson and broke the sports master's nose in a friendly sparring match.

I couldn't possibly back out, though. I just had to think of some useful dodge.

The Head didn't intend to make it a public exhibition, he said. But he let me have Bob Day for my second, so I hurried off to the form room and got Bob excused from lessons. In a few words, I told my pal what had happened.

'You mean you're going to fight the sergeant?' said Bob. 'In the gym? But he'll slaughter you, Jingo.'

'Yes,' I agreed ruefully. 'Unless –'

'Unless what?' asked Bob hopefully.

I whispered the plan that I had just thought out, and Bob gave a soft whistle.

'It might work,' he commented slowly. 'In fact, it will jolly well have to – it's your only hope.' In the gym, the sergeant, stripped to the waist, was punching the bag to get into trim. It's a fifty-six pound bag, but you'd think it weighed only an ounce the way he hit it.

Wham! Bang!

As the heavy bag swung back he met it with his fist and dented the heavy, sand-packed canvas. You could hear the thud right through the gym, yet he didn't seem to be trying.

'Sure your plan will work?' asked Bob nervously. 'What am I to say to your uncle if it doesn't?'

'Idiot! I'll be all right,' I said.

'Well, here comes the Head. We'd better hurry,' urged Bob.

The Head strode into the gym, and nodded to the sergeant while Bob fitted two large cushions to me, back and front, and roped them securely on. I needn't tell you that the cushions were invisible, thanks to the gadget, and I daresay some of you smarter chaps will guess why I wanted the cushions.

A fencing mask, nicely padded inside, went over my head, and that, too, was invisible – the mask, I mean!

There was no question of a fair fight. I didn't stand a chance. Nothing hung on the fight, so I could regard it as a fair leg pull, provided it kept me out of trouble.

The Head and the sergeant were talking as Bob rigged me up

in my invisible defences.

'You really mean to tell me, sir,' said Sergeant Bellow in a tone of almost contemptuous disbelief, 'that young Jones knocked out Alf, the Merciless Mauler. Whoever said they were there when it happened must be half-witted.'

'Is that so? Well, I was there!' snapped the Head indignantly.

'You saw it happen?'

'I – er – I was myself prone and unconscious at the time,' said the Head with some embarrassment, 'having been knocked out by Alf – at my own request.'

'At your own request?' echoed the sergeant in amazement. 'Well, sir, when you feel you need knocking out,' he added in a hurt tone, 'you don't have to go to strange boxers. I'm always around, and my punch is as good as Alf's.'

'Perhaps,' said the Head coldly, 'you, too, may soon know what it is to be knocked out if Jones delivers his K.O. punch.'

The sergeant gasped. His jaw dropped, and then he hooted with laughter.

'Jones knock me out? That's rich! Ha, ha, ha!'

'Jones! Are you ready to enter the ring with the sergeant?' the Head called to me.

'Y-yes, sir,' I said.

'You are not nervous?'

'Well –' I said.

'Ha, ha, ha!' roared the sergeant.

'I'm slightly nervous in case I might do him an injury as he's an elderly man past the prime of life, sir,' I said gravely. 'But I'll pull my heaviest punches.'

The sergeant stopped laughing abruptly at that.

'Past the prime of life?' he muttered, his eyes narrowing.

I went to my corner, and took off the blanket I had had wrapped round me. Of course the cushions were invisible, and my own figure showed up clearly, stripped above the waist.

'Pfffff,' went the sergeant, trying to smother a burst of mirth at sight of me.

Of course, if he hadn't been so amused he might have felt Bob Day hitching one end of an elastic exerciser round his waist. The other end was hitched to the ring post in his corner. Naturally, I had made the exerciser invisible.

'Time,' said the Head, who was refereeing.

The sergeant rushed at me – but I just stood my ground, put my hands on my hips and let him hammer away with his fists on the invisible cushions strapped to my chest.

Then I stepped back. The sergeant tried to follow me but was brought to a halt by the elastic exerciser.

I got just out of range to lure him beyond the limit of the elastic. He did get beyond the limit slightly, which shows how tough he is. Then he started to lean backwards as the thing pulled him.

I hit him on the chest. As punches go, I don't suppose it was terrific. But it was just enough to send him tottering back and once he tottered he couldn't seem to stop. The terrifically powerful elastic exerciser pulled him back!

He lost his balance and footing and seemed to be running backwards until he suddenly fell full length.

'Careful, Jones,' warned the Head, 'you knocked him back three feet!'

I did some more prancing and the surprised sergeant got up, looked behind him and all around.

'Someone was pulling me from behind,' he muttered.

'No one was pulling you. There was no one there, sergeant,' rapped the Head. 'It is merely that the terrific force of Jones' punch made it seem to you that you were being pulled back.'

The sergeant scowled and made a rush at me. He reached the

end of the elastic's stretch and again was stopped in his tracks. As he tottered backwards, I rushed in and hit him with the old one-two.

Back he went, almost running, and landed. The crash shook the gym, and just as he landed, in came Mr Jacobson.

'I have brought Butch,' he began. Then he looked at the sergeant and from him to me. 'Hey, what's happened?'

'Five – six –' counted the Head.

The sergeant tried to rise, but he couldn't. The reason was that the elastic exerciser was now round his chest holding him down. When he tried to sit up, he was pulled back as though fired from a catapult: and his head rocked the ring's floor.

'Eight-nine-out!' shouted the Head.

The sergeant tottered up as Bob freed the invisible elastic, and I looked across at Butch.

'You knocked him out?' he asked me, pointing to the sergeant.

'Looks like it,' I said modestly.

'O.K. That settles it. I don't fight him,' said Butch to Mr Jacobson. 'Not if he can knock out a heavyweight, even a flabby, flat-footed – Ugg!' he ended, as the sergeant, who had stood enough, fetched him a short jab in the middle.

'That's shown him,' rapped the sergeant in satisfaction as Butch went down with a terrific flop.

'My boy, my champ, you damaged him,' howled Mr Jacobson at the sergeant. 'He's never been knocked out before.'

I strode forward.

'Sergeant,' I commanded, 'leave this to me!'

Then I turned to Mr Jacobson. 'You, sir, get out of here and take your Butch with you. I never want to see your face again.'

I pointed to the door of the gym and remembering what I had done to the sergeant and the sergeant had done to Butch, Mr

Jacobson backed away quickly.

'And never come near this school again or else, see —' I said in typical fim gangster fashion. 'Sergeant,' I called, 'pick up Butch and carry him out.'

'Do as Jones tells you, sergeant,' said the Head with a wary glance at me.

The sergeant picked Butch up, and took him to Mr Jacobson's car while the Head followed with the boxer's hat, which had fallen off.

'Well, Bob, how was that?' I asked my pal.

'Grand! But it won't be if you don't take those cushions off. They've become visible!' he yelped. 'The effect of the invisibiliser has worn off!'

The one on my front had burst, but the cushion covers and the ropes were in full view, and so was the elastic, which we both noticed, trailing behind the sergeant as he went out of the door.

'Gosh, if the Head sees them, you'll be for the high jump, Jingo,' cried Bob.

'Where's the invisibiliser?' I yelped suddenly.

I remembered it was in my jacket, and where was my jacket? Bob hauled the rope and cushion off me just as the Head and the sergeant returned. I found the invisibiliser just as they re-entered the gym, but I was in such a panic that I pressed the wrong button and made both Bob and myself invisible.

'H'm, Jones seems to have gone, sergeant,' frowned the Head. 'But what's that hanging down behind you? It looks like part of an elastic exerciser. Why on earth did you put that on?'

The sergeant twisted round and goggled at his 'tail'.

'No wonder I seemed to feel something pulling me,' he said in amazement. 'But why didn't I see it?'

The Head didn't answer; he was staring at the ring.

'Sergeant, the ring is covered with small feathers. Most

extraordinary!' he cried. Then he gave a loud chortle. 'Haw, haw – evidently Jones did knock the stuffing out of you. Haw, haw!'

'Haw, haw!' echoed the sergeant nastily, scowling at the feathers.

Bob and I, still invisible, stole quietly away. I read somewhere that mystery is good for encouraging mental development, whatever that is. Well, there was mystery in plenty here for the sergeant and the Head to solve.

But despite all the clues I had left around, they never did discover the answers to where I got my amazing 'strength' – thank goodness!

Sandsprite

Sandsprite

by Ray Marr

Pleasure and anxiety were mingled in Bart Hanson's eyes as he gave the order to his pal, Bill Oldham, to 'let her roll. . . .' He heaved on a rope and the sails that towered above him tightened to meet the wind. Gently at first the yacht *Sandsprite* moved forward.

But no waves rippled at her bows, no white foam streamed out astern. For the *Sandsprite* was a sand yacht, a sleek, streamlined vessel of gleaming aluminium and scarlet enamel, mounted on three motor-cycle wheels. Bart and Bill were members of the Broadbay Sand Yacht Club and had built *Sandsprite* in the hope of winning the Broadbay Open Championship – the Sand Yacht Derby, as it was called.

Now, following the receding tide, they swept out across the wide sands of Broadbay. A tremendous expanse of hard, clean sand was exposed when the tide was fully out and it was a perfect place for sand yachting.

Bart and Bill's faces glowed as they felt *Sandsprite* surge forward, her wheels kicking up a trail of sand in her wake.

'I'm going to try her on a tack,' Bart yelled, swinging the wheel of the yacht.

The boom swung over as *Sandsprite* changed direction, and Bill leaned outwards on the outrigger to let his weight compensate for the pull of the wind on the vessel's main sheet. Four times in quick succession Bart tacked the yacht, and each time the pals, their senses alerted to the feel of the craft, had her under perfect control. Then Bart took her flat-out on the straight again.

'She's a beauty!' Bill exclaimed as the yacht swept over a low, rolling ridge.

'She certainly is,' Bart agreed. 'Look who's here, Bill – Bannock and Grale.'

Another sand yacht had been manoeuvring behind the ridge. It was a bigger ship than *Sandsprite* and even from a distance it showed its power. A tremendous mast reared skywards and its hull showed every evidence of professional workmanship.

That was little wonder. For Bert Bannock, who owned the yacht, was also the owner of the biggest garage in Broadbay.

'He'll be going all out to win the derby this year,' said Bart. 'The sports club at the aircraft factory are going to form a sand yacht section. If he can show them that his yacht is the fastest, they're likely to order a lot from him.'

The other yacht swung closer. It was painted a gleaming black with its name, *The Winner*, picked out in yellow at bow and stern. Bert Bannock's burly body was at the wheel – behind a low windscreen.

'*The Winner*,' snorted Bill. 'Well, he'll have to change that to *The Loser* when we're finished with him.'

The Winner pulled almost alongside *Sandsprite*, then deliberately Bannock kept her on the same course.

'Come on, Bart,' Bill grinned. 'Let's show him a thing or two.'

The wind was steady and the two yachts moved along together, *Sandsprite* edging a little in front all the time. Bart frowned thoughtfully as he saw Bannock's cold eyes sizing up the *Sandsprite*.

'Bill,' he said quietly, 'drop the hook.'

His pal stared at him in amazement. Then he pulled on a lever. From the centre of the *Sandsprite* a heavy steel hook, like half an anchor, dug down into the sand, acting as a brake.

At once *The Winner* began to pull ahead. Bannock turned to give the two pals a mocking wave. Hubert Grale, his crony, made a gesture of offering a tow. Bill glowered as he turned to his pal.

'Why did you do that?' he demanded. 'Bannock will be boasting that he has us beaten already.'

'Let him boast,' Bart answered calmly. 'Now he'll go to the race thinking *The Winner* is a lot faster than *Sandsprite*. He won't be worrying about competition from us.'

Bill stared, then chuckled.

'Gosh, Bart, you're right,' he answered. 'At least we'll be sure he won't bother to pull any of his tricks this time. And we'll be able to give him a surprise!'

For there had been races in the past in which Bannock had used very underhand tactics. Confident that they had outwitted their opponent, the two lads concentrated on their practice.

They would not have been so confident could they have heard the words that passed between Bannock and Grale a little later. *The Winner* had just passed over *Sandsprite's* track. Bannock had been making a contemptuous remark about its slowness when Grale pointed suddenly.

'Look!' he gasped, pointing out the track the hook had left. 'Maybe it isn't so slow. That mark in the sand means that when we were pacing them, they had their hook down!'

'Why, the young sneaks!' Bannock exploded. His face twisted in a frown.

'This is bad, Hubert,' he snarled. 'If they could keep almost level with us with their hook down – their yacht must have a terrific turn of speed.'

Bill and Bart kept making trial runs and made a few adjustments to *Sandsprite's* rigging. But Bart was still not satisfied.

311

'She's just a shade on the light side,' he observed when they headed for home at last. 'I'd like some kind of ballast aboard – small, heavy stones for preference – that we could dump if the wind became light.'

'It won't be easy to find ballast,' Bill remarked. 'There aren't many stones about. It's so sandy. Look at those blighters! They might have given us a hand!'

Bannock had brought his garage break-down lorry to the edge of the beach, and with its winch had hauled *The Winner* up to the road. It would have been no trouble for him to have helped the pals haul *Sandsprite* to the road, but Bannock ignored them as he climbed into the cab of the lorry and drove off.

Bart lived close to the Sand Yacht Club and *Sandsprite* was kept in his garden. Next morning – the day of the derby – he was surprised that Bill did not show up to help him wheel *Sandsprite* down to the beach.

'He's probably gone straight there,' Bart decided with a grin, 'or overslept. . . .'

Bart trundled *Sandsprite* down to the beach to take her place in the line-up for the first heat. The time for the start was near, but still there was no sign of Bill.

One of the young spectators was only too glad to take a message for Bart. Soon he came panting back from Bill's house.

But the message he brought deepened the frown on Bart's forehead. For Bill had not overslept. He had gone out hours before!

'Something's wrong!' Bart muttered. 'Bill must be in trouble of some kind. He would never miss the race.'

One of the officials blew a whistle. It was time for competitors to make ready. The heat would start in five minutes – and he had no crew for *Sandsprite*!

While he still peered round anxiously, a tall, athletic-looking stranger stepped forward.

'You look as if you're in trouble,' he said. 'Lost your crew? Maybe I could help. I've done a bit of sand yachting.'

Bart eyed him and thought quickly. The heat would last only a few minutes. After that he would have time to search for Bill and maybe get him back in time to crew for *Sandsprite* in the race itself. But if Bart didn't enter for the heat, there would be no race for *Sandsprite*!

'All right,' said Bart, his mind made up. 'I'd be grateful if you'd stand in for this heat.'

'My name's Mark,' said the man as he clambered aboard and looked round to familiarise himself with rigging and controls.

Now the officials were taking up their places. It was time for the start of the heat.

Away they went together in a tall cloud of shimmering canvas – all except *Sandsprite*. Though her sails were trimmed in and she should have been moving with the rest, she stayed put.

'The sand-hook!' Bart yelled. 'That lever in front of you – pull back on it.'

'Sorry!' Mark cried. 'I – I thought it worked the other way.'

Deftly he corrected his blunder. But already *Sandsprite* had lost fifty yards. Bart crouched over his wheel, coaxing the utmost out of the slender yacht. Gradually they began to make up ground. They passed the first of the stragglers.

And as they reached out into the bay, the wind increased. *Sandsprite* heeled over. They came to the first marker pylon and rounded it.

'Across!' yelled Bart. 'To the other side!' For Mark had hesitated just a fraction of a second.

A moment later *Sandsprite* would have felt the wind on her new course without the crewman's weight to steady her. Just in time to avoid a capsize, Bart nosed her up into the wind to give

Mark time to cross.

Mark apologised as he took his place. But more precious ground had been lost.

Sandsprite was fairly eating up the ground as she overhauled the leaders.

'Watch the main sheet!' Bart shouted suddenly.

Mark's attention had wandered. The sail was on the point of gybing.

Only by a lightning twist of the wheel did Bart stave off the disaster of a gybe – which might have caused the mast to snap!

'That's the third blunder he's made,' Bart thought grimly. 'I wonder – –?'

It was strange that each time *Sandsprite* was catching up Mark should make some blunder – though he seemed smart and capable enough the rest of the time.

Suspicion began to mount in Bart's mind.

'Mark,' he said suddenly, 'how much is Bannock paying you to see I don't win?'

'I – I don't know what you're talking about,' the other began.

But Mark's stammering had given him away. Bart was sure that his suspicions had been correct.

Mark had half risen.

'Look here, Hanson, I don't like – –' he began.

'And I don't like a traitor on my yacht,' Bart snapped back.

He felt the wind veer slightly. Automatically he started to turn the yacht. And then he changed his mind.

He let the yacht gybe!

Like a flash the heavy boom swung over.

Mark saw it coming for him. It was going to sweep him over the side, but he saved it the trouble.

With a squawk of alarm, he dived over the side himself. Bart had a glimpse of his flying body hitting the sand. Then, with desperate speed, he was spinning the wheel back, correcting the gybe before it could do any harm.

Sandsprite swept on. With a glance astern Bart saw Mark pick himself up unhurt and shake an angry fist.

But now Bart was sailing alone – and it took two to sail a sand yacht. Suddenly Bart had an idea.

Deftly he lashed a line to the wheel and sprang out to the outrigger, the spar that held him out from the yacht's side. There he could use his own weight to balance the yacht – and steer by his length of rope to the wheel.

Freed of the extra weight of Mark's body, *Sandsprite* was faster than ever, and though she was far behind, she came racing up now, overhauling the leaders hand over fist.

It was the wildest ride Bart had ever known and only his fierce determination to get a place in the final steeled his nerves to keep the effort up.

Sandsprite fairly ate up the ground now and the leaders came closer and closer. A cheer began to rise from the crowd, amazed at Bart's single-handed feat. If the race had been just a little longer, he might have taken first place. But as it was he sailed comfortably home third.

'At least I'm sure of a place in the final now,' he thought. 'Now to search for Bill.'

Bart had decided that Bert Bannock must be behind Bill's disappearance. Angrily he looked round for the scheming garage-owner, determined to force the truth from him.

But the second heat had already started and *The Winner* was sailing in it. There would be no chance to question Bannock until the heat was over. Glumly Bart sat down on *Sandsprite*'s deck.

Next moment a hand plucked at his sleeve.

'While you were racing, I was asking everyone if they'd seen

Bill,' said an eager-faced lad excitedly. He was the boy Bart had sent with the message to Bill earlier on.

'Well?' Bart demanded, suddenly alert.

'Old Hardcastle, the bait-digger, saw him this morning,' was the answer. 'He was walking out across the bay.'

'Where did he go?' Bart asked breathlessly. The boy shook his head.

'Hardcastle didn't watch – he was too busy digging lug-worms!' was the reply.

Bart stared out across the broad expanse of the bay. Was Bill out there somewhere? And why had he gone there?

'Somehow Bannock must have tricked him,' Bart thought.

He started towards the official platform and button-holed the club chairman to ask for the loan of his binoculars.

Dashing back to *Sandsprite*, Bart hurried up the tall mast. Glasses to his eyes, he began to scan the sands. Once he saw a trudging figure and his hopes rose. But it was only Hardcastle, the bait-digger, hurrying shorewards before the rising tide.

The yachts in the second heat were heading in towards the finishing line and Bart was grimly determined to go and drag the truth from Bannock. He started down the mast.

As he did so, something caught his eye. It was a faint flickering light from far across the sand. For a moment Bart stared. Then it flickered again.

'Dot-dot-dot, dash-dash-dash, dot-dot-dot.'

The light was flashing the Morse code signal for S.O.S. Again and again it was repeated.

'It must be Bill!' Bart gasped. 'He's trapped out there.'

He swung up the binoculars again. Through them he could see that the flashes came from a group of rocks known as the Dragon's Teeth, right out at the mouth of the bay.

At high water the Dragon's Teeth were completely covered.

If Bill was trapped there he was in deadly peril.

'I've got to get to him before the water reaches the rocks,' Bart resolved as he slid to the deck and started *Sandsprite* forward.

As the yacht swept away he had a glimpse of *The Winner* living up to her name, romping home well ahead of the rest of her heat.

'Bannock's in the final,' Bart thought. '*Sandsprite*'s the only yacht that can beat him. But rescuing Bill comes first, even if I don't get back in time to race.'

As *Sandsprite* raced out seawards, towards the towering, sheer-sided rocks, Bart had to shorten sail, for now the ground was scattered with weed-covered stones.

Bart glanced round. There was a clear path round to the right of the stones, but he realised that, if he took that route, he would lose valuable time.

'That's no good,' he murmured under his breath. 'I need every second I can save to find Bill before the tide comes in. I'll have to go through the stones.'

It was tricky work steering *Sandsprite* through the maze of stones, for Bart knew that if he ran into one of them he was liable to do some damage to his home-made craft.

He took a quick look over his shoulder landwards, and saw that the heat in which Bert Bannock was racing *The Winner* had been completed.

And yet there was no sign of Bannock's black sand yacht among the rest of the racers gathered around the club quarters.

Then as he glanced once again at the Dragon's Teeth rocks from which he had seen the flashing light, Bart caught a glimpse of another yacht which was skirting the patch of treacherous stones at top speed.

Bart gasped. It was Bert Bannock's yacht!

'What's he up to?' Bart mused. 'One thing's certain – by the time I can get up speed again, Bannock will be almost level with me. Surely he can't have come out to help me look for Bill!'

For the next few minutes, Bart paid little attention to the other craft as he concentrated on steering *Sandsprite* through the last patch of stones.

But as he hoisted more sail to gain speed for the intervening distance to the Dragon's Teeth, he noticed that *The Winner* was angling towards him, and, with the full benefit of the wind behind billowing her sails, was overtaking *Sandsprite* hand over fist.

As Bannock's yacht came closer, Bart hailed his rival.

'Ahoy, there, Bannock. What are you after? It'll be time for the race soon.'

There was no reply from the garage proprietor.

'Surly blighter,' grunted Bart, his hand rock-steady on the wheel of his yacht.

But next moment Bart got a shock, for he realised that, if *The Winner* continued on her present course, she would collide with *Sandsprite* in a matter of seconds!

'Change course, you madman!' Bart yelled at Bannock. 'There'll be a pile-up if you don't!'

But Bannock gave no indication that he was attempting to avoid ramming Bart's yacht.

Bart thought fast. It seemed obvious now that his rival was intent on smashing *Sandsprite*, and Bart was aware of the fact that his yacht would come off a poor second in a collision. Bannock's yacht was far heavier and tougher than Bart's slender craft. Clearly Bannock was relying on the superior strength of *The Winner* to take him safely through a smash-up.

A few seconds before *Sandsprite* reached the point where the two vessels would collide, Bart wrenched hard at the lever which controlled the sand-hook.

318

The hook dug deeply into the hard-packed sand, and the yacht came to an abrupt stop. Every joint of her chassis creaked under the strain.

Next moment *The Winner* streaked across her bows, leaving only inches to spare. At her wheel, Bert Bannock gave a snarl of fury at *Sandsprite*'s young helmsman.

Bart jerked up the deeply-rooted hook, and set off again in the direction of the Dragon's Teeth. Bannock had set course for the club quarters. He was not going to make a further attempt to ram *Sandsprite*.

In a matter of minutes Bart had reached the Dragon's Teeth rocks. The tide was coming in swiftly.

His gaze swept the ground round the rocks. Bill was not there.

Then he looked upward – and gasped.

For perched on top of a jagged rock thirty feet above the ground was Bill.

'How on earth did you get up there?' Bart howled.

'Never mind that,' Bill shouted back. 'How am I going to get down?'

Bart's face hardened. It was an urgent question, for already the tide had reached the seaward side of the rocks. In minutes the rocks would be surrounded. Then there would be no hope of reaching his pal.

'If only I had a ladder,' Bart thought. 'It's the only way I could reach him.'

Then his eye fell on *Sandsprite*'s tall mast.

Deftly he drove the sand yacht closer to the rock. But the tip of the mast was still out of Bill's reach, below the cliff.

Bart threw himself on to the outrigger, tilting the yacht towards the rock. Still it didn't quite reach. Bill took his courage in both hands, and leapt – straight for the top of the mast.

319

He took aim and leapt on to the mast.

For a few anxious moments it looked as if Bill would miss and crash to death or injury, and then – –

'Got it!' yelled Bill as he grasped the top of the mast and clung to it. Next moment he was swarming down to the yacht's deck.

'No time for explanations now!' cried Bart. 'We've got to get going!'

For already the incoming tide had sent a long tongue licking round the sand yacht's wheels.

Desperately the pals swung *Sandsprite* round to face the land and, almost knee deep in water, pushed her to the firm sand. Only when the yacht was humming shorewards did Bill tell what had happened.

'I got a note signed by you,' he said, 'asking me to meet you in a cave out on the Teeth because there were good stones for ballast there. When I got out I saw the ladder leading up to the cave, climbed up it, and started to look for you inside. I couldn't find a sign of you. I thought it must be someone's idea of a joke and decided to go back home. Then I found that the ladder had gone. I had a pocket mirror on me and tried to signal with it.'

'I know,' Bart nodded. 'A pity you didn't see who took the ladder away. It must have been Bannock, but if only we had proof – –'

Bill grinned and pulled a piece of paper from his pocket.

'We have,' he said.

He held it out. It was the note which Bart was supposed to have written – but on its back was a bill made out to Bannock's garage. It was plain that Bannock had overheard the pals discussing their need for ballast the previous evening and had hit on his plan to get rid of Bill. He had scribbled his note on the first bit of paper that had come to hand.

'That'll just about cook Mr Bannock's goose,' said Bill with satisfaction. 'All the same, it's a pity we couldn't have cooked it before he won the derby.'

Bart's eyes flashed defiantly.

'He's not going to win it,' he snapped. 'We are.'

And he crouched a little lower at his wheel.

Far ahead they could see the yachts being mustered for the start of the final.

Sandsprite was streaking forward now. Suddenly Bill gave a groan and reached for the sand-hook.

'Water ahead!' he yelled.

A long channel between two sand dunes had already been filled by the incoming tide and the water was three feet deep in it. Bart eyed it and then looked along the channel. It ran away to one side. To skirt it would mean a long detour, which would end all hope of taking part in the race.

Swiftly Bart made up his mind.

'Up with the hook,' he cried. 'We're going to sea.'

And as the *Sandsprite* rolled forward, he aimed it deliberately at the water. It was far too deep for the wheels to keep the hull above water. Bart was gambling on one thing – the light, air-filled tubing of which *Sandsprite* had been built.

And the gamble came off.

For instead of coming to a halt as the water deepened, *Sandsprite* floated. For a few breathless moments she became a water-borne yacht, sailing across the channel.

Then they were across and heading for the line.

Sandsprite was still some distance short of the line when the race began.

Bert Bannock's yacht took the lead almost from the moment that the starting-cannon sounded. Bill gave his pal a despairing glance.

'A stern chase,' Bart said. 'But we can still catch them.'

Officials waved *Sandsprite* on as she raced up to the starting line.

The wind was freshening all the time. Bart eyed the sky – then deliberately headed off on the opposite tack to the others.

'The wind's changing,' he shouted in answer to Bill's inquiring look.

And sure enough in a few moments the wind veered round. Now *Sandsprite* had the full advantage of it while the other yachts had to sail against it to reach the first mark.

'Good old Bart!' Bill shouted excitedly. 'This'll help to make up for out late start.'

Bart's jaw jutted grimly. His keen-eyed observation of the changing winds had given the *Sandsprite* a sporting chance – but the yacht still had a long stretch to make up before the pals caught up with even the last of the stragglers.

Like an arrow *Sandsprite* flew forward. Her lightness and the pals' careful trimming of her rigging had given her a great advantage over the other competitors in the Sand Yacht Derby.

At the wheel of *The Winner*, Bert Bannock had not seen *Sandsprite*'s late entry in the race. Suddenly his crony, Hubert Grale, gave a shout.

'Look! Hanson and that other young cub! They're in the race – and they're coming up the field fast! I thought you'd made sure their yacht wouldn't compete.'

Bannock growled.

'So I did,' he replied, his face grim with fury. 'Somehow Hanson must have got his pal down from the Dragon's Teeth and beaten the tide to get back here in time. Don't worry, Grale, they can't prove anything – and they won't catch up with us now.'

As Grale let out the mainsail, *The Winner* raced ahead at a speed that almost matched *Sandsprite*'s.

Bart's helmsmanship was superb. Under his control, *Sand-sprite* bounded forward. With the wind full behind her, she was quickly able to overtake three of the trailing yachts which were tacking to reach the next leg.

'We've got a long way to go before we catch up with Bannock,' said Bill urgently.

The two pals devoted all their concentration to the tricky task of sailing *Sandsprite* at full speed. As Bart turned the craft to enter the second leg of the race, the boom of the mainsail swung over and Bill ducked it neatly.

Now the wind was broadside on to their course, and Bart had to tack the vessel towards the start of the third leg. Under his skilful handling *Sandsprite* overtook steadily, and at the end of the leg had passed most of her rivals.

At the start of the third leg, only two craft were ahead – and the leading one was *The Winner*, Bert Bannock's yacht.

But *Sandsprite*'s wheels hummed over the firm sand, and as they reached the marker for the end of the third leg, Bart and Bill overtook the second yacht. Now only *The Winner* was in front!

On the long leg to the finishing line, Bart and Bill got the last ounce of speed out of their light craft. Closer and closer it drew to Bannock's yacht.

Bannock started to weave his yacht ahead of *Sandsprite* in an attempt to bar her way.

'We'll never pass him,' Bill groaned.

Hard-eyed, Bart was studying the sky again.

His next order startled Bill into stunned silence.

'Down mainsail,' he yelled.

The canvas came flapping down on deck. *The Winner* drew ahead – but only for a moment.

For with startling suddenness the wind changed again. It was now blowing from the finishing line.

The Winner had to bear away on a tack, for no vessel can sail straight into the wind.

But *Sandsprite*, with all sail down, rolled straight forward under the momentum of the speed she had already gained.

As *The Winner* came racing in on its second tack, *Sandsprite* crossed the line – first in the Sand Yacht Derby.

'And now for a word with Bannock,' Bart said threateningly.

But as he strode towards the black yacht, Bannock's letter in his hand, he was beaten by the tall figure of Mark, who hauled Bannock from his place and slammed a tremendous punch home to his jaw. Then he turned to Bart.

'You were right,' he said. 'I was trying to make you lose in the heat. And Bannock did pay me to do it. But I didn't know then that he was rat enough to maroon your pal where he might have been drowned.'

He pulled some bank-notes from his pocket and threw them in Bannock's face.

'Keep your dirty money, Bannock,' he snapped.

At that moment a club official came up to Bart.

'Don't worry about Bannock,' he said. 'The committee have heard about his plan to keep you from winning the race. He has been thrown out of the club – he'll never race again. Now you and Bill must come along and collect the cup – as the worthiest winners of the Sand Yacht Derby I've ever seen.'

Trouble on the Team

Trouble on the Team

by Sydney Golt

What a shot! Jack Higgins watched the blue and white shirted centre-forward slam a pile-driving shot past the leaping goal-keeper.

Jack was in the ground of Fourth Division Lepton Town Football Club, but it wasn't a league game that was being played on the pitch, and there were few spectators apart from Jack.

Lepton were playing a Thursday morning practice match, and Jack was doing one of his normal weekly jobs – cleaning the windows in the club's ground.

Jack was dead keen on football and it had been a happy moment for him when Mr Shipton, the boss of the window-cleaning firm he worked for, told him that the Lepton Town F.C. ground would be one of his regular jobs.

It would give him a fine opportunity to watch the players training, as he gave a shining polish to the club secretary's office window.

'What wouldn't I give to be out there playing for Lepton!' Jack muttered to himself. 'I wish I could change places with Fred Green, the lucky blighter!'

Fred Green was the Lepton Town inside-right, and there was a long-standing enmity between him and Jack Higgins. The rivalry began during their schooldays, when Jack had been picked for inside-right for the school team in preference to Fred. Fred had never forgotten this, and since he had managed to work his way into the Lepton team, he had taken every opportunity to gloat over Jack, who still had to work at his daytime window-cleaning job, only being able to play for a local club-team at weekends and some evenings.

Jack watched, slightly envious, as Fred Green took possession of the ball and sped down the field.

Fred was a well-above-average player, but he had one big failing – he was selfish. Once he got the ball he would never pass it until the very last moment, and then it would usually be too late.

A burly full-back ran to tackle Fred, as he neared the opposing goal.

'Pass, Fred!' yelled the centre-forward.

Fred Green took no notice of the call but tried to take the ball past the back before having a shot himself. He caught the ball a tremendous wallop with the side of his boot, and it went spinning up into the air high over the touchline.

Next moment Jack gasped. The ball was hurtling straight for the office window he had just cleaned!

Quick as a flash he leapt forward and sprang high into the air. He caught the ball smack on his chest and its spin was damped as it fell to the ground. In a flash he gained control of the ball.

Sam Stevens, the town's popular player-manager, gave a grunt of pleasure as he spotted the neat way Jack had dealt with the high-flying ball.

But Fred Green wasn't so pleased. He ran towards Jack who still had the ball at his feet.

'All right, Higgins,' he said sneeringly, 'that's enough showing-off. Give me the ball and get back to your window-cleaning. Stop trying to show us what you've learned playing for your tin-pot Saturday team.'

Jack was furious, the knuckles white on his clenched fists as he faced his rival.

'If you want the ball, you can darned well come and get it,

Jack jumped up and trapped the ball against his chest.

Green,' he said hotly. 'You nearly smashed the office window because you can't kick straight. Let's see if you can tackle any better.'

'Why, you . . . !'

Red-faced with rage, Fred Green raced forward, determined to take the ball from Jack.

But with a nimble swerve, Jack dodged the charging player. A roar of laughter went up from the other players as Fred lost his balance and fell flat on his face.

But Jack hadn't finished yet. He sped on to the pitch, the ball at his feet. Bill Simons, the good-natured Lepton right-half, entered into the spirit of the thing and ran to tackle him.

'O.K., lad,' he said, with a grin. 'See if you can beat me!' Bill was a veteran footballer, renowned for his skilful and fearless tackling, but Jack was too fast for him. In a split second he had sold Simons a dummy and had whipped past him towards the goal.

The Lepton goalie tensed as he saw the young window-cleaner racing towards him.

Next moment Jack shot. The ball hurtled for the corner of the goal like a cannonball. The goalie sprang, but he was too late! The netting bulged as the ball struck it hard.

'Goal! Well done the window–cleaner,' shouted one of the players.

Sam Stevens, Lepton F.C. player-manager, beckoned to Jack.

A trifle worried, Jack walked up to the Lepton manager.

'What's your name, lad?' Sam asked.

'Jack Higgins,' Jack replied.

'Well, Jack, that was a pretty good show of yours just now. Very promising,' said Sam Stevens. 'How'd you like a trial for the Lepton Reserves?'

Jack was amazed.

'A – a trial, Mr Stevens?' he stammered. 'A trial for Lepton? Wow! You bet I'd like it! When do you want me to turn up?'

'At 5.30 today, after you've finished work,' continued the manager. 'I'm trying out one or two other new lads. So you come along, and we'll see how you shape.'

The rest of the day couldn't go fast enough for Jack. At last he finished work for the day, and turned up at the stadium. A group of nervous-looking chaps were changing into playing kit in one of the dressing-rooms, into which Jack was ushered.

Quickly Jack undressed and donned the playing kit issued to him. He looked round in awe at the big lockers, the huge bath and well-equipped shower-room of the club buildings. It was such a startling contrast to the scruffy hut on the ground where Jack normally played.

'Hello, Jack,' Mr Stevens greeted him cheerily as he walked out on to the pitch. 'We're trying you out on the right-wing. Nip out there and do your best.'

As Jack took his place ready for the kick-off of the practice game, it felt as if butterflies were fluttering in his stomach. This was the chance of his lifetime, and if he played badly he might never get another. If only he could do well, and be taken on to Lepton's books, it would be the first step on the road to his ambition – to be a soccer star. The whistle blew, and the most important game Jack had ever played in began.

From the first Jack did well. As soon as the game started his nervousness vanished. Jack's team-mates soon realised that he was a class player, and the ball was constantly passed out to the right-wing.

Suddenly, with the ball at his feet, Jack saw an opening. He weaved his way forward, and was about to shoot when he heard a voice yell out.

'Stick to your amateur games, Higgins! You'll never be good

enough to play for Lepton!'

Startled, Jack glanced round. With a sneering grin on his face, his old enemy Fred Green stood leaning against the fence at the bottom of the terracing. It was obvious that he had come to the trial game especially to put Jack off his stride.

It looked as if he'd succeeded, too. His shout ruined Jack's concentration and cost him possession of the ball.

'Don't stand there dreaming, Jack!' bellowed Sam Stevens, who was reffing the game.

'I'll have to do better than this,' Jack muttered. 'I mustn't let that blighter Fred Green put me off. I've just got to forget all about him and play my best!'

From then on, Jack played like two men, dodging and weaving his way down the field, paying no attention to the jibes and catcalls coming from the railing.

At the close of the trial game, Jack had scored one goal and laid on another for his inside partner. Sam Stevens had no doubts that Jack had the makings of a first-class player.

The manager took him to one side in the dressing-room.

'You did well, young feller,' he told Jack. 'I want you to report here for training every evening. Your boss is an old pal of mine, so I'm going to ask him if he'll let you have a morning off once a week for extra training into the bargain.'

'Th . . . thanks, Mr Stevens,' Jack said excitedly. 'I'll be here tomorrow evening, without fail.'

For the next few weekday evenings, Jack turned up regularly at the Lepton Stadium for training. He thoroughly enjoyed the intensive sessions of body-building and gymnastics, and the special instruction in tactics and ball-control that he received from Sam Stevens.

Then one morning, his boss told him that he was to be allowed extra time off for training.

'I wouldn't do it normally, Jack,' said the boss, 'but I've the greatest respect for Sam Steven's judgment. He says you're going to prove a real asset to Lepton, and his word's good enough for me. The town's going through a bad patch at the moment; it can do with some promising newcomers. You can take off Tuesday and Thursday mornings each week.'

'Gee, that's fine, Mr Shipton!' gasped Jack. 'I don't know how to thank you.'

'There's only one way you can thank me, Jack,' his boss replied. 'That's by training hard and making yourself a credit to Sam Stevens and Lepton Town.'

Jack was determined not to waste a moment of his extra training. Every Tuesday and Thursday he made a few early morning calls to houses and offices near the stadium, and then at ten o'clock pedalled his special cycle and sidecar with its window-cleaning equipment to the stadium.

Jack shaped so well in his first two weeks that he was given a chance to play for the reserves. That first game was really tough, but the young right-winger played at the top of his form, and won his way to a regular place in the reserve team.

Jack had no further brushes with Fred Green since he had joined the club, and he began to think that his old enemy had decided to ignore him.

Then, one Tuesday morning, as Jack came off the field after an hour's intensive training, he noticed a cluster of players round the flagpole at the corner of the stadium – the flagpole from which the Lepton Town's blue and white flag flew triumphantly on match days.

Now there was a different kind of flag fluttering in the breeze – a pair of football shorts at half-mast!

'They must be the skipper's shorts,' Jack heard one of the team say.

'Some idiot must have pinched them from his locker and nailed them up there.'

'Proper insult – flying them at half-mast!' said another angrily. 'I suppose some clot thinks it's funny to make out we're in mourning 'cause we lost the game against Ramford last Saturday.'

Suddenly one of the team glanced round. Against the wall of the stadium rested a twelve-foot-long ladder.

'Lepton Town Window Cleaning Service.' The footballer read the bright green lettering on the side of the ladder. 'Window Cleaning Service? This is your ladder, Jack Higgins! What's it doing here? Was it you who nailed those shorts up to the mast?'

Jack was flabbergasted.

'Wh . . . what? No, of course I didn't!' he said. I didn't know anything about the shorts till just now. I haven't the slightest idea how my ladder got here. I left it on my sidecar in the car park.'

'O.K. We'll take your word for it,' said the other, still a trifle suspicious. 'But this is no joke. And it still looks as if you might have had something to do with it.'

Another shock was in store! When the players got back to the dressing-room they found a message scrawled on the big mirror over the washbasins:

'To all you first team deadbeats:
You lot couldn't win a game to save your
lives! Why don't you give up and make room
for some real footballers?   Lepton's chief mourner.'

'What a nerve!' exploded Jackie Denton, the first team centre-forward. 'If I could catch the blighter who wrote this, I'd show him a thing or two!'

'It must be someone in the club,' said another player thoughtfully. 'No one else would be able to get into the grounds and mess about in the changing rooms without being challenged.'

' "Lepton's Chief Mourner" he signs himself,' pointed out another. 'Must be the same chap who put the skipper's shorts on the flagpole. If only I could get my hands on him!'

Fred Green walked over to the mirror and rubbed his finger against the yellow scrawled lettering. A greasy mark smeared across the glass and came off on his fingertip.

'Some sort of yellow grease-pencil,' he said. 'If we can find the chap who's got a pencil like this, he's our man!'

'You needn't bother to look, Fred. I've found him,' a voice said curtly from the doorway.

Astonished, Jack and the rest of the players spun round. In the doorway stood Stump Harley, one of Fred Green's cronies, holding a yellow crayon in his hand.

'I know who wrote that message,' Stump said accusingly. 'Jack Higgins! I was suspicious of him after his ladder was found near the flagpole. I thought I'd take a look in his sidecar. I found the pencil there.'

'This is crazy!' Jack protested hotly. 'Look here, chaps, I don't know anything about this. I've no idea how the pencil got in my sidecar. All I know is I've got nothing to do with these stupid practical jokes.'

He looked round at the circle of faces. They were all looking at him sternly, without any friendly smiles. Clearly the players did not believe him.

Jack was pretty certain now that Fred and his friend had hatched up the whole scheme so that they could put the blame on him and get him thrown out of the club. But unless he could prove it to the other members of the club, he knew he'd really be finished.

'You say you've got nothing to do with it,' said Jackie Denton. 'O.K., we'll let Sam Stevens decide. But I can tell you, Higgins, I don't think there's a man in this club who'll play in the same team as you after all this.'

Minutes later Jack was called into Sam Stevens' office. The player-manager looked stern and thoughtful.

'I don't know whether you had anything to do with this ridiculous practical joke or not, Jack,' he said. 'But if you give me your word that you had nothing to do with it, I'll accept it.'

'I swear I didn't, Mr Stevens,' Jack said.

'O.K., Jack, I believe you,' nodded Sam. 'But you must realise that this business has caused a lot of bad feeling in the club. The other fellows think you're responsible. You've got to admit things point that way, with the ladder close to the flagpole and the pencil found in your sidecar. Unless you can *prove* that you had nothing to do with it, I'm afraid they'll go on believing you're guilty. In short, Jack, unless you can solve the mystery – prove who performed these unsporting pranks – you'll have to leave the club!'

Jack was thoroughly downcast as he walked home that night. He had spent the evening training as usual, but it hadn't been accompanied by the customary cheery good comradeship.

Convinced that Jack was the practical joker, the other players had ignored him. Once or twice Jack spotted Fred Green casting an unpleasant smile of triumph in his direction. This made Jack sure that Fred and his crony, Stump Harley, were responsible for the scheme that threatened to wreck his career.

The only bright spot in the whole evening had been Sam Stevens' warning to hold himself ready for Saturday's match with the reserve team.

A mutter of protest from the other players had been firmly silenced by Sam, but it was clear to Jack that an unpleasant situation like this couldn't continue. Either he must find the culprit and supply proof, or get out of the club.

'I'm darned sure it's Green and Harley who're responsible, but how the heck can I prove it?' Jack muttered as he walked down Lepton High Street, his hands thrust in his pockets.

'Hello, Jack! What's the matter? You look miserable.' It was Mike Sales, one of Jack's friends who ran an electrical shop nearby.

'It's a long story, Mike,' said Jack ruefully.

'I've got all the time in the world to hear about it,' grinned Mike, slapping his pal on the back. 'Come on. I'll treat you to a cup of coffee, and you can tell me all about your troubles.'

The two pals walked down the road, and Jack explained the whole business to Mike.

Mike nodded thoughtfully as Jack finished.

'I've got a little gadget in my shop which might help you – if you could dream up a way to use it,' said Mike slowly.

'What is it?' asked Jack excitedly.

'Come along with me and see,' Mike replied mysteriously.

Leaving the coffee bar, he led Jack to his electrical shop, and when the young footballer left, he was carrying a box with a handle, rather like a small suitcase.

That Saturday morning, the day that Jack might play his final game for Lepton, he set out from home with the box concealed in his sidecar, next to his buckets and leathers.

At the stadium there was the usual tactics-talk scheduled for the first team players, amongst them Fred Green and Stump Harley.

Jack knew that Fred and Stump made a habit of returning to Fred's digs for a light lunch before each home match, and his plan depended on them sticking to their usual practice today.

At the time he reckoned the tactics talk would be over, Jack rode up to Fred's digs, where he normally paid a weekly call to clean the windows.

He rang the bell, and Fred Green's landlady answered.

'Morning, Mrs Somers,' Jack said. 'O.K. if I go ahead and do your windows today?'

'Why, it's Jack Higgins!' exclaimed the landlady. 'You're early, Jack. Monday's your usual day. But it's all right – do them today if you like.'

'Thanks,' said Jack, whistling as he started to cart his ladder and gear from the sidecar and took them round to the back of the house.

It was well after lunchtime when Jack Higgins arrived at the stadium.

The skipper of the reserves greeted him coldly as he cycled up to the changing rooms.

'Left it a bit late, haven't you, Higgins?' he snapped. 'The match is due to start in two minutes. Better get changed right away.'

Jack shoved the bundle he carried beneath his arm into his locker and changed quickly. Just in time for the kick-off, he raced on to the field, to be greeted with derisive shouts from a section of the supporters.

'Get off, Higgins! We don't want the likes of you in Lepton!'

It looked as though the story of the practical jokes had leaked out.

The barracking from the spectators and the unfriendliness of his team-mates put Jack off so badly that it seemed as if he couldn't put a foot right.

The opposing team, Selbridge Wanderers Reserves, were attacking strongly, and it needed all Lepton's efforts to hold them off.

Suddenly the ball came out from a ruck of players straight towards Jack.

Normally Jack would have pounced on it like a shot, but this time it took him valuable seconds to react to the opportunity. Even as he raced for it, a Selbridge player whipped it out of reach and passed upfield.

The Lepton supporters were disgusted.

'What a player! Shake the lead out of your feet, Higgins!'

'What's up with you, Higgins? Playing for Selbridge now?'

Stung into action by the spectators' jibes, Jack played much better for the rest of the first half, but Lepton were still 1–0 down when the ref blew up for half-time.

A shock was in store for the Lepton players when they went into the changing rooms.

One of the ball-boys ran in from the bathroom, looking startled.

'There's been some more trouble, chaps. It looks as if someone's put a lot of old clothes in the bath!' he said.

The players jostled their way into the bathroom. There in the four-foot depth, tiled bath floated a mass of clothes – trousers, jackets, shirts, even a few ties!

'Old clothes be blowed!' snorted one of the playres. 'That's my sports jacket there! And I can see my new gaberdine trousers! Someone's dumped all our clothes in the bath!'

'Not all of them,' cut in another voice coldly. 'Jack Higgins' clothes are still hanging up in his locker. Of course, he wouldn't throw his own clothes in the bath. I suppose this is another of his senseless practical jokes!'

'You've hit on it, Bill!' snapped another player. 'Higgins, what have you got to say about this?'

Jack was encircled by a ring of menacing faces.

'Take it easy, chaps,' he said grimly. 'I didn't have anything to do with this – just as I didn't have anything to do with the other practical jokes. But this time I think I can prove it. Will someone please fetch Sam Stevens? I want him to hear the evidence.'

Sam Stevens was soon brought to the reserves' changing rooms, accompanied by several of the first team players.

Jack went to his locker and took out the bundle he had placed there before the game. It was a tape-recorder!

Switching it on to the fast speed, he pressed the release catch. The tape whizzed over the deck, only the noise of its fast-running motor breaking the silence.

Suddenly a high-pitched gabble squeaked from the loudspeaker. Jack snapped the switch to the slow speed he had set the machine to in Fred's room.

Fred Green's unmistakable voice rang out from the tape:

'. . . soon get that blighter Higgins just where I want him – out of the club!'

'I must say that message on the mirror was a brilliant piece of work, Fred,' Stump Harley's voice chimed in. 'And how did you like that piece of play-acting when I said I'd found the pencil hidden in Higgins' sidecar? Everyone swallowed the story hook, line and sinker!'

'Darned good, Stump. We've finished Higgins with Lepton now, right enough. But just to make absolutely sure I'm going to make things look even blacker for him. I'll dump all the reserves' clothes in the baths except his – that'll make them dead certain it's Higgins playing these jokes.'

Jack jerked the switch off. The tape recorder stopped and there was a stunned silence in the room.

'O.K., Jack. I don't need to hear any more,' Sam said. 'As far as I'm concerned you're the victim of some very unsporting dirty work. You're on the level – what do you chaps think?'

342

He dodged and weaved his way past rival players.

A mumble of embarrassed apologies rose from the Lepton players. Shamefaced, they realised how wrong they had been in suspecting Jack.

Sam rounded angrily on Green and Harley.

'I'll settle with you two after the game,' he said. 'But I'll tell you this – it'll be your last game for the club. We don't welcome blokes like you two in Lepton.'

He turned back to Jack and the reserves.

'You're due back for the second half, chaps,' he said. 'Go on out there and play the game of your lives.'

When the second half started, Jack and his team-mates proceeded to do just that.

A pass from his inside partner brought the ball out to Jack. Swiftly he set off down the wing, dodging and weaving his way past rival players.

Suddenly Jack centred. The ball sizzled through the air and fell in just the right position for the centre-forward to nod it home. It was a goal!

From then on, Selbridge didn't get a look in. Time and again, the Lepton attack cut through the Selbridge defence. They notched up three more goals by the time the final whistle blew, two of them scored by Jack!

Jack was the hero of the day as he returned to the changing rooms, with his victorious team-mates chairing him in triumph.

And there was another pleasant surprise for Jack. Sam Stevens had news for him.

'Because of injuries, it looks as if there'll be a couple of spare places in the first team, son,' he said. 'One of 'em's on the right wing. How'd you like to take a crack at it next Saturday?'

'You bet I would!' Jack replied with a grin.

The Disastrous Climb

The Disastrous Climb

by Steve Rogers

Two figures were fighting furiously on the edge of a towering wall of sheer rock. If one of them fell, he would drop to his death two hundred feet below.

I was rounding the cliff-side path just behind them, and stopped dead in horror. They would kill themselves!

The chunky fellow with the red hair was Bob Cooper, leader of the Doppenberg Mountain Climbing Expedition, of which I was a member. The other, dressed in an all-white climbing outfit, was Jack Farlow, one of Britain's best young climbers. They were both experienced mountaineers, who knew the danger of taking the slightest risk when climbing. But now they were throwing all caution to the winds as they battled relentlessly on the edge of the precipice.

I dashed forward to try to stop the fight, my eyes glued on them. Bob Cooper was trying desperately to hold off Farlow, who seemed completely unaware of his surroundings as he lunged at the leader.

'Farlow!' I yelled. 'Stop! Stop!'

But even as the words left my lips, Farlow slammed a punch at Cooper's jaw. It burst past Bob's flailing arms and smashed into his face. My heart jumped into my mouth as he staggered back, clawing at Farlow to steady himself.

His hands met empty air; he tottered on the edge of the cliff for a moment, then keeled over backwards and disappeared from view, his cry of terror echoing and re-echoing around the mountain.

Terror welled up in me. I grabbed at Farlow's arm.

'You're mad, Farlow!' I cried. 'You've killed him!'

He was a wild figure as he stood there, the wind shrieking around him, snow fluttering down on his close-cropped hair. He turned and saw me. His eyes glittered and he grasped me roughly by the lapels of my jacket and dragged me towards him.

'You haven't seen anything!' he hissed between clenched teeth. 'Understand? You breathe one word of this to anyone, Glyn Morgan, and you'll go the same way as Cooper!'

He dropped his hands, brushed past me and began to make his way down the path towards the base camp of the Doppenberg Expedition.

I stood still, almost too horrified to move. I had certainly never expected anything like this when I joined the expedition.

Every year a party of British mountaineers comes to Switzerland to climb the lofty Doppenberg on the anniversary of the first conquest of that difficult peak. I come from a family of Welsh mountaineers, and, resolved to follow in my family's footsteps, I had made up my mind that I would be chosen for this year's expedition. It had been a tough struggle, but I had made it – I had been selected to go with the team, though only as a reserve.

It was a great honour, since I was by far the youngest member of the expedition. Although it was unlikely that I would be called on to make the climb this year, there was always the chance that someone would notice me and remember me for a future team.

But the fact that I was only a reserve didn't stop me putting in plenty of training. I knew that I had to keep myself in trim just in case I was chosen to make the ascent at the last minute. I had been climbing higher up on the Doppenberg when the approaching storm had brought me hurrying down, and it was then that I came across Farlow and Cooper.

Aghast, I stared after Farlow for a moment, as he hurried away down the slope; then I moved to the edge of the drop and peered over.

I gave a gasp of relief – for there, fifty feet below me, on a narrow ledge, lay the crumpled body of Bob Cooper. By a miracle he had landed on that ledge, and had not plunged down to the screes far below.

Even as I watched, Bob stirred slightly and I realised joyfully that he was still alive. But he was still in a very dangerous position. At any moment he might move and roll off that narrow ledge. I thought of returning to the base camp for help, but then decided against it. A heavy storm was brewing. If the storm broke before the rescuers arrived, it would be impossible to find Bob.

There was no point in calling after Farlow. He had shown by his actions that he was not in the least concerned about Bob's safety. Somehow I would have to rescue him myself.

All I had with me was a coil of rope. I slipped it from my shoulder, tied one end firmly to a strong outjutting rock at the cliff edge and looped the other end securely round my body.

The storm mounted in fury. The howling of the wind rose to a crescendo. It tore at me and threatened to blow me over the edge. Snow was falling thick and fast and already Bob was just a dim figure below me.

Slowly, with infinite care, I began the perilous descent down the cliff face, the rope grasped between my gloved hands, my feet feeling for foot-holds.

The climb down seemed never-ending, but at last my searching feet struck the ledge. I glanced to the left and saw Bob's still body lying where it had fallen.

A gust of wind slammed me against the cliff face. My feet

With Bob's body over my shoulder, I started to climb.

slipped on the wet rock and for a moment I dangled in space at the end of the rope. With my heart thumping painfully, I somehow swung myself back on the ledge and dropped to my knees, panting with exertion.

I crawled slowly forward till I reached the still figure. Bob was unconscious. He seemed in a bad way. He would be quite unable to help himself up the cliff.

I made a fresh loop in the rope for Bob; then, with his limp body over one shoulder, I started on the ascent.

The climb was a nightmare. I lost all sense of time; I was only conscious of the great weight on my shoulder, the rope chafing my hands, the wind tearing at my clothing.

Confused thoughts raced through my mind. Why had Bob and Farlow been fighting? It had been more serious than an ordinary quarrel, otherwise Farlow would have come to his senses when Bob had gone over the edge and stayed to help me rescue him. What the fight had been about was something I meant to find out when I got back to the camp.

We were climbing in a white world. The dancing snowflakes cut visibility down to a few feet of grey rock. How many times the wind buffeted us against the rock face, how many times my feet slithered and lost their hold on the icy granite, I shall never know.

At last, after an eternity, I crawled over the edge of the cliff and lay sucking in great lungfuls of air, my whole body numbed and frozen. Bob lay limp, his face white and drawn. I heaved myself to my feet, got him on to my shoulder again, staggered for a moment, then started down the path toward the screes.

Half an hour later I stumbled into the base camp. Helping hands lifted Bob's heavy weight from my shoulders and carried him into the main tent. Tom Jupp, who acted as the camp's cook, thrust a mug of piping hot cocoa at me and soon there was new life in my numbed body.

'What happened to Bob?' Tom asked. 'He looks in a bad way.'

'He fell from the top of the cliff out there,' I said grimly. 'Or rather, he was pushed – by Jack Farlow!'

Tom stared at me incredulously for a moment, then broke into a roar of laughter.

'Jack Farlow?' he asked. 'Do you know what you're saying, Glyn? Jack's one of the finest mountaineers in Britain. He'd never push anyone off a cliff. You must have imagined it. Snow can play funny tricks.'

I didn't press my story. I could see that Tom would never believe me. And neither would the other climbers. Jack Farlow was very popular with them. They wouldn't believe it if I told them that he had pushed Bob off the cliff top. But he had – and I was determined to find out why.

I pushed the flap aside and entered the cheery warmth of the large tent. Bob had been laid on a camp bed and a group of climbers stood anxiously over him.

'How is he?' I asked Jim Parsons, the expedition's doctor.

'He's suffering from exposure more than anything,' Jim said. 'Only a couple of bones broken. But I'll be happier when we've got him to the hospital in the town. A mountain is no place for an injured man.'

He turned to the group of serious-faced mountaineers.

'Come on, fellers. I want four volunteers for a stretcher party.'

Ten minutes later the little party set off down the mountain-side towards the twinkling lights of the Swiss village below. The storm had abated now; the fierce wind had died to a whisper.

Norman Jackson, the second-in-command, laid a hand on my shoulder.

'You did a fine job, bringing Bob in through that storm

Glyn,' Jackson said. 'Any idea how the accident happened?'

I was about to reply when I noticed Farlow. He was standing in the corner of the tent, and I hadn't spotted him before. There was a mocking glint in his eye and he shook his head slowly. I understood that glance. Farlow, too, realised that I would be wasting my time if I told Norman that he had attempted to kill Bob. Farlow thought he was safe, but I meant to find out what was behind his attack on the leader.

I turned back to Norman.

'I saw him fall from the top of the cliff that leads down to the screes,' I said. 'He dropped on to a ledge about fifty feet down, and I went down and brought him up.'

'If you did that, Glyn,' Norman said, 'you're a better mountaineer than we thought. As Bob's out of the climb, and you're one of the reserves, you'll be going up the Doppenberg tomorrow!'

I gasped. My big chance had come, and I was only sorry that it had had to come through the loss of Bob Cooper.

I was more than ever determined now to find out what had led to the fight between Bob and Farlow. Although no one would believe any wrong of Farlow, I meant to get to the bottom of the mystery and expose him for what he was.

As Norman bade me goodnight and went off to his tent, I puzzled over the problem. Farlow must be a very desperate man to go to such lengths. Why should he want to kill Bob?

I shook my head, feeling suddenly very tired after my strenuous climb. I decided to turn in and sleep on the problem.

The next morning dawned bright and clear, and by seven o'clock five climbers were stamping their feet and swinging their arms to keep warm while they waited for the sixth member of the party to appear.

'Glyn, go and dig Jack out,' Norman Jackson called across to me. 'Tell him we're ready to go.'

I hurried over to Farlow's tent and pushed inside. It was dark in there and the hurricane lamp was burning. Farlow was holding a piece of paper up to the light studying it. The lamp shone through it, picking it out in detail. I recognised what was on the paper immediately – it was a sketch map of the summit of the Doppenberg, with a small cross marked just below the top-most peak.

Farlow turned suddenly, saw me, and stuffed the map hurriedly into his pocket.

'We're ready to move off,' I said.

'Right!' Farlow said, then, as I turned to leave: 'You've been very wise so far, Morgan. You've kept your mouth shut about what you saw yesterday. Make sure it stays that way!'

'You can save your threats, Farlow,' I said angrily. 'I don't know what your game is, but I mean to find out and prove that it was you who pushed Bob off the cliff!'

'Well, don't say I haven't warned you!' Farlow snapped and pushed past me out of the tent.

We set off. Six climbers, split into two parties of three, would set out up the east side of the Doppenberg to within striking distance of the summit. The last stage – the climb to the top – would be taken by two climbers. Jack Farlow had already been picked as one; the other would be chosen from the team that reached the head of the Doppenberg glacier first.

We marched across the screes and up the cliff path. At the top we roped up and, with Norman Jackson leading one party and Farlow the other, we began a long, tough climb up a two-thousand foot chimney of rock to the infamous glacier above.

It was a gruelling climb, but Farlow was brilliant. He clawed his way up the chimney as if drawn on by some invisible magnet, and his team-mates found it hard work keeping up with him.

Norman, myself and Jim Parson formed the other team, and experienced mountaineer though Norman was, he couldn't keep pace with Farlow.

I stared after that figure in the white climbing outfit as we moved slowly up the rock face, searching for hand and foot-holds. He was climbing at a fantastic speed. What was the hurry, I wondered. Then I remembered the map of the summit I had seen him looking at. . . .

It was late in the afternoon when we reached the top of the rock chimney. Hardly pausing for breath, we unpacked ice-axes that had been slung across our backs with the rest of our gear and began to hack our way up the face of the glacier.

It was the hardest climb of my life. Although the Doppenberg was not a particularly high peak, mountaineers had given it the name of the 'toughest little mountain in Europe'. And with good reason! The glacier sloped up at a terrifying angle, a sea of bleak ice, criss-crossed by dangerous cracks and fissures.

Farlow was beginning to tire now and gradually we caught his team up as we hacked at the ice with our axes. Another storm moved in and we reached the head of the glacier in a blinding blizzard. It was impossible to go further that day; the path to the summit was shrouded by cloud and a howling wind increased the peril of the ascent.

In the last few minutes of the struggle up the glacier, Norman, Jim and I had just beaten Farlow's team to the top, despite the fact that Norman had slipped and fallen heavily.

We erected our two small tents and made camp for the night. By the time Farlow's team joined us in our tent for a makeshift meal, Norman's right leg, which had been twisted under him when he fell, was swelling painfully.

'I'm afraid this leg puts me out of the running,' he said with a wry grin. 'It wouldn't stand up to the strain of the climb to the summit. Jim can't go either. As team doctor he'll have to remain here.' He broke off and turned to me. 'That leaves you, Glyn!'

'Me? You – you mean you want me to make the climb?' I gasped.

'You're the only one who can,' Jim said. 'Our team got to the head of the glacier first, so the choice falls on one of us. How do you feel about it, Glyn?'

'Well, just great, Jim,' I said with a broad grin.

But Jack Farlow wasn't so pleased about it. He glowered at me, his eyes half-closed. Then he got to his feet without a word and went back to his tent with his team-mates.

A few minutes later I was arranging my sleeping-bag on the hard-packed snow. I turned to Norman.

'Gosh, I'd like a nice soft pillow to lie on,' I said.

Norman grinned.

'Try this for size,' he chuckled, digging into his haversack. He brought out a large volume on mountain climbing that he always carried with him, and threw it over to me. The pages fanned out in their flight and something dropped to the ground. I caught the book, then stretch ⌐ out my hand and picked up a newspaper cutting that had fallen from it. My German was very weak, but I could make out the bold headline that said: 'Plane Crashes on Doppenberg.'

'What's this about a plane crash?' I asked curiously.

'That was last year,' Norman told me, 'during our climb. A small plane crashed on the summit. Jack Farlow and Bob Cooper were making their way up to the summit. They fetched the rest of the party and we rescued the pilot and the two passengers.'

'There was a rather unpleasant sequel, though,' Jim put in

quietly. 'The plane was carrying a packet of very valuable diamonds. They were never recovered. Suspicion fell on our party, but although we were all searched by the police when we came down, the diamonds weren't found.'

'Nobody even knew what had happened to them,' Norman said. 'It was all a very strange business.' He smothered a yawn. 'Well, I'm hitting the sack. Night all!' He blew out the lamp and we snuggled into out sleeping bags.

But I didn't drop off to sleep straight away – there were too many things on my mind.

Suddenly everything had become clear. The diamonds on top of the Doppenberg! Perhaps they were still there and that was why Farlow was in such a hurry to get to the summit.

Whatever it was that he was after on the summit, it must be pretty important for him to risk murder. He had already tried to kill Bob Cooper. Now he would probably try to kill me, too!

We made an early start next morning and by midday Farlow and I were ready to set off for the summit.

Norman, whose leg was much better after a night's rest, handed us the flag of our Alpine Club to plant on the highest point of the Doppenberg.

'Good luck, you two,' he said. 'Get back as soon as you can – I think there's another storm blowing up. If you're not back in two hours' time, we'll come and look for you.'

Securely roped together, with Farlow in the lead, we set off. But as soon as the others had disappeared from sight in the low-lying cloud, Farlow stopped and turned to me.

'This is your last chance, Morgan,' he shouted above the scream of the wind. 'If you want to stay alive turn back now!'

'Keep going, Farlow!' I yelled back. 'I'm not letting you get away quite so easily. I'm staying with you!'

Farlow clenched his fists, then turned and continued the

climb. We thrust our way up a precipitous wall of rock until we were above the cloud. Icy winds tore at us and the storm Norman feared began to close in.

The path to the summit lay up the wall of rock, across a large field of deep snow, then up another cliff of slippery, perilous rock to the peak.

We struggled across the snow-field and started up the rock face.

Then, on a narrow ledge half-way up the rock face, Farlow halted suddenly and turned to me. He had a knife in his hand.

'I gave you the chance to back out, Morgan,' he shouted. 'You've only yourself to blame. No one's going to stop me now – no one!'

The knife flashed down and severed the rope between us. His eyes glittered as he swung his arm up again. I twisted my body desperately and the knife whistled past me. But I had forgotten my precarious position on the ledge. As I moved out of the way, my feet slithered on the rock. Next moment I was falling through space . . . falling, falling.

Consciousness returned slowly. I was lying on my back, embedded in soft, clinging snow. I had fallen fifty feet from the rock face, but the deep snow had broken my fall.

I staggered to my feet and peered upwards, trying to catch a glimpse of Farlow. But snow was now falling heavily, obscuring the summit, and he was not in sight.

Blazing with anger at his cowardly attack, I floundered across the snow-field and dragged my battered body up the rock face, fighting for handholds. The cliff began to slope more gradually; once more I was moving through snow; the summit was almost within grasp.

I stumbled on and then I saw Farlow. He was on his knees, scrabbling at a small cairn of rocks.

He looked up and his eyes widened disbelievingly as he saw me. Then he twisted sideways and leaped to his feet, his hand groping for a knife. I hurled myself at him, my hand going to his arm. I forced it back and the knife dropped to the snow. Farlow snarled and brought his knee hard up into my stomach. I gasped as all the breath was knocked from my body. My legs threatened to crumple under me, but somehow I kept on my feet and slammed a punch to Farlow's heart. He doubled up. With every last ounce of remaining strength I crashed an uppercut to his jaw. He staggered for a moment, then sank to the ground.

I stared at him, my chest heaving, then turned to the cairn. It was half-open. I pushed the remaining rocks aside to disclose a small parcel. I unwrapped it with trembling hands, and there, nestling in my palm, glittering and winking, were – a dozen uncut diamonds!

I heard a sound behind me. I whirled to see Farlow on his feet, coming at me.

'I'm not beaten yet!' he panted. He lunged forward and fetched me a blow to the jaw which knocked me right off my feet.

Farlow grabbed up the diamonds that had fallen from my hand and began to run back down the snow-field. Then suddenly he stopped, turned, and began to flounder back up towards me. Four figures had appeared out of the mist. I gave a shout as I recognised Norman and the other climbers. They had come to look for us.

'After him!' I yelled. 'Don't let him escape!'

I got to my feet. Farlow was almost on top of me.

I was ready for him this time. I dived below his swinging fists and caught him round the knees. He went down underneath me and I crashed another punch to his jaw. He stayed down.

'What's going on, Glyn?' Norman demanded as he hurried

up. 'Has Jack gone berserk?'

I opened Farlow's fist and held up the diamonds.

'He was after these, Norman,' I said. 'I think I know the whole story now. Farlow stole the gems from the plane last year and hid them in a cairn, making a map to mark the spot. He was afraid to take them down the mountainside, knowing he would be searched by the police. But Bob Cooper was suspicious of him and Farlow, scared that Bob would voice his suspicions, tried to murder him by pushing him over the mountain.'

'But I thought Bob fell from the cliff,' Norman said. 'You didn't say Jack pushed him.'

'I tried to tell Tom Jupp,' I said. 'He didn't believe me and I knew nobody else would either, so I decided to keep quiet until I knew definitely what Farlow was up to.'

'Well, you do now, Glyn!' Jim said, staring at Farlow as he began to come round. 'Come on, Farlow, you cold-blooded devil. We're taking you and the diamonds to the police. When they see them it'll clear the rest of us of suspicion.'

'Just a minute!' I said. 'There's one more thing to do!'

I picked up the Alpine Club flag from the snow, climbed the last few feet, and planted it firmly in the snow on the summit.